ONCE IN EVERY LIFE

Kristin Hannah

BALLANTINE BOOKS • NEW YORK

A Ballantine Book
Published by The Random House Publishing Group
Copyright © 1992 by Kristin Hannah

Published in the United States by Ballantine Books, an imprint of The Random House Publishing Group, a division of Random House, Inc., New York, and simultaneously in Canada by Random House of Canada Limited, Toronto.

Ballantine and colophon are registered trademarks of Random House, Inc.

www.ballantinebooks.com

Library of Congress Catalog Card Number: 92-97062

ISBN 0-449-14838-6

Manufactured in the United States of America

First Edition: February 1993

OPM 29 28 27 26 25 24 23 22 21

Praise for Kristin Hannah

ANGEL FALLS

"An all-night-reading affair—you won't be able to put it down. . . . [Angel Falls will] make you laugh and cry."
—*The New York Post*

"A tearjerker. . . about the triumph of family . . . Perfect reading for hopeless romantics."
—*Detroit Free Press*

"One of the premier voices in women's fiction . . . Hannah deftly explores love in all its variations and manifestations."
—*Romantic Times*

ON MYSTIC LAKE

"[Hannah] writes of love with compassion and conviction, her characters so alive and dear you can't bear to see the novel end."
—LUANNE RICE

"Superb . . . I'll heartily recommend On Mystic Lake to any woman . . . who demands that a story leave her in a satisfied glow."
—*The Washington Post Book World*

"Marvelous . . . A touching love story . . . This page-turner has enough twists and turns to keep the reader up until the wee hours of the morning."
—*USA Today*

By Kristin Hannah
Published by The Random House Publishing Group:

A HANDFUL OF HEAVEN
THE ENCHANTMENT
ONCE IN EVERY LIFE
IF YOU BELIEVE
WHEN LIGHTNING STRIKES
WAITING FOR THE MOON
HOME AGAIN
ON MYSTIC LAKE
ANGEL FALLS
SUMMER ISLAND
DISTANT SHORES
BETWEEN SISTERS
THE THINGS WE DO FOR LOVE
COMFORT & JOY
MAGIC HOUR

This book is lovingly dedicated to my husband, Benjamin, and his family, the Hannahs, who so warmly took me in and made me one of their own. The story was conceived and written with my in-laws, Fred and Ann, in mind. Unfortunately the creative process is slow, and the publishing process slower still. Ann is now past the time when she can read my words. But I believe that somehow she knows and understands how much I love her, and that some part of her—a small, spiritual part undaunted by the reality of Alzheimer's—remembers. . . .

Also, I'd like to thank two very special women, Laura John Turner and Charlotte Stan, who read the first draft of my first book and told me it was good . . . with a straight face.

There is no death. Only a change of worlds.
—The great Indian leader Chief Sealth.
January 1855.

Special thanks to ...

Etta Egeland, founder of the San Juan Island Historical Museum, and to Alvan Hannah, for so graciously sharing his time and memories with me.

Prologue

SAN JUAN ISLAND, WASHINGTON TERRITORY 1873

Sprawled facedown on a hard-packed dirt floor, Jackson Rafferty regained consciousness slowly. For a moment he felt like a man coming out of a deep, contented sleep. Then reality hit. He'd had another blackout.

Ice-cold dread washed over him in waves. His teeth began to chatter. At his sides, his hands scraped through the dirt and formed shaking fists. A vague, amorphous fear hovered at the back of his mind, gaining momentum with every beat of his heart. It coalesced into a single, terrifying thought; the same thought he always had upon waking, the same fear.

No, he thought desperately. Not my children. I wouldn't hurt my children. . . .

Liar. The word pounded through his brain. A small, terrified moan slipped from his lips. Every morning the first thing he did was check on his children to make sure he hadn't inadvertantly hurt them in the night. It was irrational, he knew. A legacy from the horrible nightmare of his past. Now, supposedly, he was cured. Yet still, he had the terrifying blackouts. Still he awoke afraid. *Oh, God . . .*

Shaking, he got to his hands and knees. At the movement, his head spun, nausea yanked his empty stomach.

He sat back on his heels, waiting for the familiar queasiness to pass. Gradually his vision cleared. Behind him, a lantern rested on the workbench, sputtering pale golden light into the night. In its glow, he saw the shadowy outline of two stalls. The comforting smells of musty wood, dust, and fresh hay filtered to his nostrils.

The barn. He was in his own barn.

All at once he remembered coming here. His gaze shot to the workbench, where a cradle lay, half-finished and forgotten. A saw and hammer lay on the floor where he'd dropped them.

He'd been reaching for the can of nails when the storm hit. The last thing he remembered was the sudden volley of rain, pounding the roof like gunfire.

Gunfire.

Memories catapulted him back in time. He squeezed his eyes shut, trying not to remember, not to feel.

As always, he had no control; his efforts were a feeble, useless waste of time. The visions clawed at him, sucked him once again into a depression so deep and dark and consuming, he couldn't imagine finding his way out. Dear God, he couldn't live like this anymore. . . .

Breathing hard, trembling, Jack forced his watery legs to a stand, and staggered to the workbench. It was there, waiting for him, gleaming dully in the lamplight. His Remington army revolver.

Taking a deep, calming breath, he curled his work-calloused fingers around the pistol's grip. The cool metal handle warmed at his touch, felt comforting and familiar.

"So easy." The words slipped past his lips before he knew he was going to say them. It would be so easy. One shot and the misery would end. His family would be safe.

He lifted the gun. It seemed to grow heavier, uncomfortably so. The muscles in his forearm tightened in response.

Cold metal kissed his temple like an old friend. He

pressed slightly. The muzzle squeezed against his flesh; he knew from experience it would leave a small, circular indentation in his skin. His hold on the grip tightened, his trigger finger slipped into place.

It's now or never.

Sweat beaded Jack's forehead and crawled along his scalp. Warm rivulets slid into his eyes and blurred his vision. His finger vibrated against the cold steel trigger.

Do it. Do it, damn you. . . .

He deserved to die. His wife had told him so a thousand times. God knew he wanted it, deserved it, *ached* for it. Everyone wanted him to do it.

They'd be better off without him. Amarylis had made sure he understood that. Savannah and Katie were too young yet to fully understand his failure, but soon. Soon . . .

And now there would be another baby, another innocent life. The baby deserved better than to have Jack as his father. . . .

"Daddy!"

Through a fog of self-loathing and fear, Jack heard his daughter's voice. Instinctively he yanked the gun from his temple and threw it down. It clattered against the wall and skidded along the workbench. His palm immediately felt cold and damp and empty.

Maybe next time. But even as he thought the words, he knew they were another lie. He didn't have the strength of character to commit suicide.

And why should he? he thought dully. He'd been a coward for a very long time.

The barn door banged open and a gust of wind whooshed inside. "Daddy, are you there?"

"Yeah, Savannah, I'm here." He turned to look at his twelve-year-old daughter. She stood silhouetted in the open door, her hands knotted nervously in her long woolen skirt. She started to take a step toward him, then stopped. Uncertainty tugged at one corner of her mouth.

His own daughter was afraid of him. Jack felt a rush of self-hatred so strong, it made him want to smash his fist into something. But years of practice kept him perfectly still. Not a hint of emotion crossed his face or crept into his narrowed eyes. "What is it, Savannah?"

She chewed nervously on her lower lip. "Mama said to come quick. Her time's come."

"Now? But she's not due until— Shit!" He pushed past Savannah and ran into the cold, dark night. Rain pummeled his face and blurred his vision as he ran toward the house.

Christ, while he'd been putting a gun to his head, his wife had been preparing to give birth to his child.

What the hell kind of man was he?

"God forgive me," he murmured.

But, of course, he had no hope of that.

Chapter One

SEATTLE, WASHINGTON.
1993

Tess Gregory paced nervously from one end of her small office to the other, her hands twined in a cold, bloodless ball. The silence that she'd long ago learned to accept seemed suddenly oppressive, suffocating. For the fifth time in as many minutes, she glanced down at the Mickey Mouse watch on her wrist.

Twelve o'clock. She let out her breath in an anxious sigh. The results should have been back by now. Certainly if her latest experiment had been successful—

No. She refused to think negatively even for a moment.

She knew better than most the value of positive thinking. Wearing a rut in the utilitarian gray carpet and worrying herself sick wouldn't do a bit of good. The lab would get back to her in their own sweet time, and until then, she simply had to relax. To *believe.*

Tess squeezed her eyes shut. It was an old childhood trick to calm her ragged nerves, one she'd often used as the doctors poked and prodded and asked questions she could no longer hear. She blacked out the physical world and focused on the one special noise that was captured forever in her memory: laughter. As always, it came to her quickly, lifting her spirits and easing the gnawing anxiety from her stomach.

She pried her fingers apart and shoved her hands into her lab coat's deep pockets. Taking a deep breath to calm her racing nerves, she tilted her chin and sailed past the cushioned beige walls of her cubicle.

In the employee dining room, lunch hour was in full swing. Dozens of white-coated people were clustered around the long, rectangular table. Heaps of Styrofoam food and drink containers littered the wood-grain veneer tabletop. The mingled aromas of microwaved leftovers, old coffee, and hospital disinfectants hung heavily in the air.

They were all talking animatedly to one another, mouths and hands moving at the speed of light. It was like an old Charlie Chaplin movie: the only thing missing from the vibrant scene was sound.

Tess moved restlessly past the bank of vending machines and went to the room's only window. Hugging herself against the slight chill that seeped through the thin glass, she stared outside.

It was an ordinary spring day: wet and gray. The kind of day that encouraged Seattleites to seek travel packages on Maui. Ash-hued, moisture-thick clouds hung above the city, obscuring the rooftops and casting the streets in shadow. Rain pattered cement sidewalks and plunked in overfull, leaf-clogged gutters. Puddles shone on the pavement like haphazardly thrown silver coins.

A good day for miracles.

The thought came before she could control it. She knew she shouldn't even think it—thinking was the first step to hoping, and hoping was the first step to disappointment. But no matter how often or how loudly she told herself not to hope, she'd never been able to follow her own advice.

Maybe today was her mantra, her lifeline. It was the

same hope she had every morning as she stood at the corner of Third and Virginia, waiting for the bus that would whisk her here, to the Fred Hutchinson Cancer Research Center. The hope never died, even after countless failures. In fact, with each defeat, it grew stronger.

She rested her forehead against the pane, suppressing a quick shudder as the icy window chilled her skin. The answer was right under her nose; she could feel it. All she had to do was find the right key. If these tests didn't give her the answers she needed, she'd try again. And again and again and again.

That's what Tess loved about life and science—anything and everything was possible if a person truly believed.

And Tess had always believed.

The yellow light on the wall above her head blipped on and off. It was the beeper system the hospital had devised to reach Tess and other hearing-impaired employees anywhere in the building.

Excitement brought her head up. Her heartbeat accelerated. Unable to keep a grin off her face, she hurried back to her office.

Dr. Weinstein was already there, holding a manila folder of test results.

She skidded to a halt. Her heart and hopes and prayers were in her eyes as she looked up at him. Her breath caught as she waited for the results.

He squeezed his eyes shut and shook his head.

Her knees went weak with disappointment. She sank unsteadily into the tufted vinyl chair behind her desk.

Dr. Weinstein squeezed her shoulder and tossed the file on the desk. She cast him a weary sideways glance and forced a smile. "Maybe next time," she said quietly, thankful for once that she couldn't hear her own voice. She was sick and tired of saying the same thing. Over and over and over.

Tess shoved the papers in her briefcase and followed Dr. Weinstein out of her office. She needed to walk, be alone for a while. Regroup.

Shrugging into her Eddie Bauer raincoat, she hurried down the stairs and went outside. The cold dampness of a late Seattle afternoon hit her full in the face. Rain pattered the thick Gortex of her hood; she felt each drop as a vibration of remembered sound.

She turned her face skyward. Cool water splattered her cheeks and nose and closed eyelids. The icy feel of it refreshed her, reminded her with unexpected force that she was alive. With life there was always hope, and with hope, anything was possible.

Tightening her grip on the briefcase, she started down the hill toward the bus stop, moving cautiously down the rain-slicked sidewalk. Beside her, buses and cars and taxis zipped through the gray drizzle. She could feel the vibrations of the moving vehicles as a gentle humming beneath her feet. The cherished sound-memories of honking horns and blaring sirens echoed through her fertile imagination, reminding her of the days, long ago and before spinal meningitis, when the ordinary noises of life had not been withheld from her.

She was just about to step in a tire-sized mud puddle when she caught herself. She wrenched sideways at the last minute and lurched toward the curb.

After that, everything seemed to happen in slow motion. A messenger-service bicycle slammed into her back and sent her careening into the street. She stumbled on the slick pavement and skidded out of control. Her briefcase flew out of her hand and sailed through the air. It hit the pavement hard and snapped open. Papers scattered and stuck to the bumpy asphalt. Rain riveted them in place.

The acrid stench of burning rubber filled the air. She froze. Heart hammering in her chest, she spun around and saw the bus heading right for her. A scream locked in her throat and issued past her lips as a low, terrified moan.

She didn't even have time to pray.

Tess drifted gently on a tide of warm water, wrapped in layers of smooth black velvet. The world around her was soothingly dark. She washed closer and closer to the shore, and knew she should reach out and grab hold, but she was tired. So tired . . .

"Tess, wake up, honey. I've got a schedule to meet." A woman's harsh, gravelly voice pierced the blackness.

Tess edged reluctantly toward consciousness. Her eyelids fluttered, tried futilely to open.

"I think she's awake," came a man's deep, rich voice.

"Really?" The woman's voice again. "Tess? Are you awake?"

She could hear! Tess snapped to a sit and glanced wildly around.

There was nothing to see. Nothing—and no one— except a seemingly endless expanse of star-studded night sky. Tiny, eye-splittingly bright lights vibrated and blinked like the Milky Way.

She started to panic. Her heart pounded painfully in her chest, turning every breath into a burning spurt of fire.

Calm down, Tess. Get a grip.

Cautiously she eased back and found that she was sitting in one of those Art Linkletter chairs. She drew a deep, shaking breath and let it out slowly. Her white-knuckled fingers eased their clawlike grip off the cushy armrests. An easy chair. What was so weird about that?

Nothing, she told herself. Nothing at all.

Then she noticed that her feet were dangling in the air.

She gasped. There was no floor beneath her, no walls around her. She was sitting in a black chair in the middle of a black void with a thousand stars twinkling all around her. Alone.

She was dreaming, she realized suddenly. Dreaming she was sitting in a chair in the middle of space, dreaming she could hear, dreaming—

"Tess?"

There it was again, that scratchy boilermaker-and-tobacco-fed voice, coming at Tess from the nothingness around her. Surely if she were going to dream a voice, it wouldn't sound like *that*.

"Y-Yes?" she said, for lack of something better.

"I'm Carol. Your guide. Do you have any questions before we begin?"

Tess started to say, "Begin what?" then changed her mind to the more obvious question. "Where am I?"

There was a long pause before the voice said cautiously, "You don't remember?"

"Remember what?"

"The . . . bus."

Tess stopped breathing. Memory hurled her back onto that rain-slicked Seattle street. She remembered the acrid, stinking smell of burning rubber, the driver's horrified expression through the dirty windshield. Sounds she couldn't possibly have heard battered her with hurricane force: squealing brakes, a honking horn, her own strangled sound of terror.

She'd been hit by the bus. She glanced around. Maybe this wasn't a dream after all. Maybe it was . . . the other side. "Am I dead?"

There was a sigh of relief. "Yep."

Tess shivered and hugged herself. "Oh."

"Now that that's settled, let's get on with it," Carol said matter-of-factly. "This here's the theater of second chances. Your life on earth—the first one—it was sort of . . ." Carol's scratchy voice trailed off.

"Fine."

"Yes, precisely. But 'fine' isn't good enough. God, in His infinite wisdom, makes sure everyone gets one happy life before they move on. So, hon, you get another chance."

"I don't understand."

"It's simple. Your first life was so-so. Now you get to choose another. I studied your history very closely, and I think I know the problem. Your childhood in the foster care system left something to be desired. What you need is someone special and a family of your own. I've chosen a dozen suitable candidates. Each one needs you as much as you need him. All you have to do is push the button when one of them strikes your fancy."

Tess smiled wryly. "Sort of a 'Dating Game' for the dead? What's next—'Bowling for Celestial Dollars'?"

"Hey, that's good! But—oh, shh. The show is starting. Just push the button when it feels right. I'll do the rest."

A single red button appeared on the chair's stark black arm. Pale red light throbbed against the dark fabric. "It's a dream, right?" Tess said to the voice. "I'm sedated now and in surgery. Am I right?"

"Shh. Watch."

The stars sprayed out in front of Tess slowly melded together, becoming a huge white rectangle wreathed in jet black nothingness. A screen.

She leaned forward. Even though she knew it was a dream, she couldn't help feeling a quick rush of suspense. Her fingers curled nervously around the tufted armrest.

A dot of color appeared in the exact center of the white screen. It started small, no larger than a nickel. For a heartbeat it quivered, silent and alone. Then *wham!* it exploded into a full-color picture of a man in a gray flannel suit waving for a cab.

He was an attractive man. Young. Obviously affluent.

Tess settled deeper in her chair. Her finger moved toward the button, but she didn't push. Instead, she studied him with the critical, detail-sensitive eyes of a woman used to relying on sight for her impressions of the world.

The man was clutching an Italian leather briefcase as if it contained the plans for a nuclear bomb. Or, more likely, a summer house in the Hamptons. His hair was precisely combed, maybe even moussed. There were no laugh lines around his eyes. No earring marred his conservative image. His tie was a regimental blue stripe, his shirt plain white.

Her finger eased off the button.

The scene switched to a snowy hillside. A man in faded blue jeans and knee-length duster was shoving hay into a long wooden feeding bin. Breath billowed in white clouds from his mouth. Behind him was a whitewashed, porched farmhouse that looked a hundred years old.

Tess let the cowboy pass. Someone else could ride the range.

Next came a man playing volleyball on the beach. His body was well muscled, browned to tanning bed perfection. Pale blond hair clung to his sweaty face as he spiked the winning shot. Several women on the sidelines cheered loudly, and he gave each of them a playboy wink.

Tess winced. Yuck.

The stud was replaced by a knight in shining armor. Literally. He moved woodenly, clanging with every step across the stone floor, muttering words in a language Tess couldn't understand. The scene looked exactly like a production of *Macbeth* she'd once seen at a theater for the deaf in Boston.

Tess's finger didn't go anywhere near the button. Egotistical actors weren't for her. She had no desire to be the wind beneath his wings.

Men and lives merged into one another, became a hypnotic blur of color and questions and possibilities. Still Tess sat there, her finger hovering over the red button that would supposedly grant her another life. She didn't believe a word of it, of course, but somehow she couldn't hit the button—even to play along. Especially not with the kind of men who kept showing up. (Currently there was a man in a space suit hovering in front of her.)

The spaceman melted away. Slowly the color onscreen softened. A man appeared, standing alone and in the shadows. He was standing beside an old wooden crib, staring down at a baby wrapped in a bundle of woolen blankets. His big shoulders were hunched, his fingers were curled tightly around the crib's top rail. The quiet strains of his breathing reached her ears, filling her senses like long-sought-after music.

Tess felt his quiet desperation like a noose around her neck.

He moved forward, and the shadows fell away, revealing a once handsome and now haggard face framed by jet black hair badly in need of a trim. He stared down at the child. One finger at a time, as if each motion were fraught with danger, he lifted his hand and reached toward the baby's cheek. Halfway there, he froze. His fingers trembled. Tears glistened in the corners of his eyes, and he yanked his hand back.

God, how he loves that child.

Then he was gone.

Tess slammed her palm down on the button.

"He's the one?" Carol's voice sounded soft and deceptively close.

Tess nodded slowly, shaken and confused by the intensity of the emotions she'd felt. As someone who'd spent a lifetime isolated and alone, *watching*, she knew little of stormy passions and wrenching heartache. And yet, when she'd looked into his eyes, she'd seen pain, real pain, and something more. Some dark, aching emotion that ripped past her natural optimism and frightened her.

There had been something about him, something in his defeated gaze that cut like a knife blade through her heart. She'd learned long ago to read people's eyes and see beyond their words, yet never had she glimpsed a soul in such agony.

"I don't know," she murmured. "I felt such . . . pain."

"I understand, hon. You've always been a healer at heart. Good luck. You'll need it with that one."

There was a wisp of rose-colored light, a scent of smoke, and then nothing. Tess knew without question that she was alone again.

"What now?" she asked of no one in particular, and flopped back in her chair.

Except there was no chair. No chair, no floor, no walls. There was only an immense sky of midnight black spackled with stars so bright, they hurt the eyes.

Tess whizzed by the moon and kept falling.

Chapter Two

Pain. Immense, incalculable pain.

Tess lay perfectly still. She tried to breathe and found that even that simple action hurt. Every square inch of her body felt battered and broken. Even her breasts ached.

Why? Why did she feel like this?

She'd been hit by a bus.

The memory came at her like a hard right punch, catching her square in the gut. Her breath expelled in a sharp rush. Her lungs burned at the effort. No wonder she hurt. She was lucky to be alive.

Or was she?

Am I dead?

She remembered uttering that small, quiet question, remembered the endless star-spangled night sky and Carol's barroom voice. *Yep.*

Just as she'd thought. It had all been a dream. Or a painkiller-induced hallucination. Or one of those near-death experiences inquiring minds loved so much.

She moved a fraction of an inch and immediately regretted it. Red-hot pain twisted her midsection, brought a surge of nausea so strong, she thought she'd vomit. All thoughts of life after death vanished.

She *felt* as if she'd been hit by a bus.

It *had* all been a dream. There was no second chance for

Tess; no family to join or ability to hear. No man standing
by a crib, reaching out.

She was surprised by the sharp regret that flashed
through her. She'd really wanted that second chance at
life. At love. No one in this life would have missed her.

Disappointed, she closed her eyes and sank back into
the darkness of oblivion.

She was dreaming she could hear.

". . . blood loss . . . don't know . . . not good . . ."

Tess clawed her way to consciousness. The pain was
still there, gnawing with dull teeth at her midsection, but
it was more manageable now. She said a quick prayer to
the God of anesthesia and coaxed her eyes open.

She was in a huge bed, looking up at the floor. She
frowned in concentration, willing her tired eyes to do their
job, and her equally tired brain to function. Blinking, she
tried again.

It wasn't a floor. It was a ceiling built of oak boards.

"Dead? Don't know . . . possible."

Tess gasped. She'd heard that! She struggled up to her
elbows. The effort left her shaking and winded and in in-
conceivable pain. Her head pounded. She found a station-
ary lump of black and focused on it.

The lump became a shadow, the shadow became an old
man. Sparse gray hair studded his pointed, balding head.
Thin wire-rimmed glasses perched precariously on his
beaklike nose. Rheumy eyes stared into her own.

"Mrs. Rafferty? Are you okay?"

Tess glanced around for Mrs. Rafferty.

He scooted his stool closer. The wooden legs made a
squeaking, scraping sound. He laid a skeletal, blue-veined
hand on her shoulder and squeezed gently. "Welcome
back."

This was no dream. She could really hear.

"Whaas—" Tess tried to speak, but her throat felt as if she'd been screaming for hours. She signed her question instead: *What's wrong with me?*

The man glanced over his shoulder at the shadows in the room's corner. "It's like she's trying to say something. . . ." He leaned closer and peered into her eyes. "I'm Doc Hayes. Do you recollect me?"

She shook her head no.

He frowned and pushed to his feet.

Even in the midst of her pain, she marveled at the slow, tired shuffling of the doctor's footsteps. After so many years of silent nothingness, the common, everyday sound of his bootheels scuffing across the floor was indescribably wonderful.

He melted into the shadows by the door. "I don't know, Jack. It's the damnedest thing I've ever seen. I was pretty sure she was dead. This ain't the sort o' thing one sees ever' day. She might be sort o' . . . different for a while. Who knows? Appears her memory's shot to hell."

"What can we do for her?" It was another male voice, softer and richer. The warm, brandy-soft sound of it sent a tingle slithering down Tess's spine.

"I don't know," the doc answered. "But if she gets a fever or takes a turn for the worse, send someone for me."

The shadows moved. The door creaked open, then clicked shut. She was alone.

Confusion swirled about her like a thick, gray fog, drawing her into the mists. Tiredly she glanced around her hospital room, but the shadows were so thick, she couldn't make out much beyond her own bed. Yet something about the darkened room felt weird. Apprehension tingled along the back of her neck. She'd been in enough hospitals to recognize one, even in the dark. Where was the familiar antiseptic smell and muted buzz of fluorescent lighting? And docs hadn't made house calls since Welby.

Minutes ticked by, quietly, without the marching tick of a clock to herald their passing. She stared up at the strange ceiling, feeling the warmth and light from the lamp beside her bed. The acrid scent of a burning wick teased her nostrils.

So strange, she thought. Everything was so damned strange.

Before she could figure out why, she was asleep again.

Tess tried to force her eyes open, but the painful throbbing behind them made it impossible. She tossed uncomfortably.

Something cool touched her forehead. It felt unbelievably good. A soft sigh of relief slipped past her parched lips.

After a few moments she was able to open her eyes. The first thing she saw was that weird floor/ceiling again.

"Oh, crap," she mumbled. She thought for sure she'd waken to the comfortingly familiar sight of white acoustical tile and long tubes of fluorescent lighting.

The cool, damp rag on her forehead vanished. A flesh-tone smear wobbled in front of her eyes. She blinked, tried to focus. Gradually the blur coalesced into a man's face that seemed both familiar and unfamiliar at the same time.

He shoved a too long lock of black hair out of his eyes and bent closer. Tired, bloodshot eyes peered questioningly into her own. Stubbly, dark hair accentuated the hollowness in his cheeks and the hard, masculine line of his jaw. Tess frowned. A wisp of memory winged through her head, and she tried desperately to chase it down. Somewhere she'd seen this face before.

It came to her in a flash. He looked sort of like a young Sam Elliot . . . on a very bad day.

But why did the man look so utterly exhausted, as if he'd sat vigil by her bed for endless hours? There was no one who cared about her so much.

An intern, she realized suddenly. He had to be the intern assigned to her case. She'd seen that ragged, haggard look before—it was a surgical intern on the tail end of a three-day round.

"Amarylis?"

"No, thanks, I don't drink." The moment the words were out of her mouth, she realized that something was wrong with her voice. It sounded . . . southern. *I doan draank.*

"What?"

A headache jackhammered across her head. She squeezed two fingers against her temples. "Forget the liquor. What I need is an Excedrin the size of Baltimore, and a look at my charts."

"Charts?"

It took a supreme effort to remain civil. "Just tell the doc in charge of my case that I'm conscious and I'd like to consult about my condition. Okay?"

"H-He's not here."

One eyebrow cocked upward. "Golf day at the club?"

"Golf?"

Tess clamped her dry lips together and didn't say a thing. It was best that way.

He offered her a tense smile. "Do you want to see the baby?"

Tess frowned. She thought he'd said "baby."

She was about to suggest he get some sleep when a question crept cautiously into her consciousness. What if Carol hadn't been a dream? What if—

She chewed nervously on her lower lip and stared up at him. "Baby?"

"You . . . don't remember?"

She winced. The last time someone had asked her that question, Tess had forgotten getting run over by a bus. That kind of memory lapse did nothing to inspire confidence. Cautiously she said, "No."

"Yesterday you had a baby. Our son."

She started shaking, and all of a sudden remembered where she'd seen this man. He wasn't an intern. He was the man she'd chosen in the theater of second chances.

"Oh my God . . ." She clamped a hand over her mouth.

It had been real. *Real.*

The bus had killed her. She'd died in Seattle and been reborn in the body of a woman who'd died in childbirth. Questions and concerns and hopes and fears tumbled one after another in her mind. What did one do at a time like this? Laugh, cry, scream—what?

One thing at a time, Tess. Only one.

She took a deep breath and offered him a tenuous smile. "I—I need some time here. To think. How about getting me that aspirin?" At his utterly blank stare, she added, "Acetaminophen is fine, too. Whatever you have. That and a glass of ice water would be great."

"Aceta—what?"

"Tylenol."

He shook his head. "I don't understand, Amarylis. What are you asking for?"

Tess shoved her hand through the bunched-up sheets in search of the nurses' button. Except there was no button; no button, no metal railing, no utilitarian food tray. There was only a splintery, old-fashioned wooden bed.

The woman had given birth at home?

Tess shivered. No wonder the poor woman had died.

She glanced around the room for a bottle of something—anything—that would take the edge off her migraine. Sunlight spilled through a small, thick-paned window and splashed across a dull, planked floor. Blue gingham curtains hung listlessly on either side of the small window, their hand-hemmed edges bleached from too many days in the sun. No flowers peeked through the glass or brightened the sill. Against the far wall, standing alone and unadorned with photos or knick-knacks, was an oaken washstand with a tilted mirror. A white crockery ewer and basin sat dead center on a wrinkled white scrap of lace.

A prickly-hot feeling crawled through Tess. Reluctantly she shot a look sideways, and immediately winced. The bedside table was a fruit crate turned on its side, and the lamp was a small, triangular glass jar with a wick sticking out of the narrow top. Tucked beside the crate was a pink porcelain chamber pot.

Horror rounded her eyes. She thought of the cowboy and the knight in shining armor, and shook her head in denial.

No, Carol wouldn't do that to me. . . .

"What is it?" the man asked anxiously. "Should I call Doc Hayes?"

"Where am I?"

"At home . . . on San Juan Island."

Tess felt a tiny stirring of relief. At least she was still in Washington; she could get home from here.

But her location wasn't really the issue, and she knew it. She took a deep breath and squeezed her eyes shut. It took every scrap of courage she possessed to ask the next question: "What year is it?"

There was a heartbeat's pause before he said quietly, "It's 1873."

"Oh, no." She covered her mouth with her hand. "Oh, *shit* . . ."

Eighteen seventy-three.

No television, telephone, electricity. And that was just

for starters. How was she supposed to live without showers, razors, tampons?

"No way." She curled her hands into fists and screamed at the top of her lungs. "CAROL!!!"

Chapter Three

Carol? Jack thought. *Who the hell is Carol?*

He stared at his wife in confusion, unable to think of a single damn thing to say.

She looked . . . different. The hard, calculating look usually in her eyes had softened. She looked frail and frightened and alone.

He had an inexplicable desire to brush the hair from her face and tell her everything would be all right.

His mouth twisted into a grim parody of a smile. God, how she would laugh if she could read his mind right now.

She would never accept comfort from him, and the realization that even now, after years of silence and hurt, he still wanted to be in love with her was enough to make him sick.

His broad shoulders hunched in defeat. *Jackson Rafferty, you're a goddamn fool.*

She hated him; she had since the moment he'd told her the truth about himself. In that split second the love in her eyes had metamorphosed, congealed into something cold and dark. Not once in all the years of their marriage had the hatred lessened. She despised him and his cowardice with an intensity that continued to amaze him. Wound him.

Amarylis had married Jack for one thing, and one alone. Security. She'd come from a family labeled poor white trash by the whole county, and Jackson Rafferty had been her ladder out of poverty. When things had changed, when *he* had changed, she'd felt betrayed, and in the years since, her sense of betrayal had grown, turning finally into an icy knot of hatred. She had never—would never—forgive his weakness. It had taken her dreams of respectability and wealth and left her with nothing but a crazy shell of a man and a broken-down sheep ranch in the middle of nowhere.

He knew all that, and more. So why did he see in her eyes right now an impossible softness? Amarylis was never frail and frightened; he knew that. It was all in his mind, as were so many things.

He ran a shaking hand through his hair. Too well he knew what she was capable of doing to him, and he wouldn't let it happen again. Her contempt and hatred wouldn't push him over the edge. He had the children to fight for, even if he didn't have himself.

"I'm not your wife, you know. What's her name, Amaretto?"

Jack's head snapped up. "Huh?"

"She died. Go ahead and mourn her passing. There's been a mix-up. I never agreed to any time change. Eighteen seventy-three." She shuddered. "How am I supposed to function without a microwave and a computer? And what about my work?"

"You mean the household chores?" He frowned. "But you don't do anything."

She drew in a tiny, squeaking breath. "Nineteenth-century chores?" she said, gasping. "What do I do, make soap from tree bark and scrub floors? Oh my God. Carol! Get down here. Now!" She looked wildly around the room, as if she expected someone—or something—to answer her cry. The name, *Carol*, vibrated on the air, then died away, plunging the bedroom back into its thick, awkward silence.

The lamp beside the bed sputtered. Light wobbled, splashed across the red and white wedding-ring-pattern quilt and glittered on his wife's classically beautiful face. Her eyelids quavered for a moment and closed. The dark brown lashes looked like smudges against the paleness of her skin.

He thought he heard her mumble "shit" as she sank tiredly back into the pile of feather pillows, but that wasn't possible. Amarylis Rafferty—the perfect southern lady even on a backwater sheep ranch—never cursed.

Jack scoured his brain for something to say. But it had been years since he'd spoken civilly to his wife, and longer yet since she'd wanted to hear it.

He had just decided to try something incredibly banal and inoffensive, like *Are you thirsty?* when footsteps sounded outside the door. After a flurry of whispers, a knock thudded.

Jack tensed. All thoughts of comforting his wife vanished. He remembered in a rush just who she was and the pain she was more than capable of inflicting on all of them.

A headache pounded behind his eyes. He rubbed his throbbing temple. The kids were his life; all he had or ever hoped to have. He had to protect them from their mother's vituperative anger and explosive hatred, and there was only one way to do that. No matter how much it pained him, how much each aching silence cost him, he had to appear detached and uncaring. Because if Amarylis thought—even suspected—how much he loved his children, she'd find a way to make them all pay. The children most of all, for in hurting them, she hurt Jack. And hurting Jack was always her primary goal. She wanted him to remember, every day in every way, that he'd betrayed and ruined her, and that she would never forgive him.

He still remembered the last time he'd tried to shield the

girls from his wife's biting tongue. She had smacked him—a stinging, flat-palmed crack to the cheek—and told him that if he said another word, *ever*, she'd leave.

See how the girls would do then, you sniveling coward. They'd grow up as twisted and crazy as you are. Do you want that? Do you?

A chill crept up his spine at the memory. "It's the girls. They've been asking to see you."

She looked at him sharply, her eyebrows pulling together in a slight frown. "The girls?"

He searched her face for a hint that she was toying with him again. But there was no trace of pretense, no sign that she was faking her memory loss. "Our daughters, Savannah and Mary Katherine."

"Oh . . ." She nodded, but the confusion remained in her eyes. "Okay."

"Come on in, girls," he yelled.

The door opened. Savannah entered first, carrying the baby. She stopped at the foot of the massive bed. Katie followed quickly, melting like a formless apparition into the shadows behind her older sister. Only the jet black outline of her hair and a hint of lemon yellow ribbon were visible at Savannah's crooked elbow.

Jack stared through dull, tired eyes at his children. Their frightened faces tore at his heart. As always, the magnitude of his sin and shame sickened him. He and Amarylis had turned two vibrant, loving girls into shadowy, silent wraiths.

This marriage had been a bloody battlefield for years. And these two perfect, beautiful girls, their own children, had become the casualties. Prisoners of a war they couldn't understand.

"H-How are you, Mama?" Savannah asked in a hushed, respectful voice.

Tess sat up a little straighter in bed. There was something wrong here. Something ... strange. "Come closer, girls. I want to see you."

The taller of the two girls moved hesitantly forward. As she moved into the lamp's circle of light, Tess's heart wrenched. The girl was trying desperately hard to keep her chin cocked at a defiant angle. Her huge blue eyes stared emotionlessly forward, as if the wall were of utmost fascination. She was completely motionless except for the trembling in her chapped, work-reddened hands.

Behind her cowered a smaller child, her small, pink fingers clutched tightly in the blue gingham of her sister's floor-length skirt.

"Which one of you is Savannah?"

The older girl seemed startled for a moment, then said, "I—I am."

"I assume that's Mary Katherine behind your skirts?"

She nodded, flicking a long, mahogany-hued braid over her shoulder.

"How old are you?"

"I'm twelve. Katie's seven."

After the quick answer, silence descended once again. Tess got the distinct impression that it was the normal state of affairs with this family. Then someone cried. It was a hiccuping, sputtering sound like the whining cry of an ungreased engine.

Tess's gaze lowered to the bundle in Savannah's arms. "Is that the baby?"

Savannah bobbed her head.

Tess swallowed thickly. Fear and excitement merged together, bringing a slow, hesitant smile to her lips. "M-May I see him?"

Surprise flitted across Savannah's face. She stood rooted to the spot.

The truth washed over Tess in a cold wave, made her feel

sick and twisted-up inside. "You're afraid to let her . . . I mean *me* hold him."

Savannah blanched. Chewing nervously on her lower lip, she edged closer to the bed and gently placed the baby on Tess's distended stomach. "N-No, it's just that you never wanted to hold Katie. I—I thought . . ."

Instinctively Tess reached out to comfort the frightened girl. "It's okay, honey."

Savannah stiffened and jerked out of reach. Before Tess could respond, the bundle in her arms started wriggling furiously.

Gingerly she peeled back the homespun blanket. Murky, swollen-lidded eyes peered up at her from a beet red, wrinkled face the size of a tea saucer.

Hesitantly she stroked his velvet-soft newborn skin. At her touch he sucked in a shuddering, hiccuping breath and stopped crying. His unfocused gaze landed on her face, and she had the unmistakable sense that he was studying her. After a moment he gave a quiet, contented sigh. Snuggling deeper in the blanket, he went back to sleep.

Tess felt his acceptance and trust like a tangible presence. For the first time, she understood the meaning of the word *awe*. Her eyes widened with it, her heartbeat slowed to a crawl. Tears scalded her eyes.

She looked up suddenly, expecting to see her awe mirrored on the faces around her. Instead, she saw anxiety and suspicion.

Savannah immediately reached out for the baby. "Here, Mama, I'll take him. . . ."

Katie, who'd peeked her head around her sister's elbow, jerked back into invisibility behind Savannah.

Tess frowned. What was wrong with this family? They acted as if they expected her to fling the baby across the room. Savannah and Jack were standing on guard, waiting for the explosion, regarding her with the wary, nervous glances normally accorded a hand grenade with a pulled pin. And poor Katie was following the first rule of warfare: Keep your head down and stay in the trenches.

There was so much pain here, so much she didn't understand. She felt again the involuntary urge to help, to touch, to heal. Just like when she'd seen Jack huddled piteously near the crib . . .

She wanted to say something light and easy, something that would ease the heartache from the faces around her. But she couldn't think of a thing.

She tried to reach for Savannah, but the infant restricted her movement. All she could do was raise a single pointed finger toward the girl.

Only her finger didn't point at Savannah. It pointed at the door. At the gesture, Savannah's skin went ashen. Before Tess could utter a word, Savannah swirled and ran from the room. Katie followed at a scamper. The door slammed shut.

Jack leapt to his feet. "Damn you, Amarylis! Would it have hurt you to *talk* to them? They've been worried about you, for God's sake."

"I thought—"

"Ha!" He surged toward her. The hollow sound of his bootheels slamming against the floor rang in Tess's head.

"You know what you're doing to her, goddamn you."

"I just wanted—"

He laughed. It was a harsh, bitter sound without a trace of mirth. "I know what the hell you want. Everyone does." He stared at her again through cold, narrowed eyes, then turned away from the bed as if sickened by the sight of her. He crossed the small room in three steps and yanked the door open, slamming it shut behind him.

Tess stared at the door, feeling—stupidly—another woman's guilt and regret.

Amarylis, it seemed, had not been a very good mother.

* * *

Jack slammed the door so hard, the rafters rattled. The girls jumped like scared rabbits and spun around to face him. Katie slunk behind her sister's full skirts.

He wanted to push past his children and run from this cursed house, and keep on running until he couldn't run anymore.

"Is Mama all right?" Savannah asked.

Jack looked at his eldest daughter and felt a jolt of emotion so strong, he almost cursed out loud. She was looking at him with a mixture of hope and love and desperation that serrated his heart.

How? he thought angrily. How could she love him after everything he'd done . . . and not done?

Need rose in him like a sudden wave. He wanted—ached—to get down on his knees and take them in his arms.

But, of course, he didn't move. His hands remained bolted to his sides, and not a hint of softness crept into his hardened gaze. The only protection was in distance. If he cracked—even for an instant, as long as it took to say, "I love you"—the evil in his soul would slip out and devour his children.

But he wanted to. Sweet Christ, how he wanted to.

He swallowed the boulder-sized lump in his throat and prayed the emotions in his heart didn't reach his eyes. "She's fine. Doc Hayes says she'll be confused for a while. Might even forget some things. We're supposed to help her out."

Katie peeked her head out from behind Savannah. "Caleb's a good name."

"Caleb, huh?"

"Mama won't like it," Savannah said tonelessly.

Because we do. Jack had no trouble finishing the sad sentence. She was right, and all three of them knew it.

Amarylis took pleasure in stealing their joy. Jack knew he should say nothing, should simply turn his back and walk away. But God help him, he couldn't. Before he knew it, he found himself saying, "Well, maybe we should try it now, while she's . . . confused."

At Savannah's sudden smile, Jack felt a new wave of despair. It took so little to make his girls happy. So very, very little. And, damn his soul, he gave them even less.

"Carol," Tess hissed as soon as the door closed. "Get down here. *Now!*"

Tess moved higher in bed. "Carol!"

No answer.

Tess let her breath out in a frustrated sigh. She hadn't really expected Carol to answer. Apparently ghostly intervention was reserved for postdeath experiences. New lives were a new slate.

What was she supposed to do now? Be a pioneer wife? She shuddered at the thought. She didn't even like *movies* about pioneer wives. The women were always so dirty and overworked.

She glanced down at the baby curled so peacefully beside her and felt a rush of confusing emotions. Fear, hope, excitement. Mostly fear.

She didn't know the first thing about being a mother. Or a wife, for that matter. She'd never really been part of a family in her life. She'd never been in love, and now here she was, the matriarch of an apparently frightened, dysfunctional family and the mother of three—including a newborn. She didn't cook, clean, sew, understand children, or communicate particularly well.

She should have chosen the knight in shining armor. At least she could have outrun him.

"It's perfect, Carol," she said sarcastically. "I should fit right in."

The sarcastic words were barely past her lips when she heard the doorknob turn. Seconds later, the family filed into her bedroom like a contingent of mute, defeated soldiers, with Jack in the lead. He stood tall and proud, far enough away from the girls to keep his distance, and yet close enough to make Tess wonder why he bothered to keep himself separate. His unkempt hair hung in wavy disarray to the broad shelf of his shoulders, where it lay curled like shavings of jet. Piercing green eyes impaled her from beneath a row of thick black eyebrows.

Savannah moved stiffly forward, her hands balled together at her waist. With her long, auburn braids and huge blue eyes, she looked like Dorothy facing the Wizard.

Tess leaned sideways in an attempt to see Katie. But the moment Tess shifted her weight, Katie scooted the opposite way. Again there was nothing to see but the child's drooping yellow ribbon and a flash of black hair.

Strange family, Tess thought again.

"Mama?" Savannah said quietly.

It took Tess a moment to remember that she was now their mother. Cautiously, she said, "Yes?"

"We . . . We thought Caleb might be a nice name."

Tess glanced down at the baby in her arms. "Caleb." The word rolled off her tongue with just the right sound. Of course, it wasn't her place to name the baby, and she wouldn't have presumed to disagree, and yet, strangely, they had chosen exactly the name she would have picked. She nodded, smiling slowly. "It's perfect."

Katie poked her head out. "It is?"

Tess smiled softly at the little girl. "Did you think of it?"

Katie blushed furiously and disappeared again.

"And who diapered him?" Tess asked.

Savannah chewed on her lower lip. "I—I did. But if you want, I can do it a—"

"You did a perfect job. Thank you."

Blood rushed to Savannah's milky white cheeks. "I gotta go." Turning quickly, she raced out of the room, with Katie fast on her heels.

Jack stared at Tess with an inscrutable expression. She couldn't tell if he was pleased or angry. Time stretched out, turned thick and uneasy. She wanted to speak, but couldn't think of what to say. The fiasco of the finger pointing had proved to Tess what an emotional minefield this family was. A person could say the wrong thing and get her head blown off.

The silence made Tess distinctly uncomfortable. She'd spent years—a lifetime—living in aching silence. It was something she'd never do again.

"Jack, I—"

"Don't worry, I'm leaving." He spun on his heels and barreled for the door.

It slammed shut just as Tess said, "—think we should talk."

She stared at the door for a while, feeling strangely betrayed. Then, with a resigned sigh, she melted deeper into the pillows and closed her eyes. The unfamiliar scents of weathered wood, hand-washed cotton, and burning oil wreathed her senses. Sounds reached her ears and made her smile; soft, quiet noises that most people probably wouldn't notice. Creaking, settling boards, wind tapping against the windowpane, Caleb's steady breathing. To Tess, deaf since the age of seven, these sounds were a glorious explosion. A gift from God.

"Okay, Carol," she said quietly. "I'm here. I accept that. But what the hell am I supposed to do?"

There was no answer; she hadn't expected one. As usual, Tess was on her own.

She rocked Caleb gently back and forth until he fell

asleep, then she peeled back the covers and started to get out of bed.

Pain stopped her cold, reminding her forcibly that her body had just given birth. Slowing considerably, she shuffled toward the cradle and gingerly put the sleeping baby to bed.

Straightening, she pressed a fist to her aching back and turned around. The mirror winked at her, drew her. She moved cautiously toward the looking glass, feeling very much like Alice.

What she saw made her breath catch. Silky, cornsilk-blond hair wreathed an exquisite Grace Kelly face. Huge, liquid-soft brown eyes peered questioningly back at her.

She shook her head in amazement, mesmerized by the way the light caught and tangled in her long, golden hair. "Whew, when God gives you a second chance, He means it," she said in a smooth southern drawl.

Hobbling back to the bed, she snuggled under the heavy quilt. For the first time in her life, she went to sleep thinking she was beautiful.

Chapter Four

A loud crash woke Tess.

Groggy, disoriented, she wedged her elbows behind her and struggled to get up. It took her a minute to remember where she was. *When* she was. She shot a quick glance at the cradle. Caleb was sleeping peacefully.

Relieved, she surveyed the room through bleary eyes. Nothing seemed to be different or disturbed—although she couldn't be sure. Pale moonlight came through the silvered windowpane, but otherwise the room was dark and still.

She shoved the quilt back and sat up. At the movement, pain wrenched her abdomen, shot down her thighs. It took all her strength of will not to flop back into the pillows like a dead fish.

She squeezed her eyes shut, concentrating on each breath until the blazing hurt ebbed into a dull, manageable ache. Then she swung her stockinged feet over the edge of her bed. Cool evening air skipped along her flesh, bringing a flurry of goose bumps. Shivering, she limped slowly toward the door.

"Johnny! No!"

The screamed words reverberated through the room and brought Tess to a dead stop. She waited, listening for another outburst, but the house was silent once again.

Reaching for the flannel robe flung along the foot of the bed, she shrugged into the warm fabric, eased the door open, and hobbled from the bedroom. At the end of the hallway, she paused to regain her breath. Clutching her aching midsection, she cautiously peeked around the corner.

The living room was dark except for the throbbing orange glow of a dying fire. Pulsating red-gold light licked the floor and cast sinewy fingers into the darkness. The furniture was a series of shadowy clumps, without form or substance.

Tess frowned. Easing away from the wall, she walked into the room.

Like an apparition, Jack materialized in front of her. Startled, Tess stumbled backward and hit the wall with a thud. He closed the distance between them in a single step. She felt the weight of his stare on her face, but she couldn't see his eyes.

"What the hell are you doing here?" The question was spoken quietly, though somehow the softness was more frightening than any yelling she'd ever heard. "You know the rules."

Tess wished she could take even one step backward, but the wall had her trapped. "I . . . I heard a noise."

"Go away." He spun away from her and began pacing. His movements were stiff and overly controlled, the rigid actions of a man who wanted to run but was forcing himself to stay. After a few moments, he covered his ears with his hands, as if there were great, booming noises only he could hear.

"Jack, I—"

He spun back around and grabbed her by the shoulders, yanking her to him. She hit his chest hard and bit back a gasp of pain. "Don't do this to me, Amarylis." His voice cracked. "I'm not strong enough to play your games right now."

She stared up at him, her breathing ragged. His gaze

seemed to grab her around the neck and squeeze. Suddenly he let go, as if he'd just realized he'd touched her.

She slid down the long, hard length of his body. Her bare feet hit the cold floor with a muffled thump.

"And don't forget the rules again. It doesn't matter what you hear. You don't come out here after dark. Not ever."

Tess leaned against the wall, struggling to catch her breath. She squeezed her eyes shut. Jack's bootheels thudded atop the floor, his every step matching the echoing beat of her heart. She heard the rough, ragged strains of his breathing and the crackling hiss of the dying fire. She tried to concentrate on the sounds she'd waited a lifetime to hear, only the sounds, but somehow she couldn't take joy in them. All she felt was alone and afraid and frighteningly out of her element.

She thought of Carol and her promise, and at the thought, sadness washed through her, leaving in its wake the sting of betrayal. Carol had lied to her. Jack Rafferty wasn't someone special at all.

She tried to be strong, tried not to care, but she couldn't help herself. Disappointment crept through her, tugging the corners of her mouth downward. For some absurd reason, she felt like crying.

She gritted her teeth, battling the unfamiliar wave of self-pity. Then she snapped out of it. She wasn't one to give up. She never had been before, and she damn well wouldn't start now. And besides, it wasn't all Carol's fault. Tess had chosen this life. This man.

"Damn it," she said to him. "This is my house, too, now. I have every right to go where I want, when I want. And right now I want to go . . ." She had to think a minute. "To the bathroom."

Forcing her chin up, she pushed away from the wall and headed toward the hallway.

"Where are you going?" he growled as she hobbled past him.

She tilted her chin a little higher. "Not that it's any of your business, but I intended to use the bathroom." She reached for the door in front of her.

"In the girls' room?"

Tess's hand froze inches from the knob. Frowning, she turned around and walked slowly toward the living room. "But there aren't any other doors."

"That's right. Not in the house, there aren't. There's the chamber pot in your room. Or, if you're feeling braver than usual, you can go—"

No. Don't say it, don't say the toilet is—

"—outside."

"Outside," she repeated dully. "Of course."

Hugging her cramping abdomen, she felt her way along the sofa and shuffled painfully into the kitchen. At the front door, she hesitated. The thought of putting her bare backside down on some shadowy pit toilet made her stomach writhe in revolt. But she didn't much feel like squatting over a porcelain pot in her bedroom, either.

She glanced back at the living room, searching the shadows for Jack. He was still standing by the window; she could see the outline of his torso against the pale curtains. "If I'm not back in ten minutes, call 911."

"What?"

She opened the door and went outside. Cold night air, thick with the scent of the sea, splashed her face and slid along her exposed neck. She clutched the robe tighter to her throat and stepped cautiously forward. Tired, white-washed boards creaked beneath her feet.

She hobbled down the wide, covered porch that stretched along the front of the house. At the top step, she paused, waiting for the pain to melt once again into something she could manage.

She glanced around. Midnight blue shadows and black shapes surrounded her, all of them wreathed by ghostly split-rail fences. A huge, opalescent moon hung in the star-spangled sky. Below it, the Straits glittered like an endless sheet of hammered steel, its surface rippled with moonlight. A row of shadowed, farmy-looking sheds led the way to a rickety, isolated old building that had to be the outhouse.

She clutched the wobbly handrail and slowly descended the few steps. By the final step, she was breathing heavily again. Pausing, she wiped the sheen of sweat from her brow and walked stiffly up the yard's grassy incline.

With each step, her stomach sank a little bit more. Wincing, trying not to breathe, she reached for the drawstring latch and opened the door. It swung on squeaky hinges and smacked hard against the wooden wall. The whole structure shuddered at the impact.

She peered inside, but couldn't see anything except a shower-sized, jet-black opening.

Cautiously she inched her way into the darkened stall. Night air immediately closed around her like black velvet. The expected odors curled around her throat, turned thick and ugly.

Clamping her lips together to keep from breathing, she lifted her nightgown and planted her bare behind on the cold wooden rim.

Suddenly the door banged shut, plunging her into tomblike darkness. Her imagination ran riot. She saw bugs and snakes and all kinds of nameless wild things creeping under the door and slithering toward her. Animal and night noises that any other time might sound whimsical and exciting, sounded ominous.

1873, she realized then, was not for sissies.

* * *

Savannah huddled under the thick blanket, her whole body shaking. She had a long-forgotten urge to suck her thumb again. She fisted her hand tightly and pressed it to her stomach. The unmistakable sounds of a parental fight crept beneath her door and hovered like a bad odor in the cramped room.

"Vannah? How come Daddy always yells about Johnny?"

Savannah shrugged in the darkness. Her throat was too thick with unshed tears to say anything. But Katie didn't expect a response. They'd lived through this same scene too many times to expect much of anything from anyone.

"You think Daddy's okay?"

Savannah swallowed. "Yeah." The word slipped out on a tired breath, with no conviction.

Katie crawled out of bed. Her bare feet thumped on the hard wooden floor. "I'm gonna go peek."

Savannah shoved her coverlet back and swung her stockinged feet out of bed. " 'Mere, Katie."

Katie shuffled toward her sister and took her hand. Together they crept cautiously toward the door and eased it open.

Daddy was standing in front of the fire. In the yellow-red firelight, they could see the trembling in his hands, but other than that, he was as still as stone. His quick breathing sliced through the darkness.

Mama walked to the back door. "If I'm not back in ten minutes, call 911."

"What?" Daddy yelled.

Mama ignored him and went outside. There was a minute of breath-laden silence, then Daddy swiveled away from the fireplace and started pacing. The loud thudding of his heels and the quickened tenor of his breathing filled the room, giving everything a dangerous edge.

"Damn you," he hissed into the darkness, "damn you."

Spinning toward the wall, he drew his arm back and slammed his fist into the wooden wall.

Savannah flinched. Katie melted against her sister, making tiny mewling sounds of fear. Savannah clutched her midsection. The need to go to him, to touch him and tell him she loved him, was like a burning ache in her heart. She took a hesitant step forward, then froze. He wouldn't want her comfort. He never did.

"Damn you," he yelled again.

Savannah fought the sting of tears. In the quavering firelight, she saw the smear of blood on the wall, and the sight made her sick to her stomach.

Don't hurt yourself, Daddy, she prayed. *She ain't worth it.*

Silently Savannah and Katie went back into their bedroom and shut the door. Crawling into bed together, they huddled close, drawing strength from each other. They didn't speak; there was nothing to say. It was a long time before either one of them stopped thinking about their daddy. And longer still before they fell into a fitful, troubled sleep.

The next morning Tess was wakened by a gurgling, mewling sound. Blinking tiredly, she pushed to a sit.

"I'm coming, Caleb," she said. Shoving the quilt back, she hobbled over to the cradle and cautiously picked him up.

"Morning, Caleb," she cooed, staring down into his pink, unbelievably cute face.

He blinked up at her and started crying. Tess felt a tremor of anxiety. Suddenly he didn't look so cute. He looked . . . intimidating.

All at once, the magnitude of her responsibility hit Tess like a shot between the eyes. She was a mother now. A *mommy.* That was more than picking out clothes and reading stories and kissing downy cheeks. It was *everything*. His tiny, innocent life was in her hands.

A vague, formless fear bit into her self-confidence as she made her way back to the bed and crawled under the quilt. She swallowed thickly. Nothing in her solitary, isolated life had prepared her to take care of this baby. She was a doctor of microbiology, for God's sake, not a caretaker. She didn't know how to stop a baby from crying, and she had no time to learn. The responsibility of Caleb's life was hers. *Now.*

She wished to hell he'd come with an instruction book.

Timidly, Tess stroked the velvet-soft side of his face with fingers that were suddenly shaking and cold. "Shh, baby, shh . . ." The words tumbled from her lips over and over again in a hypnotic, tranquil roll.

Except that Caleb was not hypnotized or tranquilized. His cry strengthened, took on an ear-shattering quality. His face turned an unattractive shade of red.

Her breasts started to tingle. Moisture gushed across the front of her nightgown, dampening the fabric. She unbuttoned her gown. The wet fabric fell open to reveal her naked breasts.

Tess took one look and screamed.

Startled by her outburst, Caleb sucked in his breath and stared up at her for a heartbeat. Then he squeezed his puffy eyelids shut and let out a banshee wail that set Tess's ears ringing.

The door flew open and cracked against the other wall. Jack barreled into the room. "What is it?" he panted.

Too horrified to be embarrassed, Tess pointed sickly at her chest. These couldn't be my breasts, she wanted to say. They couldn't be *anyone's*.

Jack stared at the Hall-of-Famer set of mammaries. "Y-You ready to be wrapped?"

"Wrapped?"

"You know, to stop the milk flow."

"Milk. Of course." Tess felt like an idiot for forgetting that a body that had just given birth would produce milk.

"I'll go get Savannah," he said, turning for the door.

"No! I don't want to be wrapped. I want to breast-feed him."

"What?"

"It's well documented that mother's milk is full of necessary nutrients and antibodies." She smiled down at Caleb. Warmth spilled through her body, and for a second, she really felt like his mom.

"But, you've never . . . nursed the kids."

Tess shrugged. "How hard can it be?"

An hour later, Tess had to admit it could be very difficult indeed.

Caleb was crying bloody murder, a high-pitched bleating sound that pinged up and down every vertebra and rattled in her head like an off-key rendition of "Jingle Bells." Jack was standing along the far wall, arms crossed across his chest, eyes riveted on the drama unfolding in the bed. He seemed completely unwilling to help in any way.

"Come on, Caleb," she murmured for the thousandth time, "let's try again." She eased him toward her left breast. He grabbed hold with both tiny hands and tried to suckle, but her breast was so hard and swollen, he couldn't latch on.

"Here you go, sweetie, try again." She curled Caleb in a new hold and pressed his face to her other breast. His mouth was a hairsbreadth from her swollen nipple.

Please, oh, please—

He screamed in frustration.

Tess felt like screaming right along with him. Tears stung her eyes and blurred her vision. Caleb became a squirming red blur with a gaping mouth.

Fear curled around her throat and made it difficult to draw a breath. She wouldn't be able to feed him. Oh, God, how would he live if she couldn't feed him?

Oh, God . . .

"Are you all right?" Jack's quiet voice filtered through the fog of Tess's frustration and made her cry. Aching, soundless sobs that shook her entire body and parched her throat.

He moved to the end of the bed and stood there, waiting. "Amarylis?"

She couldn't look at him. She felt so humiliated and afraid. No wonder God had never given her children in her previous life. She was useless as a mother.

He sat beside her. The tired old bed creaked, and the mattress buckled beneath his weight. Shaking and afraid, she looked up at him. "I can't do it. I can't . . ." Tears clogged her throat until she couldn't speak. All she could do was sit there, helplessly staring at him.

"You don't have to."

"Please," she whispered, tears streaming down her cheeks. "Help me . . ."

Surprise widened his eyes, and Tess knew instinctively that it had been a long time since Amarylis had asked for his help. She thought for a moment he was going to refuse, then quietly he said, "I'll get Savannah."

He started to get up, and she grabbed his sleeve. He paused, turned toward her.

"Thanks." It was a watery, pitiful little word that didn't say nearly enough, and yet she couldn't push anything more past the huge lump in her throat.

"Sure," he answered stiffly. Then he was gone.

Tess sat there, holding the crying baby, crying herself, for what seemed like hours. *Please, God,* she prayed over and over again, *don't let me be a failure as a mother. Please . . .*

Finally someone knocked at the door.

"C-Come in." She tried to yell the words but couldn't. They slipped past her lips as a tired sigh.

"Mama?" Savannah opened the door and poked her head around.

Tess bit her bottom lip to stop its trembling, and swiped the wetness from her cheeks. She tried to smile, and failed miserably.

Savannah came in the room carrying a metal bucket full of steaming water. Thick cotton towels were draped across her forearm like a maitre d' at a posh restaurant.

She set the bucket on the floor and sat down on the bed. Scooting close, she eased one of the towels off her arm and dropped it in the water. As she pulled the soaking rag out and efficiently twisted off the excess water, she frowned at her mother. "Daddy said you had a . . . swelling problem."

Tess would have burst out laughing if she hadn't been in so much pain. "You could say that."

"Hot rags might help. We done that for Bessie last—"

"Bessie?"

"You know . . . the cow."

Tess forced a weak smile.

"Anyhow, I done this on Bessie when her teats gummed up last spring. It worked good. Here, I'll just set these hot towels on your . . . chest. There, like that."

The hot rags brought immediate relief. Steam wafted upward, curled across Tess's nose, and plucked at the straggly curls of hair along her brow. Her milk released in a rush. The terrible, aching tautness began to lessen. She closed her eyes and let her head bang back against the wooden headboard.

Savannah bent closer. "Better?"

"Yes," she said shakily, "I think it's helping. . . ."

After about ten minutes and an equal number of towels, Tess felt like a new woman.

"Do you want to try feeding him now?"

Savannah's voice eked through the almost hypnotic state Tess had slipped into. She smiled sleepily and lifted Caleb to her breasts. "Come on, baby Caleb, let's try again."

This time Caleb latched on as if he'd been doing it all his life. His tiny fingers unfurled and planted themselves on either side of her breast. In the blink of an eye he became more than just the baby she'd been holding; he became a part of her.

Tess stared down at him and felt an emotion so big, so profound, she knew she'd never feel its like again. Awe, pride, humility, love, peace. The feeling filled her soul and lit it with brilliant, white-hot light. She got a hint—a fleeting glimpse—of what motherhood could be, and it made her ache with longing. She felt . . . *needed* right now. Important. And not as a scientist with a brilliant mind, but as a human being. A person. It was a feeling she'd sought all her life, at first with desperation, and then with a nagging sense of despair.

She looked up suddenly at Savannah, eager to share this moment with someone.

The cold, guarded look in Savannah's eyes sliced through Tess's happiness. The words backed up in her throat, became a tangled mass. She closed her mouth.

Her joy bled away, turned into another aching sadness. All her life she'd waited to find someone with whom to share her joys and sorrows. Someone to love. And now here she was in the midst of the one thing she'd always sought—a family of her own—and she was more isolated and alone than ever.

She lowered her lashes to hide her disappointment. "Thanks."

Savannah lurched to her feet. "I gotta go start dinner."

She was halfway to the door before the words were even out of her mouth.

After she'd left, Tess stared at the closed door for a long time. It was older, with antique hinges and splintery wood, but it was still just another closed door between Tess and a family. She'd been looking at them all her life.

Hours later, Savannah stood at the kitchener, stirring the rabbit stew she'd made for dinner. Steam slipped through the cracks of the iron oven door, carrying with it the mouth-watering aroma of baking cottage bread. On the back burner, a heavy cast-iron pot full of slow-boiling water rumbled.

She wiped her sweaty forehead with the crook of her arm and plucked a healthy pinch of salt from the ornate wooden box beside the stove. The pine lid thumped back in place as she sprayed the coarse white granules into the stew.

She ran her hands along her rumpled white apron and headed for the larder. When the pat of freshly churned butter and the crockery jar of last summer's strawberry jam were settled alongside the silverware and plates, she allowed herself to sit down.

Dinner would be ready in about five minutes. Not that anyone would notice . . . or care.

She plopped an elbow on the table and cradled her small chin in her palm. Her breath expelled in a sigh too deep and lonely for a twelve-year-old girl, but Savannah didn't know that. She was unaware that loneliness wasn't the normal course of things, for it was all she'd ever known.

Until recently. Her pale cheeks flamed at the memory. She quickly scanned the room to see if anyone was lurking around to see her blush.

For once, she was happy to be alone.

"Jeffie Peters." She whispered his name and closed her

eyes, lapsing into a gentle state of whimsy. Sounds filtered through her mind: books cracking shut, children laughing, booted feet shuffling hurriedly along a hardwood floor. The bell heralding the end of the school day pealed gaily.

"Savannah?"

She spun around. Jeffie Peters was standing beside her. She felt the whisper-soft brush of his elbow against her arm, and the contact made her pulse thump like a rabbit's.

"Yeah?"

"Can I walk you'n Katie home?"

Savannah's eyes opened. Heat crept up her cheeks again, leaving a blazing trail of shame and embarrassment. She hadn't even had the presence of mind to answer him. She'd just stared at him, her mouth gaping and snapping shut like a freshly landed trout. Then she'd grabbed Katie's chubby hand and dragged her stumbling baby sister out of the one-room schoolhouse.

It didn't make a lick of sense. Jeffie Peters had been her classmate for years. So why all of a sudden did she get all tongue-tied and stupid whenever he said her name? And why did he want to walk her home anyway? She'd been doing just fine on her own for years.

A miserable little groan escaped her. If only she had someone to talk to about the strange things she was feeling lately. Not just about Jeffie, either. She had strange feelings about lots of things. Even her body was changing. Her breasts were getting sort of sore, and her stomach was upset an awful lot lately.

Katie peeked her head around the corner. "Dinner ready?"

The emotion slid off Savannah's face effortlessly; it was a trick she'd learned from her father. Better to hide one's feelings and smile than to cry. "Yeah. Get Daddy."

"I'm right here."

As usual, the sound of her father's deep, baritone voice

filled Savannah with a sort of formless longing. She ground her teeth together and gave him a shallow, awkward smile, but he wasn't looking at her. The smile died. She tried desperately to hide her disappointment.

Rising stiffly, she rubbed her damp palms on her apron and strode purposefully to the kitchener.

She had to stop this. It was a useless waste of energy, this trying to capture his attention.

It was all because of *The Times*. That's how she thought of them in her head, capitalized, wreathed in silent awe. The times when all of a sudden she'd look up and find him staring at her. Those precious seconds when she was a somebody to him swelled in her lonely soul like grains of gold in a beggar's hand. One look, one touch from him, and it started all over again. She started wishing, hoping, praying. . . .

But the moments were so rare, so transient, that she was often left wondering whether she'd imagined them. Usually she came to the conclusion that she had.

She heard him coming toward her, and she stiffened instinctively. He stopped beside her, peered over her shoulder at the stew bubbling softly in the cast-iron pot. Then he reached toward her.

For one heart-stopping moment, she thought he was going to touch her arm or pat her shoulder. She leaned infinitesimally toward him, enough so she might brush his sleeve and feel the heat of his skin or smell the woodsmoke scent of his chambray work shirt.

He reached past her and eased the kettle off the heat. "Smells good."

Savannah squeezed back tears. What was wrong with her? Why was she so unlovable? Other children were hugged and kissed and loved by their parents. She'd seen that kind of affection at her friend Lila's house, and every time she saw Mr. Hannah pat Lila's shoulder or kiss the top of his daughter's head, Savannah felt a dull, throbbing ache in her midsection.

It had to be something wrong with her; she'd faced that truth a long time ago. Something dark and ugly that made her parents turn away.

She bent tiredly and opened the oven door, carefully extracting the golden loaf of bread. Using her apron to shield her hands, she moved the loaf to a riddle board and started to slice it thickly.

Katie went to the table and sat down. Her little elbows thumped on the scarred wooden surface. The steady thump-thump-thump of her toes hitting the chair's solid legs was a welcome end to the silence. "What's for dinner, Vannah?"

Savannah slopped a ladleful of stew into a bowl, balanced a plateful of bread on top, and headed for the table. "Rabbit stew, cottage bread, and some of those pickled cucumbers Mrs. Hannah gave us."

Katie wrinkled her nose. "Rabbit stew . . . again?"

Savannah set the food on the table, and gently cuffed her baby sister on the head. "Watch it, you," she said, smiling as she buttered her sister's bread. "Or you'll get it for breakfast, too."

Daddy dished himself a heaping bowl of stew and laid two slices of bread on the bowl's rim. Balancing it carefully, he mumbled, "Thanks," to Savannah and headed to the back porch to eat in solitude.

Savannah headed back to the stove and got herself a small bowl of stew. Then she went over to her usual dinner spot. Leaning against the dry sink, feeling the towel rack jabbing against her lower back, she ate her dinner.

No one spoke, and the entire meal was over in less than ten minutes. After Katie left, Savannah carried both of their bowls to the dry sink and set them on the wooden drainboard. Filling the metal washbasin with the hot water from the kettle, she set about washing the evening dishes.

The kitchen door squeaked open, then banged shut. Footsteps thudded toward her. The floor boards shuddered with each step he took.

"Savannah?"

She stared intently at the murky gray water. *Don't care. Don't care.* "Yeah, Daddy?"

He came up beside her and stopped. "I'll take a bowl to your mama."

"Okay."

She waited for him to move away. He didn't. He stood there for a moment longer, and Savannah had the ridiculous thought that he wanted to say something to her.

She waited.

"I'll get it, don't you bother."

Savannah sighed. "Sure, Daddy."

Chapter Five

Jack raised a fist to the rough-planked door and knocked.

"Come on in."

Come on in? Tension crept through Jack's flesh and tightened his spine. Something wasn't right; Amarylis had never sounded so friendly or casual. Certainly not to someone wanting to enter her sanctuary. Certainly not to him.

He balanced the tray of food in one hand and turned the knob. The brass felt cool in his fingers as he pushed the door open and entered his wife's bedroom.

She sat propped up amidst a billowing mirage of grayed pillows. Her straight blond hair was pulled deftly to one side, where it cascaded over her shoulder like a length of moon-spun silk and puddled on the red and white quilt.

She didn't look up immediately, which was normal enough. What wasn't normal was why she didn't look up. It wasn't the usual calculated snub.

She appeared, quite simply, to be too captivated by the baby in her arms to wrench her gaze away.

But that couldn't be. She'd never bothered to look twice at her other children. Why would she start now? He eyed her suspiciously, wondering what new game she was playing.

She looked up all of a sudden and smiled at him. *Smiled.*

"God, he's so tiny, isn't he?"

Jack stared at her in mounting confusion. What the hell was going on here?

"Come see your son," she said in a quiet, almost hesitant voice.

The butter-soft tone of her voice hit him hard in the midsection. It had been years since he'd heard her voice without the brittle edge of contempt. For a moment he was flung back in time to the early years, when they'd been so desperately in love. God, how he'd loved her. . . .

He forced the tired memory from his mind and shuffled across the room. Setting the tray down on the table beside the bed, he said, "I brought you something to eat."

She patted the bed beside her. "Sit."

He stared at the indentation left by her hand in the thick comforter. Before he could stop it, longing spiraled through his body. The desire to sit beside her was like a dull ache in his soul.

But he knew better. The years had given him an emotional armor. She was toying with him again; using his weakness and his need for love against him. She was stronger, so much stronger than he. Of that, there had never been a doubt. And these games of power amused her. They were her way to get back at him, still and again, for betraying her dreams of wealth and turning her into a poor, cowardly sheep rancher's wife.

He wouldn't let her humiliate him again. Never again. He'd resist her until they both dropped dead. "No." He cleared his throat. "No, thanks. I'll stand."

Disappointment flitted through her eyes, and she looked away. Jack knew he should feel proud that he'd beaten her at her vicious little game, but he couldn't quite manage it.

"You'd better eat to keep up your strength," he said for lack of something better to say.

She didn't answer. Instead, she peeled the blue home-spun blanket away from Caleb. The baby's soft, sleepy breaths fluttered upward.

As he stared down at the baby's wizened, old-man face, Jack felt a surge of emotion so strong and pure, he knew he had no right to feel it. At his sides, his hands fisted into useless blocks. There was a tightness in his chest that made his breathing speed up.

He had no right to feel these things, no right to feel a father's love.

He stepped backward, unsteady on his feet. "I'll go now."

Amarylis looked up at him then, and there was a soft-ness in her gaze that almost brought him to his knees. "Is it her?" she whispered. "Has she done something to make you this way?"

It was a stupid, incomprehensible question, and Jack was relieved he didn't have to answer. With a curt nod, he turned his back on her and left the room.

Tess eyed the bedpost, wondering if she should start notching it. The way the days were blurring together, pretty soon she'd wonder how long she'd been here in soli-tary confinement. So far, it had been five days; five of the longest, most boring days of her life. Correction, she thought, of her lives.

She glanced down at the baby in her arms, and felt a now familiar rush of maternal love. The highlight of the last week had been the chance to bond with Caleb. She was actually beginning to *feel* like the baby's mother.

But as exciting and fulfilling as the budding emotion was, it didn't make up for the nagging sense of isolation which now surrounded her. Sometimes, especially when

Caleb slept and she was left alone in her big bed and too-silent bedroom, she felt a lingering sadness.

God, she was tired of being lonely.

"So, kiddo," she said to Caleb, "what do you think about global thermonuclear war? Or the greenhouse effect—do you believe in that?"

He burped a little and spat up.

For a split second there, she'd thought he was going to answer.

She was cracking up. Her scientist-sharp mind was turning slowly, irrevocably, to mush. She was inches—centimeters—away from going stark, raving mad.

The last few weeks had been almost unbearable. She hadn't had an honest-to-God discussion with a human being since the night Jack had yelled at her for breaking some unknown rule. In retrospect, that little tête-à-tête looked pretty good.

She couldn't live like this. She'd tried. She'd told herself to simply melt into the woodwork, do what was expected of her, and everything would be fine.

The problem was, nothing was expected of her. Nothing. Everyone walked around Amarylis as if she were a lighted stick of dynamite—quietly and quickly, without looking back. She felt like a ghost, unwanted and invisible.

Tess couldn't stand it. Here she was, a healthy, hearing woman who spoke with a lilting southern drawl, and she had no one to talk to. And nothing to hear. Just as before, she lived in a world of aching silence and isolation.

They ignored her. Completely.

Oh, Savannah came in twice a day, bearing a tray of food and a pile of folded towels for Tess's "you know, womanly needs." She nodded silently to her mother, occasionally mumbling, "Good morning"—that was a very good day in Tess's book—but more often saying nothing.

She set the tray down on the bedside table, plucked up Tess's small bucket of used towels, then spun away from the bed and disappeared.

Tess wouldn't see another soul until dinner. Then Savannah went through the same ritual again. Jack and Katie hadn't even peeked their heads in to say hello.

Seeing a single person, and no one else, for over a month, especially when that person looked at you as if you were Typhoid Mary, just didn't cut it.

The first few weeks hadn't been so bad. In fact, it had been sort of nice, being catered to. She'd been in so much pain, and between feedings she'd desperately needed to sleep. But now Caleb was sleeping almost through the night and she felt pretty good. The pain and bleeding had passed, and she was breast-feeding like a champ. There was no reason for her to spend all day lounging in this room or this bed.

This was her life now. It was a realization she'd come to accept in the last few days. There would be no further soul switching, no last-minute "It was just a joke" from Carol.

It was done. This was Tess's life. She was Amarylis— she was going to have to do something about the name— Rafferty now, and she damn well had to make the best of it.

If there was one thing Tess knew, it was how to fit in. As a kid, she'd changed foster homes like some kids changed underwear. Things were always the same. She came into the family alone, a skinny, silent deaf girl who didn't—couldn't—belong. The first few days she spent closeted in her room, trying not to cry, wishing things were different. Then she realized that things *weren't* different. She lifted her chin, rolled up her sleeves, and set about fitting in.

It was time for that now. She'd waited and hoped for

someone to invite her into the family, then she'd moped because the invitation hadn't come.

No more, she decided. It was time to make her own invitation.

Tess bided her time patiently all day, waiting for just the right moment to make her move into the family. With this group, she figured it was like merging into a Los Angeles freeway; one had to move cautiously and signal first.

After feeding Caleb, she crawled back into bed, awaiting Savannah. As night pressed against the bedroom window, she began to hear the telltale sound of cooking.

Tess smiled for the first time in days. Soon she would make her move.

Savannah was right on time with supper. She knocked lightly on Tess's door, then glided silently across the room, a tray of food balanced perfectly in front of her. She set it down on the bedside table with practiced ease and mumbled, "Evenin', Mama," then turned to leave.

Tess grabbed her sleeve. "Savannah? May I talk to you?"

Savannah turned back around, eyeing her mother warily. "'Bout what?"

Tess patted the quilt. "Sit down."

The girl sidled to the bed and perched like a frightened bird on its very edge, her gaze glued to the fascinating floorboards between her feet. "Yeah?"

Tess wet her lips. "Well, I was wondering what your ma—I mean, what *I* do all day."

That got Savannah's attention. She actually looked at Tess. "Do?"

Tess frowned. "I must do something."

Savannah shrugged. "Well, you embroider a lot."

"Embroider ... How exciting that must be."

"You read a lot o' them *genteel* books."

"Don't I do anything outside?" she asked hopefully. "Like gardening?"

It was Savannah's turn to frown. "Well . . ." the word was drawn out, as if she were really searching. "Sometimes you set on the porch swing and sip lemonade."

Tess sighed. "In other words, you're the real mama in this family. I'm just a . . . lady."

"A *southern* lady," Savannah corrected quickly. "You always say that's a right important thing to be."

"Do I? How magnanimous of me."

Savannah's eyes bulged at Tess's use of the word "magnanimous." She popped to her feet. "I gotta go wash the dishes."

"Just one more question," Tess promised.

"All right," Savannah said without turning around.

"What time do you get home from school?"

" 'Bout three-thirty or four. Unless it's rainin', then the walk takes longer."

"And then you cook dinner and clean the house and put Katie to bed. Thanks, Savannah. For everything."

"Sure." Before the word was out of her mouth, Savannah was gone.

Tess smiled. Now she had a place to start. Someone had to help that poor, overworked kid.

Tomorrow—heaven help them all—the new-and-improved Amarylis was coming out.

The next morning, Tess finished nursing Caleb and gently put him back into his cradle. She waited a moment to make sure he wasn't going to wake up, then she flung the heavy flannel wrapper around her shoulders and tiptoed to the window. Outside, the farm lay shrouded in darkness. Only the barest hint of gold along the horizon heralded the approaching dawn.

Tess smiled with satisfaction. All she had to do was get

to the barn without being heard, and she could put her plan into action.

She left her bedroom and crept soundlessly down the hallway, her fingertips trailing lightly along the rough wooden walls. With every step her heartbeat increased, her breathing quickened.

At the living room, she poked her head around the corner and scanned the darkness for Jack. He was a series of black humps against the slightly less dark sofa. The quiet, even strains of his breathing filtered through the shadowy room.

Tess released her breath. She was okay.

She bent her head down and hurried through the darkened house, closing the kitchen door silently behind her.

She raced across the dew-dampened grass toward the barn and eased the huge wooden door open. By the time she'd found a lantern, matches, and the milking stool, dawn was slanting through the cracks in the barn's plank walls in streaks of pinkish gold.

"Mooo." Bessie's angry bellow echoed through the still, cold air.

Tess jumped. Her fingers spasmed reflexively around the milk can's thin metal handle.

"It's okay, Bessie," she said hesitantly, "I'm here to milk you."

Bessie swung her big brown head around and stared at Tess.

Tess moved cautiously forward, placing the milk can down between the cow's back legs. Then she put down the stool, yanked up her heavy nightgown, and planted herself on the hard wooden surface.

Bessie's hugely swollen udder filled her vision.

Tess grimaced sickly, and instinctively clamped a hand over her own bulging breasts. "Okay, Bessie, here we go."

She gently plucked at the teat with her forefinger and thumb. The pink appendage bobbed uselessly.

Clearly this was not the best approach.

She tried again, this time grabbing hold of the teat and yanking hard.

Bessie mooed loudly and swung her head around. Long-lashed brown eyes stared unblinkingly at Tess.

Tess smiled weakly. "Not quite right, huh? How about this?" She tried again, a bit more gently.

Bessie smacked Tess in the face with her tail.

"Mama?"

Tess swiveled in her seat and saw Savannah standing just inside the barn door. "Savannah!" Tess cried. "I'm so glad you're here. Milking isn't quite as . . . instinctive as I'd thought it would be."

Savannah's mouth dropped open. "Mama, you never—"

"Ah, never say never. Here—" she got to her feet "—have a seat and show me what to do. I've decided to become an active member of this family. And that means doing chores."

Savannah gave her mother a wary are-you-an-ax-murderer look. "Th-Thanks, Mama."

Tess bit back a smile as the girl sidled past her. When Savannah sat down on the stool, Tess scooted over and kneeled beside her. "What do you do first?"

Savannah curled her fingers around one of the teats, then squeezed once and pulled hard. A stream of milk shot from the teat and hit the empty bucket with a ringing sound. Steam spiraled upward, bringing with it the humid scent of fresh cream.

"How did you do that?"

"Here, watch." Savannah did it again. "Squeeze, pull, let go."

Milk squirted from two of Bessie's teats. The rapid-fire

squirt-ping-splash of each stream hitting the bucket sang out in the quiet barn.

Tess lifted her gaze from the milk and studied Savannah, who was staring intently into the bucket, her lips drawn into a thin, colorless line.

Tess eased a straggly lock of hair from Savannah's face. "You've tried to keep this family together, haven't you?"

"Family? Ha." Savannah said the words harshly, then realized what she'd said. She paled. "Oh, I didn't mean—"

"Shh, it's okay," Tess murmured. "It's not much of a family, from what I can see."

Savannah's shoulders sagged, her head bowed. Tears sparkled in her eyes but didn't slip past her lashes.

The girl's silent misery twisted Tess's heart. No one knew better than she what it felt like to grow up alone, without a mother to lean on or turn to. From the day of her mother's death until now, this very second, Tess had carried inside her soul a tiny, nagging ache. A void.

It was, she knew, the same void that pulled the color from Savannah's cheeks and stole the smile from her lips.

You've always been a healer, Tess. The words came back to Tess, and she realized the truth in them. She had to help this poor, frightened girl.

She tried to find something to say, anything, that would be a start. "I—I know I'm your mother on the outside, and you don't trust me, but on the inside I've . . . changed."

Savannah didn't bother to look at her. "What do you mean?"

"I'm ashamed of the way I've treated you and Katie and Daddy."

Savannah went so still, she seemed to stop breathing. She turned slightly, staring at Tess through huge blue eyes. "Really?"

The single, softly spoken word revealed a spark of hope, buried deep inside a mountain of mistrust. Tess could see how desperately Savannah wanted to believe. Wanted to but couldn't—not yet.

"I'll tell you what," Tess said. "I'll make you a deal."

"What?"

"You teach me to be a mother—you know, cooking, cleaning, stuff like that—and I'll teach you and Katie to have fun."

Savannah regarded her warily. "We already know how to have fun."

"I don't think so."

"Besides, you're already a mother."

"Not much of one, from what I can tell. But I'd like to change that. Will you help me?"

Savannah studied her for a long, silent moment. Then, slowly, she nodded. "Sure, Mama."

Tess grinned. "Thanks, honey. I won't let you down."

Tess carried the heavy bucket full of steaming milk toward the house. Dawn was just breaking across the rolling, rocky pasture and filling the gray sky with streaks of pink and purple. Sheep were scattered through the fields like puffy clumps of dark cotton.

She paused and looked around. The small farm lay shrouded in semidarkness, but she could see how well the place was tended. The fences were straight and strong, the house was nice and white. Everything was in perfect repair. But there were no loving touches. No flowers lining the walk or curling around the base of the oak tree, no flower boxes along the porch. No wind chimes hanging from the overhang. There was only a scrawny, half-dead wild rose that twined around the porch rail and crept up the post.

She set the bucket down. It hit the rocky dirt road with a sloshing clank, spilling warm liquid across Tess's bare feet. Turning, she glanced back at the barn and thought about her talk with Savannah. It had gone well. Talking was just a little thing, a gentle movement forward, but it was something. A beginning.

Tess thought about her own lonely childhood, about how much it would have meant for someone to take a moment to reach out to her. She'd been so starved for acceptance and affection that even a simple little thing like a smile would have meant so much. Somehow, she was certain that life was similar for Savannah. The girl was afraid to believe in Tess because her mother had obviously ignored her for a very long time, but through the fear was a kernel of hope. A wish and a prayer.

For the first time since waking up in this century, Tess felt a sense of purpose and a stirring of hope. A shadow of her old zeal came back. She could help these people. Ease their tired hearts and make them laugh. And maybe she could bring a little laughter into her own soul at the same time.

She'd known the moment she'd seen Jack that he needed someone desperately. The pain in his eyes had drawn her; the pain and something more. She hadn't known what it was then, but now she understood. She'd been drawn by a sadness she understood all too well. The aching loneliness of someone who longs to be part of a family and can't quite fit in.

No wonder she'd been drawn like a moth to the flame of his heartache. They were kindred spirits, people on the fringe of happiness. Close enough to touch it, yet too frightened to reach out, too afraid of rejection to step up and say, "I want."

But no more. She and Jack and these children were connected now. A family. And they all needed one another.

All she needed now was a plan. She bit her lower lip and frowned, trying to analyze the situation. She had to look at this family as a long-term project. She wouldn't solve it all at once, wouldn't heal a lifetime's worth of wounds with a single bandage, but she was used to that. She'd spent ten years of her life in cancer research—the first four had been spent isolating a single cell. Yes, if there was one thing Tess had, it was patience.

She thought about Jack and smiled. If there was one thing she'd need in dealing with him, it was patience.

By the time the girls had left for school, Tess was beginning to think she'd been a tad optimistic. Cancer seemed like a bump in the road compared to the ills in the Rafferty family.

Breakfast had been a horrible affair. She'd been so flabbergasted by the tension in the family that she hadn't been able to offer anyone more than a wobbling, tentative smile. And that had only served to make everyone jumpier.

They didn't even eat together. Katie sat at the table—alone—pushing her food around with her fork and rarely taking a bite. The whining squeak of tin on crockery rang in the too quiet room like fingernails on a chalkboard. Savannah stood at the sink, wolfing down her food without ever speaking or making eye contact with anyone. And Jack.

She sighed. *Jack.* He hadn't even remained in the house. He'd eaten out on the porch.

The whole ordeal had lasted less than ten minutes. Tess had been just gearing up to say something—although she hadn't figured out *what*—when Jack rammed his dishes in the sink and disappeared. The girls gulped down the rest of their food, shoved the dishes in a bucket of water, and followed him out.

Tess had been left alone, stunned into silence by the show.

It had been almost an hour since they'd left the house,

and she still hadn't moved. She sat at the kitchen table, her elbows planted on the hard wood in front of her. A cup of strong, bitter coffee was between her elbows.

Tess plopped her chin in her hand and let out a sigh. She couldn't help it. She was . . . lonely. The house was depressingly quiet.

At least at the foster homes, people had *talked* to her. This morning with Savannah had just served to reinforce how isolated she was here. How alone.

Suddenly Jack burst into the room. He saw her and stopped dead. The door banged shut behind him.

"Amarylis!"

Tess felt a flood of relief at simply seeing another person. She grinned up at him. "Hi."

He glanced uncomfortably out the window. For a moment she thought he might jump. "I guess I'd best get going—"

"Wait." She lurched to her feet. "Have a cup of coffee with me. We could talk."

His eyes bulged. He stared at her as if she were deranged. "I don't think so."

"Okay, I'll talk. You can sort of . . . grunt and nod."

"Christ," he muttered, shaking his head.

"Jack, I can't just *sit* all day. I have to do something. But I can't . . . remember much about farm work."

He strode into the living room and snatched up a pretty little basket. "Here," he said, shoving it at her.

Tess lifted the lid and saw a bunch of cotton and thread. "Embroidery. How . . . stimulating."

He glared at her. "You never wanted to be stimulated before."

An entirely inappropriate twentieth-century retort popped into Tess's head. She grinned.

"What's so goddamn funny?" he hissed.

Tess tried to rein in her smile, with limited success. "Nothing. Really."

He eyed her warily. "Amarylis, do whatever you want. Just stay the hell out of my way."

Chapter Six

Do whatever you want.

Tess thought about it. What did she want to do?

She wanted to turn these four dysfunctional, frightened people into a family. As stupid and Snow White–ish as it sounded, she just wanted everyone to be happy. It was up to her to be the beginning. She had to start being an honest-to-God mother, then maybe they'd become a family around her.

"Okay," she said, taking a sip of coffee, "how?"

What did mothers do? Unfortunately, the question answered itself. Cooking, cleaning, laundering, scrubbing.

"Yuck." No wonder she'd always hated those movies about pioneer wives. While the men were out herdin' dogies and riding the range, the women were home cleaning floors and making butter.

She set her cup down and stood up. Unpleasant tasks, she knew, were a part of life, and ignoring them didn't make them go away. If Tess wanted to be the center of this family, she had to get started. Somehow she had to figure out how to be the perfect pioneer woman.

Getting dressed was probably a good start, she decided. Donna Reed never spent the day in her nightgown.

She went to the bedroom and checked on Caleb, who was asleep.

Then she opened the armoire and chose a waistless,

scoop-necked gingham nursing gown. Dressing quickly, she tied on a wrinkled white apron, rolled up her sleeves, braided her hair, and went to work.

Four hours later, Tess crawled into the last corner of the kitchen. Dragging the bucket of soapy water behind her, she scrubbed the dirty floor and dried it with her now filthy towel. Then she applied the last bit of the beeswax furniture paste she'd found and polished the boards until they gleamed like bright new pennies.

Sitting back on her heels, she dropped the rag in the water and let out her breath in a deep, satisfied sigh. The house was clean. She grabbed the chairback and got tiredly to her feet, pressing a fist to her aching back as she surveyed her handiwork.

Beneath her feet, the floor was a panel of richly polished oak. The table, its imperfections concealed by a stark white tablecloth, was a profusion of early spring flowers. On the dresser's long, open shelves, the blue earthenware plates, tin coffeepot, and crockery jugs sparkled like new. Even the stove, now soot- and grease-free, looked as if it belonged in *Country Home* magazine. A fire burned low behind the iron-barred grate, glowing orange-red and sending off fingers of woodsmoke-scented heat.

Outside, heavy footsteps pounded up the porch steps. A second later, Jack broke through the kitchen door at a run.

A comical look of disbelief crossed his face as his heels skidded across the slick floor and whooshed out from underneath him. He hit the floor like a ton of bricks.

Tess gasped. "Are you all right?"

"What the hell—"

Her lips twitched. "Maybe I shouldn't have waxed the floor."

Jack shook his head. "If you're trying to kill me, how about using a less painful method?"

Tess smiled down at him and offered a hand.

Ignoring her, he grabbed hold of the chair and hauled himself to his feet. He looked around, noticing the kitchen for the first time. The customary scowl settled on his face.

"I suppose it's *too* clean?" Tess said.

"What the hell are you doing? You know goddamn well—"

She winced at the loudness of his voice. "Oh, for God's sake, Jack. Shut up."

He was stunned into speechlessness. "What?"

"Your attitude sucks."

"What?"

"I've got plans for this family—big plans. But frankly, I can't do squat if you're going to be running around yelling at me all the time. So we'd better come to an understanding."

He laughed.

"Laugh all you want, just listen."

He crossed his arms across his chest and studied her through slitted, uncompromising eyes. But he didn't leave. That was something, at least.

She curled her fingers around the chairback and stared at him. "Does the word 'reincarnation' mean anything to you?"

"No."

She frowned. "Well, some people think that after death, a soul can . . . go on. You know, change bodies and get another life. Some of these people believe that time doesn't really exist, that everything—past, present, and future—is actually happening now. You believe that?"

"No."

Tess cocked an eyebrow. "That could present a bit of a problem."

"Why?"

She let go of the chair and moved toward him, noticing

the way his eyes flinched at her every step. Directly in front of him, she stopped. "I'm not your loving wife."

He snorted. "No shit."

She laughed. "No, I don't mean I'm not loving; I'm mean I'm not your wife. She died."

He blanched. "You remember that?"

"Death isn't one of those things that escapes your notice. It makes an ... impact. Anyway, she died, and here I am. Get it?"

He leaned back against the dry sink. "I should be so lucky."

"No, it's true. I'm—"

"Yeah, and I'm the King of England."

Tess sighed heavily. She searched his gaze, probed the guarded green depths for a hint of open-mindedness.

It was a useless effort. She could tell that he wouldn't believe. There was no room in Jack's ideology for the reality of soul swapping. "Okay, Jack, have it your way. I'm Amarylis back from the dead. But I'll tell you right now: I'm not the same woman I was before."

The guarded, wary look crept back into his eyes. "What do you mean?"

"Well, obviously I didn't *really* die; I mean, here I am. What I meant was I've ... changed. Like one of those improved toothpastes. Something new's been added."

He looked at her as if she were a science experiment gone horribly awry. "And what would that be?"

She shrugged. "I guess we'll find out together. Won't it be fun?"

"Fun? *Fun?* You expect us to have fun?"

"You make it sound like I asked you to jump off the Brooklyn Bridge."

He backed away from her. "I don't know what the hell you're talking about."

She winced. "Yeah, mentioning the bridge was a mistake. I think—"

He surged toward her and grabbed her. His strong fingers bit deep in the fleshy part of her arms. "Have all the goddamn fun you want, but don't drag me into it. Got it?"

Tess glared up at him. Enough was enough, damn it. In the past week she'd been hit by a bus, given birth, and died. She was trying to make the best of this life, but nothing—nothing—said she had to let this man yell at her.

She wrenched out of his arms. "It's about time to set some rules, Jack."

He drew back. "Huh?"

"Good comeback. Now, are you going to hit me?"

Surprise registered in his eyes. "Now?"

"Ever."

"I've never hit a woman."

She eyed him suspiciously. "Are you *trying* to be evasive?"

"No. Goddamn it, you know I'm not going to hit you."

She stepped closer, staring dead into his eyes. "Then quit trying to scare me. It won't work. I'm doing my best to help out this family, and damn it, I expect you to put forth a little effort, too. Okay?"

He stared at her, too stunned to reply.

"Okay?" she repeated.

His mouth opened—no doubt for a stinging retort—then snapped shut with a click of teeth. Anger crawled in a red wash up his throat. "I'm leaving."

He pivoted away from her and surged through the open door, slamming it shut behind him.

Tess sighed and crossed her arms, staring hard at the closed door. That hadn't gone too well.

Suddenly this lifetime stretched out before her like an endless, waterless desert. If she didn't do something, she'd spend sixty years fighting with Jack. Just the thought was enough to make a calm, levelheaded scientist go mad.

She should have picked the spaceman.

Katie stared up the hill at the schoolhouse. The clapboard wooden structure sat alone amidst a stand of just-greening trees. Kids ran back and forth in front of the woodpile in a game of tag. High-pitched giggles peppered the air. A few horses—owned by families who could afford to let their kids ride to school—stood tied along the three-slatted wooden fence that bordered the yard.

Katie slowed down. Her fingers curled in a death grip on the wire handle of her lard tin. The cold metal bit into her sweaty palm.

"It's all right, Katie," Savannah whispered. "They won't laugh at you."

They both knew it was a lie; knew they *would* laugh at her.

Katie bit down hard on her lower lip to keep it from trembling. Tears stung her eyes as she stumbled along beside her sister.

It don't matter what those dumb old kids think anyway.

But it did matter. It mattered more than anything.

She clung to Savannah's hand and kept moving, trying to be grown-up, trying not to be afraid.

If only she weren't so stupid. Then everything would be okay. The kids wouldn't laugh at her. Her mama would love her. The teacher—

"Are you ready to go in?"

Savannah's voice cut through Katie's thoughts. She yanked her head up and found that they were almost there. Anxiety spilled through her blood like ice water.

She turned to her sister. "I don't feel so good, Vannah. Maybe I should go home."

Savannah dropped to her knees and touched her sister's cheek. "Aw, Katie . . ."

She flung herself into her sister's arms. Savannah hugged her tightly, stroking her hair and mumbling soft, soothing words of love.

Savannah drew back and looked up at her.

Katie did her very best not to cry. Tears burned behind her eyes and blurred her vision, but not one slipped past her lashes. It was a trick all the Raffertys had learned. "I-I'm fine." She rubbed her sweaty palms on the nubby wool of her skirt and clutched her strapped-up schoolbooks to her chest.

Savannah got slowly to her feet. Hand in hand they climbed the creaking steps and opened the schoolhouse door. The tired whine of the hinges drew every eye. A dozen small heads cocked in their direction.

Shivering, Katie drew back.

Savannah laid a comforting hand on her shoulder and held her in place. "I'm right here," she murmured soothingly.

Katie made a beeline for her desk. The small, sturdy heels of her heavy leather walking boots clicked loudly on the planked floor. With each footfall, the rising cadence of giggling nipped at her self-confidence. She moved faster, her schoolbooks bolted to her chest, her gaze nailed to the wood beneath her feet.

She sidled into the steel-backed chair with an audible sigh. Savannah eased in beside her. The comforting warmth of her sister's body gave Katie the courage to set her things on the desk in front of her. With trembling fingers, she unstrapped her books and pulled *McGuffey's First Eclectic Reader* out from beneath her math primer. The small brown book nearly disappeared into the scarred wood of the desk.

Katie wished fervently that it would really and truly disappear.

In the front of the room, Miss Ames rapped sharply on her desk and stood up. "Let's begin by reading aloud."

Katie squeezed her eyes shut. In her lap, her fingers crossed tightly, then curled into fists. *Please don't pick me. Please don't—*

"Susan Jacobs, why don't you begin? Page nine of the reader."

Katie's breath expelled in a sharp sigh of relief. She opened her eyes slowly and turned to page nine. She stared hard at the paper, trying to read along with Susan.

It was impossible. The black ink swirled and danced and changed positions. Letters were meaningless, melting together to form words that weren't words. Sentences that were pure gibberish. Not a single word that Susan read appeared on Katie's page.

Tears burned her eyes. What was wrong with her? She tried so hard—harder than anyone else in the class. Every night she hurried to her room right after supper and studied the mishmash of letters in her primer. Every night she failed, and miserably, to make sense of even one word.

"Thank you, Susan, that was very good. Now, how about you, Mary Katherine? Will you pick up where Susan left off?"

Katie's head snapped up. A wordless, aching "no" slipped past her lips.

Miss Ames leaned slightly forward, waiting. Every student turned to look at Katie.

She felt Savannah's hand on her bent elbow and knew her sister was trying to comfort her. But it wasn't working; not now. She was too cold to feel even the meager warmth of Savannah's touch.

She swallowed thickly and forced her gaze downward.

The yellowed pages blurred before her eyes. She blinked rapidly, swiped the moisture from her eyes.

You can do it this time. You can.

She stared hard at the first word: h-T-e.

Panic sucked at her, made her heartbeat thud in her ears. *h-T-e m-n-a h-a-s a n-e-p.*

She mouthed the first word, but knew before the effort that it was no word at all. She tried again, focusing on each letter.

Kids started whispering. The sound of laughter penetrated her concentration. She knew it was probably all in her imagination—Savannah had told her that a dozen times—but she could never make herself believe it. The giggling sounded so real. So close.

She jerked her head up and stared wildly around. Countless eyes stared back at her. Sally Burman's skinny lips were curved in a triumphant smile.

Katie lurched unsteadily to her feet and whirled away from the wobbly desk. Tears of shame and frustration coursed down her face and burrowed into her mouth. They felt warm and wet and salty. Like failure.

"Katie!"

She ignored her sister's call and ran as fast as she could. Blasting through the door, she hurtled down the creaking steps and kept running.

Savannah scooped up the books strewn across her desk and stood up. "I'll go get her, Miss Ames."

"Me, too!"

Before Savannah could respond, Jeffie Peters was standing beside her.

She looked at him. He looked at her. A confusing rush of emotions hurtled through Savannah, sparking a flood of heat across her cheeks.

"Y-Yuh want me t' carry them books for yah?" he stammered.

Savannah felt every eye in the room on her. Mumbling, "No thanks," she clutched the books to her chest and ran for the door. Barreling through, she thundered down the sagging steps and came to a shuddering, breathless stop by the fence. The books slid out of her hands and hit the dirt.

Behind her, the door banged shut again. "Hey, Savannah—wait up!"

She wanted to run away and find a nice quiet place to be alone, but her feet wouldn't move.

"Why'dya run like that?" Jeffie said, coming up beside her.

Savannah pinned her gaze on the water pump. It took a wagonload of willpower not to twist her fingers together, but she remained perfectly still, her chin tilted high, her eyes straight ahead. "I was worried about Katie."

"Yep. Seems she ain't the best reader."

"No," she said stiffly, "she ain't."

Savannah waited uneasily for him to say something else. He waited for the same thing. Then, in a rush of awkwardness, they both dropped to their knees and dove for the fallen books.

Their fingers brushed. Savannah jerked her hand back and buried it in her lap.

Jeffie turned to look at her.

They were close, closer than they'd ever been. Savannah could see the smattering of freckles across his brow. Intelligent, caring brown eyes stared intently into her own. He leaned infinitesimally forward, as if he were about to say something.

Fear made her heart race. She warned herself to sit perfectly still. But then—somehow—she was leaning just the tiniest bit toward him.

"Savannah, I . . ." His gaze slid away from hers. Color

crept up from his collar and fanned along his jawline.
"I . . ."

She was suddenly afraid of what he was going to say.
Of what she was going to feel when he said it. She
snatched the books to her chest and vaulted to her feet.

She started to spin away from him, but her feet tangled
in the heavy woolen folds of her skirt and she stumbled
sideways. Jeffie was on his feet in an instant, holding her
elbow, steadying her.

"Thanks." She pulled away from him without meeting
his gaze. "I gotta go now. My ma—"

"C'n I walk yah home?"

For one terrifying moment Savannah thought she was
going to throw up. Shaking her head "no," she clutched
her books to her chest and whirled away from him, running down the hill as fast as she could.

She was out of breath and had a stitch in her side by the
time she reached Katie, who was sitting forlornly beside
the road. Still breathing hard, she came up beside her baby
sister and dropped to her knees in the hard-packed dirt.
The books and lunch pail landed beside her with a
clanking thud.

"There's somethin' wrong with me," Katie said in a
small, quavering voice. "I'm stupid."

Anguish coiled around Savannah's heart and squeezed
hard. "No, you ain't," she managed past the lump in her
throat.

Katie plopped her trembling chin onto her bent knees
and squeezed her eyes shut. Tears slipped past her thick
black lashes and streaked down the puffy little-girl pink-
ness of her cheeks.

Savannah felt a surge of frustration and anger. Her
hands curled into fists as she stared at the immense blue
sky above. She wished she could tell Mama about Katie's
problem, but there was no point. Mama would only laugh

and confirm Katie's fears that she *was* stupid. Savannah didn't believe for a second that her mama had changed.

Daddy would help. The thought came as it always did, quickly, bringing with it a heartbeat of hope.

Then, just as quickly, it was gone, plunging Savannah back into the pit of hopelessness. Once, she'd almost told him. She'd been close, so close, at Katie's birthday party. Katie had been laughing about something—all three of them had, she remembered—and Savannah had looked across the table at her father and seen something almost magical in his eyes.

She'd thought then it was love. Her heart had skipped a beat. Anticipation and hope brought her awkwardly to her feet and drew her toward him. She'd said his name, softly. He'd looked up, met her gaze. The truth about Katie had hung on her lips, heavy and waiting. The truth about so many things . . .

Suddenly the laughter ended, leaving in its wake a silence thick enough to make Savannah sick to her stomach.

He'd lurched to his feet and spun away from them, thundering across the kitchen and disappearing into the yard. Savannah had waited hours for his return, until finally, exhausted, she'd fallen asleep on the sofa.

She'd wakened in her own bed. The moment's connection with her father had been gone, leaving her to wonder if she'd imagined it. That had been about five months ago, when Katie's problem first became noticeable.

Savannah had never even been close to telling anyone again.

"Come on, Katie, let's go home," she said tiredly.

Katie looked at her. Tears magnified her eyes. "I don't want to," she whispered.

Savannah clasped her sister's small, cold hand. "I know. Neither do I."

They sat there all through the long, hot spring day, waiting in heavy silence for the pealing clang of the school bell that indicated it was time to leave.

"It's time," Savannah said quietly as the last metallic clang faded away.

Katie nodded, dashing the moisture from her eyes. Together, hand in hand, they got to their feet and started walking toward home. The grass-studded dirt road stretched out before them, seeming to twist beyond forever in the miles between the farm and school. Neither of them wanted to continue, but they did.

It was simple. They had nowhere else to go.

Tess stood in front of the stove, staring at the huge black metal monstrosity with a mixture of dread and anticipation. She tried to tell herself this was a challenge, and she'd always loved a good challenge.

Somehow this time it didn't work.

There was no doubt in her mind that cooking was not one of the things she would be good at in this—or any other—life. In 1993 she hadn't had to worry about it. Between the takeout joints, delicatessens, restaurants, and frozen-food sections of her local grocery store, there'd been no reason to cook, but now, in 1873, she had no choice. She wanted to lift some of the burden from Savannah's shoulders, and she wanted to be a mother. Cooking achieved both her goals. And so, cook she would. She'd given herself plenty of time. It was just after midday. The girls wouldn't be home from school for hours. All she had to do was start.

She kneeled and stared through the heavy, soot-stained grate. Thin, twisted, black remains jutted from a pile of cold, gray ashes. The acrid scent of a long-dead fire seeped through the iron bars and stung her eyes.

Using two fingers, she started to ease the door open.

She realized her mistake immediately. The door

weighed a ton. It crashed downward, whacked hard on her bent knees, and knocked her off balance. With a stuttered cry, she flailed forward and smacked her head against the warming oven.

When she woke up, she was sprawled on the kitchen floor with her blue gingham gown up around her middle.

She took one look at herself and burst out laughing. Ten seconds in the kitchen and she'd already knocked herself unconscious.

Rubbing the goose-egg-sized bump that was forming above her left eye, she got to her knees and stared into the cold dead ashes. A sinking feeling tugged at her empty stomach. Ignoring it, she got to her feet and stood confidently in front of the stove. She tried her best to feel cheflike.

It was like trying to squeeze into a size four with the saleslady watching.

"Okay," she said aloud, "I'm going to cook dinner." She paused, thinking. "The first thing to do is make a fire."

She smiled, feeling better already. Yes, that seemed like a sensible plan of attack for someone hell-bent on cooking a meal. Make a fire.

There was a small, neatly piled stack of kindling alongside the stove. She opened the grate door and propped it open with her knee. Then, leaning sideways, she grabbed a few sticks and dropped them in the steel hole.

A quick search of the kitchen revealed no paper. So she set the kitchen towel on fire and dropped it on the pile of wood.

Thick, gray-black smoke spiraled up from the burning rag and crept along the ceiling. She waved it aside and peered into the hole. The smallest stick had caught on fire. Things were looking good.

Whistling at her success, she ambled around the cluttered kitchen, looking for a cookbook. She took this search considerably more seriously than she had her inspection for paper, and opened one cupboard after another. Next she tried the drawers. When she found herself lifting up the silverware to see what was underneath, she knew she was getting panicky.

There were no cookbooks.

How in the hell was she supposed to cook without instructions?

She flung the pantry door open and stared into the neatly aligned shelves. That sinking feeling immediately came back into her gut. The food was in industrial-sized sacks, stacked one after another and tied up with fraying rope. And jars. There were hundreds of glass jars brimming with colorful globs that reminded her of an eighth-grade science lab. Each jar proudly bore a date—as if people chose food by date rather than content.

Anxiety began to unravel Tess's self-confidence. She squeezed her eyes shut and sought divine help. *Okay, I believe in reincarnation. So ESP must be real, too. Mom, give me a recipe. Or you, Carol. Come on, don't be shy. Jump on in.*

Long minutes passed. No one answered.

Apparently deceased relatives and guardian angels were like cops. There was never one around when you needed them.

She opened her eyes. A thick sack of flour filled her vision.

Flour. Okay, what did a person make with flour?

Bread. She dismissed that idea immediately. She may not have been a great cook, but she'd been a world-class shopper. Bread makers sold for two hundred dollars—anything that expensive had to alleviate a ton of hard labor. She had to start small.

Small bread. Biscuits! She could do that.

Smiling broadly, she got out everything she thought she

needed—flour, salt, eggs, and milk. She plopped the ingredients on the table and got to work.

Two hours later, she had five carefully cut out, pancake-sized circles of dough scattered amidst a mountain of flour. Grimacing, she pinched off a section from the biggest one and tasted it. The dough hit her stomach like a lead balloon.

"No more," she mumbled, feeling decidedly ill. She was through taste-testing. This was batch number six, and there was enough dough in her gut to make a large pizza.

She didn't care if the biscuits tasted like shoe leather. She was done. Period.

She backhanded the sheen of sweat from her brow and tucked a flour-coated lock of hair behind her ear. Straightening, she set down the rolling pin and clapped the excess flour from her hands. For the first time in two hours, she looked up from the table.

And winced. The kitchen was . . . trashed. There was no other word for it. Dozens of pots and pans were strewn across the floor, their existence forgotten as she'd searched for a cookie sheet. Flour covered the table and lay like a dusting of new-fallen snow on the floorboards. Smoke clung to the ceiling.

Cooking, apparently, was a dirty business.

Oh, well, she thought. You didn't make an omelet without breaking a few eggs. Turning back to the now hot stove, she dragged a huge cast-iron pot toward her. It bumped and scraped and clanked atop the metal stovetop.

She lifted the lid and tossed in the potatoes, onions, and preserved carrots she'd cut up earlier. Setting the lid down carefully alongside the pot, she filled the pot to the top with water, added salt from the box alongside the stove, and dropped in the haunch of meat she'd found in the mesh container hanging above the dry sink.

She watched it simmer for a few moments, then shoved

her hands in her apron pockets and slowly turned around. The magnitude of the mess struck her again, and she winced. It made her tired just *looking* at the chaos around her.

Sighing, she walked over to the table and slumped on the hard wooden seat. She knew that if she didn't do something—and fast—she'd fall asleep right there and then.

Tiredly she pushed to her feet, grabbed two buckets from beneath the dry sink, and headed outside.

Her breath caught at the beauty of the afternoon. Lush grass rolled out from the house and dropped gently toward the sea. Thousands of wildflowers peeked colorful faces up from the rolling, golden-green grass. Far below, the steel-blue water of Haro Strait sparkled. Sunlight gilded the softly rustling leaves of the oak tree.

She closed her eyes, listening to the sounds of springtime. Birds chirped, wind whistled, leaves fluttered, bees buzzed. To Tess, so many years in silence, it was like the finest of symphonies. Nothing in Carnegie Hall could be so grand.

Humming, she ambled lazily toward the cistern and threw back the heavy wooden lid. Clear blue-green water caught the sunlight and sparkled up at her.

It took her forever to fill and heat sixteen buckets of water, but when she returned to the kitchen and poured the last bucketful into the full-length copper tub she'd found in the shed, she knew it had all been worth it.

She stripped out of her waistless nursing gown and tossed it over the nearest chair, eagerly climbing into the tub.

The water was barely more than lukewarm, but it felt heavenly just the same. She scrubbed her hair and body with lavender-scented soap until her skin tingled and glowed. Then she rested her head on the tub's copper rim and closed her eyes. She'd just relax for a few minutes before she had to clean the kitchen. . . .

Before she knew it, she was asleep.

Chapter Seven

Jack was dead tired as he climbed the sagging steps to the house. At the closed door, he stopped, trying to find the icy numbness he would need to deal with Amarylis. It was difficult—he was so damn tired—but he kept trying, searching his soul for the shield of detachment he needed so desperately with his wife. Steeling himself, he yanked the door open and strode inside, running right into the copper bathing tub. An echoing clang echoed through the humid room.

Jack looked down. His blood immediately ran cold.

Amarylis was asleep in the tub, her arms draped casually on either side, her knuckles resting on the wooden floor. Moonlight-pale hair cascaded all around her, puddling on the floor in swirling, touchable pools. And her skin. Sweet Jesus, her skin . . .

The pink outline of her nipples shimmered through the colorless water. Desire flashed hot and hard through his body. God, how he remembered the feel of her flesh, how pliable and warm and willing she'd once been.

The door slipped out of his nerveless fingers and banged against the wall with a loud *thwack*.

She came awake with a start. "What? Huh?"

That's when Jack noticed the kitchen. He latched on to anger as a preferable emotion to desire. "Christ Almighty!"

"Jack?" she said sleepily. "It must be you. I'd know that pleasant voice anywhere."

"It looks like a cannonball landed in here. What in the hell are you doing?"

"Jack!" This time his name was a shriek, as if she'd just realized she was naked in the tub. She flung herself sideways and grabbed a towel, plastering it to her body.

"What are you doing?" he demanded again.

She got slowly to her feet, the damp towel clamped protectively across her body. "Cooking."

"You can't cook."

"You can say that again."

"I said you can't—"

She burst out laughing. "I didn't mean it literally, Jack."

"Goddamn it, Amarylis, you know I hate a mess."

She sobered instantly and looked at him. He tried to shield the desire in his gaze, but he had a sick, certain feeling that she'd seen it. She eased her death grip on the towel and stepped toward him. "You're afraid," she said quietly, her voice filled with wonder.

Jack stiffened and tried to retreat, but his feet felt nailed to the floor. He stood there, breath held. His senses were so alive, so sensitive, he heard each droplet of water as it streamed down her naked legs and plopped in the bathwater. The quiet, quickened strains of her breathing stabbed through his midsection like hot needles, making him shiver and want and ache.

He riveted his gaze beyond her, staring dull-eyed at the stove. He forced himself to remain perfectly still, even though his skin felt too tight for his body, and he wanted desperately to run.

The touch was so soft, he barely noticed it at first. But when he did, the gentle caress felt like a slap. He grabbed her hand and yanked it away from his face. "Stop it," he said in an embarrassingly husky voice.

Her eyes captured his, held his gaze in a fire-hot grip. "I think I guessed that about you."

Her voice, so soft and edged in the memory of the South, slid down his chest and landed hard in his groin. He opened his mouth to say something, anything, but nothing came out.

"About hating messes, I mean," she went on. "You're the kind of person who slaps a coat of paint on a crumbling wall and calls it new."

The clean lavender scent of her wreathed him, lulled him. His damp palms tingled with the need to touch her, to feel the silky softness of her skin.

"Not me," she whispered, never once taking her gaze from his eyes. "I might make a mess—a hell of a one, actually—but when I'm done, there's a brand-new wall. Strong and lasting."

Jack felt as if he were being sucked over the edge of a huge, crumbling precipice. Any moment, if he didn't break away, he'd go tumbling into the fathomless brown depths of her eyes, and he'd never come out alive. The realization gave him a surge of strength. He grabbed her by the shoulders and shoved her backward enough to hold her at arm's length. "Clean up your goddamn mess."

"Okay."

Her easy acquiescence unnerved him. Frowning, he added, "And don't go around building any walls, either."

She smiled enigmatically. "Don't worry, Jack. Apparently I have to tear down a few first."

Hours later, after the kitchen was clean, Tess stood beneath the oak tree with Caleb in her arms, waiting for the girls to come home from school. A cool late afternoon breeze ruffled through the grass and plucked at her skirt hem. The crisp springtime scents of freshly turned soil, new grass, and blooming flowers filled the air.

But, for once, the beauty didn't capture Tess's attention. She couldn't stop thinking about her confrontation with Jack.

She rocked Caleb gently in her arms, moving in time with the whistling cant of the wind.

Something had happened today with Jack. Something she'd never expected. When he'd walked in on her, she'd felt . . . sexy.

Tess had been many things in her life, done many things. She was no virgin, but neither had she ever felt really comfortable with her sexuality. She'd always thought it was because she wasn't pretty, or because her deafness made intimacy difficult.

Today Jack had set her to wondering about all that. From the moment their eyes had met, it was as if she'd been struck by lightning. Strong, undeniable sexual currents had been loosed in the room, splaying back and forth between them like a live wire. She knew Amarylis was physically pretty; she'd seen that in the mirror. But that didn't mean a whole lot to Tess. She'd learned long ago that beauty was on the inside.

But today, in Jack's eyes, she'd seen her own beauty. Seen her own desirability.

It stunned her even now to realize how much that meant to her. How it had made her feel. Without even thinking, she'd been on her feet, clutching that ridiculous cotton towel to her dripping body as if it protected her modesty.

His eyes had drawn her, left her powerless to resist their dark, hypnotic pull. It shouldn't have surprised her, this deep, almost primal attraction to Jack, but somehow it had. All along she'd thought she was drawn to his pain or his heartache or his need. Now she saw the truth: she was drawn to something deeper, something beyond the pain. To the man himself.

For the first time she'd seen him not as a father, or a

man in pain, or an adversary. Today he'd been simply a man. And she hadn't been the pudgy, frightened deaf loner, or the makeshift mother to his children. She'd been just a woman, moving toward a man who attracted her.

She'd moved with a grace she'd never before possessed, looked at him with a seductive strength she'd never even imagined.

And when she'd touched him—a simple, nothing little brush of skin on skin that lasted no longer than a heartbeat—she felt as if she'd touched fire.

What on earth had possessed her? She knew he hated his wife, had known it from the moment he first looked at her.

But now she knew something else; something dangerous and surprising and more than a little frightening.

He wanted her.

And even more frightening was the fact that she wanted him, too.

"Mama!"

The shrieked word ripped Tess from her daydream. She brought her head up and saw Savannah and Katie skidding to a stop in front of her.

"M-Mama," Savannah said again, twisting her lard tin's steel handle. "What are you doing out here?"

Katie stumbled in her haste to hide behind her sister's skirts. Cautiously she peered around Savannah's elbow.

"I don't know," Tess said. "It was just so pretty, I thought I'd get some fresh air before supper."

Savannah blanched. "Oh, I'll get started right n—"

"The stew's on."

The girls gasped.

Tess laughed. "I don't know how it'll taste, but I decided to try cooking. Why don't you girls go have some fun? I'll call you when it's time to wash up."

Neither one of them moved.

Finally Savannah said, "How?"

The question caught Tess off guard. Startled, she looked at the girls. Their sad, frightened eyes tore at Tess's heart. If only she could ease their pain, help them. But how? She'd never spent much time with children. She'd probably say something wrong and botch the whole thing. It was undoubtedly better to hang back and study the situation a bit more before diving into the fray.

Then it struck her. She was their mother. It didn't matter to them that Tess didn't know the first thing about parenting. All they knew was that they were lonely and afraid, and neither of their parents seemed to care. Until now.

Tentatively she said, "H-How about if we go pick some wildflowers together?"

Surprise widened Savannah's blue eyes. "Really?"

Tess knew instantly that she'd done the right thing. "Yes, really."

They started to come toward Tess.

"Wait," she said.

They froze. Fear rounded their eyes.

Tess winced. What had Jack and Amarylis done to these girls to make them so damned afraid? Smiling softly, she said, "You can leave your books and lunch pails here. That's the first rule of having fun. You need your hands free."

They went to the porch and plunked their lard tins and books down on the bottom step. Then, slowly, they turned around.

Tess smiled with a new sense of confidence. "Okay, let's go."

She tried to keep up a steady stream of banter as she led the girls through the sheep pasture. The indigo rays of a late afternoon sun glanced off the grass hillside, illuminating dozens of multicolored flowers. A soft breeze came up from the Straits, ruffling the tall grass.

"That's a wild rose," she said, pointing to a scraggly little bush that was just beginning to bud. "I'll have to pull that up and plant it by the house. That way we'll be able to see the flowers when we sit on the porch at night."

"We ain't never sat on the porch at night," Savannah said matter-of-factly.

"Well, that's about to change. Oh! Look!" Tess clutched Caleb more tightly and hurried toward the small cluster of maple trees up ahead.

"What—"

"Come on." Tess bent down and found a few maple seedcases. The girls closed ranks around her. Frowning, they watched as she picked through the winged seedcases for just the right ones and then stood. Shifting Caleb to her left arm, she flicked a seedcase into the air. The boomerang-shaped seed whirled and danced in the night breeze like a helicopter before it floated slowly to the grass.

"Here." She placed some in the girls' hands.

Savannah stared down at the seeds in her palm. "You want me to throw them in the air? Why?"

"It's fun."

Savannah frowned. "Oh."

Tess took another seedcase and flicked it hard to the right. It twirled around and hit Tess in the eye. "Aagh!" She clamped a hand over her eye and slumped dramatically to the ground.

Savannah and Katie rushed to her side. "Mama! Are you all right?"

Tess grinned up at them. "Of course I am."

There was a moment of stunned quiet before the girls burst into laughter. Tess felt a surge of happiness at the sound. She knew then why the sound had always stayed with her, even in the muted darkness of her deafness.

Grinning, she got to her feet. "Okay, see that tree down there? Let's see who can hit it."

Savannah and Katie giggled and sidled beside Tess. And the Seed-twirling Olympics began in earnest.

Later, Tess smoothed out the beautifully embroidered tablecloth and carefully set the blue earthenware plates and silverware in just the right spots. A lightning jar full of purple and pink wildflowers sat in the exact center of the table. Dented tin containers of salt and pepper flanked the jar.

Everything was perfect.

Whistling softly, she turned and went into the bedroom. Opening the armoire, she stared at the clothing lined up so neatly inside.

She wanted to find something special to wear. After the wonderful time she'd had with the girls, she felt unexpectedly hopeful about this life. She was fitting in, and she was beginning to make a difference. Tonight would be their first family dinner, and she wanted to look her best.

The first thing she pulled out was a pair of ankle-length muslin pants with a drawstring waist and no crotch.

"Pretty racy," she muttered, dropping them on the floor.

Next came an hourglass-shaped, boned corset just the right size for a Barbie doll. The corset hit the floor next to the pants. She would *not* be squeezing her postpartum body into that thing.

As she pulled out garment after garment, Tess became increasingly aware of two things: One, none of the dresses would fit her unless she wore the corset, and two, women in 1873 were supposed to be uncomfortable.

She stripped out of the flour-dusted gingham gown and tossed it in a heap at the bottom of the armoire. Then she yanked on the muslin crotchless pants and covered them with a floor-length white muslin skirt with pretty lace along the hem. Last came a sleeveless, scoop-necked, short-waisted white blouse that looked like something Ralph Lauren might create for spring.

She went back to the washstand and studied herself in the mirror, turning this way and that. The pretty white fabric belled and swirled. She felt incredibly feminine and beautiful.

Satisfied, she left the bedroom and went into the kitchen. After another quick check on the supper, she called for the girls.

Savannah and Katie came running out of the bedroom. The moment Savannah saw Tess, she stopped in her tracks. Katie rammed into her sister's backside and giggled loudly.

Tess frowned. "What's the matter?"

Savannah shot a nervous glance at the door, as if she was afraid Jack would come through any minute. "You're wearing your . . . unmentionables."

Tess glanced down, surprised. "Really? This is underwear? All of it?"

Savannah nodded.

Tess laughed. "What a hoot. Well, this should get old Jack's attention, don't you think?"

Savannah started to say something else. Then she noticed the kitchen table. Her eyes bulged.

"*Now* what's wrong?" Tess asked.

"That's the good Sunday tablecloth. We ain't used it since Reverend Weekes came for dinner last year."

Tess winced at the word "ain't" and made a mental note to start grammar lessons tomorrow. "What day is it?"

"Thursday."

"Close enough. Now, wash up. Your daddy will be here soon."

* * *

Jack pushed the battered gray Stetson higher on his head and backhanded the sweat from his brow. Squinting against the fading purple twilight, he glanced down the row of fence-line he'd built today.

God, he loved it out here. Alone, working his land like in the old days. Here he wasn't afraid or lonely or filled with regret. No one expected anything of him or looked at him through hurt- or hate-filled eyes. He was just plain old Jack Rafferty, San Juan Island sheep rancher. Not Jackson Beauregard Rafferty III, disowned, cowardly son of the wealthiest planter in Georgia.

Not for the first time, he felt an almost suffocating wave of regret. They could have had a good life here. If only Amarylis had given the island—given him—a chance. But, of course, she hadn't. Within ten seconds of landing in Garrison Bay, she'd dismissed the island and all its residents with an airy sweep of her pale hand. No one, she declared, but poor white trash would live in such a backwater place. And Amarylis Rafferty refused to have anything to do with trash. Jack had seen Savannah wince at her mother's words, seen the lonely pain creep into his daughter's eyes. A pain that had been born on that day and grown every day since, until now Jack couldn't remember what she looked like without it.

He stood there for a long time, watching wind scurry through the gilded grass and ripple across the water far below. The slow-moving breeze rustled softly through the leaves overhead, then died away, leaving in its wake an almost preternatural silence.

With a last swipe at the sweat on his forehead, he headed in for supper. As he rounded the barn, the house came into view, and his rare good mood fled. His stomach twisted into a coil.

He crossed the yard and ascended the stairs slowly. Each step reverberated up his stiffened spine. After the bathing debacle this afternoon, he felt like a man walking on an emotional tightrope. One misstep and years' worth of hard work would be wrenched away.

Taking a deep breath, he opened the door and stepped inside.

"Hi, Jack," his wife drawled. "Welcome home."

He was too stunned to hide his reaction. "You're wearing your . . ."

"Unmentionables. I know. Savannah told me." Humor—honest-to-God humor—twinkled in her brown eyes. *"C'est la vie."*

"Say la what?"

"It means—roughly—such is life. Anyway, my boo—" She glanced over at the children, and amended her sentence. "My breasts are covered, so who cares?"

Savannah and Katie covered their mouths to keep from laughing.

Jack glanced around the kitchen, looking for something—anything—to take his mind off the creamy swell of cleavage that looked so damned inviting. "You're using the Sunday tablecloth."

Dumb, Jack. Really dumb. Now she'll rip it off the table and throw it at—

"Thursday."

He frowned. "Huh?"

"Now it's the Thursday tablecloth. Tomorrow it'll be the Friday tablecloth. Then I think we'll have a picnic. What do you think, girls? Wouldn't a picnic be nice on Saturday?"

"A picnic? You must be joking."

"It may rain, of course, so we'll have to have a contingency plan—like dinner in the barn."

He wondered suddenly if she'd been hit on the head or fallen down the porch steps. "Amarylis? Are you all right?"

"I'm glad you brought that up." She bent over the table and collected the plates.

Jack felt a headache start. It swelled behind his eyes like a giant wall of pressure. She had to be toying with him. She *had* to be. . . .

He rubbed the bridge of his nose and squeezed his eyes shut, fighting for the strength to remain numb. When he thought he could speak without raising his voice, he said, "Brought what up, Amarylis?"

"My name. It stinks. What could her—I mean, *my* mother have been thinking?"

Jack opened his eyes and stared at her. "You always liked your name. You said it showed good southern breeding."

"*Breeding?* What am I? A pig? Here, follow me."

Without waiting, she went to the kitchener.

Reluctantly he followed.

She peered into the pot and started ladling stew onto the plates. "Now, about my name . . . Hmph, it's sort of runny."

He was holding on to his temper by a thread. "Your name?"

She laughed. It was a clear, guileless sound that made his headache double in intensity. "Of course not. The stew is runny. My name is just plain ugly. I've been giving it some thought lately, and I've decided to change it . . . at least a little. Sort of a nickname." She paused, frowning. "How do you spell it, anyway?"

It was a few seconds before Jack felt it was safe to answer. "A-M-A-R-Y-L-I-S."

"Ugh. Sorta limits my choices. I'd love to choose, say . . . Tess, but I don't think that's quite right. After all, a new life deserves a new name. How about Amy?"

Jack was pretty sure it was a rhetorical question, but he couldn't think of a damn thing to say anyway.

"No," she said finally. "Too young. Mary's too traditional, and Maryl probably hasn't been invented yet." Her frown deepened for a moment, then vanished. "I've got it! Lissa." She cocked her head and looked right at him. "From now on, I'd like to be called Lissa, okay?"

They were so close, he could feel the whisper of her breath against his lips. Jack stiffened, fighting the urge to leap backward.

She gave him a smile that sent feelers of warmth shooting into his groin. Then she reached out to touch him.

This time he did leap backward. "Lissa is fine," he said through gritted teeth.

"Great, I'm glad we got that settled. It's pretty, don't you think? Now, let's sit down."

"Together?" Savannah's voice came out as a surprised squeak.

Tess set the plates down. "Of course, together. We're a family, aren't we?"

Jack gave her a sick look. "Don't tell me. Supper's one of those 'new and improved' things."

She pulled out her chair and sat down, patting the back of the chair nearest her. "Here you go, Jack. Head of the table."

He edged past her and took a seat, careful not to touch so much as her little finger.

"Savannah and Katie, y'all—my, what a great word that is—y'all sit on either side of your daddy."

When everyone was seated, Tess went to the stove and eased the oven door open. Dry heat whooshed out at her, bringing with it the scent of done-to-a-turn biscuits. Grabbing a towel, she pulled out the heavy pan and set it on the riddle board, then snapped the door shut with her hip and ventured a proud look at her biscuits.

Her smile fell flat.

Her biscuits were flatter.

She stood there a long time, staring at her failure, trying vainly to figure out what she'd done wrong. After a few minutes, Savannah came up beside her and peered around her shoulder.

"Gosh, them biscuits are flat. Look hard, too. You musta forgot the soda."

"Oh," Tess said. She felt a moment's worth of disappointment, but years in the scientific trenches had taught her to discard it easily. Then she had a flash of inspiration. "They aren't biscuits, they're— No, I'll save that for later. Come on, let's sit down."

The four of them came together at the table and sat down like a regular family. They looked everywhere except at one another. Gazes darted like wildfire, up, down, across, away. Obviously no one knew what to do, or when to do it.

"Everyone take hands," Tess said in a voice that brooked no argument.

"But—" Savannah started.

"Now." Tess reached a hand toward each girl. Katie's small, pudgy, pink hand slipped into her own warm one, and Tess gave the girl's cold, trembling fingers a reassuring squeeze. Then she took hold of Savannah's hand.

Jack looked studiously at the flowers on the table, his hands in his lap. For a moment Tess thought he wasn't going to comply. Just as she was about to say his name, he brought his hands to the table and clasped his daughters' hands.

Tess bowed her head and waited for everyone else to do the same. One by one, they did. "For what we are about to receive, may the Lord make us truly grateful. Amen."

"Amen," mumbled the rest of the family. Immediately everyone yanked their hands back.

With a sigh, Tess eased her napkin out from beneath the

silverware and plopped it in her lap. Plucking up the soup-spoon, she took a sip of her stew, and frowned.

The broth tasted like bottled water that had been left in the sun. No, it was saltier than that. Seawater, maybe.

She reached for the pepper and poured a load in her stew. "What did I do wrong, Savannah?"

"Nothing, Mama. It's great."

Tess laughed easily. "Sure, if you *like* drinking dirty dishwater . . ."

Savannah struggled with a smile. "The vegetables and meat are good. Maybe next time you could add some flour to the broth. It'll thicken it."

"God knows you can find the flour," Jack muttered.

Surprise brought Tess's head up.

Jack flashed her a smile that lasted no longer than a heartbeat, then his mouth drew back into its customary scowl.

Tess felt as if she'd been struck. The memory of his smile lingered long after he'd looked away from her, floating down to that small, dark, frightened corner of Tess's soul, and brought with it a quivering ray of light. Somewhere deep inside Jack was a sense of humor, and with laughter there was always hope.

Tess smiled. For the first time since meeting Jack, she thought maybe she could really, truly fall in love with him. *Maybe* . . .

Chapter Eight

After supper was finished and most of the dishes had been washed and dried and put away, Tess clapped her hands for attention.

Jack regarded her warily. "What now? You want us to call you Queen Victoria?"

"Vicky is fine," she shot back with a grin.

"Mama, what do you want me to do with these . . ." Savannah eyed the flat brown patties, as if uncertain whether they deserved the title biscuits.

"I'm glad you asked," Tess answered, tossing her soggy dishrag over the dry sink's rim. "I'm going to go check on Caleb, and while I'm doing that, I want you three to go stand by the tree swing. I'll be right out."

Savannah looked at her in horror. "But—"

"Damn it, what—" Jack cut in.

Tess ignored them. "Go on, all of you. I'll be out in a minute." When they didn't move, she looked pointedly at Jack. "I could cook something else. Maybe a nice three-layer cake."

Jack flinched. "We're going. Come on, girls."

They filed out of the house like silent, resentful soldiers. Tess checked on the sleeping baby, then grabbed the biscuits and ran outside.

The fresh, salt-limned night air immediately filled her with a giddy feeling of anticipation. Moonlight illuminated the three people standing in the small yard. Behind them, the farm buildings were a charcoal-hued range of shapes and rooflines. The barn was a hump of black in the distance.

She looked around. "Do we have a dog?"

Katie burst into nervous laughter.

Jack's eyes narrowed. "No, we don't have a dog."

"Too bad." Tess plucked up her hem and balanced the heavy pan on one hip, making her way carefully down the steps. "Gather round, y'all. We're going to play Frisbees."

They shuffled reluctantly toward her. Tess set the pan down in the middle of the dirt driveway. "Savannah, run down there to the edge of the chicken house. I'll wing one to you."

As Savannah did as she was told, Tess grabbed a biscuit from the pot. "Here it comes," she yelled, flipping the leadlike pancake with an expert flick of the wrist.

The pale brown circle flew through the air.

"Catch it!" Tess hollered.

Savannah reached high and just missed. The biscuit glanced off her fingertips and exploded against the chicken house wall. Rock-hard bits flew everywhere.

"Is the wall still standing?" Tess yelled.

Beside her, Katie clamped a hand over her mouth.

Tess touched the girl's shoulder. "You can laugh," she said softly.

Katie looked up. In the meager light, her brown eyes appeared huge in the small, pale oval of her face. "Can I try it?" There was a quaver in her voice that tugged at Tess's heart.

"Of course. You go on down there, and I'll send one your way."

Katie hurried toward her sister and turned around, hands outstretched.

Tess lobbed a slow, easy one. The biscuit rolled through the air and landed in Katie's tiny hands.

"I got it, Savannah! I got it!"

Tess was so caught up in watching the girls, she didn't hear Jack come up beside her. "What are you doing?"

She jumped in surprise. Whirling around, she found herself almost in his arms. There was a flicker of surprise in his eyes, but the emotion lasted for less than a heartbeat. His gaze narrowed, pinned her in place.

"Answer me, damn it."

His nearness sent strange sensations tingling through her body. Her throat felt thick and tight. For a second, she couldn't breathe.

Moonlight spilled through the branches and illuminated their faces. They stood motionlessly, close enough to touch but careful not to.

She tilted her face up and met his troubled gaze.

He's afraid, she realized suddenly and without question. Tess had learned long ago to trust her instincts about people. She was rarely wrong. For some reason, Jack was afraid of his wife, and his sarcastic anger was just a cover, a way to keep his precious distance. She'd bet her last dollar on it.

"Jack." she whispered his name in quiet wonder.

He didn't move, just stood there, staring down at her through those narrowed, unreadable eyes. Their faces were close, no more than a hand's span apart. She could smell the masculine wool and leather and woodsmoke perfume of his clothing, feel the whisper-soft threads of his breath against her lips.

"What are you doing?" he asked quietly.

Tess swallowed thickly. After years of deafness, she knew what it meant to listen. In his voice she heard things a non-hearing-impaired person would never notice. Fear, exhaustion, despair. And something else, something that took her heart and twisted it in half.

Loneliness.

In that moment, she knew. She could be a part of this family. Tonight when she'd picked flowers with the children, and taken their hands at prayer-time, Tess had felt . . . as if she belonged.

This was the second chance Carol had given her. It wasn't just about another body in another time. It was about finding the kind of emotion she'd only dreamed about, about exploring a side of herself she'd never known existed.

And it was even more than that. This chance belonged to all of them. Together they could help one another, heal one another.

The realization freed her, gave her a sense of daring and *rightness* she'd never known before. Made her feel . . . brave. As if she could take on the world—or one very frightened, very lonely man.

Tess blinked up at him, knowing her eyes were filled with all the pent-up hopes and dreams of a woman who'd lived alone too long. Knowing that the emotion in her eyes would scare the hell out of him, but unable to shield her gaze. She'd never been good at pretending not to care.

He backed away from her suddenly, his hands raised in the air, his head shaking slowly in denial. "I won't let you hurt those kids any more than we already have."

She reached for him. "Jack . . ."

He jerked away, stumbling backward in his haste to escape her touch. "I mean it," he said quietly. "Don't hurt them."

Tess watched him go. With every step he took, she felt an aching sadness creep through her chest.

She realized then the risk she was taking. If she let herself fall in love with this family, with Jack, nothing would ever be the same again. If they—if *he*—rejected her, it would hurt as nothing in her life had ever hurt before.

Jack stood at the window, his forehead pressed against the cool glass, watching his wife toss flat biscuits to his giggling daughters.

He squeezed his eyes shut and tried not to think about what was happening to him. What *she* was making happen with her sudden smiles and casual touches.

He had to remain numb; he knew that. Years ago, when his wife's hatred for him had just begun, he'd learned to squelch his hurt and need beneath a veneer of icy calm. When Amarylis laughed at him, he turned away; when she slapped him, he turned the other cheek.

It had always worked. He'd walked around this house silent, alone and lonely, like an undead thing in the world of the barely alive. After a while, she had stopped even trying to bait him. They lived like strangers, all of them, each one distant and unconnected with the others.

He hated it, of course, but it was the only way to protect his precious children. It was the one thing he and Amarylis had always agreed upon. He was a danger to them all. It was distant, his insanity, but not forgotten. Even now, years after the breakdown, he went to sleep each night afraid, and woke each morning in a cold sweat. He was always desperately afraid that the darkness would take him unaware and that, during a blackout, he'd hurt someone. Maybe even his babies . . .

He accepted his isolation from his loved ones as a fact of life, another ramification of his cowardice, and mental defect.

But now things were changing. Until Caleb's birth, he couldn't remember the last time one of Amarylis's cruel games had actually angered him. He watched her manipu-

lations from afar, through eyes that understood and antic-
ipated her every move. And that had given him the edge.

Now he was losing that edge. She was doing the unexpected, changing her routines. Every time she did something new, he felt it like a hard punch in the stomach.
Emotions hurtled through him with frightening velocity—
pain, shame, fear. But the strongest of them, the emotion
that made him the angriest of all, was need. He'd thought
the need for her had died years ago, buried in the icy cof-
fin of her hatred.

Only now it was creeping back, suffusing his senses and
sucking the strength from his soul. God, when she smiled
at him, the need for her was like a hammerblow to his
heart. It had been so long since she'd smiled, he'd almost
forgotten. Almost . . .

"Ignore her," he said quietly to himself. Ignore the
changes, the smiles, the touches. Ignore it all, and remember who she is and why she hates you.

The sound of Savannah's carefree laughter seeped
through the half-open door and filled the small, darkened
kitchen.

Jack groaned and pulled away from the window. Turning, he paced across the room, trying not to see the tablecloth and flowers.

Changes. More goddamn changes . . .

Ignore it.

The lilting strains of laughter came again. This time it
was his wife's soft, throaty chuckle that filtered through
the cool night air.

A sharp stab of longing almost shoved him toward the
door, but he planted his feet and remained motionless.

"Please, God," he murmured, "I've never asked you for
much, and I know I don't deserve help, but I need it. Please,
don't let me start believing in her again. *Please . . .*"

* * *

Tess woke in the middle of the night to feed Caleb. Half-asleep, she nursed the baby, then rediapered him and put him back to bed. She was almost at her bed when she heard a strange, scraping noise coming from the living room.

You know the goddamn rules.

Jack's words came back to her, reminded her that she shouldn't leave her room.

She stared at the door. The old Tess—the one who'd grown up in so many foster homes—wouldn't have questioned Jack's edict. A rule was a rule. A person didn't go where she wasn't wanted.

But the old explanations didn't soothe Tess this time. Something had happened to her tonight. When she'd stood in the moonlit yard, close enough to touch Jack, feeling his breath as a caress across her lips, she'd realized how desperately she wanted to get to know the man who was her husband. And there was only one way to do that. Break a few rules.

Slipping into her wrapper, she went to her door and eased it open. Pale golden light spilled into the hallway from the living room.

Cautiously she made her way down the darkened corridor and paused at the corner of the room.

Jack was sitting on the stone hearth, his body backlit by the red-gold glow of a fire. Between his legs was a large piece of wood. The slow, steady *scrape-thunk* of a knife slicing along skinned wood filled the room.

Tess narrowed her eyes, trying to see what he was making.

A rocking horse. She could just make out the pointy ears and triangular head, and the huge arched rockers.

Tess's heart twisted. He was up, alone and probably lonely in the middle of the night, making something for the children he loved so deeply. Children he never spoke to and rarely looked at, but spent his every waking moment trying to protect.

What happened to you, Jack Rafferty? The question burned on the tip of her tongue, spiraled through her mind. What had happened to make him so desperately afraid of showing his love?

She tried to remain motionless and silent, tried to respect his privacy, but she couldn't. Before she knew it, she was moving toward him, her hand outstretched, her heart in her eyes. "Jack?"

His head snapped up. "Amarylis? What are you—"

"Lissa," she answered softly. "And I couldn't sleep." She walked to the couch and sat lightly on its ragged edge. "What are you making?"

"Please," he said in a broken, tired voice. "Leave me out of it."

"Out of what?"

"Whatever new game you're playing. Just leave me and the kids out of it."

"What's wrong with games?" Her voice was so quiet, he had to lean forward to hear it. "Maybe you could use a little fun in your life."

Despair filled his eyes. He ran a shaking hand through his hair and looked away. "I'm doing the best I can," he said quietly. "Don't push me."

The aching words tore at Tess's heart. The silent pain in his eyes wrapped around her throat and squeezed hard.

She took a single step toward him, then stopped. She had to move slowly with Jack, take the relationship step by step. Tonight was the beginning, the starting place, and it was important that she do it right. If only she could figure out what "right" was with Jack . . .

Suddenly he lurched to his feet. The rocking horse hit the hardwood floor with a clatter as he strode toward the kitchen.

"Jack." His name slipped from her lips before she had anything to say.

He didn't even pause. He tore through the kitchen and left the house. The door banged shut behind him.

Tess stared after him for a long time. Then she went over and picked up the half-finished rocking horse. Running her fingers along the scratchy wooden surface, she felt the sting of tears come to her eyes.

He was running from something; she was sure of it. Something dark and dangerous that scared him to death.

And he was alone in his fight. Desperately, achingly alone.

Somehow she had to ease that burden from his shoulders, had to let him realize that she wouldn't hurt him. If she could bring him into the family, make him lighten his heavy load, they could begin the healing—and melding—process together.

Somehow she had to figure out a way to get past Jack's angry facade and touch the man behind the mask.

It came to her the next morning as she was cleaning out the pantry. *The Plan.*

Phase One was deceptively simple. Force Jack to react.

She knew now that he was working hard, very hard, to remain distant and aloof from his wife and children. The scene by the crib proved how much he loved them, and how terrified he was to show his love.

She had no idea why he acted so angry all the time, but Tess was fairly certain it was a carefully constructed facade. A way to keep his children from loving him.

All she had to do was slowly, layer by layer, peel away his angry defenses. She had to force him to interact with his family. If she could just bring him into the circle of his family, maybe he would relax a little. Maybe he'd even try to be a dad.

Tess knew how he felt, knew the pain of being an outsider in your own family. She knew, too, how the girls felt every time he turned his back on them or failed to meet their gazes. Each rejection, no matter how small, was like a tiny slice of the surgeon's knife. As an orphan, a reluctant stranger in someone else's family, Tess had learned a lot about what children needed, and even more about how it felt to get less or nothing at all. Kids needed love and laughter and a place they felt safe. The Rafferty girls had none of those things.

Until now, Tess vowed. Somehow she'd change that; somehow she'd bring laughter and love into these walls.

Laughter. That was the key. She had to teach Jack to laugh. It seemed like a simple thing, too simple, but Tess was certain that everything hinged on that. If he could let go of his anger long enough to laugh, or even to smile, maybe the real Jack would come out of hiding.

But how to make him smile? That was the question that had kept her awake half the night. But about ten seconds ago she'd dusted off a jar of pickles, and it had come to her.

Do the unexpected. Get him off guard, and keep him off guard. She'd done it once already, when he'd interrupted her bath. Seeing her naked had shaken him up so badly, he'd forgotten to be mad for a while.

Now she just had to get him that off balance with her clothes on.

It would work. She was certain of it.

All she had to do was figure out what he expected of her. And do the opposite.

Tess was waiting on the porch for Savannah and Katie when the girls got home from school.

"Hi, girls!" she yelled cheerily, waving.

Savannah gave her a tentative smile and waved back. "Hi, Mama."

Tess plucked up her heavy skirt and hurried down the steps, crossing the grassy yard to meet them. "I've been waiting for y'all to get home from school. I've got a great idea."

Katie perked up. "Really? What?"

Tess linked arms with each girl, and together they walked toward the house. "You'll see, but first I want to ask you a few questions."

Both girls immediately tensed, their brisk walk slowed to a hesitant shuffle, then stopped altogether.

Kneeling in the grass, Tess gathered them close. "Don't be worried. It's nothing major. I just wondered what things are usually like around here."

Two blank stares.

Tess tried a more specific question. "I mean, what does your daddy expect around the house?"

Savannah frowned in thought. "You mean like having supper on time?"

Tess grinned. "Exactly! So your daddy expects his meals on time. What else?"

"Well, he likes things quiet."

"Uh-huh. What else?"

Savannah shrugged. "I dunno. He don't like messes."

Tess's grin softened to a thoughtful smile. "You're right about that." She turned to Katie. "Can you think of anything he expects, sweetie?"

Katie's eyes bulged in surprise, as if she couldn't believe her mother was asking her for advice. Then she screwed up her little face in deep concentration. "Nobody's 'posed to touch his tools 'n' stuff in the barn."

"That's perfect, Katie. Just perfect!"

Disbelief rounded the little girl's eyes. "It is?"

Tess nodded. "The best. And now, here's the hard part. What does he expect of me?"

They both answered at once. "Yelling."

Tess laughed happily. "No problem. I hardly ever yell. Now," she said. "How about that game?"

"Are you sure?" Savannah asked, eyeing Tess warily. "Daddy don't like games like this."

Tess gave her a look of complete innocence. "But *everybody* likes hide-and-seek."

"I like hide-and-seek," Katie piped up, her pudgy pink fingers wrapped tightly around the bunch of spoons Tess had given her.

"There, you see," Tess said to Savannah. "Everyone likes hide-and-seek. Now, Katie, you go hide the rest of the silverware while Savannah shows me *again* how to baste this damned bird without getting burned. Then wash up your hands and go get your daddy."

Jack wiped the gritty dirt off the pitchfork's prongs and carefully hung it on the barn wall. The perfectly aligned pitchforks, hoes, rakes, and other farming instruments glinted dully in the late afternoon's fading light. Turning away, he eased the hammer from his belt and hung it on its hook above the workbench. It hung perfectly straight in its place alongside the trowel.

"Daddy, supper's ready!"

"Supper?" Jack turned away from the workbench and saw Savannah standing just outside the barn door. A gentle breeze rustled her skirt and lifted the curly ends of her long hair. Her cheeks were flushed, and there was a brightness in her eyes he hadn't seen in a long time.

Confusion rendered him momentarily speechless. She looked . . . happy.

"C'mon Daddy. It's ready."

He fished the pocket watch from his pants pocket and flipped it open. He immediately frowned. "But it's only four o'clock. We don't usually eat for another hour."

Savannah shrugged. "All I know is, Mama said to get you for supper." She glanced back over her shoulder toward the house. "Now I gotta go. We're playing games."

Before Jack could say a word, she was gone, skipping across the grass for home.

"Games?"

He glanced at his nice, orderly tools and felt a flash of fear. "What now? Amarylis?"

Reluctantly Jack left the barn and headed for the house. As he passed the oak tree, he heard a happy, high-pitched giggle coming from the open kitchen window.

He paused, frowning. *Laughter?*

Then came Savannah's voice: "Here it is, Mama. Under the pie safe!"

And more giggles.

Jack's stomach tightened into a small, anxious knot. He climbed the steps slowly, wincing at each creak of the tired old wood. The doorknob felt cold and strangely unfamiliar in his hand as he entered the kitchen.

The first thing he noticed was the mouth-watering aroma of roasting chicken. The second was the pandemonium.

Amarylis and Katie and Savannah were running around the kitchen and living room, giggling, crawling under furniture, lifting lamps.

"Here's a soupspoon!" Katie yelled, laughing, as she produced a spoon from beneath the sofa's cushion.

Jack frowned and quietly shut the door behind him. As he moved into the room, he noticed the table.

"What the hell . . ."

The table was set with flowers, plates, cups, silverware,

even salt and pepper. The only problem was, all of the utensils were painted onto the tablecloth in bright red.

He studied the strange artwork, trying to figure out what in the hell was going on.

"Hello, Jack. Welcome home."

He heard his wife's softly spoken words, and cringed. Ramming his hands deep in his pockets, he grudgingly looked up at her. She was standing in front of the kitchener, her hands clasped together like the well-bred southern lady she had always claimed to be.

And yet, she looked . . . different. Disheveled. Her cheeks were flushed from steamy heat and laughter, and there was a sparkle in her eyes that made him ache with longing. Once, long ago, she'd looked like this whenever they'd been together.

She watched him study her, making no move to turn away. A slow, sensuous smile curved her full lips. Crazily, he felt it was a smile meant for him and him alone.

He clenched his jaw and looked away.

The oven door creaked open, then banged shut. The aroma of roasting chicken and potatoes filled the small room.

Jack searched for something to say that would sever the ridiculous feeling of rightness seeping into his consciousness. "Why is supper so damned early?"

Staring at the bizarre tablecloth, he waited, arms crossed, for her to answer. She didn't.

"Amarylis?"

Still nothing.

He crossed the kitchen in two giant steps and came up beside her. "Goddamn it, I'm talking to you."

She looked up at him, the very picture of innocence. "You were?"

"You know I was."

"How would I know that? In normal communication,

one *looks* at the person to whom they're talking. I thought perhaps you were addressing the painted flowers."

"Damn it, Amarylis—"

"That's a problem as well."

Jack was so goddamn confused, he didn't know what to do. His hands balled into frustrated fists. *"What?"*

"You called me Amarylis."

"Yeah."

"So naturally I assumed you were speaking to the flowers. I am Lissa. From now on I refuse to answer to anything else." She grinned. "Unless you want to call me honeybun or sweetie pie."

Jack stared at her in disbelief, then spun away from her innocent eyes and smiling mouth. He strode to the dresser and grabbed a plate. Wedging it under his arm, he yanked the bottom drawer open.

It was empty.

He turned back toward her. "Where's the silverware?"

She moved the chicken to a small platter, carefully arranged the potatoes in a ring around it, and set the food on the table. "I'm not sure."

He went to the table and sat down hard. "You're not sure where the silverware is? It hasn't moved in years."

She sat down across from him, steepled her fingers, and rested her chin on her fingertips. A challenging smile sparkled in her eyes and curved her full lips. "That's right."

"I'll get you some, Daddy; it's in—"

"Your daddy can get his own silverware, Savannah," Lissa said in a matter-of-fact voice that brooked no argument.

Jack shot a quick glance toward the living room. The girls were standing side by side in front of the sofa, staring at him. They both looked ready to dive beneath the sofa at a moment's notice.

He sighed tiredly, suddenly exhausted by everything. The changes, the smiles, the laughter. *Everything.*

"Okay, Lissa, what's going on?"

"The girls and I were playing hide-and-seek. We were sure you'd want to join in."

He snorted at the obvious lie. "Well, I don't. So now that the game is over, let's eat."

"Why would you think that?"

He frowned. A headache flared behind his eyes. "Think what?"

"That the game's over."

He glanced at the girls again, then back at his wife. "Who's hiding now . . . Caleb?"

She smiled. "We weren't hiding people. We were hiding things."

Jack knew he shouldn't ask. "What things?"

Her smile grew into a grin. "The silverware."

Jack's first reaction was to explode. The last thing he needed at the end of a hard day was a game of hide-and-seek for the silverware.

He squeezed his eyes shut, rubbed his suddenly throbbing temples, and concentrated on remaining calm. He refused to give her the satisfaction of making him angry.

"Jack?" she said in a taunting, singsongy voice. "Are you all right?"

His eyes popped open and drilled her. "Yeah." He bit the word off. "I'm fine."

"Good, then how about we all go into the living room and find—"

"No."

Her sentence snapped in half. She looked up at him, obviously surprised by his refusal.

Their gazes locked across the table. He was breathing a little heavier than he'd like, but other than that, Jack thought he looked pretty damn calm for a man slowly being sucked over the edge.

"We hid *all* the silverware," she said smugly.

It was Jack's turn to grin. He reached for the chicken and wrenched off a succulent, still hot leg. "Then it's a good thing you made chicken."

Surprise flitted through her eyes. She studied him for a moment longer, and he would have sworn he saw a glimmer of respect. Then her lips twitched slightly and she turned away.

Jack allowed himself a triumphant grin. He'd one-upped Amarylis for the first time in years, and goddamn, it felt good.

It would have felt even better if she hadn't laughed.

Chapter Nine

Jack lay on the couch, shivering. He thrashed side to side, fighting the nightmare's frightening grip. A low, miserable moan escaped him. Restlessly he pulled the flimsy woolen blanket tighter to his chin. His teeth chattered in staccato bursts of sound.

A red haze crept across his closed eyes, turning his world into a twisting quagmire of dripping blood and oozing mud. Screams of the dead and dying reverberated through his head. Gunfire exploded all around him.

Suddenly he was awake.

The darkness was coming. Oh, God, it was coming. He could feel it, circling him like hungry wolves, closing in for the kill. Fear washed through him, closed around his throat. Hot, aching breaths pushed past his trembling lips. He curled into the fetal position and lay there, panting, praying it would go away this time. Praying this time he could forget . . .

Rain splashed at the windowpane behind him, rattling the house. The sound rocked Jack to the core of his soul. He wrapped his shaking arms around himself, trying desperately to hold himself together until the storm stopped. But it didn't do any good. He could feel the darkness, feel its cold, icy breath on the back of his neck, feel the brush of its fingertips along his arms. It was coming.

Thunder boomed through the night, echoed through the too still house like a volley of cannonfire.

A scream of pure terror wrenched up Jack's throat. He had to protect his family.

He lurched to his feet, not bothering to find his shoes in his panic to flee. Only half-awake, he lumbered to the kitchen and grabbed his coat, plunging his arms into its sheepskin-lined warmth.

Panicked, desperate, he wrenched open the door and raced onto the porch. Rain hammered the overhang above his head and ran in sheets of silver, rattling the floor-boards. The wind whistled, screaming, through the night.

"Oh, God," he moaned, feeling the darkness get closer. Closer.

He closed his eyes in a hopeless prayer, then stumbled down the rain-slicked steps and ran.

He had no idea where.

Tess woke with a start. *Something was wrong.*

She pushed to her elbows and gazed around the room through bleary, unfocused eyes. The first rays of dawn were pushing through the glass, but otherwise the bedroom was dark and quiet. Nothing *looked* wrong.

She flipped back the coverlet and reached for her robe. Shrugging into the warm flannel, she went to the cradle and checked Caleb. The baby was fast asleep, sucking on his fist.

She hurried down the hallway and peeked into the girls' bedroom. Relieved to find them both asleep, she headed for the living room.

The sofa was empty except for the brown woolen blanket slung haphazardly across its back. Crossing her arms across her chest, she walked toward the kitchen and peered out the window. Dawn was just beginning to creep through the shadowy grass. Last night's lingering rain clung to the leaves, making them appear rich and glossy green.

It was so quiet, Tess could hear the raindrops falling from the leaves and plunking in the still wet grass.

Cold seeped through the thin pane, making her shiver. But it was more than the cold that sent a skitter along her flesh.

Something is wrong.

"No," she said aloud, taking comfort from the strength and certainty of her own voice. Nothing was wrong. Jack was simply out before dawn, working his fields as always.

And yet, she didn't quite believe it.

She stared across the farm's rolling, grassy pastures, willing herself to see a lone figure. Somewhere. Anywhere.

"Where are you, Jack?" she murmured. "And what's wrong?"

Jack opened his eyes and thought for a moment he was blind. The world was a smeary wash of black and midnight blue and deep purple, of impossibly shifting shapes and imposing shadows.

Dread slammed through his body, tensed his every muscle until he ached. He rolled onto his stomach and lay panting, trying desperately to remember something. *Anything.*

Nausea thrummed his stomach hard, coiled around his insides. He swallowed thickly, praying he wouldn't vomit, and crawled shakily to his knees. On all fours he paused, head hung low, taking deep, measured breaths.

Gradually he became aware of the scent of fresh green grass and wildflowers.

He sat back on his heels and looked wearily around him. The headache had already begun, pounding behind his eyes like hammerblows. His vision swam in and out of focus.

The west pasture.

He was in his own field.

"Thank God," he whispered in a raspy, scream-weakened voice.

He started to get to his feet, but as he moved, his knee ground into something hard and cold. He shifted sideways, reaching blindly for the object. His fingers curled around something long and narrow and chillingly cold.

A knife.

Jack squeezed his eyes shut, feeling a flash of terror so icy, so consuming, he thought for a moment he was going to vomit after all.

His hands started to shake. Curling his fingers tighter around the cold blade, he lifted it up. It seemed to grow heavier, colder. Sweat crawled in an itchy trail down his forehead. Fear radiated through his body, echoing with every painful throb of his headache.

What have I done? The familiar question drove like an icepick into his brain.

No, he thought desperately, I wouldn't hurt my children. Please, God, not my children . . .

Weary, shaking with fear and shame and despair, he opened his eyes and looked at what he had in his hands.

A piece of metal. Just a goddamn piece of metal. Not a knife at all.

He got to his feet and started the long walk home. With every step, every breath, his fear escalated until, by the time he saw the outline of the house in the distance, he was wound tighter than a badly made clock.

"Please, God," he mumbled time and again, his hands curled into white-knuckled, shaking fists, "not my children. Not my children. Please . . ."

* * *

Tess crept across the darkened yard and slipped into the chicken pen, latching the gate behind her. Sighing, exhausted, she plunged her hand into the burlap sack and scooped up a fistful of grain.

"Here, chicky-chicky-chicky," she called, scattering the golden kernels across the shadowy yard. Dozens of birds ran into one another, squeezing together in a great, feathered mass in their haste to peck the fallen grain.

Tess stared at the cluster of birds without seeing them. Her mind was a million miles away. *Jack?* she thought for the thousandth time today. *Where are you?*

She was so deep in thought, it took her a moment to notice the sound. She paused, listening.

Footsteps.

Jack!

Tess spun around, accidentally dropping the bag of grain in her haste. Corn spilled across her feet. Birds surged toward her, ringing her skirts and pecking feverishly at her feet.

She immediately dropped to her knees and started scraping the grain back into the bag.

"What are you doing?"

Tess heard Jack's scratchy, angry voice and thought it was the most wonderful sound she'd ever heard. She'd been so worried. . . .

Smiling, she looked up.

He was standing about ten feet away from her, legs braced in a fighter's stance, arms crossed. Pale moonlight silhouetted his body, outlining the tired droop of his shoulders. His face was a dark void beneath an even darker hat.

Tess opened her mouth to speak, and was surprised to find a lump in her throat. "Hi, Jack," she said quietly. "We missed you."

"How . . . how long was I gone?"

Tess felt a momentary confusion at the question. Her eyes narrowed, focused on the shadowy area of his face.

He sighed, and it was the tiredest, *oldest* sound she'd ever heard. "Fine, don't answer me. I don't give a shit."

That's when Tess knew. He wasn't mocking or taunting or teasing her. He was asking her a real, honest-to-God question. He didn't know how long he'd been gone. And he was scared.

"I think you left just before dawn ... today."

His shoulders sagged downward. Another ragged sigh escaped him. "Thanks. So, what are you doing out this late?"

"Feeding the chickens."

"At this hour?"

"I ... I couldn't sleep."

His shadow shifted slightly. "Why not?"

Tess grabbed a handful of skirt and scrambled awkwardly to her feet. She wanted to move toward him, wanted to touch him and reassure herself that he was really back. But she didn't move. She forced herself to remain perfectly still. "You were out."

"So?"

"So ... I was worried."

"Ha!" His burst of laughter was as sharp as glass, and filled with a pain so deep and drenching, Tess felt ill. He pivoted, heel grinding into the gravelly dirt, and strode away.

Toward the barn. *Damn.*

Tess winced. She should call him back, find some excuse, however feeble, to keep him from going into the barn tonight. But he wouldn't listen. Wouldn't stop. She felt a sick tensing in her stomach.

He wasn't going to be amused by what she'd done. Not tonight.

He disappeared into the barn. Tess waited.

There were about two minutes of blessed silence, and then came a bloodcurdling yell.

"Get in here, Lissa. Now!"

Tess thought briefly about running into the house, but knew it would be pointless. He'd find her.

"Lissa!"

Tess clutched the grain sack to her midsection like a protective shield, tilted her chin, and headed for the barn. It was all part of the plan, she reminded herself, and the plan was for his own good. She had to get him off guard and keep him off guard. She had to make him react.

And what she'd done in the barn would certainly do that.

She sidled past the huge wooden door. Jack was standing with his back to her. He stood stiff as a fence post, staring at the enormous yellow flower she'd painted on his workbench. Beside him was a huge, beribboned barrel that held all of his farming tools.

"What the hell did you do?"

Tess jumped.

He spun around. "Talk!"

Tess bit her lower lip to stop it from trembling. All at once she realized the error in her plan. She didn't know this man, didn't know what he was capable of. The mouse had blithely baited the lion. . . .

"Now!"

"I painted your workbench and rearranged your tools."

"I see that." His voice was quiet. Too quiet. Another icicle of fear streamed down Tess's stiffened back. "What is it you painted, a daffodil?"

"Tulip," she said in a small, strangled voice.

He grabbed her by the shoulders and yanked her to him. She hit his chest hard and let out a tiny yelp of pain.

He glared down at her, breathing hard. She looked up.

Pale lantern light highlighted the hard, unforgiving angles of his face. "This is my place, goddamn it. *Mine.*"

Tess was just about to say something—she had no idea what—when she saw it. Deep, deep in his eyes, beyond the fury and the disbelief, lay pain.

Her fear dissolved and was forgotten. Jack was hurting right now. Hurting so badly, he couldn't summon enough detachment to cover it up. His pain touched something deep in her soul, something small and frightened that had never been touched before. He needed her. And she needed him. Maybe together they could escape the fear and loneliness that shrouded both their souls.

She touched his face, laid her palm against the stubble-coated hollow of his cheek. At the touching of their flesh, she shivered. Her gaze turned warm and liquid and melted into his. "What's the matter?"

His hold on her shoulders tightened, bit deeply into her tender flesh. Tess's breathing quickened. With each inhalation, she felt her breasts brush the hard wall of his chest. "Jack . . ."

He flinched. Without the high color of anger in his cheeks, his skin looked ashen and old. Aching, desperate pain filled his eyes.

"Please," he said in a husky voice, "don't do this to me, Lissa. Please."

"What has she done to you?"

Jack let go of her as if he'd been scalded. "Leave me the hell alone."

He shoved past her and ran for the door.

She watched him. "I don't think I can do that, Jack."

He slowed. She thought for a second he was going to turn around. She leaned forward, waiting.

Then he regained his footing and disappeared into the darkness beyond the barn.

He never looked back.

* * *

Be numb. Be numb. Be numb. The words circled in Jack's brain, gathering force with each repetition.

He knew it was the only way he could survive this new game of hers, knew it as certainly as he knew his name.

He paced back and forth in the darkness behind the barn. Moonlight crept through the bank of gray clouds and cast the pasture in uncertain, blue-tinged light. The world tonight was quiet, so quiet he could hear the whisper of the wind through the tall grass. It sounded like a woman breathing.

Like *her* breathing. He walked to the edge of the barn and glanced at the house.

She was down there. Just a few steps away. Maybe she was even waiting for him. . . .

Groaning, he closed his eyes and leaned tiredly against the rough wooden wall. But the self-imposed blindness didn't help. He could still see her face, and though it was a face he'd seen since childhood, it looked different now. And it was that difference that was killing him. Slowly. Inch by agonizing inch.

In his mind he saw her smiling. The vision held the dreamlike quality of a favorite memory. As if in slow motion, she turned, hair flying around her like strands of sunlight, and glanced down at Katie. Pride and love shone in her brown eyes, gave her a radiance she'd never had before. A softness that made him ache with longing. It hadn't been so long ago—not so long, really—that she'd looked at him that way.

She couldn't be changing, not really. No matter what he saw—or thought he saw—in her eyes, she couldn't really be changing. It was just another game designed to hurt him.

No matter what she said or did, he had to remember that

it was just another game. The changes, the smiles, had to be in his sick, twisted-up mind.

Be numb. Be numb. Be numb.

The words came back to him, and he focused his thoughts on them with single-minded determination. He could do it; he could resist the need washing through his body.

He'd been resisting it for years.

Jack stared at the closed door, knowing he shouldn't go in. He wasn't strong enough to fight her again. He should just turn around right now and run to the safety of the barn. Except that he was tired of running, so tired. For the last two hours he'd paced the darkness, fighting a need he'd thought long forgotten. Now he was so damn tired he could hardly stand.

Slowly, cautiously, he opened the door.

Amarylis was waiting for him by the stove. "Hi, Jack."

He had to remind himself again that she wasn't relieved to see him, because goddamn, she *looked* relieved.

She looked breathtakingly beautiful, too. Tousled, unbound hair framed her pale, upturned face in a halo of unbelievable light. Her cheeks were flushed and pink from standing over a hot stove. He could smell the sweet aroma of cinnamon and peaches that clung to her like expensive perfume.

She looked and smelled like . . . home. Against all reason, he found himself thinking about cozy nights curled around a fire and early mornings spent softly talking.

"I knew if I waited long enough, you'd come back."

Jack couldn't think of a single word. He stood there, dumb as a post, staring into her luminous brown eyes and praying as hard as he could. *God, don't let her touch me now. Not now . . .*

She came toward him. Her skirt hem breezed across his

ankle like a caress. She started to reach for him. He shrank backward. She paused. Slowly, frowning, she eased her hand away from his arm. "I've drawn you a bath. Savannah and Katie are sleeping. We're alone."

Alone. The word was like a dagger in his heart. He shook his head. "No."

Her gaze slid casually from his face. He felt suddenly self-conscious, realizing for the first time how he must look. Torn, ragged red long johns streaked with dirt; hair that hung in planklike sheets of muddy black; filthy, earth-caked feet.

She stared at his dirty face and tried not to smile. "You don't *want* to bathe?"

Jack felt as if he were being strangled. "No."

Their gazes met, held. For a moment he thought she was going to mock him, but she didn't. She just stood there, still as a stone, her strangely focused eyes searching his face. He sensed that she saw more—far more—than he wanted her to.

"Your clothes are filthy. Why don't you bathe with them on?"

She was trying to make him comfortable. At the realization, his mouth dropped open in surprise. Amarylis was doing her best to make him comfortable.

She moved closer, her hand outstretched. "Come on."

He started to say something—he had no idea what—but the words jammed in his throat when her fingers brushed his sleeve. He felt the warmth of her touch, and something inside him, something deep and dark and desperately weak, melted like wax. "Amarylis, I—"

"You can hate me again tomorrow."

"Hate you?" The words seemed to be ripped from the last remaining portion of his soul. "I wish to hell it was that simple."

She touched his cheek. "I know you're tired."

He shivered, chilled by the heat of her caress, and squeezed his eyes shut. It was true; he was tired. So goddamn tired . . .

She took hold of his wrist. In a gentle but firm motion that brooked no resistance—even if he had been able to summon the strength for it—she led him toward the copper tub already half-filled with water.

"Get in," she commanded. "I'll get more water."

He shouldn't do it. Of that, he had no doubt. He knew also, and the knowledge caused a sinking feeling in his stomach, that he was going to do it. He was too exhausted to fight her. With a ragged sigh and a hopeless prayer, he climbed into the tub.

Warm water curled around him, lapped gently against his stomach and thighs. He closed his eyes and leaned his head back, letting his arms dangle over the tub's metal sides.

Amarylis shuffled quietly toward him. She stopped by the side of the tub. Tensing, he waited for her to say—or do—something.

She added water to his bath. The falling stream drove between his legs in a gush of powerful heat. His eyes flipped open, but she was already gone. He twisted around and saw her standing at the stove.

Leaning tiredly against the metal rim, he closed his eyes again.

"Jack?"

He heard her saying his name, but her voice seemed to be coming at him from the end of a long, dark tunnel.

"Jack, wake up."

He blinked awake and lurched to a sit. Water sloshed against his chest and splashed over the sides. Feeling like an idiot, he glanced up at her. She was standing beside the tub, holding a bucket of water and a bar of soap. "Yeah?" he said cautiously.

"I'm going to wash your hair."

He shook his head. "No, thanks."

"You'll notice I didn't ask a question. I made a statement. I'm going to wash your hair." She moved behind him. He heard the metallic clank of a bucket hitting the floor, then the telltale thump of bone on wood as she kneeled.

The moment her fingers touched his scalp, he groaned. He tried desperately to sheathe his emotions in ice. But it was a useless attempt. At the whisper-soft circling of her fingertips in his hair, he shivered. Need and desire merged into a single, red-hot response and sent fire shooting into his groin.

"Relax," she said in a soothing, soft-edged voice he'd never heard before. "Relax." She said the single word over and over again. "Relax . . ."

He drifted on the gentle tide of her voice, feeling the fear and anxiety drain from his body. The night just past seeped from his memory and was forgotten.

By the time it was over, Jack was more relaxed than he'd ever been in his life.

"Come on," she said quietly, helping him to his feet. Like a sleepwalker, he allowed himself to be led into her bedroom. She handed him a clean pair of long johns and a towel. Wrapping himself in the warm towel, he peeled out of the wet underwear and slipped into a new set.

When he was done, she took his hand again and led him toward the bed. Her bed.

One look at her bed and Jack's sense of well-being and relaxation vanished. He stiffened, yanked his hand out of her grasp. "That's your bed."

"Tonight it's yours," she answered. She turned back the coverlet and gestured for him to get in. "I'll sleep on the couch."

He shook his head and started to draw away. "I don't think—"

"Good. Now, get in."

They stared at each other for a long time. Later Jack would wonder what it was he'd seen in her eyes, wonder if it was simply another manifestation of his weakness. But right now, in this instant, he saw a woman he'd never seen before. A gentle, caring woman who wasn't trying to hurt or destroy him. Someone who simply wanted to help.

"Please," she whispered. "You're tired."

She was right. He was too tired to fight her now. He could wage the battle tomorrow; maybe he could even win it. But that was tomorrow. Tonight he needed sleep.

He crawled into bed and pulled the coverlet tight to his chin. She kneeled beside the bed and began to stroke his unshaven cheek. The quiet, even strains of her breathing caressed his lips.

"Why are you doing this?" he murmured.

"Because you need it."

He didn't know what he expected her to say, but that wasn't it. He searched her eyes for some hint of cruelty or irony or playacting. In the dark brown depths, he found nothing but compassion. It left him utterly speechless.

"Where were you tonight?" she asked, still stroking his cheek.

He winced at the question. *I don't know. God help me, I don't know.* The truth almost slipped out; he wanted to tell this woman who was his wife and yet wasn't. This woman who touched him with a softness he'd always ached for and never known. It took all his inner strength to say, "Out."

She seemed to sense his anguish. "It's okay, Jack. Just go to sleep. Shh. Shh."

He closed his eyes. The last thing he remembered was the velvet-soft stroking of her fingers against his cheek.

* * *

The next morning dawned bright and hot. Tess hiked her skirts up to her thighs and straddled the small chair, scooting closer to the table. An array of jars was spread out before her. Beside her, a book lay open to a page titled *Fruits and Vegetables: A Canner's Guide.*

Today, by God, she was going to teach herself to can. She flipped open the instruction book and turned to the section on preserves. She was concentrating so hard, she almost missed the sound of a wagon driving into the yard.

Visitors!

Tess flew out of her chair and raced to the window, flinging the flimsy curtain aside. A wagon rolled up in a cloud of dust. The driver tossed down the reins to Jack, who tied the horse to the railing alongside the chicken coop.

Jack pushed the hat higher on his head and smiled up at the small, hunch-shouldered man sitting alone in the wagon. The man doffed his hat, revealing a nearly bald head that reflected the hot spring sun.

The men talked for a moment, then they both looked uneasily toward the house.

Tess waved.

Jack gave her a tense, humorless smile.

The old man frowned for a second before he cautiously waved back.

Tess concentrated on reading Jack's lips.

"Come on in and see her, Doc. She's . . . different."

"Doc Hayes," Tess said to herself. "Of course." She let go of the curtain and went to the door, opening it and stepping onto the porch. "Hi, Doc!" she called out, waving again and tenting her eyes against the glaring sun. "Would you like a glass of . . ." She frowned. What did people offer other people in 1873? Chardonnay was definitely out. "Water?"

"That'd be right nice," he answered, letting Jack help him down from the wagon.

The two men walked toward the house and followed Tess into the kitchen.

"What's all this?" Doc asked, eyeing the jars on the table.

Tess pulled out a chair for him. "I'm trying to figure out how to make jam."

Both men looked uncomfortable with her response.

"Sit down, Mrs. Rafferty," Doc said.

"But your water—"

"Sit down."

Tess shrugged easily and sat in front of the doctor. "Okay. Sure."

"How do you feel?"

"Fit as a fiddle."

He frowned. "Really?"

"Really. Things are going great around here. I'm fitting right in."

"And the baby?"

Tess smiled softly. "Oh, Caleb is doing beautifully. He's already grown so much. I had a little trouble breast-feeding at first, but now it's going great."

Doc shot a sideways glance at Jack. "Sorry, Jack, but I have to ask this."

Jack nodded tensely.

Doc turned back to Tess. "Do you remember coming to me when you first conceived?"

"No."

Doc paused for a moment, as if carefully considering his words. "You wanted to . . ." He blushed slightly. His voice deepened. "Well, you weren't happy about the baby."

Tess gasped. Her hand flew to her mouth. "Oh, my God. You mean I wanted to terminate the pregnancy?"

"Yes."

Impulsively Tess reached out and took the old man's hands in hers, squeezing his big-knuckled fingers affectionately. "Thank God you didn't." Tears stung her eyes. "Thank God."

Doc studied her, his rheumy eyes narrowed behind the small ovals of his spectacles. "What's your husband's name?"

"Jack."

"His whole name."

"Jack Rafferty."

He looked at Jack, who shook his head.

Quietly Jack said, "Jackson Beauregard Rafferty the Third."

Tess's eyes widened. "You're kidding. That's a great name."

Doc gave her hands a quick squeeze, then got slowly to his feet. "Nice to see you again, Mrs. Rafferty. Jack, walk me to the wagon."

The two men left the kitchen and headed slowly across the yard. Beneath the oak tree's huge canopy, Doc touched Jack's arm and they stopped.

Tess eased the curtain open slightly and peered at the two men, her eyes focused on their lips.

"What the hell's wrong with her, Doc?"

"Amnesia, I reckon."

"How long will it last?"

"Who knows? Could be you got yourself a new wife. Could be the old one'll be back tomorrow."

"You mean, these changes could be . . . real?"

"The brain's a funny thing, Jack. Ain't nobody understands it. Damn sure not a country doctor like me."

"Damn it, Doc, that isn't good enough. These changes are killing me. She's so . . . different."

The doctor patted Jack's shoulder. *"I didn't mean to*

scare you, son. Just be patient. I'm sure she'll be her old self in no time."

Jack stiffened. *"Yeah. That's what I'm afraid of."*

Tess let the curtain flutter back into place. Then, slowly, she smiled. Jack was afraid of her. It was a reaction, and it wasn't anger.

The plan was working.

Chapter Ten

Savannah tucked her feet underneath her and plopped her lunch pail on her lap. Sunlight streamed through the pine needles overhead, spangling her brown muslin skirt.

Katie sat silently beside her, burrowing through her tin pail.

Savannah sat back on her heels, staring down the grassy hillside. She was so intent on her own thoughts, she didn't hear the crunching of footsteps coming her way.

"Savannah?"

She looked up with a start and found Jeffie Peters standing beside her. He was staring down at her, his lard tin clutched to his chest with white-knuckled fists. His face was paler than usual. "C'n I set with you?"

Savannah's throat seized up. Her stomach gurgled loudly and threatened to embarrass her. She opened her mouth to say no,

"Sure, Jeffie," Katie said, taking a crunchy bite of pickle.

Color rose in Jeffie's face like a wave of red paint. "Thanks!" He dropped to his knees beside Savannah and began earnestly rummaging through his lard tin.

Savannah's mouth closed with a click of teeth. Stiffening, she lowered her lashes and studied Jeffie.

He looked . . . nervous. His fingers were all fidgety and

135

clumsy as he peeled the thin cheesecloth away from his wedge of cornbread.

Suddenly he looked sideways and caught her watching him.

Heat blazed across Savannah's cheeks. She wrenched her gaze away and buried it in the ankle-high grass.

"Savannah?"

Reluctantly she glanced his way. "Yeah?"

He blushed. "I was wonderin' . . . I mean, the shearin' dance is comin' up, an'—"

"That ain't for weeks," Katie interrupted.

Jeffie shot her an irritated look, then swallowed hard. His Adam's apple bobbed up and down his skinny throat. "Anyway, it ain't *that* far away, an', well . . . I was wonderin' if you'd go with me." He stared at her through huge, earnest eyes.

A confusing rush of emotions hurtled through Savannah. For no reason at all, she felt like crying. "I can't."

"But—"

Savannah's mouth trembled and turned down. "You know my mama. I couldn't even if . . ."

"Even if what?"

She swallowed the lump in her throat and said quietly, "Even if I wanted to."

"Oh." Jeffie carefully wrapped up his crumbling cornbread and plunked it back in his pail. Slowly he got to his feet. " 'Bye," he said, then turned and walked away.

Savannah stared at the ground through the stinging haze of unshed tears.

"Maybe you should talk to Mama," Katie offered. "She's been sorta . . . nice lately."

Savannah's pent-up breath released. "What would I say? She wouldn't understand what's wrong with me."

"There ain't nothin' wrong with you," Katie answered defensively. "You're perfect."

Savannah gave her baby sister a weak smile. "Thanks. Now, eat your lunch."

They lapsed back into a companionable silence. Savannah tried to concentrate on eating, only eating and nothing more. But Katie's words came back to her time and again.

Talk to Mama.

If only I could, she thought.

She bit into her slice of bread and chewed tiredly. Of course she couldn't talk to Mama; there was no doubt about that. It had been years since she'd even tried. Mama would just tell her what she already knew: She was acting plum crazy around Jeffie Peters. There wasn't no chance at all Mama would tell her what she really wanted to know.

Why she was acting that way.

Craaack. The ax slammed into the thick log and split it down the middle. Jack paused, backhanded the sweat from his brow, and realigned the half log.

As he raised the ax again, he heard a strange sound. He paused, listening.

A sweet sound rode the gentle spring breeze, underscoring the gay chirping of the swallows and finches careening overhead. The song was at once familiar and unfamiliar, with a strange stop-and-start rhythm, as if the words had been memorized but never actually heard before. But the voice—ah, the voice—now, that was something he'd never forget.

He turned slowly, knowing as he did that it was a mistake.

Amarylis was sitting on the porch swing, singing Caleb the strangest version of "Rock-a-bye Baby" he'd ever heard. The wistful strains of her song brought a bittersweet smile to Jack's mouth. No wonder the song sounded strange; she'd never sung to her children before.

If only. The thought was there before he could stop it.

If only she were really the loving, gentle soul she appeared right now. He thought about the bath, remembering the almost narcotic sense of peace it had given him to be ministered to by her. For a few short moments it had been like the old days, when he'd trusted her with his soul and crawled eagerly into her bed. When he hadn't been afraid.

She looked up suddenly and saw him. Their eyes locked, his narrowed and filled with a longing he couldn't dislodge, hers wide and filled with joy. She smiled brightly and waved him over.

He shouldn't go; he knew that. He should turn his back on her and keep cutting firewood. But he wanted to go. Just this once. The ax slipped from his hand and hit the dirt. Shoving the Stetson higher on his brow, he sidestepped the pile of half-chopped wood and headed toward her.

She was still smiling when he reached the porch.

"Hi," she said quietly, scooting sideways in silent invitation.

He stared at the empty space beside her. Damn, it looked inviting. . . .

"Have a seat," she said when he didn't move.

He swallowed thickly and forced his gaze to her face. "I shouldn't. . . ."

She smiled. "I won't bite."

The look in her eyes drew him like a magnet, stole his free will. Before he knew it, he was climbing the steps and sitting down beside her. The porch swing creaked beneath his weight.

He stared out across the rolling, sheep-filled pasture, his eyes riveted ahead, his hands balled in his lap.

Silence descended between them. The hot sun bore down on him, seeping through his shirt and dampening his flesh. He waited for her to say something angry and stinging; she waited for the same thing. Then they both spoke at once.

"Sure is hot—"

"Nice weather—"

Amarylis burst out laughing. It was a throaty, seductive sound that wound around Jack's vitals. "So," she said, "it seems we agree on the weather, at least."

Jack fought the urge to smile with her. Then the fact that he *wanted* to smile sunk in and caused a red-hot burst of anger. Damn her for being so good at manipulating him, and damn him for being such a weak-willed fool. He rammed the hat lower on his forehead and lurched to his feet.

"I . . . I gotta get back to the woodpile."

She looked up at him. There was a sadness in her gaze that hadn't been there before, and he had the absurd notion that he'd hurt her feelings. "It was nice talking to you."

Jack pivoted and strode down the steps. It was all he could do to keep from running.

Later that night Tess sat at the kitchen table with Savannah. Behind them, Katie was busy burrowing through the silverware drawer.

Idly, Tess picked up her spoon and stared into it. She tried not to think about Jack right now, but it was impossible. Ever since last night, since the bath, she'd been unable to stop thinking about him. Dreaming about him. She felt like a sixteen-year-old girl in the throes of her first crush. It was ridiculous.

A slow smile pulled at her mouth. It was also exciting, invigorating, and energizing. Now she was more certain than ever that there was something special between her and Jack. She knew now why she'd chosen him, and it was more than just the heartache and fear she'd seen in his eyes as he reached out for his child. It was his capacity for love. For even as she'd seen him standing by the crib, she'd known that he was desperately afraid to be there, afraid to need his child's love, and yet, as afraid as he was, he'd stayed there, reaching out. Most people retreated from life and gave up on love. Tess knew; she'd done it herself. But not Jack. He'd sheathed himself in anger and tried his best to forget, but he'd never walked away. And that meant he'd never given up.

Last night, in the moments before he'd fallen asleep, she'd seen her first glimpse of the real Jack, the man beneath the angry mask. And he was a frightened, lonely man who was tired of being alone. So much like her . . .

She thought about the times she'd caught him smiling, or looking at the girls with love, or carving a rocking horse in the middle of the night, and her heart swelled with emotion. At the memories, something inside of her broke free. Deep inside her, in the tiny, oft-overlooked corner of her soul where she'd long ago put her dreams of love and family and forever, something stirred. Something that had been asleep for a very long time.

Tess felt the heavy weight of Savannah's gaze on her face. She looked up suddenly, and found Savannah staring at her intently. "What is it, Savannah?" she asked quietly.

Savannah shook her head slowly. A sad little frown plucked at her mouth. "Nothin'."

Tess reached over and squeezed Savannah's hand. Their eyes met and held. "You know, Savannah," Tess whispered, "I'm here for you if you ever need me. For anything."

Savannah swallowed hard. "Th-Thanks, Mama."

Katie thumped her elbows on the table. "Mama, you promised to show me how you done that thing with the spoon."

Tess smiled and slowly withdrew her hand from Savannah's. "Okay," she said. "Here goes. First you blow on it.

Like this." Tess blew on the spoon until it steamed up nicely. "See? When it looks like that, you stick it on your nose." She placed the spoon on her nose like an expert.

"It works!" Katie cried, clapping her hands.

The spoon fell off Tess's nose and hit the table with a clang. "Of course it does. A mother never lies."

Savannah's eyes narrowed. "Really?"

Tess's smile faded as she looked at Savannah. There was a long, quiet moment as they studied each other. Tess got the distinct impression that she was being tested. "Really."

"C'n I try it?" Katie asked eagerly.

Tess and Savannah looked at each other for another second or two, and then Tess turned to Katie and nodded. "Of course you may."

Katie frowned in concentration. Cautiously she blew into the bowl of her soup spoon. The metal turned a dull, milky gray, and she gently set it on her nose. The spoon stuck fast.

Her eyes bulged open in surprise, and a quick, excited giggle dislodged the spoon. It clinked onto her empty plate.

"Okay," Tess said. "Now all together."

Jack stared at the house. Advancing night shrouded the small clapboard structure, turning the whitewashed wood a deep gunmetal gray. The porch railing was nothing but dark lines and shadows cast along pale wooden planks.

Wind chattered through the leaves of the oak tree. The rope-swing's slatted seat thumped methodically against his left leg.

Jack's gaze moved up the porch and along the shadowy building. Thin, ghostlike strands of smoke spiraled up from the brick chimney, its trail a momentary whisper of gray against the midnight blue sky. Amber light blurred the kitchen window, made it look like a square of captured sunlight in the middle of a cold, darkening night.

The kitchen curtains were open, as if the inhabitants were no longer soldiers under siege, but, quite simply, a farm family waiting for someone to come in from the fields. The house he'd built so many years ago looked like something it had never been: a home.

He shoved the swing out of his way and turned away from the house. Staring out at Haro Strait glittering far below, Jack tried not to think about the window that looked so inviting.

It's an illusion, Jackson, just a damn illusion.

But he couldn't quite make himself believe it this time. Somehow the changes seemed more substantial, more tangible.

More dangerous . . .

He thought about the doctor's words, wondering if maybe—just maybe—the changes he saw in his wife were real. Lasting.

Maybe she really is changing. Maybe . . .

"Damn." He shoved a cold hand through his hair and sighed loudly.

Damn it, he couldn't let himself believe in her. He'd done that once, long before, and it had cost him—and the kids—nothing but pain.

But what if it's real this time?

It was that question more than any other that fueled Jack's fear and turned his stomach into a writhing coil of anxiety. He'd spent a long time building emotional armor strong enough to keep his one-sided love contained. If the walls came down, even for a second, he didn't think he'd ever get them back up.

And then what would happen to him?

You know damn well what would happen. It would be like before.

He shivered at the thought and flipped his collar up.
Before.

Then it had taken him years to find his way back to
sanity—if, in fact, he ever had. Years of wandering, alone
and hungry and friendless; years of praying to find his
way. Years spent huddled in the blackest void a man could
imagine.

He had to remember what kind of woman she was, how
easily she used people and how well she pretended. Nothing about her was real except her hatred of him.

Think about the night Caleb was conceived.

All she'd had to do that night was smile and touch
Jack's cheek, and he'd run to her bed like a callow school-
boy. And given her another innocent weapon to wield in
the war of their marriage.

The "change" had lasted less than an hour, and then
she'd been back, hating him with a vengeance. Day by day
he'd watched her swell with child, and every hour of every
day he'd had to fight the need and shame in his own soul.
Every day she'd taunted him with the manner of the baby's conception, laughed at how weak and easily led Jack
was.

*"All I have to do is smile, and you come running. You're
pathetic."*

Jack winced at the memory. It was true, God help him.
He'd always wanted to be loved by her.

Every day he'd seen her stomach grow, seen her secret,
deadly smile when she looked at him. Every night he'd
lain in his lonely bed, dreading the moment of the child's
birth. Knowing he'd condemned an innocent soul to a life
so cold and lonely, it amounted to purgatory. No wonder
he'd wakened that morning in the barn, alone, with no
memory of where he'd been or what he'd done. The strain
of her pregnancy had nearly killed him.

He wouldn't let her manipulate him again. He would

not. There was no way he'd let himself believe in her this time.

Remember, he told himself. *Remember.*

Jack crossed the shadowy yard. With the wooden steps of a man walking to the gallows, he climbed the porch steps and eased the kitchen door open. He was completely unprepared for the scene that greeted him.

Lissa and Katie and Savannah were sitting stock-still at the kitchen table. None of them turned to look at him.

It didn't surprise him, considering they had spoons hanging from their noses.

"Jack!" Lissa turned suddenly. Her spoon flew off her nose and clattered on the floor.

Katie and Savannah immediately flinched and looked up. Their spoons crashed to the table.

Lissa got to her feet and pulled out a chair for him. She patted the seat. "Here, sit down. The food's ready."

Jack eyed all three of them warily, noticing the quivering smiles that hovered on their faces. They were having fun; he could feel it in the air. Longing spilled through him and twisted up his insides. He wanted so desperately to join them. Stiffly, trying not to look at their smiling faces, he moved to the table and sat down.

Lissa hurried to the kitchener and dished up supper. Then she returned and set the plates down.

Jack stared down at his plate in confusion. Three eggs, all with broken, overcooked yolks and blackened edges, were lined up alongside three crusty, burnt pancakes. There was a low layer of smoke clinging to the crockery plate. "This is supper?"

She gave him a bright smile and sat down at the opposite end of the table. *"Bon appétit."*

On either side of him, the girls tried hard not to giggle. They did not completely succeed.

Jack frowned. "It's breakfast."

Lissa looked down at her plate. "Is it?"

He slammed a fist down on the table so hard, the salt and pepper rattled. "Goddamn it, Lissa, you know it is. You're serving breakfast for supper."

She blinked innocently. "I thought I just woke up." She glanced at the girls. "Am I wrong?"

Jack lurched to his feet. "I can't take any more of this. Not today." He started to leave, but as he turned, his stomach rumbled loudly.

"Stay, Jack," she said quietly. "You're hungry."

Slowly he turned back around. She was smiling up at him, but this time there was no taunting curl to her lip. She was simply smiling. There was a silent invitation in her eyes that clawed at his self-control and made him want to stay.

He *was* pretty hungry, he told himself.

Before he was aware he'd made a decision, he was lowering himself onto the chair once again. He scooted close to the table. Careful not to look into her dangerous eyes again, he kept his gaze riveted to the food on his plate.

"I know what you're thinking," she said.

He snorted. "Yeah?" Reluctantly he looked up, met her gaze. "What?"

"You're thinking you've got to be pretty hungry to eat this food."

He smiled before he could stop himself.

"See?" she said in a voice so quiet, he knew it was meant for him alone. "It doesn't hurt a bit."

He felt himself pale. The easy smile slid off his face. He looked into her warm brown eyes and felt a stab of longing. "You're wrong. It hurts like hell. Now, let's eat . . . breakfast before it gets cold."

Lissa glanced down at her smoldering eggs and grinned. "I think we've got plenty of time."

* * *

After the supper dishes were done and put away, Tess went outside and sat on the porch swing. Holding Caleb in her arms, she rocked gently back and forth, staring across the darkened fields to the tarnished, moonlit water far below.

Caleb gurgled playfully and squeezed her finger in a red-fisted grip.

Tess laughed quietly, gazing lovingly down at him. "Hey, kiddo, that's quite a grip you have."

He gave her a gummy grin.

Behind her, the door creaked open. "Mama?"

"Yes, Savannah?"

"Can I . . . talk to you?"

"Sure, kiddo. Sit down." She scooted sideways, making room.

Savannah perched tentatively beside her. Back stiff, eyes straight ahead, hands coiled in a nervous ball at her lap, she didn't say a word.

Tess waited silently.

After about three minutes of bone-jarring silence, Savannah cleared her throat. "I . . . I was wondering about . . . Oh, this is stupid. Never mind." She popped to her feet.

Tess reached out and grabbed her hand. Savannah turned, looked down at her.

"Is it about a boy?"

Savannah gasped. Her eyes rounded. "How did you know?"

Tess smiled. "I was twelve myself once."

Savannah slowly lowered herself back onto the swing's slatted seat. "It's Jeffie Peters." She turned suddenly, pinned a confused adolescent stare on Tess. "When he talks to me lately, I . . . I feel like I'm gonna throw up."

Tess nodded sympathetically. "You like Jeffie?"

Savannah nodded solemnly.

"There's nothing wrong with that. Nothing at all. It's perfectly normal."

"Then why do I feel all afraid and stupid when he talks to me?"

Tess smoothed the hair from Savannah's cheek and tucked a curly ringlet behind the girl's ear. "It's all part of growing up. It's nothing to be afraid of. And you know what?"

"What?"

Tess leaned closer. "I'll bet he feels the same things when he looks at you."

"Really?"

Tess smiled. "Really."

Savannah threw her arms around Tess and Caleb. Tess hugged the girl tightly. Finally Savannah drew back and looked at Tess through huge, overbright eyes. "Thanks, Mama. I . . ." Her voice dropped to a throaty whisper. "I love you."

Tess gasped. Emotion tightened her throat. Tears burned her eyes. "I . . . I love you, too, sweetie."

Savannah smiled and swiped the tears from her eyes. Then she clambered to her feet and disappeared back in the house.

Tess sat there, too stunned to move.

I love you, Mama. The simple words circled around and around in her brain, each repetition bringing with it a pang of joy so strong, Tess almost couldn't breathe. All her life she'd waited to hear those simple words—ached to hear them. And now she knew why. They filled her soul with a brightness she'd never even imagined before.

The next day dawned sunny and beautiful. Perfect for Tess's plan.

"Why'd you have Vannah make all this food, Mama?"

Katie asked, watching Tess load a jar of pickles into a big basket.

"Because no one would eat my cooking," she answered easily. "Savannah, honey," Tess said over her shoulder. "Go get your daddy out of the barn. Tell him to hitch up the team."

"Why?"

"We're going on a picnic."

Savannah and Katie gasped.

"Daddy won't wanna go on no picnic," Savannah said.

"He won't want to go on *any* picnic," Tess corrected.

"I know. That's what I said."

Tess turned around, wiping her dusty hands on her apron. "He'll go."

"But, Mama, Daddy won't go—"

The door swung open suddenly. "Where won't I go?"

Savannah jumped guiltily and crammed her hands together. Katie froze in the middle of the room.

"Oh, hi, Jack," Tess said brightly. "You're just in time to hitch up the wagon. We're going on a picnic."

He laughed sharply. "No we're not."

Tess walked over to him, smiling broadly. "I guess you didn't hear me. The work week is over, and this family is going on a picnic."

He crossed his arms. "It'll be a long walk."

"No it won't. We're taking the wagon."

"Oh?" One eyebrow cocked derisively upward. "You know how to hitch it up?"

"No. I don't need to. You will. Or else." She squared off with him, toe to toe.

He laughed again. "Or else what?"

"Ever heard of a strike?"

He stared at her in disbelief. "You'd *hit* me?"

"Of course not." She tried to remember when strikes had been invented. Apparently sometime after 1873. "A strike," she informed him, "is a refusal to work until you get what you want."

"And the relevance of this fascinating bit of trivia is . . ."

"The girls and I won't work this week unless you hitch up the team and take us on a picnic. Today."

The girls gasped.

Jack's head jerked up. "Are you two in on this?"

There was a long silence.

Tess crossed her fingers. *Come on girls, come on . . .*

"Are you?" he yelled.

"We—" Savannah's voice was a squeak. She cleared her throat and tried again. "We are."

Jack glared at Tess. Tension emanated from him like heat waves. He was fighting hard for control. Or the appearance of control.

"Don't do this."

She blinked innocently up at him. "Do what?"

"Make us a goddamn family."

The frightened plea almost broke Tess's heart. There was a bleakness in his eyes that hit her hard in the stomach. He looked lost and aching and alone. And desperately afraid. "We already are."

He paled. "It's not safe."

"Yes it is."

His anger came back, replacing the momentary flash of emptiness and fear in his eyes. "Fine. I'll do it for them. But don't try this . . . strike thing again. I'm a man of limited patience."

He spun back around and stormed through the open door. He was on the bottom porch step when Tess called out his name.

He paused and reluctantly turned toward her. "Yeah?"

"Just for the record, Jack, you're a man of *no* patience. But don't worry, I've got tons."

Jack stared at her, speechless for a heartbeat, then he turned and walked away.

Tess flashed the girls a triumphant grin and gave them a thumbs up. "Way to go, girls."

Five minutes later, Katie was still staring at her mother. Mama was lying on the floor, tickling Caleb's toes and laughing.

Katie turned to her sister, a grave look on her small face. "There's a stranger in Mama's body," she said quietly.

Savannah nodded. She, too, was staring at her mother. A faraway, wistful look crept into her eyes. "I hope she stays."

Katie slipped her hand into Savannah's and squeezed it tightly. "Me, too."

Two hours later, Tess stacked the last basket in the back of the wagon. Clapping the dust from her hands, she eyed the spread with a critical eye. Basket and boxes lined the wagon's planked side, their interiors filled to overflowing with fried chicken, cold potato salad, hard-boiled eggs, fresh-baked bread and homemade jam, pickles, and canned peaches. A bottle of cider stuck up amid a stack of plates and cups, its metal lid glinting silver in the morning sunlight.

The girls buzzed around the loaded wagon like excited, nervous bees. Every now and then one of them would laugh, and the clear, high-pitched sound assured Tess that she was doing the right thing. This family needed— desperately needed—to have some fun.

"Get in," Jack said in a gruff, angry voice that cut through the girls' laughter like a hot knife.

Katie flinched, paled. Dropping her gaze to her feet, she shuffled wordlessly to the wagon and climbed aboard.

Tess grabbed Jack by the sleeve and spun him around. "Remember when you asked if I'd hit you?" she hissed.

He nodded, eyeing her warily.

"Well, speak like that to your children again and I'll knee you in the groin so hard, you'll hit the dirt. Do we understand each other?"

The wariness turned to outright disbelief. "Lissa?"

She gave him a dazzling smile and let go of his arm. "Of course. Who else would it be?"

He frowned and shook his head. "Yeah. Right." Turning his back on her, he snatched up the reins and began studiously examining the leather.

Tess reached down for the long, narrow basket beside her. Within it, folded in layers of pale brown homespun, Caleb wiggled and squirmed. Bright blue eyes blinked up at her.

"Hi, honey," she said, lifting the basket and setting it gently in the wagon. Savannah and Katie immediately scooted close to the basket and started entertaining the baby.

Tess waited patiently for Jack to help her to her seat. He didn't. She tapped her booted toe in the dirt and crossed her arms. "Jack. It's time."

He cast her an angry sideways glance.

She smiled and held out her gloved hand. Grudgingly he threw the reins onto the wagon and helped her aboard.

"Thanks," she said, primly fanning her butter yellow muslin skirts out around her.

"You're welcome," he answered. "A whole hell of a lot."

"It's probably best not to curse in front of the children," she said.

Jack gave her a look that would curdle milk, then snapped the reins. The horse dropped its head and slowly plodded forward.

Tess's plan was in motion. The Rafferty family's first adventure had begun.

Chapter Eleven

Tess saw the perfect spot and practically lurched off the wagon's hard seat. "There!" she yelled, pointing at the huge madrone tree up ahead.

Jack didn't even bother to look sideways at her. "I take it by your screech that you've chosen the picnic site."

Tess beamed. "Exactly right, Jack. And here I was thinking you didn't understand me."

He mumbled something in response. The words were unintelligible, but the message was clear: *Leave me alone.*

She decided to answer the unspoken message. Just to shake him up a bit. "Sorry, Jack, I can't do that."

He stiffened. "What did you say?"

She turned and gave him a bright, challenging smile, which he studiously avoided. "I said, I'm sorry, but I can't leave you alone. It's not part of my plan."

The flesh at the corner of his eye flinched in a quick, angry tic. He said nothing, simply stared silently ahead.

Tess studied his profile, noticing the sudden narrowing of his eyes, the tightening of his mouth into a grim, gray line, the way his fingers curled convulsively around the reins.

The plan was working, she realized. He was reacting. Oh, he was trying hard to be cool and calm, but the anger was there. Building, hovering just below the surface. All she had to do was bring it out and disarm it. Let him know that the other emotion, buried even deeper, was okay, too. She was sure it was there—it was there in everyone. Somewhere in Jack's dark, frightened soul was the desire to be happy.

All she had to do was find it.

He yanked back on the reins and brought Red to a stop. "We're here," he said through gritted teeth. He jumped down from the wagon.

Tess stared down at him.

He glared at her. His eyes narrowed even further.

"Wow," she murmured. "I wouldn't have thought that was possible."

"Go ahead, Amar—"

"Lissa." She smoothed her skirt.

His voice lowered. "Go ahead, *Lissa*, have all the god-damn fun in the world. But leave me the hell alone." He leaned forward, resting one gloved hand on the wagon's splintery side. "You got it?"

Tess sidled sideways along the wooden bench until she was within touching distance of Jack. Her knee brushed against his hand. She leaned down, staring at him. She was close enough to see the tiny gold flecks that lightened his green eyes. "I swear, we keep having the same conversa-tion. No, Jack, I don't got it. And neither, apparently, do you. This is a family picnic. You are part of this family. Therefore, you *will* picnic."

"What the hell does that mean?"

She shot a smile at the girls, who were huddled close to-gether in the back of the wagon with Caleb, apparently waiting to see who would win this battle before moving. "It means eating outside, enjoying the sunshine, and—" she looked back at Jack, and this time it was her eyes that narrowed "—having some fun."

He stared at her for a long time, measuring her. Then he

let out his breath in a weary sigh and shrugged. "Do whatever the hell you want."

Yes, Jack, she thought. *Get tired of fighting me. Get really, really tired of it. Let your guard down.*

"Why, thank you," she said sweetly. "I will. Come on girls, let's unpack the food and spread the blanket out beneath the tree."

Tess plucked up Caleb's wicker basket and held him close to her chest. She sat at the edge of the seat, waiting patiently.

Then not so patiently.

Behind her, she could hear the sweet, high-pitched giggling of the girls as they struggled to smooth out the huge plaid blanket. Jack was up at Red's head, fiddling with some leather thingamajiggy. Tess was pretty sure it was a diversionary tactic. No doubt the leather thing was perfectly clean and adjusted correctly.

It was time to force his attention.

"Oh, Jack," she called out in her best I'm-a-southern-lady-in-distress trill, "I could use a hand."

"I'm busy," he muttered without looking up.

She cleared her throat. "The longer I sit in the wagon, the longer we'll be here."

He groaned—and Tess was fairly sure there was a curse buried in the sound. "Fine."

Tess smiled. "Fine."

He wrenched the reins around a smaller cedar tree and expertly tied a bulging knot. Then, smashing his hat lower on his forehead, he stalked across the knee-high grass to the wagon and shoved his hand up at her.

"You'll need both hands."

Eyeing her, he cautiously offered her his other hand.

Before he could say a word, Tess placed Caleb's basket in his outstretched hands. Jack glanced down at the bundle in his arms, then up at her. The color seeped slowly out of his cheeks; his mouth dropped open.

"He's your son," she said softly.

Fear darkened his eyes. Tess felt a sudden stab of empathy for this man who was trying so hard, so desperately, not to care. It was all she could do to keep from touching his face and murmuring his name. "Just . . . just take him to the tree and set him down. I'll be right there."

He swallowed hard. "I might drop him."

"No you won't."

"Don't do this to me, Amarylis. Please . . ."

"Lissa," she said gently.

They stared at each other, neither speaking. Behind them, sounding at once far away and comfortingly close, the girls were giggling gaily. The carefree laughter melded with the soft sighing of the wind through the leaves.

He looked at her through eyes filled with unbearable pain and the hopelessness of a man who didn't—couldn't—believe in himself. His silent agony drove like a dagger through her heart.

Drawn irrevocably, undeniably, Tess scooted closer to the seat's edge. She leaned toward him. Closer. Closer . . .

Her tongue darted out, nervously wetting her lower lip. He leaned infinitesimally toward her.

Suddenly Tess realized where she was and what she was doing. She *wanted* to kiss him, wanted to be kissed and held and loved by him.

Oh, God . . .

Her heartbeat picked up speed, hammered in her chest and ears. "Jack, I . . ." She didn't know what to say, so her sentence trailed off, disappearing in the gentle, grass-scented breeze.

He took an unsteady step backward. "C-Can you get down by yourself?"

Tess heard the husky emotion in his voice and knew

he'd felt the same bone-jarring jolt of reaction she had. "Yes, go on."

He clutched Caleb's basket tightly to his chest and pivoted away from her, blazing a trail in the tall grass as he walked to the tree.

Tess watched him go. Gradually her heartbeat slowed down and her breathing normalized. She realized her hands were shaking. She'd almost done it, almost put her fear on hold and reached out for what she wanted.

Almost. But not quite.

Jack kneeled cautiously on the blanket and set the basket down. He tried to look away—really tried—but it was pointless and impossible. Against his will, he found himself drawn to the child in the basket. His son.

Caleb blinked up at him, his red-cheeked face looking impossibly small and helpless against the mounds of brown homespun.

"Hi, Caleb." The greeting sounded harsh and tired, and Jack was unable to push anything else past the lump of emotion in his throat.

He thought about touching the tiny cheek, and changed his mind. It was best not to get involved, best not to . . .

Amarylis plopped to her knees beside him. "Isn't he perfect?" she said in a quiet voice.

The lump in Jack's throat swelled to watermelon size. He nodded and looked away, right at the thick brown tree trunk beside him. The bark swam embarrassingly before his moist eyes.

Christalmighty. He staggered to his feet and stumbled backward, putting a safer distance between him and his stranger-by-the-moment wife. "I'll get the food." Spinning away, he ran for the wagon.

By the time he got there, he was out of breath and his heart was pounding, and he knew it had nothing to do with the length of the run. It was because of the goddamn changes. They were killing him.

She was killing him. The woman he'd loved for more than half his life had finally found a way to kill him.

Feeling suddenly tired and ancient and unbearably alone, Jack turned around. Lissa and Savannah and Katie were holding hands and skipping around in a circle. Their joy-filled voices rose into the air.

"Ring-around-the-rosie, pocketful-of-posies. Ashes, ashes, we all fall down!"

They collapsed in a giggling, writhing heap of elbows and billowing skirts.

Jack felt his solitude like a fist to the heart. He leaned heavily against the wagon and dropped his head, staring at the golden-green grass. Sadness and longing and regret coiled together and crept through his chest until it hurt to breathe.

". . . We all fall down!"

Reluctantly, knowing he shouldn't but unable to help himself, he lifted his chin and glanced their way.

Lissa hit the ground first, and the girls piled on top of her. They hugged one another and rolled down the hill, skirts flapping, hair flying. The happy sound of their laughter tore at his heart, slicing a piece of it away.

"Oh, God," he breathed. Christ, how he wanted, *ached*, to join in. To just once be a part of them. The need was like a burning pain in his chest. His hands curled into tight, shaking white fists.

All of a sudden Lissa looked up at him.

Jack's breath caught in his throat. She lay sprawled in the tall grass, her hair sprayed around her face like a golden waterfall, her skirts hiked up to reveal pale, shapely legs.

She pushed to a sit slowly, never taking her eyes off his

face. Then, unbelievably, she cocked her head. "Join us," she mouthed. "Come on . . ."

Jack clutched the wagon for support. He felt as if he were being slowly, inexorably, sucked over the edge of a steep, straight-edged cliff. Below lay a fall that would shatter his soul and leave him in a thousand irretrievable pieces.

He licked his lips nervously. *Don't go, Jackson.*

But he was already moving toward her, drawn by a need he'd felt more than half his life, a love he'd never been able to forget or deny.

It wasn't until he'd gone about fifteen feet that he realized what he was doing. He was falling, hell, he was running, right into her goddamn trap. He stumbled to a halt and forced himself to look away. He stared at the madrone tree and turned numbly toward it. "I'll sit over here."

He thought he heard her sigh.

"Okay, Jack."

He glanced quickly at her, surprised by the sad echo in her voice. "Lissa? Are you all right?"

She smiled, but somehow it, too, was a dismal shadow of itself. "I'm fine, Jack. I was just going to teach the girls to make daisy chains. Want to learn?"

He shook his head, afraid to let himself speak.

"Okay. Well, maybe you can learn by watching."

He went to the blanket and lowered himself onto its bumpy surface. Drawing his knees close to his chest, he glanced down at Caleb, who was sleeping, then looked again at his wife and the girls.

Lissa was showing them how to thread the dandelion stalks together to form a crown. Katie and Savannah looked mesmerized.

It occurred to Jack then, as he watched his wife, that he had called her Lissa. He hadn't even thought of her as Amarylis.

Changes, he thought with a grim tightening of the mouth. More changes.

Ignore her. Just goddamn ignore her.

Jack said the words to himself over and over again, but try as he might, he couldn't make himself do it.

The sight of her mesmerized him, flung him back in time to a distant place and time. He stared at her in silent, heart-wrenching awe, willing her not to move.

She sat in the tall grass kneeling, her burr-studded skirts tucked carelessly around her body. Her hair, the color and texture of spun gold, fell around her shoulders and spilled down her arms. Bright yellow dandelions wreathed her head like the finest of crowns. She was smiling, an honest-to-God smile that took his breath away.

Beside her, the parasol she should have had perched over her head lay planted firmly in the ground, its white, lacy expanse shielding Caleb's naked body from the bright noonday sun.

The girls chattered happily back and forth, and every now and again Jack caught wisps of their conversation, but more often than not, he sat stone-still in a hazy half world of his own. A world of long ago and far away.

Everything about Amarylis was blazingly new and yet achingly familiar. He felt as if he'd stumbled back in time, to a past—their past.

She looked . . . different. Younger. Almost like the caring, joy-filled girl he'd courted when they were both younger and still believed in God and love and each other.

And yet, even that wasn't quite right. There was a tenderness in her now that was new and compelling. He saw it in her every move; the way she smiled at Katie or nodded encouragement to Savannah, the way she absentmindedly rubbed Caleb's naked back as she talked.

It was that softening more than anything that made him wonder. Made him almost believe.

She looked up suddenly, as if drawn by his perusal. Their eyes locked. A friendly smile shaped her lips.

Without thinking, he smiled back.

Surprise widened her eyes. A pink blush spread through the peach-hued softness of her cheeks as her smile slowly faded away.

Jack felt like an idiot. He looked away.

"Don't," she breathed, shaking her head slightly.

Reluctantly he looked at her. "Don't what?"

"Don't stop smiling. I . . . I like it."

Jack felt as if he were falling again. He reached uncomfortably for the cup of water beside him, not surprised at all to find that his hand was shaking. His fingers curled around the sun-warmed tin and he clung to it, feeling ridiculously like a drowning man hanging on to a rapidly sinking oar.

Suddenly he remembered Doc Hayes's words: *Could be you got yourself a new wife.*

Jack felt something he hadn't felt in a very, very long time. Something he'd vowed never to feel again. And try as he might, he couldn't bury or ignore the emotion.

God help him, he felt a spark of hope.

Tess leaned back against the cracked bark of the madrone tree.

"Mama! Look! It's a twirling seed." Katie raced up to Tess and dropped to her knees, skidding through the tall grass. "I found it all by myself."

"That's great, sweetie. Show your daddy how well you can throw it."

Katie scrambled to her feet and deftly threw the maple seedcase. It whirled through the air and floated to the grass. Katie jumped and shrieked with joy, then ran over to tell Savannah about the flight.

Tess glanced over at Jack. He was looking at Katie, and there was a soft, faraway look in his eyes.

"She's quite a girl," Tess said quietly.

He smiled. "Yeah."

Their eyes met, and in that instant, that look, something powerful passed between them. Something special and filled with promise.

All of a sudden Tess felt beautiful and wanted and welcome. She felt—for one bright and shining moment—loved.

Then it was gone. Jack looked away, and the connection vanished as if it had never been. She let out her breath in a shaking, depleted sigh. The world seemed to drop out from underneath her. Once again she felt like the little deaf girl waiting—always waiting—to be invited into the warm, cozy home.

Waiting. The thought made her angry. She'd always been waiting. Always.

And it was her own damned fault. She'd *let* her life be put on hold by being too scared to reach for love. She'd always been terrified of rejection—of being told she wasn't pretty enough, or talented enough or loving enough. After enough adoptions that didn't come through, enough parents who didn't want her, she'd stopped even reaching out. She'd lived in lonely safety, her heart in no danger of being broken again.

No more, she thought suddenly. She'd been given another chance at life, at love, and by God, she wouldn't wilt away from possible heartache this time. She wanted Jack to love her, and she wanted to love him.

She had only two choices. Either wait in lonely silence for him to come to her, or go out on that shaky, too slim limb and reach for the stars.

It was no choice at all.

Chapter Twelve

Tess's latest attempt at cooking breakfast was another dismal failure.

"We could use it to tack down area rugs," Lissa said brightly, washing down her second bite of oatmeal with a big swallow of milk.

"It'd hold up wallpaper," Savannah added with a grin.

Katie giggled. "It'd catch rabbits, too. Just throw a bunch on the ground." She pounded her little fist on the table for emphasis. "Bounce, bounce, stick."

The three of them dissolved into laughter. The carefree, happy sound tugged at Jack's heart. He glanced around, studying each one of them in turn. Savannah looked prettier than he'd ever seen her. Bright splashes of pink spotted her cheeks, and her blue eyes glowed with happiness.

His gaze turned lovingly to Katie. His Katydid. Her big brown eyes were shining and bright with laughter. The sight of her made his chest ache with longing for the relationship he'd never let himself develop with her, for the thousands of lost moments and lost opportunities.

Maybe they're not lost anymore. Maybe . . .

He glanced across the table, and his breath caught. His wife was looking right at him, and once again her eyes seemed to see too much.

Once again he thought: Maybe. The small pod of hope buried deep in his heart sent roots twining around his soul.

The tentative tendrils that had been planted at yesterday's picnic began to sprout and grow.

A soft, beguiling smile shaped her lips. Crazily he knew it was a smile meant for him alone. She dipped her head in an almost invisible nod.

His heartbeat picked up speed. So did his pulse.

I'm not imagining this, he thought suddenly. *It's real. She's changing—really, truly changing.*

For the first time in years, he allowed himself to believe. Maybe—just maybe—there was hope for him and Lissa. Hope for them all.

The school bell rang out loud and clear, indicating the end of the school day.

Katie let out her breath in a long sigh of relief. In her lap, wedged tightly between her skirted thighs, her fists relaxed. She'd made it through the day without getting laughed at.

Beside her, Savannah was busy collecting her books and restrapping them together. Katie scooted back in her chair and stood up. Staring down at the books spewed across her desk, she reached shakily for the shortened leather belt.

Concentrate, she told herself. *It ain't that hard. It can't be. Everyone else does it all the time.*

Course, everyone else did lots of things that came hard for her.

With exaggerated care, she began stacking her books in a pile atop the open strap.

"Savannah? Katie?"

She froze. It was Miss Ames's voice.

"Yes, ma'am?" Savannah answered.

Katie swallowed reflexively and forced her chin up. Miss Ames was staring right at her. She felt a shiver of fear at the hardness in the teacher's eyes.

Miss Ames walked crisply toward them, her heels clattering rapid-fire along the wooden floorboards. Each *click-click-click* hit Katie like a slap on the cheek. At her sides, she clutched the heavy wool of her skirt and twisted it nervously.

Miss Ames held out a small scrap of paper. "Savannah, I want you to take this home to your mother. I expect her to call on me in the next few days about—" her disapproving gaze cut to Katie "—your sister's deplorable laziness."

Katie whimpered quietly and pinned her gaze on the scarred wooden tabletop.

"She ain't lazy, Miss Ames. She works real—"

"Don't tell me my job," Miss Ames interrupted with a sour look. "I've been teaching longer than you've been alive, and believe me, any child who can't read by the age of seven is just plain lazy. Or stupid."

Savannah reached sideways and clasped Katie's trembling hand, giving it a reassuring squeeze.

Katie clung to her sister's hand. Tears of shame and humiliation burned behind her eyes. The blackboard blurred into a charcoal-colored smear against the wooden wall.

"Run along now," Miss Ames said, whirling around and striding briskly back to her desk at the front of the classroom.

Savannah swept up Katie's books and strapped them together in a practiced movement that made Katie feel even more stupid and clumsy.

"Let's go, Katie." She clutched the books to her chest and led her sister into the aisle.

Katie kept her head down and tried desperately to stop crying as she stumbled along beside her sister. She stared hard at her feet, watching each step and trying not to trip. Down the aisle, through the doorway, along the sagging wooden steps, and onto the soft new shoots of grass.

"You can look up now," Savannah said softly. "Everybody's gone."

Katie forced her trembling chin up. The fenced, treed school yard blurred into a wash of green grass and blue sky.

"Miss Ames is wrong. You ain't lazy. You're just . . ."

"Stupid." The humiliating word burst from Katie.

"No!" Savannah's books fell from her arms and hit the dirt with a thud and a puff of dust. She whirled around and dropped to her knees, grabbing Katie by the shoulders. "You ain't stupid. Don't you believe that. Not even for a minute."

Huge, aching tears squeezed past Katie's lashes and streaked down her cheeks. "I try so hard."

Savannah's eyes filled with tears. "I know." Her voice was barely more than a croak of sound.

It made Katie feel even worse to see Savannah cry. "Come on," she said thickly, "let's go home."

Savannah pulled Katie into her arms. "I'll help you," she whispered against her neck. "I swear I will. I just don't know how."

Tess stared at the note in shock. She snapped her chin up, a stinging comment poised at her mouth.

Then she noticed the girls. Savannah was wide-eyed with fear, her skin pale and chalky. And Katie had fallen into her old habit of hiding behind her sister's skirts. They were scared to death.

Tess forced herself to appear calm and in control. She was too angry with that witch at the schoolhouse to talk with the girls rationally right now, but she would later. And by the time she was through, neither one of them would ever be afraid again.

"Don't worry, girls," she said softly. "I'll handle this."

Jack heard determined footsteps coming toward the barn, and he winced. He knew that brisk, no-nonsense gait all too well. It wasn't part of any "new and improved" wife. It was the old Amarylis all the way. And it was trouble.

Crunch—crunch—crunch.

Every time her heel hit the dirt, he flinched.

"Jack?"

He steeled himself and turned slowly around. "Yeah?"

She stopped about a foot from him and stuck her hand out. A small, white scrap of paper, its edges curled from nervous handling, lay in her palm. "Look at this."

He frowned. "What is it?"

"Read it."

"Just tell me what it says."

She snatched her hand back and brought the paper closer to her face. "Dear Mrs. Rafferty, I must meet with you regarding Mary Katherine's deplorable lack of attention and laziness in the classroom. Any afternoon shall be suitable for our conversation. Sincerely, Rebecca Ames."

Shock, then anger, blazed through Jack, turning into a cold, hard knot in his chest. His fingers tightened painfully around the hammer.

He thought instantly of the last time Miss Ames had sent a note home. The memory of his wife's reaction was seared into his brain.

That note, like this one, was short and sweet. *Dear Mrs. Rafferty, I believe you should be aware that Mary Katherine is experiencing significant difficulty in learning the fundamentals of reading. If you would like to speak with me regarding her laziness, I would be pleased to set aside some time. Sincerely, Rebecca Ames.*

God, how Amarylis had laughed. Even now he could hear the grating, almost hysterical sound. She'd torn the note up and tossed it in the fireplace.

"What is there to talk about, Jackson? Our daughter's

stupidity?" Then she'd cast him a glance that would burn through steel. *"Blood will tell, after all. . . ."*

"*Say* something, damn it," she yelled.

He eyed her suspiciously, wondering what the hell she expected of him this time. "Like what?"

"Like *what*? The old bat just called your daughter stupid!"

Jack stared at her in confusion. It sounded as if she were . . . angry. But that couldn't be. She didn't give a shit about Katie.

Disgust narrowed her eyes. "You're some piece of work, Jack Rafferty. Let's go."

"Go? You don't mean—"

She crushed the paper in her fist and rammed a pointed finger against his chest. "We're going to see the teacher."

Stark, icy desperation washed over him. He backed away, shaking his head. Not this.

"Hitch up the team. I'm going to go feed Caleb, and then we're leaving."

Panic clawed through his enforced calm. He couldn't go with her. Not now. Not until he found some way to control his emotions. God knew if he heard that bitch call his Katydid stupid, he'd probably belt the woman.

Amarylis would see his weakness, his love for Katie, and use it to hurt them all.

"I won't go."

"No?" A grim, humorless smile curved her lips. It was an expression he knew well. Determination turned her eyes into cold brown chips. "Thirty minutes, Jack." Then she pivoted and strode out of the barn.

"Damn it, Amarylis, I can't."

She didn't even turn around.

Tess sucked in her breath and held it. With shaking fingers she wrenched the corset-strings together and tied a knot.

A small squeak escaped her lips as she tried to exhale.

Stumbling sideways, she clutched the wooden bedpost and tried to remain standing. Scorching pains coiled around her rib cage and squeezed until she was dizzy and panting for air.

She collapsed onto the bed and lay perfectly still, wondering how long a human could live without air.

Ha. Ha. Ha. Each carefully taken breath sounded like laughter in the quiet room.

Gradually the white dots crept out of her field of vision and the aching pain in her lungs subsided. Cautiously she rolled onto her side. Then, inch by agonizing inch, she eased to a sitting position.

Ha. Ha. Ha.

Barely lifting her feet from the floor, she shuffled to the armoire and got dressed. The lovely forest green muslin gown she'd selected earlier settled around her shoulders and fell to the ground in folds.

Breathing a little easier, she moved to the mirror. If she'd had any breath in her body, her reflection would have taken it away. She looked . . . beautiful.

Smiling in spite of her discomfort, she turned swiftly. Too swiftly, she realized immediately as stars once again careened across her eyes. She clutched the washstand for support.

Ha. Ha. Ha.

"I'll . . . just stand here . . . for a minute."

She needed to come up with a plan of attack anyway. She couldn't just waltz—all right, she conceded, hobble—out to the barn and whisk Jack off his feet. It would take a plan of some sort to get his help. And by God, she *would* get his help. This time he was going to be a part of this family whether he wanted to or not.

"Okay," she said to the exquisitely beautiful woman in

the mirror, "how shall we handle this? It won't be easy.
He won't want to go."

No, she realized, that wasn't quite right. It wasn't that
he wouldn't want to go. It was that he was afraid to go.
Whatever water there was under the bridge of Jack and
Amarylis's marriage—and the word *tsunami* came to
mind—it kept Jack from being the parent he wanted to be.

He was afraid to show an interest in his children.

Still, the old bat schoolteacher had called Katie lazy,
and Tess couldn't let that pass. It was the sort of thing that
scarred a child for life. Tess knew.

So, how to enlist Jack's aid without causing a fight?

It had to be a nonconfrontational meeting, she decided.
One that wouldn't get him—or her—riled up. No more
temper outbursts like she'd shown today. Angry demands
were what he expected of his wife, and Tess knew she had
to do the unexpected.

She had to keep the discussion light. Not a hint of anger
or even irritation could surface.

Keep it light.

Yes, that would work. No matter what he did or said or
didn't say, she'd keep smiling.

Because if there was one thing Tess had learned in the
past few days, it was that her smile knocked Jack completely off guard.

It took Tess about twenty minutes to get to the barn, but
she considered it a major victory. She was, after all, conscious when she arrived.

"Jack?"

"Yeah?" His answer came from the darkened corner.

She clutched the workbench's splintery end and slowly
turned around. Her gaze narrowed as she searched the
black, cobwebby corner. "Jack?"

"I'm here. What do you want?"

"I'm waiting for you to hitch up the team."

He stepped out of the shadows. A twig snapped beneath his heel, and the sound echoed through the still, silent barn. "You'll be waiting a long time."

"Are you saying you won't take me to the school?"

"I said you'd be waiting a long time for me to hitch up the team."

Tess fought a wave of impatience. *Keep it light.* "Yes, I heard the *words* you used, I was inquiring as to your meaning."

Jack was in front of her in a heartbeat. "I meant that if you want to go to school, go ahead. You can take Red."

Tess got a sinking feeling in her stomach. "Red?"

Jack smiled and cocked a thumb toward the nearest stall. A big, Roman-nosed sorrel snorted in response. "*Big* Red."

Tess swallowed thickly. "Do I ride?"

"Only thoroughbreds."

"Somehow that doesn't surprise me. Well, saddle them up."

His smile faded. "Them?"

"I'm not going alone."

"I'm not going with you."

"Of course you are. How else would I find the school?"

Jack stared at her as if she were something stuck to the bottom of his shoe. "You don't remember where the school is?"

The plan fell in her lap. Perhaps a little . . . misinterpretation was the best way to deal with Jack. She batted her big brown lashes at him. "Did I ever know?"

"It's just up the road about—"

She cleared her throat.

He stopped midsentence and glanced down at her.

"And what road would that be?"

"Lissa, I swear—"

She shook her head. "Please don't. I'd rather not hear it."

Jack squeezed his eyes shut. Tess got the distinct impression that he was envisioning himself strangling her. "Lissa." His voice had that tight-edged calm that bespoke a storm of emotion underneath. "You know damn well—"

"I thought we only had a cistern."

He blinked. "Huh?"

This time her smile was blazingly bright. "You were saying something about a well."

His eyes narrowed. For a split second she wondered if she hadn't pushed him too far.

"Fine." The word shot from his mouth like a poison dart. "You want to go to the school, we'll go to the school. But don't expect me to say a damn thing."

Tess had a nearly irrepressible urge to throw her arms around him. At her sides, her gloved fingers curled into fists. He was going to go with her! The plan had worked. She'd gotten him to be a parent, at least for the moment.

She smiled. It was a start.

A few minutes later, Tess stared at the sidesaddle in disgust and wondered if her plan had been as good as she'd thought.

"I'm supposed to . . . perch on that thing?"

Jack nodded, making no effort to conceal his smile.

Tess gritted her teeth. "Help me up."

"I don't know, Lissa, wouldn't you rather—"

"I'd *rather* get behind the wheel of my Jeep, but since that isn't too likely, what I'd like is a hand up."

Jack let his reins drop to the ground and gathered hers in his hand. "Here."

She took the flat leather reins and shoved them in her mouth, biting down hard. Then she reached for the leather thingamajig that stuck out from the top of the saddle. Stepping cautiously into Jack's laced fingers, she flung her other leg over the seat.

Jack cleared his throat.

Wincing, she pulled the dusty-tasting reins from her mouth and glanced down.

He shoved the battered black Stetson off his eyes. "You aren't going to ride like that, are you?"

"It's more comfortable this way," she lied. It was the most uncomfortable contraption she'd ever been in.

He shook his head. A smile lurked in his green eyes.

She hazarded a guess. "This is unladylike."

"Very."

She leaned over a tiny bit and studied the two curls of leather that sprouted from the side of the saddle like rabbit ears. "Let me guess: I slide down and dangle my right leg over this . . . thing."

The smile slipped to his mouth and turned into a grin. "You got it."

She grabbed hold of Red's mane and slid cautiously into place. "This can't be right. I feel like a bug on the side of a car antenna."

He frowned at her description. "You always say a lady—a southern lady—doesn't care about comfort."

She smiled thinly. It took a great deal of self-control not to snap at him. "Obviously not. Shall we go?"

First surprise, then anger, flashed in his eyes. "You still want to?"

"Of course."

With a bitten-off curse, Jack mounted up and turned his horse toward the road. "Come on Turk, let's go."

It was a long, silent ride to the schoolhouse.

The one-room building came into view as they turned the last corner on Portland Hill Road.

Jack stared at the small clapboard structure that served as meeting hall, church, and summertime schoolhouse, and felt anger at the woman who dared to call his Katie lazy creep uncontrollably back into his chest.

Don't do it, he thought. Don't let yourself feel rage or fear or pain.

The familiar litany didn't work this time. He tried again and again, getting more and more desperate with each attempt. He couldn't distance himself from his emotions, not this time. They were roiling around inside of him like liquid fire, coiling around his gut.

"What a pretty little building. Is that the school?"

Jack's fingers tightened around the reins. Tension drew his mouth into a grim, colorless line. "Yes."

"Good. Okay, let's talk about how to handle this situation."

Her sentence hit him like a cold wind. "What did you say?"

"We need a plan of attack, so to speak. A way to enlist the old bat's help with Katie. We have to be calm and pleasant at all costs." She frowned in thought. "Maybe buttering her up would help."

Terror stole through his body. Surely she didn't mean for them to speak to the teacher together. As *parents*. He could never remain numb if he actually heard the condemning words about his baby. "*We* won't do a damn thing. I showed you where the schoolhouse is. My job's done."

"Sorry, Jack. It takes two to tango."

"What in the hell does that mean?"

"It means it took both of us to create Katie. And it'll take both of us to help her through this crisis."

Both. Create. Help. The words hurled at him like cannonballs. He tried to feel angry, and failed. All he felt was cold and frightened and more alone than ever. "I'll wait," he said dully, "but I won't go in."

They'd reached the schoolhouse by the time she finally answered. "Yes, Jack, you will."

Chapter Thirteen

Katie sat cross-legged on the rag rug, staring forlornly at her own feet. "What'dya think's happenin' now?"

Savannah held her finger out to Caleb, who was lying on the floor between them. He curled his tiny red hand around her forefinger and squeezed. "I dunno. Prob'ly ain't there yet."

They lapsed back into silence.

"Mama seemed pretty mad when she saw the note," Katie said quietly, plucking a wrinkled strip of blue flannel from the rug.

"Not like last time."

"No . . ." Katie shuddered at the memory of "last time." Mama had smacked her hard and yelled at her for being such a stupid, lazy little girl who didn't want to be no better'n her crazy daddy.

"Don't think about that." Savannah touched Katie's knee. "It ain't gonna be like that again."

Katie looked up. Stupid, stinging tears filled her eyes, but she couldn't hold them back. "You don't know that," she whispered. "Could be she's just tryin' to trick us again."

Savannah swallowed hard. "I know, but . . . but I don't think so. She seems . . . differ'nt."

A tear slipped down Katie's cheek and plopped on the hand fisted so tightly in her lap. She was so scared, she felt sick and twisted-up inside. Savannah was just tryin' to make her feel better. They both knew what was gonna happen when Mama got home. It was gonna be just like last time.

And there was nothin' they could do. Nothin' that would change anything. They just had to wait.

"Mary Katherine shouldn't be in school."

Tess thought she'd misheard. "Excuse me?"

Miss Ames peered down at them from her position in the front of the room. Planting her palms on her desk, she scooted her chair out from behind her and stood. A thin, humorless smile stretched her lips. "I said, Mary Katherine has no right to be in this school. She's lazy, inattentive, and obviously has no intention of learning to read." She paused, frowned. The wire-rimmed spectacles slid down her bumpy nose. "Perhaps she's not all there. In the head, you know, somewhat—"

"Don't you dare say it," Tess hissed.

Miss Ames pursed her lips in disapproval. "It seems Mary Katherine's poor manners are learned at home."

"How dare you imply such a thing about a seven-year-old child? Has it ever occurred to you that there's a *reason* she learns more slowly than the other children?"

Miss Ames sniffed loudly and pushed her spectacles back onto the bridge of her nose. "I don't believe I understand you."

Tess took a deep, shaky breath to maintain her calm. *Remember, Tess, you want this lady's help.* She twisted her hands together in a nervous ball and forced a polite smile. "I—I think perhaps Katie needs a bit more of your time than the other students. You're so helpful, so smart. Certainly you can find a way to . . . help Katie. What is it . . . exactly that's problematic?"

Miss Ames thought about that for a moment. A small

frown pleated the skin between her eyes. The glasses slid down her nose again. "Well, the pressure of reading aloud seems to be particularly challenging to Mary Katherine."

Tess leaned slightly forward, resting her palms on the rough-hewn desktop. "Maybe during your lunchtime . . ."

"I suppose I *could* spend a few spare moments with her then."

Tess nodded encouragement. "I'll work with her at home. Every night."

Miss Ames allowed herself a cautious smile. "You will? All right, then. We shall try this approach and see if it works. Thank you for coming in, Mrs. Rafferty." She shot a no-nonsense nod to Jack, who was still sitting stiff as a board at the back of the room. "Mr. Rafferty."

Tess shook the older woman's bony hand. "No, Miss Ames. Thank *you*."

Miss Ames strapped up her pile of books and strode briskly out of the schoolhouse. When the door banged shut, Tess threw her hands up in the air and let out a whoop of laughter. "We did it. She'll help her, Jack!"

When she turned back around, Jack was gone.

Grabbing a handful of skirt, she ran down the aisle and pushed through the half-open door. Jack was sitting on the top step. Hunched over, chin in his hands, he was staring at the ground.

She skidded to a stop and sat down beside him. Her fanny thumped on the sagging wooden slat.

"You shouldn't have done that," he said dully. "Pretending only makes it worse."

"Pretending what?"

"To care. It'll only hurt Katie more when you go back to your old ways. Don't—" He turned to her. Pain as raw as a new wound filled his eyes. "Don't get her hopes up. Please . . ."

Tess touched his face in a feather-stroke of compassion.

"Why?" The lone, softly spoken word slipped out before she could stop it.

He flinched at her touch. "Why what?"

"Why are you so afraid of her?"

His breath expelled in a tired, ragged sigh that skimmed her cheeks. The agonizing pain in his eyes tore at her heart with tiny, shredding fingers. "Lissa, please . . ." His voice was frayed with emotion.

Tess moved toward him, drawn by the same dark, aching feeling she'd had when she'd first seen him. She touched his face again; this time the touch was a caress. Her eyes probed his, tried desperately to see past the fear. "I'm not the same, Jack. I won't hurt you again. I promise."

For a split second, she thought she saw hope in his eyes; then, as quickly as it had come, it was gone. "Sure, Lissa. I believe you."

"Believe this." She took his face in her hands. His eyes widened in sudden realization and he tried to pull away from her.

"Lissa, don't—"

She leaned toward him, knowing it was too early, knowing he wasn't ready, and doing it anyway.

She was going to kiss him. Jack's whole body tensed. He knew he should wrench out of her grasp and fling himself backward, but he couldn't move. He was frozen in place by the raw need of a man who'd been in love alone.

He wanted to feel her lips on his, wanted it so badly, he felt weak. He'd dreamed of this moment ever since he'd seen her half-naked in the bath. Like a prisoner left too long in dark solitude, he dreamed of the sunny warmth of her touch. Ached for it. And right now, with the memory of Miss Ames's condemnation strong and bitter on his tongue, he needed this. Needed her . . .

He felt her lips touch his, whisper-soft at first, just a whirring of breath and no more. A shiver skidded down his spine.

"Oh, God." The words slipped from his mouth in a groan of pleasure and pain. Trembling, he brought his hands to her face and held her, his fingers burrowing possessively into her hair. Need washed through his body in a red-hot wave. The love and desire he'd hidden for so long filled him. God, he wanted her. . . .

He clung to her, lowering his mouth to hers and kissing her hungrily, greedily. His tongue forced her mouth apart and plunged inside the moist warmth. The kiss was everything he'd wanted, dreamed, and yet there was something in it that surprised him. Her lips felt as soft as always, and the scent of lavender clung to her as it always had, but there was a gentleness in this kiss that was new. A caution that bespoke inexperience and just a touch of anxiety. It reminded him of their very first kiss, so long ago, when they'd both believed in love.

Slowly he drew back, keeping his eyes closed. He didn't want to see her right now, didn't want to take the chance that the coldness had crept back into her gaze. With that single, hungry kiss, he'd given her the ammunition she needed to crucify him. All she had to do was laugh.

"Jack." His name sounded soft and hesitant on her lips, as if she were as scared and shaken as he.

Surprised, he opened his eyes and looked at her. And was lost.

Her huge brown eyes were glistening with tears. Her mouth trembled. She tried to smile, and failed miserably.

Jack felt as if he'd been punched in the gut. He stared dumbly at her. She looked breathtakingly beautiful and suddenly fragile, as if she could actually be wounded by him. Her breasts rose and fell in rapid, shallow breaths.

His knuckles slid down her damp cheek and brushed her

tears away. He stared at the moisture on his fingertip and swallowed thickly. "What's going on, Lissa?"

"I'm scared." There was a quaver in her voice that tugged at his heart and made him almost believe.

He stared at her long and hard, trying to reconcile the quiet, fragile person sitting before him with the brittle, angry woman he'd known for half his life. His emotions tangled into an unmanageable mass. Feeling suddenly tired and depressingly alone, he pushed to his feet. "We'd better get back."

Lissa stood beside him. She looked up at him. Pale silver lines streaked her flushed cheeks and reminded him forcibly that she'd cried. *Cried.*

She pushed a damp lock of hair from her eyes and nervously tucked it behind her ear. "Will you talk to Katie with me?"

"Don't do this to me, Lissa." His voice was a low, agonized whisper. "Please . . ."

"But—"

"No." The word came out in a strangled mixture of shame and pain. Jack squeezed his eyes shut, feeling the hot sting of emotion. He'd never in his life felt as much like a failure as he did right now.

A long, breath-laden silence stretched between them. Jack felt every second, every heartbeat, like a blow to the heart. *Don't make me talk to Katie; not now.* If he saw his Katydid right now, he'd never be able to keep from scooping her into his arms and kissing her tears away. And he couldn't do that, couldn't let her trust him until he was sure Lissa had really changed. God knew they'd hurt the kids enough without adding more.

"Okay, Jack. I'll do it, I'll talk to her. But on one condition."

His eyes popped open in surprise. "Condition?"

She dashed the last tracings of tears from her eyes and smiled shakily. "Yes."

"What?"

"I want you to try."

He froze. "Try what?"

She stepped closer, her face tilted up to his. Soft afternoon breezes ruffled through her hair, filled the air with the scent of fresh grass and wildflowers. "Just try to be a dad."

Jack swallowed hard. She was asking the impossible; to try, he had to believe. In her. In himself.

"I . . . can't."

"Yes, Jack, you can." Her gaze caught his in a silken grip and wouldn't let him go. "Trust me."

Savannah saw her parents ride into the yard, and yanked her hand away from the curtain. The tired fabric fluttered back in place and once again blocked out the fading rays of the setting sun.

Spinning around, she bustled over to the stove and tried to focus her thoughts on the frying rabbit.

"Did Mama look mad?" Katie asked quietly, hugging her worn, floppy rag doll to her chest.

Savannah knew it was useless to pretend ignorance. Carefully setting down the wooden spoon, she turned and drew Katie into her arms. She stroked her baby sister's tangled hair and sighed wearily. "I couldn't see her face."

"Maybe I'll pretend to be too sick to eat."

Savannah let her hand fall back to her side. "It wouldn't do no good."

Katie squeezed the doll harder. Her lower lip trembled. She opened her mouth to speak, but nothing came out. Savannah understood perfectly. What was there to say?

"You better set the table. She'll be in any minute."

Katie flinched at the reminder, then nodded. Slowly,

mechanically, she went to the dresser and started gathering the plates and cups. Her feet shuffled softly across the floor as she went back and forth from the dresser to the table. Silverware and plates clanked in her wake.

Savannah felt tears rise in her throat, and she turned quickly back to the stove before Katie could see her weakness. *Please don't call her stupid, Mama. Please . . .*

The kitchen door swung open. "Hi, kids."

Savannah spun around and saw her mother standing in the doorway. Smiling, Mama whipped the shawl off her shoulder and flung it over the nearest chair. "Wow, something smells great. What are you making?"

Savannah stared at her mother's smiling face in confusion. They *had* gone to talk to Miss Ames, hadn't they?

Katie eased toward Savannah and disappeared behind her skirts.

Savannah forced an uncomfortable smile. "It's rabbit, Mama. Your favorite."

She frowned. "I eat bunnies?"

Savannah hesitated. "Not bunnies, rabbits."

"Oh." Mama pressed a hand to her stomach and said weakly, "Great. Thanks."

Savannah couldn't wait another second. She had to know what happened at the school. "H-How did it go?"

Mama's smile faded. She looked at Savannah through suddenly narrowed eyes, and Savannah felt a wave of sick fear.

"You're trying so hard to be grown-up," Mama whispered. Then she smiled, a soft, loving smile that made Savannah want to cry, it was so pretty. "It went well, I think."

"It did?" Katie squeaked behind her.

"Come here, Katie." Mama held out her hand.

Katie peeked her head around Savannah's arm. "Do I have ta?"

She nodded.

Katie inched her way out from behind her sister. Savannah grabbed Katie's hand and stopped her for a second. "You . . . you ain't gonna . . . punish her, are you?"

Mama paled and squeezed her eyes shut, and when she opened them again, they were filled with tears. "Oh, God . . ." She hurried across the room and dropped to her knees in front of them, taking Savannah's hands in hers. "Everything is going to be fine. I promise. I had a long talk with Miss Ames, and I think we've figured out a way to help Katie."

Savannah felt as if the world had been lifted from her thin shoulders. The tears she'd held back for so long stung her eyes. "I—I tried really hard to help her."

"I know you did. It's not your fault she can't read."

"It ain't hers, either," Savannah said defensively.

"I know that."

"You *do*?"

Mama smiled and stood up. "Yes, I do. Now, come on, Katie, we're going to have a talk. Savannah, you watch Caleb till we get back."

Tess took Katie by the hand and led her to the door. There she stopped, and turned back to Savannah. "You helped her the most, you know, just by loving her."

Savannah felt a surge of pride and love so strong, she didn't care if she did cry. Tears rolled down her cheeks and burrowed into the corners of her mouth. For once, they tasted good. Clean. "Thanks."

The evening was cool and crisp and stained lavender by the setting sun.

Tess and Katie walked down the porch steps and up the road, veering off into the tall grass at the top of the hill.

"Where're we goin'?"

Tess squeezed her hand and kept walking. "To a special place."

Katie pulled her hand free. "What special place?"

Tess felt keenly the loss of Katie's tiny hand in hers, but knew that kind of trust was something she'd have to earn. "I don't know. I haven't seen it yet."

They trudged through the pasture, passing wild rabbits, granite rocks, and sheep along the way. Finally the land dipped and rose, creating a perfect grassy pinnacle over-looking the house, the pasture, and Haro Strait. Tess led Katie to the special spot and sat down.

Evening was just beginning to mask the fading sun. Wind burrowed through the tall grass, carrying with it the scent of twilight and wildflowers.

They sat side by side. After a few moments, Tess scooted closer and touched Katie's chin. "Katie?"

Katie resisted the pressure for a heartbeat, then turned her head slightly and looked up.

Fear and uncertainty darkened the child's brown eyes. Tess understood perfectly. There was a time when Tess had felt the very same things. It was a pain not easily for-gotten.

She squeezed her eyes shut in a quick, silent prayer. *Please, God, don't let me screw up. . . .*

"I . . . I know how much it hurts when people treat you as if you're . . . dumb."

Surprise widened Katie's eyes. "You do?"

Tess nodded. "When I was about your age, I . . . I mean a friend of mine . . . got a disease called spinal meningitis. She got really, really sick—the doctors didn't think she would live, but she did. Only . . . not all of her got better. When it was all over, she couldn't hear."

Katie frowned. "Nothin'?"

"Not a thing. It made everything really difficult for her because she didn't know how to communicate anymore.

So ..." Painful memories catapulted Tess back in time. Suddenly she was a child again, seven years old, being led across the schoolyard to the rickety old portable that housed the special education class.

This is Tess Gregory, the principal said, signing the condemning words at the same time. *She belongs here....*

"Mama?"

Katie's voice yanked Tess back to the present. She dashed the film of moisture from her eyes and cleared her throat. "Sorry. Anyway, they put ... my friend in a special class at school—a class for people who were different. It was hard for her. After a while people forgot she couldn't hear and started treating her as if she was ... stupid. And the other kids, who weren't in the special class and used to be her friends, laughed at her and then forgot...."

"Gosh, that's terrible."

Tess forced a shaky smile. "Yeah. Then my friend's mom died, and she went to live with another family." *The first of many foster families* ... "She was sad for a long time, and then something wonderful happened."

"What?"

She smiled, remembering the day Jane Essex had walked into the special ed class. "She made a friend in her class. Her friend had something called dyslexia."

"What's that?"

"It's a problem lots of people have." Tess took hold of Katie's small hands and drew them into her lap. "It's where letters get all jumbled around in your mind and seem to blur and dance on the page. Is that what it's like for you?"

Katie swallowed hard and nodded. "Uh-huh."

"Her friend was smart as a whip, too."

"Did ... did she learn how to read?"

"She sure did. It took her a little longer, but she worked really hard and learned how." Tess stroked Katie's hair, looked deeply into her eyes. "I know how you feel. But you're not dumb. Do you want to learn to read?"

Katie's bottom lip quivered. Tears flooded her eyes and streaked down her cheeks. She tried to look away, but Tess wouldn't let her.

"Katie?"

A watery sob escaped her. "I'm afraid."

"Will you let me try to help you? I learned a lot watching my friend."

She hiccuped. "I dunno. What if—"

"No what ifs, Katie. You can do it. You *can*. All you have to say is yes."

Katie swallowed thickly and wiped the tears from her eyes. "I wanna learn to read," she said quietly.

Tess felt a sense of accomplishment and pride and love so big, she couldn't believe it. Smiling, she ruffled Katie's hair. "Come on, kiddo, we better get back to the house before your daddy and sister call out the National Guard."

"The what?"

Laughing, Tess got to her feet and brushed the burrs and grass stalks from her skirt. Together, hand in hand, they walked back to the house.

Chapter Fourteen

High overhead, the hot sun peeked through a layer of cottony clouds. The sapphire-blue sky melted into the equally blue Straits, its watercolor wash broken only by the huge green hump of Vancouver Island.

Jack poured a bucket of water into the long metal trough. At the splash, sheep turned in unison and herded together, moving in a huge dirty white bubble toward him.

He shoved the hat back on his head and reached down, grabbing the empty pails. Buckets clanking, he walked down the gravelly dirt path toward home.

"Hey, Jack!"

Jack yanked his head up and looked at the road above the farm. A wagon was rumbling past in a cloud of dust.

Jack forced a thin smile and waved back. Damn, he'd forgotten that the Hannahs were coming today with the supplies he'd ordered.

It wasn't surprising that he'd forgotten. He'd been sort of ... unfocused today. No matter how much he tried to bury himself in work, he hadn't been able to concentrate. Hadn't been able to forget.

The kiss.

He groaned, feeling again the wave of desire and need that had coursed through his body as her moist, tempting lips had touched his. The kiss had been ... special. He couldn't think of any other way to put it. Like Amarylis and yet unlike her. Crazily, he thought it was like the woman she'd become recently—caring, tender, loving. Like Lissa.

Jesus, he was starting to lose his mind.

"Shit," he cursed softly, his fingers tightening involuntarily around the thin metal handles.

All morning he'd reminded himself of who she was and what she was doing. Over and over again he'd told himself it was simply another game, another ploy to ultimately hurt him and the kids.

But, God help him, this time he couldn't make himself believe the damning words. Every time he thought of the cruel things she'd done in the past, he saw her as she was now. Laughing, smiling, standing up to that old battle-ax at the school, throwing burnt biscuits, kissing Caleb's tummy.

Maybe. It was that word, and everything it represented, that kept tangling up his mind. Maybe she really had forgotten the old hatreds, the old wounds. Maybe this time it was all real. Maybe . . .

He said under his breath, "Christ, don't let me believe it unless it's true."

Tess heard the unmistakable thud of running feet, and paused in her work. Wiping her sweaty hands on her apron, she went to the kitchen window and peeked outside.

Jack was running toward the house. She let the curtain fall back in place and nervously rewiped her hands.

She hadn't talked to Jack since yesterday. Since she'd kissed him. They'd sat across from each other at supper, each silent and thoughtful, then Jack had bolted from the house and disappeared in the barn. Not surprisingly, he'd stayed there until long after Tess went to bed, and left the house before she wakened this morning.

She'd wanted to talk to him. She'd even thought about

barging into the barn this morning and demanding that they talk. But about what? That was the question that had stopped her.

What could she say about that kiss that would make sense to either one of them? That she shouldn't have done it? Or that she was glad she had?

She shivered although the room was stiflingly hot, and crossed her arms. The spicy, cinnamon-thick scent of baking pie swirled around her. Closing her eyes, she remembered the soft, hesitant feel of his lips on hers. The way his tongue had darted out and touched hers, the bolt of electricity that had rocked through her blood at the moist, hot contact. It had been unlike any kiss she'd ever experienced, filled with the fiery heat of passion and the comforting warmth of caring. She felt as if she'd kissed him before—long ago in a time now forgotten.

Suddenly the door burst open and Jack barreled into the kitchen. He stopped, breathing heavily, and stared at her. "Lissa? The Hannahs—" He stopped midsentence and noticed the kitchen.

His gaze darted from place to place, pausing at each carefully placed bric-a-brac before it moved on. He noticed every change. "What are you doing?"

The brandy-smooth tone of his voice slid down Tess's back, reminding her again of the kiss they'd shared.

She licked her lower lip nervously. Suddenly it was important that he appreciate what she'd done here. What she could do. "I'm making your house a home."

He flinched, the flesh at the corners of his eyes tightening. "My house, huh?"

Tess moved close enough to be taken in his arms. She felt the heat of his body radiating toward her, warming her. The soft exhalations of his breath slid across her forehead. He didn't move; he remained stiff and wary, his hands bolted to his thighs.

"Look at me, Jack."

Reluctantly he looked down at her.

She tilted her face up and met his wary gaze. This was it, she realized. Taking a deep breath, she climbed out onto that rickety limb and handed him her heart. "You're right. This home is ours."

He paled, but didn't look away. They stood there, close enough to touch and yet careful not to, their gazes locked.

Tess wanted to say something more, wanted to break through the silence they'd obviously lived in for years, but she didn't know how. She felt as if it was suddenly within reach, that elusive *something* she'd sought so desperately all her life. All she had to do was lean forward and let him kiss her. . . .

The sound of wagon wheels crunching over small rocks seeped through the half-opened kitchen door and broke the spell.

"Jim and Minerva are here with the supplies," Jack said lamely. At her blank look, he added, "From the farm next door. Be nice to them, okay?"

"Of course."

Jack turned to go, but at the door, he stopped. "Uh . . . the house looks nice," he said quickly. Then he was gone.

Jack ran down the porch steps as if the Devil himself were on his heels, and raced to the safety of the Hannahs' wagon.

"Good morning, Mr. Rafferty," said Minerva Hannah from her perch on the wagon's wooden seat. "I've brought a few things for Mrs. Rafferty. I would have come sooner, but I only just saw Doc Hayes and heard about the baby."

"I'm sure she'll be pleased by your thoughtfulness, Mrs. Hannah. May I help you down?"

"Thank you." Minerva offered a gloved hand to Jack and allowed herself to be helped to the ground.

Jim slid across the low-slung seat and jumped down beside her. "Lordy, it's a hot one for May," he said, shoving the straw farmer's hat higher on his head. "I got all them supplies you asked for. They're in the back."

Minerva smiled softly and touched her husband's arm. "Jim, honey, if you get me that box out of the back, I'll run on into the house while you men talk."

"Sure thing."

Jack stared at Minerva's small, gloved hand, noticing the gentle, possessive way her fingers lingered against the rough wool of her husband's sleeve. He stood rooted to the spot, motionless and unblinking, thrown suddenly into a world all his own. A world in which once, long ago, his wife had touched him like that.

Ours. Lissa had said the word so quietly that at first he thought he'd imagined it. *Ours.*

If only it were true . . .

The thought came so fast, so unexpectedly, that he had no armor raised against it. Longing and despair spilled through in its wake, bringing with it the inevitable fear. Need closed around his neck with cold, suffocating fingers.

What was she doing to him?

Suddenly he felt as if he were standing on a slippery slope of mud instead of firm, stable farmland, fighting a battle he'd thought he'd gained the upper hand in long ago.

He was losing his will to fight. Even knowing how easily she could manipulate him didn't keep him from seeing the impossible softness in her eyes. The softness that had left her gaze long ago and never really returned.

Except, of course, in his mind. There it had never left. There, in that crazy, cowardly, mixed-up place where nothing was what it seemed, and nothing seen could be believed, she'd always looked at him like that.

Only now the line between reality and fantasy was blurring. He wasn't sure if *anything* about her—about them—was real. . . .

God help him, for one moment in the kitchen, when she'd whispered *ours*, he'd believed in her completely.

"You're a fool," he muttered.

"What was that, Mr. Rafferty?"

Minerva's voice wrenched him back to the real world. Jack shook his head to clear it. What the hell was wrong with him? It was just another game, another goddamn way to hurt him. Anything to make him feel, and once he did, anything to make him hurt. Amarylis had been playing the game for years. Like the night Caleb had been conceived. That wonderful, magical night . . . and the horrible, humiliating morning . . .

He had to remember that night, the way she'd manipulated and shamed him. No matter what she did, or how she appeared, he had to remember that she hated him with a singleness of spirit that made her iron-strong.

He squeezed his eyes shut as a cold wave of regret washed through him. If only he weren't so damned weak.

If only he didn't love her so goddamn much . . .

When the knock on the door came, Tess ran her hands down the coarse linsey-woolsey of her dress and glanced quickly around the kitchen.

Satisfied, she rushed to the door and pulled it open, finding a tall, thin, beautiful woman standing on the porch. A flowered straw bonnet hid her hair, but the blue-gray eyes that sparkled beneath its brim were bright and intelligent. The woman smiled tentatively. "Good morning, Mrs. Rafferty. I trust I'm not disturbing you?"

"Are you kidding? I'm thrilled to have a grownup to talk to. Come on in."

A moment's confusion passed through Minerva's eyes.

Tess was reminded of Jack's warning to be nice. No doubt Amarylis had been rude to the neighbors.

Tess put forth her best don't-be-shy smile. "Please," she said, motioning to the kitchen table. "Come on in."

"Thank you, Mrs. Rafferty," she said, following Tess into the kitchen.

"Call me Lissa."

Minerva eyed her warily. "Certainly. And you must call me Minerva."

"Great. Now, what do you have in that box? It smells heavenly."

Minerva set the slatted wooden box on the floor. "Nothing much. Just a cold meat pie and bread. Doc Hayes said you'd had a rough time of it. I thought you might like a break from cooking."

"That's very thoughtful of you." Smiling again, she crossed quickly to the stove and put water on to boil. The quiet click of the door being opened got her attention. Turning, she saw Minerva leaving.

"Minerva, wait!"

Minerva peered cautiously over her shoulder. "Yes, Mrs. . . . Lissa?"

"H-Have I done something to offend you?"

The confusion returned to Minerva's eyes. "Why, no, of course not. It's just that . . ." She shrugged. "Well, to be honest, you've always asked me to leave before."

"Wow."

"Excuse me?"

Tess hurried to the door and put a hand on Minerva's shoulder. "Please forgive my rude behavior in the past. I'd like to start fresh, if that's all right. I've had sort of a change of . . . heart since this baby."

Minerva stared into Tess's eyes for a moment. Then, slowly, she smiled. "I'd like that."

* * *

Jack couldn't believe his ears. There was laughter com-ing from the kitchen. It floated through the open window and danced on the light spring breeze.

Jim yanked the last bag of oats off the wagon and slung it over his shoulder. "Sounds like the girls are having fun," he said, flopping the heavy burlap sack beside the oak tree.

Jack swiped his damp brow with his shirt-sleeve and stared at the window. The quiet murmuring of voices, pep-pered now and then by bursts of laughter, aroused his cu-riosity. He tried to ignore it, tried to pretend he couldn't care less.

But he couldn't quite manage it. She'd never given two whits about the neighbors. As far as she was concerned, anyone not born to money in the South was poor white trash. She'd made a point of not being nice to the island-ers, as if she was afraid she might actually be happy here.

"That coffee sure smells good," Jim said.

Jack glanced up, surprised that Jim had spoken. Jim im-mediately looked away and reached for another bag of grain.

He thinks I'm a loose cannon, Jack thought. And why not? After last Fourth of July, the whole damn island thought Jack was crazy as a bedbug. He couldn't figure out why in the hell the Hannahs didn't steer clear of him, like everyone else.

"Sure does," Jack answered. "What do you say we go have a cup?"

They crossed the yard and bounded up the sagging wooden steps two at a time. Jack had only a moment's hesitation as he turned the knob and opened the door.

Sitting at the table, Lissa glanced up in surprise. The eggshell-thin rim of her teacup kissed her full lower lip. Steam wafted up from the cup and tugged at the wispy golden strands along her brow.

"Hi, Jack." Her voice was as warm and rich as the aroma of coffee hovering in the room.

Jack felt as if he'd been flung back in time. He had to be dreaming the softness in her eyes. He *had* to be.

He was moving toward her; he could feel the movements of his body, and yet he had no control over them. Before he knew it, he was beside her. She smiled up at him. Her hand landed on his forearm with butterfly softness and lingered there.

God, you're beautiful. He stopped the words just in time and lurched backward.

"Jack?" All three voices said his name at once, and Jack immediately felt like an idiot.

"Sorry," he said "I stumbled."

"And no wonder, with as hard as you two have been working," Minerva said easily.

"Sit down," Lissa said. "I just finished making a pot of coffee, and if I do say so myself, it's pretty good."

Jim shot her a questioning look as he sat down. "You sound surprised. Why wouldn't—"

"Don't ask, Jim," Jack said, sitting beside the man. "And—just a bit of friendly advice—don't drink the coffee."

Lissa poured two more cups of coffee. Plunking them down on the table in front of the men, she took a seat across from Jack. "My husband has some doubt regarding my culinary skills, Jim." She looked up at Jack. "Shall I offer them a biscuit?"

Jack almost spit up his coffee. He glanced up from his cup and found himself staring across the table into her eyes. Flyaway hair curled around her face in a halo of honey gold light. Her eyes were on him, only him, and for the space of a heartbeat, he would have sworn she was looking at him with genuine affection. Absentmindedly she tucked a lock of disobedient hair around her ear. Her hands moved with a grace he'd never seen before.

Jim started talking about shearing. The words rumbled together, became meaningless as Jack stared at his wife. She was sitting perched on the end of her chair, as if she were really listening. Her elbows were planted lightly on the table—something no southern lady would ever do—and her chin rested on the knuckles of her left hand. The wedding ring he'd given her so long ago glowed dully against her pale flesh.

"Jack? Jack?"

He was staring so intently at his wife, it was a moment before Jack realized that Jim was speaking to him. "What? Uh, sorry, I was thinking about the west pasture. What were you saying, Jim?"

"I was talking about the British evacuation of the island. I heard that . . ."

Jack's attention turned away from the casual conversation. Try as he might, he couldn't concentrate on Jim's words. All he could think about was Lissa, and the way she'd just touched him. Even now he could feel the vague, remembered warmth of her fingers against his arm. He stared at the flowers in the middle of the table until they became an unfocused blur of color.

"Jack?"

His name was a whispered caress against his ear. It sent a bolt of fire through his body. He stiffened.

She was standing behind him, her hand curled possessively around his shoulders. He felt the heat of her touch beneath the soft chambray of his shirt, smelled the lavender-laced sweetness of her skin.

When had she gotten up?

She leaned toward him. A finger-thin lock of hair slipped out from behind her ear and fell against his cheek. "Would you like some more coffee?"

He cleared his throat. Jim and Minerva looked at him, and he realized then that they hadn't even noticed Lissa's strange behavior. They'd simply kept talking, as if it was normal for a wife to get up and touch her husband in the middle of a conversation.

"N-No, thanks. I've got more work to do."

Jim immediately got to his feet. "Me, too, Jack. As much as I'd like to chew the fat, I've got a broken stall door that needs mending, and Minerva likes to be home when the kids get home from school. Well, Mrs. Rafferty, thanks for the coffee. It was delicious."

Minerva followed suit. "Yes, Lissa, it was lovely."

Lissa smiled. "I'm so glad you stopped by. It was lovely to meet ... uh, I mean see you again."

They all walked to the wagon together, and Jack and Lissa stood side by side as the Hannahs left.

"What nice people," Lissa said as the wagon disappeared around the bend.

Jack cast her a startled sideways glance. "Yeah," he said slowly, "they are."

Turning away from her, he headed back to the barn. All the way there he tried to think about the sheep—only the sheep. But try as he might, he couldn't dislodge the memory of her smile.

Strangely, he found himself thinking about that life-after-death thing, and suddenly it didn't seem half as odd as the changes in his wife.

The next day, Jack was still trying to forget the quiet way she'd whispered his name and the gentle pressure of her hand on his arm. Huddled in the dark privacy of the tack room, he tried like hell to tell himself it was all another lie meant to hurt him. But he couldn't believe it this time. Not even for a minute.

Thunk. Thunk.

Jack paused in his thoughts and listened.

Thunk. Thunk.

Frowning, he laid down the heavy black harness and can of neat's-foot oil.

The noise came again. *Thunk. Thunk. Thunk.*

Jack tossed his oil-soaked rag down on the workbench and headed out of the barn. Following the steady beating sound, he walked through the yard and around the corner of the house. His wife stood at the top of the hill above him.

He stopped dead.

She was wearing a pair of his old work pants, and one of his new blue shirts, with the sleeves rolled up to her elbows and the shirttail hanging to midthigh. Gripping a hoe, she lifted it high in the air and brought it down with a resounding *thunk*. Rich brown earth flew everywhere, speckling her hair and disappearing in the tall grass just beyond.

Flinging the hoe aside, she bent from the waist and clawed at the ground. Her shirttail flipped up, revealed the rounded curve of her buttocks.

Jack gasped. The old, often-washed wool of his pants curled enticingly around her body, leaving far too little to his imagination.

His throat went dry. Desire twitched deep in his groin. A hint of breeze rippled the fabric against her shapely calves and thighs. Without warning, he remembered what he'd spent years trying to forget. The perfection of her body, the softness of her skin, the feel of her body beneath him—

All of a sudden she flew backward. Skidding butt-first through the blackish soil, she landed with a shriek at his feet.

Spitting dirt, she brushed the hair out of her eyes and got to her knees. Crawling forward, she turned around and saw him. She immediately smiled. "Phew, that's the second time I've done that. This hill's a bitch."

Jack stared at her in shock as she brushed the dirt from her shirt and shook her head. Clumps and particles of earth pattered his chest. His gaze swept her from head to foot, noting the thick rope belt that anchored his pants to her small waist. "Why in the hell are you wearing my Sunday clothes?"

She had the grace to wince. "These are your good clothes?"

He nodded.

"Sorry. But I couldn't garden in that torture device. Every time I lifted the hoe, I'd have passed out."

Suddenly it hit him. She was *gardening*. He glanced at the freshly turned earth and frowned. "What the hell . . ."

"I'm planting a vegetable garden. I've already gotten in the radishes, potatoes, lettuce, peas. I was just starting on the corn."

"*You're* working in the garden?"

She looked at him with a strange expression. "Let me guess: I don't garden either?"

"You always said it was beneath you."

She glanced down at the newly turned ground. "Maybe I meant it literally."

He stopped a smile just in time. "Is this part of the 'new and improved' Lissa?"

"Yes, I suppose it is." She grinned up at him. "I was going to gather some wild roses to plant alongside the porch. Want to help?"

He tried not to look at her, but couldn't help himself. She was staring up at him through wide, concerned eyes. Dirt speckled her pale, flawless skin and clung to one corner of her mouth. Her unbound hair was a curtain of moonshine that slid down her shoulder and swung gently against the soft curve of her hip.

"Is this real?" His words were a whisper, a thought inadvertently spoken aloud.

She moved toward him, smiling a soft, beguiling smile that made his knees go weak. And suddenly he was afraid of what she was going to say. "Don't say anything," he whispered harshly. "Please, no more . . ."

Her gaze held him captive. "It's real to me, Jack."

He flinched. Was it possible?

Don't think it. Not for a goddamn minute.

But it was too late. He'd already thought it. And he was lost. "You really don't remember how we were . . . before?"

"No."

"God help us," he moaned.

She touched him with a butterfly-soft caress. "Only if we help ourselves, Jack."

He stared at her in horror. The old Amarylis wouldn't have thought a statement like that. Not ever. Not even to hurt him. It implied a caring they'd given up on long ago. A commitment that had ended on the day he returned from the hospital.

He backed away from her and spun around, running blindly away.

"Jack!"

Her voice followed him, spurred him to run faster.

He couldn't help himself, goddamn it, he *believed* her this time. Believed her completely.

It was the most dangerous thing he could imagine.

As Tess watched him run away *again*, her breath expelled in a tired sigh. Disappointment tugged at the corners of her mouth.

"What has she done to you, Jack?" she whispered into the whistling wind. "What?"

She rested her hoe in the broken, rich-looking soil and

leaned wearily on its rounded wooden end, her gaze focused on the lonely figure walking slowly toward the barn. With every step he took, the sinking feeling in her stomach increased.

Stop it, Tess.

She shook her head slightly, forcing the frown from her mouth. She'd spent a lifetime dealing with rejection and disappointing setbacks. And she'd be damned if she'd let them beat her now.

It'll just take time, she reminded herself.

She almost smiled. Time, fortunately, was the one thing she had plenty of.

That, and patience.

Chapter Fifteen

Tess sat back on her heels and studied the supplies laid out on the grass in front of her. There were two pound-sized bags of paint powder, two empty extralarge glass jars, and a can of linseed oil. Sunlight spilled through the leaves of the oak tree and turned the tired old burlap sacks a pale golden hue. Beside her, sprawled in the middle of a huge plaid blanket, Caleb lay quietly.

She shot a quick sideways glance at the small building behind her. Jack was still there, watching her. The knowledge sent a tiny jet of warmth shooting through her—a feeling she studiously tried to ignore. She had a job to do.

Scooting forward, Tess grabbed the largest jar and began pouring in linseed oil with a scientist's precision.

"Are you going to tell me what you're doing or not?"

She didn't take her gaze off the oil splashing in the jar. "Or not."

"Well, I gotta get back to the herd."

She waved over her shoulder. "I will, thanks."

"Will what?"

Tess turned and tossed him a bright smile. "Have fun. I always do. Nice talking to you."

A slow, cautious smile tugged at his lips.

Tess felt the impact of that smile all the way to her toes. She had to force herself not to get up and go to him.

"I better go," he said, indicating the barn.

She nodded. "By all means."

He didn't move, just stood there, arms crossed, hat pulled low, studying her from beneath the brim of his dark hat. Tess felt the heat of his gaze like a caress along her flesh.

Finally he spoke. His words were so quiet, she could barely hear. "Really, you don't have to do that. But it does look good."

Tess's eyebrows drew together in a small frown. "What looks good?"

This time he grinned. "That apple cider you've got there."

Tess couldn't believe it. She smiled. "Why, Jack Rafferty, you *do* have a sense of humor."

His smile faded. Tess felt its loss as acutely as if a cloud had covered the sun. She got quickly to her feet and poured him a glass of cider from the pitcher. "I liked the smile," she said softly, holding the glass toward him.

His fingers curled around the sun-warmed glass just above hers. There was a brush of flesh on flesh, and then slowly he eased the glass from her hands and took a sip. "Thanks."

Tess looked up at him. For a split second she saw him not as he looked at this instant, sipping cider, but as he'd looked ten seconds ago, with a carefree smile transforming his face.

She started to lean toward him. When she realized what she was doing, she froze. Her heart thumped in her chest and her breathing sped up. She'd been going to kiss him again.

Steeling herself, she eased backward. A shaky laugh escaped her.

"What is it?" he asked, but his voice was husky, and she knew that he'd felt it, too, that sudden, unexpected rush of desire.

"I was going to kiss you," she answered simply.

He flinched, swallowed hard. "Oh."

"But I changed my mind." She closed the infinitesimal gap between them. She tilted her face up and gave him a challenging stare. "The next time we kiss, Jack, you'll be the one who starts it."

He gazed down at her, his breathing rushed. His tongue darted out, nervously wet his lips. Tess stared at the glistening trail and felt a gut-wrenching pang of need.

She lurched backward, forcing a bright smile. "Well, I'd best get back to work."

"Yeah. 'Bye." He stared at her for a long, breathless moment, then pivoted and strode away.

Tess watched him leave, a silly, ridiculous grin on her face. For the first time since she'd realized she was falling in love with him, she felt honest-to-God hope. They'd been close there for a moment. Really close.

It was only a matter of time before they got even closer.

Tess was just setting the cradle back in its place below the window when she heard Savannah and Katie come into the yard. She gave the sleeping, just-fed baby a quick kiss on the cheek and hurried out to the porch.

"Hi, girls!" she called out.

"Hi, Mama," they said at once, both smiling.

Tess felt a rush of pride and warmth at their easy smiles. "I have a project planned for us. Here are a couple of old sheets—at least, they *looked* old. I cut out head and arm holes."

Savannah's smile faded. "You did what? But—"

"Come on," Tess said with a laugh, "put them on. We're painting."

Savannah's smile came back. She dropped her lard tin and books on the ground near the bottom step and hurried over to Tess. Katie followed right on her heels.

"Okay," Tess said. "Put them over your head like this." She slipped into one as an example.

The girls put on their sheets and followed Tess to the oak tree, where the paint, paintbrushes, and bedroom curtains were carefully laid out.

"There you go, girls. Go to it."

Savannah cast her a confused glance. "Them are our curtains."

"*Those* are your bedroom curtains," Tess corrected. "And don't you think they're a little . . . dull?"

Both girls looked at the curtains, then back at Tess. Neither of them said a word.

"Well, I do," Tess said. "No child should grow up in a blah room. So fix it."

"You want us to paint our curtains?" Savannah asked.

Tess grinned. "Isn't it a great idea?" She bent down and snatched up two paintbrushes. "Here, take 'em."

Savannah studied the brush as if it were a two-headed snake. "I really don't think—"

"Paint," Tess said firmly.

Savannah kneeled in the lush grass and cautiously dipped her brush in the red paint.

Then, careful not to spill a drop, she started painting a solid red border along the bottom.

Tess waited for a spark of creativity, but none came. Savannah was focused on the border with the concentration of a brain surgeon.

Tess squatted down beside her. "Savannah, honey, do you *like* borders?"

The paintbrush lifted. There was a long pause, then: "No."

"What do you like?"

She shrugged. "I never thought about it."

"Think about it now. What sort of things do you like?"

"I like . . . stars."

"Okay."

"Okay what?"

"Okay, paint stars."

Savannah gave her a surprised look. A smile hovered in the corners of her mouth. "Really?"

"Really. Go on."

Savannah turned back to the curtain. Dipping her brush in the red paint, she scooted closer to the fabric and started her first star.

Tess glanced over her shoulder. Katie was standing as far away from the sheet as she could without losing sight of Savannah's star. Her small hands were curled into fists at her sides.

Tess got to her feet and walked toward her. Katie stiffened and stared at the curtain.

Tess gently smoothed a lock of hair from the girl's face. "It's kind of scary to try something new, isn't it?"

Katie turned to her suddenly. Stark fear had stolen the color from her cheeks. "I ... I can't do stuff like this—remember? I get all ... flustered."

Tess's heart twisted. She had to force her next words past the lump in her throat. "You can. All you have to do is—"

"I *can't*." She stared longingly at the paint. Her voice fell to a throaty whisper. "I wish I could. . . ."

Tess kneeled in the short grass and took Katie by the shoulders, turning her gently until they were face-to-face. "Remember our talk?"

Katie nodded, chewing on her lower lip.

"Okay. Now, let's take this one step at a time. What is it that's hard for you?"

Tears magnified Katie's eyes. She struggled valiantly to keep them back. "I don't write so good. The letters get all mushed together."

"You can paint without having to write."

"I . . . can?"

Tess smiled encouragingly. "Your sister's making stars for her window. How would you like to make rain on yours?"

Katie nodded fervently.

Tess reached for the can of yellow paint and held it up to Katie. "Dip your brush in."

Katie gripped the paintbrush in shaking fingers. Frowning with concentration, she dipped the bristles in the can and gingerly withdrew the brush. Sunshine yellow paint clung in globs to the black tip.

"What now?"

Tess cocked her head toward the curtain. "Fling it."

Katie's mouth dropped open. "You mean just throw paint at the curtain?"

"That's what I mean."

Her eyes rounded to the size of quarters. "But that'll make a big mess."

Tess grinned. "Yep."

"Daddy don't like messes."

"Do you see your daddy around here?"

Her nervous gaze darted around the yard. "N-No."

"Go on," Tess urged with a smile. "Fling it."

Katie took a deep breath and moved closer to the curtain. Squeezing her eyes shut, she flicked her wrist toward the ground. Bright yellow paint flew everywhere, speckling the curtain, the tree, the grass.

"Aah!" Savannah lurched backward just as yellow splattered across her star.

Katie's eyes popped open. When she saw the mess she'd made, humiliation made her lower lip tremble. "I'm sorry, Vannah. I was just—"

Savannah stopped her apology with a smile. "It's beautiful, Katie. Just like the Milky Way."

"It is?" Katie stared down at the yellow-speckled curtain. A slow, cautious smile began to tug at the corners of her small, drawn mouth. "It looks like rain, Mama. It does!"

Tess felt a surge of pride and love so strong, her knees went weak for a minute. Never in her whole life had she been prouder of someone than she was of Savannah at that moment. She nodded. "It sure does, sweetie."

The sun was melting into the pewter-colored sea by the time they finished. Katie's curtain was an explosion of yellow spots and red handprints. Savannah's creation was a perfect Milky Way with hundreds of tiny yellow spots, a crescent moon, and big, bright red stars.

"Last one!" Katie giggled as she flicked her wrist toward the curtain.

At that precise moment, Jack turned the corner and strode into the yard. Yellow paint hurtled through the air and splatted across his face and shirt.

He stopped dead.

There was a moment of stunned surprise, then Tess burst out laughing.

"You think this is funny?" he said incredulously, wiping a particularly large glob out of his eye. It smeared in a war-paintlike streak across his cheekbone. Anger drew his mouth into a grim line.

Tess catapulted past the girls and grabbed his arm. Her yellow-tipped fingers tightened warningly. "Jack Rafferty, if you yell at these children right now, I swear I'll . . ."

"What?"

"Punch you right square in the stomach."

Surprise widened his eyes. Then he did the last thing in the world Tess expected: He laughed. It was a rich, baritone sound that sent heat spilling through her body.

Tess's death grip on his arm lightened, became a friend's touch. "Would you like to see what we've done?"

He nodded. Together they walked over to the girls and kneeled down in the grass. It never occurred to Tess to take her hand from his arm.

He reached out and touched the drying red star.

Savannah turned to him with wide, eager eyes. Her hands were in her lap, twisted together in a pale, nervous ball. "Do you like it?"

He turned to his eldest daughter. "It's perfect."

Savannah's eyes glistened. "Th-Thanks, Daddy."

"What do you think of mine, Daddy?" Katie whispered.

Jack studied her painting very seriously, then gave his daughter a bright smile. "It's wonderful."

Katie looked as if she'd been given the most precious gift in the world.

Jack pushed to his feet. "Now you'd better clean this mess up."

Tess got to her feet beside him. Casually she pressed onto her toes and brushed a paint-globbed lock of hair from his eyes. Their gazes met, held. Something fluttered around Tess's heart and made her breathing quicken. She remembered their kiss, the butterfly-soft meeting of their lips and tongues.

A slow, seductive smile curved her lips. What she felt right now had nothing to do with families, or kids, or even belonging. It was a selfish need to touch this man, to hold him and kiss him and hear the richness of his laugh.

He grabbed her wrist. The smile slid off his face. An infinitely bleak expression filled his eyes. "Do you know what you're doing to me?"

The words were spoken so quietly, and with such despair, that Tess felt as if she'd been punched.

What has she done to you? Tess wanted to cry out. *What?*

Then the fingers encircling her wrist were gone. And so was he.

Jack lay on the couch, the woolen blanket pulled tight to his chin. It had been years since he had slept well; he'd always been so afraid of the nightmare that he lay awake as long as physically possible. Tonight was different. He *longed* to sleep, but his mind wouldn't stop working. He'd been lying here, wide-awake, for countless hours.

Restlessly he shifted from side to side. For the first time in years, the damn couch was acutely uncomfortable. And he knew it had nothing to do with the couch itself.

It was Jack who was uncomfortable.

He wanted to be in his bed. With his wife.

"I was going to kiss you, Jack."

He groaned and rolled onto his back. The window glowed dully in the darkness of the room, its surface tarnished by the pale light of a slivered moon.

"She can't be changing," he whispered aloud, trying to take comfort from the sound of his own voice.

"Could be you got yourself a new wife."

Jack remembered Doc's words again, and this time they seemed edged in a certainty that had been missing before. She *could* be changing.

But could Jack? He'd mistrusted her for so long, lived in the shadow of her hatred and manipulation for so many years. How could he just let go of his armor and let himself believe in her? If he stripped away the sarcasm and anger, he'd be naked to her attack.

And what if it was all a lie? Or temporary? How would he and the kids survive if it was all just another deadly trap? If they became a family and then tomorrow, or the next day, or next week, she turned on all of them and smiled that cold, frightening smile of hers and told them it was all a game . . .

He shivered and drew the blanket tighter against his body.

He'd never been so goddamn confused in all his life.

Sunday morning, Tess got up bright and early. She patted Caleb's shoulder, murmuring soft mommy-babble words to the tiny face resting on her shoulder.

"What do you think, big fella? Is oatmeal, eggs, and bacon enough?"

Caleb made a quiet gurgling sound that seemed affirmative.

Tess kissed his soft cheek. "That's what I thought." Moving toward the hot stove, she peered into the big cast-iron pot and frowned. The oatmeal didn't look too good. Fortunately the eggs and bacon showed definite promise.

She glanced into the living room and saw that Jack was still asleep on the sofa. A soft, wistful smile touched her lips as she stared at him.

He had to be dog-tired. Last night she'd heard him muttering and pacing long after she'd closed her bedroom door. She smiled at the thought. Hopefully he'd been thinking about their kiss.

Moving quietly, she set the table. The tablecloth, silverware, and plates were in place, and she was just arranging the flowers as Savannah and Katie tiptoed into the room.

"Mornin', Mama," they whispered together. Savannah pointed a finger toward the living room. "Daddy's *sleeping.*"

Tess smiled. "I know. Sorta strange, isn't it?"

Both girls nodded.

Tess shot a glance at the mantel clock. "Unfortunately, we're going to have to wake him up or we'll be late for church."

Savannah's eyes bulged. Her mouth dropped open.

Tess had already guessed that the Raffertys weren't a churchgoing family. Savannah's thunderstruck expression only confirmed it.

Tess smiled broadly. Change was good for a family—especially this family. "Is there a problem, Savannah?"

"Daddy won't go to church," she blurted out. "He says God's a hoax."

"I'm sure he meant host. As in heavenly."

Savannah looked skeptical. "I don't think so."

"Well, then it's best if I tell him the plan for today. Why don't you serve up breakfast?"

The girls looked at her as if she were out of her mind, but they didn't say a word. Biting back a smile, Tess headed toward the living room.

As she passed the girls, someone tugged on her sleeve. Pausing, she turned back around.

Savannah had her arms outstretched. "You better give me Caleb. It might get—" color suffused her cheeks "—loud."

Katie nodded solemnly. "Really loud."

This time Tess had to smile. She handed the baby to Savannah, then moved soundlessly toward the sofa. She perched on its hard edge and stared down at Jack's profile. Even in sleep he looked tired and drawn. The stubbly growth of hair that fringed his jawline was thick and black, a stark contrast to the paleness of his skin. Gray-blue shadows smudged his cheeks and discolored the flesh around his eyes. He looked like a man who hadn't slept well in years.

And now she would wake him. Regret nudged Tess and made her reevaluate her plan.

They could go to church next week. Perhaps—

Suddenly Caleb let out an ear-shattering cry. Tess

gasped and spun toward the girls, plastering a finger to her lips.

Jack screamed and bolted upright. His knee came up and rammed into Tess's backside. She slid off the bed and plopped on the floor.

She looked up; he looked down. After a second of confused silence, Tess burst into laughter. Behind her, the girls began to giggle. Caleb drew a shuddering, surprised breath and stopped crying.

The wild, terrified look in Jack's eyes disappeared. He relaxed, unfurling from his board-straight sit, and glanced down at Tess. "Sorry."

She smiled. "Not yet, but you will be."

"What do you mean?"

"I cooked breakfast."

He groaned. "No, thanks, I'll just gnaw on the table leg for a while."

"Leather's closer. Try your shoe."

His mouth quivered in a quickly suppressed smile. Throwing back the thin wool cover, he swung his legs around and stood up, stretching his arms high above his head. His red long johns pulled taut across his chest.

Tess popped to her feet beside him. "You'd better get dressed. We'll be late for church."

He froze midstretch and looked down at her. "I'm not going to church."

She grinned. "Yes you are."

"No I'm not."

She moved toward him, laid her hand on the warm cotton of his sleeve. The heat of his flesh crept through the flimsy fabric and warmed her fingertips. Tilting her face, she gazed into his sleep-puffy eyes. Tiny white lines crisscrossed his flushed cheeks. "Please?"

He swallowed hard. Beneath her fingers, Tess felt the

muscles in his arm tense. "Okay." The word slipped from his lips on a quiet sigh.

She smiled brightly. "You won't be sorry."

He snorted. "You're wrong. I already am."

Chapter Sixteen

The horses moved forward slowly, their hooves striking the hard-packed dirt road in a plodding, thudding gait. Overhead, birds chirped gaily, dipping and diving. The throbbing clang of the school bell filled the air.

At the fence, Jack reined the horses to a stop. Yanking his Stetson low on his forehead, he jumped down and tied the horses to the top rail.

Savannah and Katie climbed down quickly and waited. Tess was saddened to see that their earlier excitement had fled, leaving in its place a stoic silence.

She started to reach for Caleb, but Jack's voice stopped her cold.

"Get me that cider, will you, Lissa?" he asked.

Tess glanced over her shoulder at him, her eyebrow quirked upward in a silent question. She waited patiently for his explanation.

"I—I thought I'd drink some out here while I'm waiting," he said, yanking his collar away from his throat as if it were suddenly too tight.

"And what is it you'll be waiting for?"

"For you to get done with church."

"Oh, that." Tess swept Caleb into her arms and eased herself off the wagon without Jack's help.

Jack smiled. "I knew you'd see it my way. I don't want to go to—"

"Hell. Of course you don't." Tess cut him off with a determined smile. In the stunned silence that followed, she turned to the girls. "Go on inside. I want to speak with your father."

Savannah moved protectively toward her dad. "But—"

"Don't worry, I won't hurt him. Now, run along."

"But—"

"Now," Tess repeated firmly.

The girls grabbed hands. Together they ran pell-mell across the school yard and up the sagging wooden steps, disappearing into the makeshift church without a backward glance.

They know the makings of a good fight when they see one. Smiling, Tess set Caleb's basket down and crossed to Jack, stopping directly in front of him.

He started to back away but was pinned in place by the fence. A hunted, wary look narrowed his eyes. "What do you want now?"

"I want you to go into that church with me and pray."

He gave a harsh, derisive laugh. "For what?"

She felt a wrenching wave of sadness. Never, not in all the long, empty, soundless nights after her mother's death, had Tess ever questioned her faith. It was the bedrock of her soul, and she felt an almost overwhelming pity for this man whose soul was anchored by nothing at all. "Well, for starters, how about an honest-to-God laugh instead of that pitiful, bitter bark?"

He ran a hand through his hair and looked away. "Ah, Christ, Lissa . . ."

"Will you trust me?"

He started to shake his head, then stopped. At his hesitation, her heart soared with hope.

"I won't let you down," she added softly.

He turned to look at her, and there was a bleak hopelessness in his eyes that tore at her heart. "What do you want from me?"

She pressed up on her toes and laid her hand against his cheek. "You don't have to be so alone. God—"

"Ha."

She moved her hand from his cheek to his heart, feeling the thudding beat beneath her palm. "You invoke His name all the time, Jack Rafferty. I know you believe. Or you did once."

He glanced down at the small white hand plastered so protectively atop the faded blue chambray of his shirt. Slowly he lifted his gaze and looked into her eyes. He tried to find a light, bantering response that proved how little he cared about her God, but his throat was dry and swollen with emotion. She was right. Once, long ago, he had believed in God. And in himself.

"You don't have to carry everything inside you, Jack," she said softly. "God will help you. *I* will help you."

God had better help him, he thought dully. Because he wanted to trust her. Christ, how he wanted to; it was like an ache in his soul. And still he couldn't speak. He could only stare down into her warm, loving brown eyes and nod dumbly.

She flashed him a smile that was like a knife in the gut. For a second his knees went weak.

"Come on, let's go," she said.

"Okay," Jack answered in a voice that was a husky shadow of itself.

At her buoyant grin, he felt himself begin to relax. A slow, hesitant smile pulled at his mouth.

"Why, Jack Rafferty, I do believe you're smiling."

He bit down hard and obliterated the smile. "Come on, Lissa, let's get this over with."

He walked over to the basket and picked it up. Forcibly

he kept his gaze off the babe sleeping so quietly inside. Then, together, they walked toward the schoolhouse.

Savannah heard the door open and she cringed. The townspeople had mistrusted her daddy ever since the July Fourth picnic last year when he'd gone crazy. Every head turned as Mama and Daddy walked through the open doorway.

Her parents stood close together—closer than she'd ever seen them. The congregation scrutinized them, eyeing Daddy suspiciously. Sunlight streamed all around them, making them look golden and beautiful.

Neither of them batted an eye, as if they didn't even notice the people studying them. Then Mama did the most amazing thing. She slipped her hand in his.

Daddy jumped at the contact, but he didn't pull away. Instead, he looked down at her. His eyes were wide with wonder. She smiled up at him.

At the front of the schoolroom, the reverend pounded hard on his makeshift pulpit. "Welcome, worshipers," he intoned in his nasal voice. "Today's sermon will be on forgiveness."

One by one the townspeople turned away from the couple at the back of the schoolroom and gave their full attention to the sermon.

The preacher launched into a fevered lecture on the merits of forgiveness, but Savannah couldn't concentrate on his words. She kept thinking about her mama holding her daddy's hand. It gave her a warm, cozy feeling. Every last scrap of doubt about Mama disappeared. If Mama could change, then anything was possible.

Maybe they could even become a real, loving family. Smiling, she closed her eyes and prayed.

Jack stared at the open Bible lying in his lap. The small, yellowed pages should have looked old and dingy against the rough brown wool of his trousers, but somehow they didn't. Quite the opposite, in fact. As he studied the dog-eared, worn pages, he felt a thin strand of hope wending through his thoughts, leaving in its wake the sparkling promise of *maybe*.

He squeezed his eyes shut. For years he'd been praying for help and guidance, but never once in all those times had he believed. The words he'd spoken were meaningless shells, devoid of emotion or hope or trust. Simply the vague, formless longings of a man who'd given up.

Now he wondered if it took more than empty words and end-of-the-line pleas to engage the Almighty. Maybe God, like human beings, demanded more of a man than desperate, soon forgotten prayers. Maybe belief, honest belief, made the difference.

He brought his work-callused hands together, threading his fingers tightly. Resting his clasped hands on the open Bible, he bowed his head.

But the prayer wouldn't come. There were so many things he wanted, so many mistakes to be rectified and sins to be forgiven. The magnitude of it all swallowed his feeble sense of hope and overwhelmed him. Frightened him.

His breathing quickened. Despair sucked him in, pulling his thoughts into the blackness that so often clouded his mind. A man like him, a cowardly, crazy shell, had no right to ask for forgiveness, no right to say, "I need."

At first he hardly felt a thing, but gradually he became aware of warmth seeping into his cold fingers. Then the pressure, gentle and yet firm.

He eased his eyes open and saw his wife's pale hand curled tightly around his own, touching him, protecting him. Wordlessly, without even a glance, she was telling him that she was there. Beside him.

A calmness unlike any he'd ever known spilled through his body, cocooning him in warmth. His fear began to ebb away and was replaced by a quiet, firm belief that his wife had somehow changed. It was real, and he was ready to believe in her.

There's always a beginning, he thought suddenly. *Always.*

He closed his eyes again, and this time there was no jumble in his mind, no confusing morass of fear and desperation and despair. There was only the soul-deep, heartfelt desire of a man to begin again. A man who was ready to believe again in God, and in his wife.

Jack had no idea how long he sat there, head bowed, eyes closed, hands clasped in prayer, seeking help from God. Time dwindled and became unimportant.

It seemed like hours; it seemed like minutes.

"Jack?"

Lissa's quiet voice brought him out of his trancelike state. He lifted his head and opened his eyes. The unexpected light made him blink.

Her hand eased off of his. He immediately felt a sharp stab of loss.

"The sermon's over," she said, standing.

Suddenly it was gone. The calm he'd fought so hard for disappeared, leaving him feeling betrayed and more alone than ever. He strove to find that thread of hope once again, to make himself *believe.*

He found it, buried deep but still intact. He sighed with relief. It hadn't all been a figment of his worthless mind. For once, he'd found something of value within him. All he had to do now was cling to the kernel of hope he'd found. Nurture it. It wouldn't be easy; he'd undoubtedly fail, but for once he wanted—wanted desperately—to try.

Lissa sidled closer, touched his arm. He could smell her scent, wildflowers and promise. Turning, he looked down into her huge, earnest eyes and felt like a man who'd just been let out of jail. He smiled. "Thank you."

"I didn't do anything, Jack," she said quietly. "You did."

Hours later, Jack curled his fingers around the swing's thick, scratchy ropes and planted a booted foot on the plank seat. The wood creaked and groaned. In the falling darkness of night, he stared at the house. Pale light emanated from the open window, carrying with it the scent of roasting meat.

He'd come home. Finally, after all the years of searching and emptiness and doubt, he felt as if he'd come home at last.

A smile spread across his face. Today in church he'd let himself believe in Lissa. In that instant all the emotions he'd hoarded and hidden for years surged to the forefront of his heart, and he'd fallen in love with her all over again.

He was scared—damned scared—but he was excited, too. He felt as if he were perched on the edge of a brand-new life. All he had to do was take a single step forward.

He let go of the swing and sauntered across the yard. From far below came the echoing whoosh of the sea, and the unexpected cry of a hungry gull. The moon shimmered behind a filmy purple cloud.

He bounded up the steps and eased the kitchen door open. The aroma of beef, cooking carrots, cinnamon, and sweet dough greeted him. No one seemed to notice his arrival. Quietly closing the door behind him, Jack glanced around.

Katie was sitting with her back to him, her small body hunched over the kitchen table. In a hesitant voice, she was calling out letters. Savannah sat beside her, drawing pictures of the letter in the air. Caleb was gurgling playfully in his cradle.

Every now and then, Lissa, who was busily checking something in the oven, would gently correct Katie. "No, sweetheart, the word is w-a-s. Was, not saw. Put your finger right under each letter and see if you can tell the difference."

Lissa straightened. The oven door banged shut. "Well, supper's just about ready. Now all we need is your father." She turned and saw Jack standing at the door. Smiling, she wiped her hands on her apron and walked toward him. "And here he is."

Savannah's head jerked up. "Daddy!"

Katie lurched to her feet. Her feet tangled in the chair and knocked it over. The book she was reading skidded across the table and thumped to the floor.

Lissa stopped in front of him, apparently unaware of the bedlam going on around her. She tucked a curly, sweat-dampened lock of hair around her ear and smiled up at him. "You'd better get washed up for supper."

The softness of her voice was almost more than Jack could handle. He had a swift, terrifying urge to take her in his arms and never let her go.

"Jack?"

He cleared his throat. "Sorry. I'll be right back."

He ran for the bedroom and slammed the door behind him. It took him five minutes to change out of his sweat-and-dirt-stained work clothes and five more to calm his racing heart. He paced restlessly back and forth, then sat lightly on the bed's very edge.

He had to get control of his emotions. This thing had to be taken slowly, one step at a time. God knew he didn't feel like humiliating himself again.

"Jack?"

Her voice slid through his turbulent thoughts. He snapped to a board-straight sit and shot a glance at the door. She was peeking just around the corner.

"Supper's ready."

Supper. *Sitting together as a family, holding hands, talking quietly.* The images made him sick with longing. And suddenly he was afraid. Trusting in her was one thing; rejoining the family, being a father, that was another. He wasn't strong enough to do that. He loved his children too much, too desperately, to ever let them down. And sooner or later he let everyone down.

"I'm not hungry."

She breezed into the room in a swirl of marigold yellow skirting and dropped to her knees directly in front of him. For one terrifying moment he thought she was going to touch him, but she didn't. She clasped her fingers together and looked up. "I made the supper myself—most of it, anyway. Savannah told me it was your favorite."

Jack tumbled into her deep brown eyes and was lost. "You made it for me?"

She nodded. Waited.

Don't do it. Don't— "All right."

"Great!" She got to her feet and offered him her hand. He stared at her pale fingers, remembering with crystalline clarity the silky softness of her skin. A numbing coldness crept along his flesh and made him shiver. Trembling, he stood up. God, how those hands had once set him afire. . . .

He swallowed thickly but couldn't look away.

"Jack?" She wiggled her fingers to get his attention.

Slowly, as if every motion were fraught with danger, he reached out and touched her hand. Their fingers threaded together, curled tightly. The moist warmth of her palm made him think of other things, other places.

"Let's go," he said gruffly.

Smiling, she plucked up her skirts and led him out of the bedroom. Through the doorway and down the hall, they walked. She chatted gaily about something—he had no idea what. Nothing got through the jumbled confusion in his mind except the exquisite warmth of her touch.

And then it was gone.

"Here you go, Jack," she said, pulling out his chair.

Jack's trancelike state snapped as clean as a whistle. He watched her bustle toward the stove, then turned his attention to the carefully laid table. In the center of the white-clothed surface was a small, chipped lightning jar filled to overflowing with daffodils and bright red tulips. Each place setting consisted of a blue crockery plate, blue and white napkin, and newly polished silverware. All in all, it looked like a perfect family dinner table.

"I set the table, Daddy. Ain't it—I mean, *isn't* it pretty?" Savannah said shyly as she pulled out the chair next to him and sat down.

Jack turned to his eldest daughter. She was staring at him through eyes that concealed nothing.

She loved him. Still, after everything.

Please God, he prayed, *don't let me disappoint her. Not again . . .*

He swallowed thickly and nodded. "It looks great."

Surprise widened her eyes and crawled in a wash of pink across her cheeks. "Thanks, Daddy."

Lissa set down a huge platter. A small roast was ringed by fried potatoes, carrots, and onions.

When they were all seated, Lissa poured four glasses of milk, then set the pitcher down. "Shall we pray?" she said, placing a hand on either side of her plate. The girls eagerly placed their hands in their mother's.

They were not so quick to hold Jack's hand. Two small heads turned hesitantly toward him.

"Daddy?" Savannah ventured softly.

Jack's heart did a painful twist. Without meeting his daughter's gaze—he couldn't bear to see the uncertainty in her eyes—he brought his hands to the table.

Savannah was the first to take his hand. Warm, slim fingers slid along his upturned palm and slipped between his. Rough, bitten-down nails prickled his flesh. She gave his hand a squeeze, and it was a moment before he realized that *she* was reassuring him.

He stared at the flowers, feeling a sharp sting behind his eyes. He swallowed the thick, bone-dry lump of emotion that lodged suddenly in his throat. *God, how he loved them. Sweet Christ . . .*

"Daddy? Is it okay if I hole your hand?" Katie's quiet voice crept into Jack's thoughts and brought his head up.

Jack looked at his baby girl. She gave him a shy, hesitant smile. Love curled around his heart and squeezed so hard, his chest ached. "I . . . I'd like that."

Katie's mouth dropped open. "You would?"

He nodded, unable to speak.

Katie's pink hand moved across the white tablecloth and slipped into Jack's. His long, brown fingers slipped between her pudgy ones and curled tightly.

"Dear God," Lissa began softly, "we thank you for the many gifts you've bestowed upon this family. And for what we are about to receive, may we be truly grateful."

Jack started to lift his head, but she wasn't done. He quickly dropped his chin again.

"Savannah," she said, "why don't you tell God what you're thankful for."

"I'm thankful for Katie learning to read."

"Katie, honey?"

Katie shifted uncomfortably on her chair. Moisture seeped from her tiny hands and dampened Jack's palms. He detected a tremor in her fingers.

"I-I'm thankful we're eating supper together."

"It's my turn," Lissa said. "I'm thankful for having such bright, beautiful, loving girls to call my children, and such a darling baby boy. Jack?"

Jack flinched. His hold on the girls' hands tightened.

The silence expanded, turned vaguely awkward as everyone waited to hear his answer.

He cleared his throat. "I'm—I'm thankful for my children." Jack blurted out the damning confession, and waited for Lissa to laugh. When she didn't, he cautiously looked up, and found her staring at him. For a second, there was no one sitting at the table except the two of them.

"Amen," she said softly, and the prayer ended. Only this time, they kept holding hands. Everyone looked up. Gazes slid from face to face around the table, and for once, there was no looking away, no awkwardness.

It was Lissa who withdrew her hands first. "So, who wants some of this delicious supper?" she said, reaching for the platter.

"Wait!" Jack said without thinking.

They all glanced up at him, and Jack immediately felt like an idiot. He couldn't imagine what had prompted him to speak. "I . . . uh . . . I mean I'm the father. I'll carve the meat."

He took the carving knife from her and stood up. Towering over the small table, he carefully began slicing the roast.

Lissa and the girls lapsed into quiet conversation. The ordinary sounds of clanking forks and cutting knives peppered suppertime air.

Jack paused, the knife poised at the roast's blackened hump, and glanced around. Lissa was at the foot of the table, cutting her potatoes and talking animatedly about the troubles she'd had in the garden. Katie sat hunched over her plate, her elbows resting on the table as she listened with rapt attention to her mother's story. Savannah was laughing.

Jack felt a surge of emotion so raw and powerful, he went weak. He swayed unsteadily. His hand crashed onto the table and held him upright.

Glasses clinked against crockery plates at the sudden movement. Everyone looked up. Three pairs of concerned eyes landed on his face.

No one said a word.

"Sorry," he mumbled.

The girls turned their attention back to their plates, but Lissa didn't look away. A slow smile curved her lips. She stared at him, and crazily, he felt as if she were seeing inside his soul, seeing that black, twisted place, and finding it not so very dark after all.

"It's nice, isn't it?" she said quietly.

He knew exactly what she was talking about. Glancing at his daughters, then at his wife, he smiled. "Yeah, it is."

After the supper was finished and the dishes washed and put away, Savannah and Katie hurried off to bed. Jack and Tess were left standing in the kitchen. The air thickened with anticipation. Both of them wanted desperately to reach out, but neither one knew how.

"I ... I guess I'd better put Caleb to bed," she said lamely.

He nodded stiffly. "Yeah. I guess so."

They stood there, staring at each other. Waiting. Hoping.

Finally he said, "Maybe ..."

Tess's heart tripped. "Maybe what?"

He yanked on his collar as if it were suddenly too tight. "Maybe we could have a cup of coffee together after you're done."

Warmth spread through Tess. She grinned. "I'd like that."

"You would?"

"A lot."

A hesitant smile tugged at his mouth. "All right. I'll make the coffee."

Smiling, she picked up Caleb and held him to her breast. It was all she could do to keep from skipping out of the room.

Tess fed Caleb in record time, then hurried from her room. Jack was hunched over the hearth, starting a fire. The first tentative red-gold flames licked at the log. Behind him, two cups sat on the rough-hewn table. Aromatic steam wafted through the darkness in swirling streams of gray.

Nerves fluttered in her stomach. She twisted her fingers nervously together. "Hi, Jack."

He dropped the log he was holding. It hit the grate with a thunk. "Hi, Lissa," he said without turning around.

The flames took hold, zipped along the mossy log and burst into a crackling, popping fire.

Tess reached for her coffee and took it in both hands, curling her fingers around the warm cup. The brew's comforting, familiar smell wafted across her nostrils.

She sat down on the couch. Waited.

Jack pushed to his feet and turned around. Reaching down for his coffee, he took a seat beside her on the couch.

They sat there, stiff and afraid, both staring into the dazzling display of fire. The smell of fire and woodsmoke filled the room.

He cleared his throat.

Tess leaned forward, waiting.

"So . . . so you're teaching Katie to read."

Tess smiled. It was a start. "She's making some progress. I've found that if I draw the letter in the air, she sees it better than if it's written on paper."

"She's a smart little thing."

The ache in his voice twisted her heart. *Why?* she wanted to ask. *Why do you keep yourself so apart? What are you afraid of?*

It was the only thing keeping them apart; she was sure of it. If Tess could break through his fear and force him to admit his love for his children, everything would change. They would have a chance. *He* would have a chance.

"She loves you, you know."

Jack stiffened but didn't say a word.

"So does Savannah. Even Caleb—"

"Don't." The word came out as an agonized whisper.

Instinctively Tess set her coffee down and turned to him. Taking his face in her hands, she forced him to look at her. The bleak despair in his eyes was like a knife in her throat. She found it difficult to breathe.

They were close, no more than a hand's span apart. She could feel his proximity like a layer of warmth against her body. The soft, commingled sound of their breathing melded with the crackle and hiss of the fire and filled the small room.

"We're here for you, Jack. All of us. All you have to do is open the door."

"I . . . I want to."

Tess's breathing stumbled. "You do?"

He nodded. "But it's been closed for so long. . . ."

"Maybe . . . maybe we could open it together."

"Together." The quietly spoken word was filled with wonder. Tess smiled. Hesitantly Jack slipped his arm around her shoulders and drew her toward him. They leaned back against the couch's hard back and closed their eyes, each lost in thoughts of the other.

They sat that way until the coffee turned cold and the

fire melted into a dull reddish glow. Sometimes they talked, often they didn't. It didn't seem to matter. For now, for tonight, it was enough just to be together.

Chapter Seventeen

Savannah burst into the kitchen, clutching her side. "I'm back, Mama," she said breathlessly.

Katie looked up from her primer, which lay open on the kitchen table.

Tess was lying on the floor, with Caleb on her stomach. "Hi, honey," she said, curling her arm around the baby and getting awkwardly to her feet. "What did Minerva say?"

"She said she'd love to go for a walk with us. We're supposed to give her ten minutes, then come on over."

Tess smiled. Ten minutes was perfect. It gave her just enough time to set her plan in action. She'd told Jack she'd help him open the door to his heart. And she was going to do just that.

"Okay, girls, run into your room and put on your work dresses. I'll throw a few things in a basket and we'll be off."

Tess hurried into her bedroom and pulled a long, navy-striped muslin skirt and pretty calico scoop-necked blouse from her armoire. Dressing quickly, she braided her waist-length hair and threw on a serviceable white sunbonnet.

She was ready to begin.

"Okay, Caleb," she murmured softly, stroking his silky thatch of black hair, "it's time." Placing him gently in his cradle, she turned to leave.

She hadn't even made it to the door when he burst out crying.

Perfect. Tess gave him a soothing smile. "Don't worry, honey, you'll be okay in a minute." With a last lingering look at him, she headed out of her room and strode into the kitchen. Savannah and Katie were waiting.

"Okay," Tess said, plucking the basket of supplies off the table. "Let's go."

Savannah's smile faded. "But Caleb's in the bedroom...."

Tess grinned. "Oh? Did I forget to mention that this was a 'girls only' expedition? We have serious business to attend to, and a baby would get in the way."

Katie and Savannah exchanged confused glances, then spoke at once. "But who's gonna watch him?"

Tess's lips twitched traitorously. "Your father."

They gasped.

Tess waved her hand in an airy gesture of impatience. "Let's go."

"But he's cryin', and Daddy won't—"

"Trust me. Now, we'd best get moving. Mrs. Hannah is waiting." Tess breezed past the gape-mouthed girls and left the house. Furious whispering erupted in the kitchen and followed Tess down the steps.

She had just passed the chicken coop and was halfway to the barn when they made up their minds.

"Wait, Mama!" Savannah yelled.

Tess paused and turned around. "Well, hurry up. We haven't got all day."

Grinning, the two girls bounded down the steps and ran to catch up with her.

Jack was splitting fence rails behind the barn when they reached him. He paused in his work and pushed the tired old hat off his forehead, swiping the sweat from his brow with the back of his arm.

"Hi, Jack." Tess carefully shielded the contents of the baby basket in her arms. "How are you?"

"Fine." He glanced at the girls, noticing their drab, much-washed work clothes. "Where are you girls going dressed like that?"

Savannah shrugged. "Mama's takin' us someplace special."

Katie nodded solemnly. "We got wimmen's work to do."

Jack smiled down at her. "Do you, now? Well that's mighty important. Have a good time."

"Jack," Tess said solemnly, "I left something in the house for you."

Katie let out a quick giggle and immediately smothered it with her pudgy hand.

Jack shot his youngest daughter a questioning look. Then he looked back at Tess. "What is it?"

Tess was the picture of innocence. "A surprise."

"Really?"

Savannah struggled with a smile of her own. "You'll be real surprised, Daddy."

Jack set down his ax. "All right, then. See you soon."

Tess let her grin loose. "Great. 'Bye."

" 'Bye, Daddy," the girls said together.

Jack frowned at them. " 'Bye." The word came out in a slow, confused drawl, as if he suddenly suspected something very strange was going on.

It is, Jack, Tess thought. *Welcome to fatherhood.*

"Come on, girls," she said, "let's go." With a quick wave, Tess and the children took off through the hilly pasture at a run.

Jack watched them run through the tall grass and crawl under the fence at the far end of the field. The carefree sound of their giggling peppered the cool spring air.

Curling his thumbs around his fraying red suspenders,

he strode purposefully to the house. His bootheels drove deeply into the dirt road, crunching over pebbles with each step. He passed the shady oak tree and climbed the porch steps.

He hadn't even opened the back door when he heard crying.

Jack's step slowed. Dread, as cold as ice water, spilled down his back and made him tremble. No, he thought desperately. *She wouldn't have done that to me. She wouldn't have* . . .

Cautiously he opened the door. High, bleating screams echoed through the house.

"Oh, my God." Jack spun around and bounded down the steps, racing down the dirt road. *"Lissa!"* He screamed her name, but the sound was lost within seconds, vanished in the breeze. There was no answer.

He shot a frightened look back at the house. Even from here, he could hear the reed-thin echo of Caleb's crying.

Jack's hands curled into shaking fists. Panic rushed through him and made his breathing speed up. *Oh, God, oh, God, oh, God—*

"Stop it," he yelled at himself. Slowly, one breath at a time, he forced himself to calm down. He squeezed his eyes shut. *You asked God—and Lissa—for a new start. This is it. Don't be such a goddamn coward.*

He lifted his head and looked back at the house. The plaintive echo of Caleb's wail rode the breeze and beckoned Jack. There was no one else to help the baby.

His son.

Swallowing a thick, acrid lump of fear, he forced himself to return to the house. The door creaked open and banged shut behind him. He felt another surge of fear.

What if he hurt him? What if he had a blackout? What if—

"Enough." Lifting his chin, he crammed his fists against his thighs and walked slowly toward his wife's bedroom.

He pushed open the closed door and stood in the doorway. Through the slats of the cradle he'd made, he could see Caleb's tiny body writhing, his small fists batting at the air. The blue blanket was a twisted heap along his side.

Jack tried to move, but couldn't. Fear and dread immobilized him. He was afraid, desperately afraid, to reach out to this child—his own son—and try.

The realization made him sick. His stomach twisted into a knot. He was such a coward, such a goddamn useless coward.

Caleb sucked in a shuddering breath, and there was a moment of blissful silence.

Jack's own breathing stumbled. Maybe he wouldn't have to move, maybe—

Then Caleb started up again. This time his cry was a high-pitched, quavering wail that pinged down every vertebra in Jack's tightened spine.

He's afraid, too.

The thought came out of nowhere. He tried to talk himself out of it, tried to tell himself the baby was hungry or sleepy or just plain mad, and that he couldn't possibly know what the hell his son was feeling. None of the feeble explanations made any difference.

He couldn't make himself believe them. *Your son is alone and he's afraid. He needs you.*

"Not me," he whispered. "He needs a father. Not some broken-down shell . . ."

You're all he's got.

He moved hesitantly forward. With each step a noose seemed to tighten around his throat. By the time he reached the cradle, Jack was trembling and couldn't breathe worth shit.

Shakily he kneeled. "Hi, fella, what's the matter?"

Caleb cried harder.

Jack edged closer and reached over the wooden railing, touching his son's tear-moistened face. "There, there."

Jack felt like an idiot. His voice was thick with emotion, and he couldn't think of a single thing to say. What the hell good was "there, there" to a baby who wanted to be comforted?

Cautiously he let his fingers slide under Caleb's tiny back and curl soothingly under his arm. The warm contact seemed to have some effect. Caleb hiccuped loudly and drew in a shaky breath. His tiny fists unfurled.

A tiny thread of hope crept through Jack's fear. He brought his other hand to the cradle and gently picked Caleb up.

Caleb blinked up at him in surprise. Huge, quivering tears clung to his tiny lashes.

Jack stared down at the small, beet red face and felt a fierce wave of love. He pressed the baby tightly against his chest, and walked slowly to the bed.

He sat down with a sigh of relief. He hadn't dropped Caleb. *Thank God.*

When his heart stopped racing, he stretched out on the soft tick and let his iron-hard hold ease. Caleb lay quietly on Jack's chest, his murky blue-gray eyes fixed on Jack's face.

He's knows, Jack thought tiredly. He knows what a feeble excuse for a father I am.

Then Caleb yawned and blinked heavily. His eyelids fluttered shut. With a final sputtering sound, he pushed his thumb in his mouth and laid his head on Jack's chest. He was asleep in moments.

Jack lay there, stiff as a knife blade, afraid to move lest he disturb the sleeping baby. He stared in awe at the small, black-haired head pressed so trustingly against his chest. An odd sense of peace slid through Jack's body as he watched his son sleep. Without thinking, he brought his hand up and stroked Caleb's soft cheek.

He doesn't know, Jack thought suddenly. Caleb had no idea his daddy was a coward, and a crazy one at that. He didn't know Jack wasn't worthy of unconditional love. He knew only that without his parents, he was alone.

Try.

That's all Lissa had asked of Jack. That he try. Try to be a father, try to express his love for his children.

He wanted to. Christ, how he wanted to. But he was afraid. What if he tried and failed? Wasn't that worse than not trying at all? Better to be no parent, as his own father had been, than to be a father who hurt his children. . . .

Try.

Don't do it. You'll fail. You'll hurt them all.

Of course he'd fail—that was a given. He'd failed at everything he'd ever tried.

They deserve better, Jack. He glanced down at Caleb, and this time it was Jack's eyes that filled with burning tears. Emotion curled around his heart and squeezed so hard, his whole body ached.

He swallowed thickly, tasting the metallic aftertaste of tears. He owed them a father who at least tried.

The way it was now, he was being the father he'd been taught to be. The realization sickened and shamed him. Hadn't he sworn not to extend the circle of pain begun by his own self-centered, silently cruel, unforgiving parents? Hadn't he and Johnny sworn it together?

Johnny.

Jack let out his breath in a pain-filled sigh. He and Johnny had sworn to be good, loving parents. But Johnny never had the chance to fulfill that vow.

Jack had the chance, but he'd thrown it away. He was so afraid of failing, he'd never let himself even try.

In church he'd vowed to make a new beginning.

Don't be afraid. Be a man. For once, be a man. . . .

"Please, God," he murmured, "show me the way. Show me what to do. . . ."

He closed his eyes and prayed. And for the first time in many, many years, he was absolutely certain someone was listening.

Jack woke to the sound of laughter. He blinked sleepily and pushed up to one elbow, careful not to disturb Caleb, who was still sleeping peacefully against Jack's chest. He cradled the baby in his arms, staring down at his son's perfect, innocent face.

There was the sound of feet thumping down the hallway, then Katie burst breathlessly into the bedroom. "Hi, Daddy!" she said with a gap-toothed grin. "We got somethin' for you."

Savannah came up behind her sister, and she, too, was smiling broadly.

Jack lifted one eyebrow derisively. "Another surprise?"

Katie's smile fell, and Jack immediately cursed his thoughtless sarcasm. He forced a smile. "If it's half as good as the last one, I'll be happy."

Katie grinned again. "It is, really and truly."

She and Savannah hurried to his bedside. "Don't look, Daddy; close your eyes."

Jack did as he was told. He heard the rattling clank of little hands pawing through half-empty buckets.

"Okay," Savannah said, "open your eyes."

Jack opened his eyes and found himself staring at four shallow, wooden-framed boxes that were lined carefully against the foot of the bed. Each box had a pressed, perfect-looking flower fastened to its slatted back, and beneath each flower was a single word. Together they read: *Happy Father's Day, Daddy.*

Jack's throat closed up. Emotion rendered him speechless.

"Happy Father's Day, Jack," Lissa said quietly from the doorway.

Jack turned to look at her, and immediately felt as if he'd been punched in the heart. She looked breathtakingly beautiful. Her hair was a leaf-and-twig-infested curtain of honey gold that slid down her arms and curled against her hip. Her pale skin had been darkened to a peachy pink by the warm sun, and her full mouth was curved in a heart-breaking smile.

He swallowed thickly. "What's Father's Day?"

A frown passed across her brow, then disappeared. "Oh. I guess I just invented it. It's supposed to be in June sometime, but I figured May was close enough." She smiled. "It's a day to tell your father how much he means to you. How ... much you love him."

"Daddy? Are you okay?" Savannah asked quietly.

Daddy. The word twisted Jack's heart. He hadn't been much of one to her—probably couldn't be if he tried. But he was sick and tired of pretending not to care. Tired of living in an isolated, lonely world full of aching silences and wrenching regrets.

Don't do it. You'll fail. At the thought, Jack felt a rush of fear. It was easier somehow to be a father to Caleb; he was an infant. Caleb wouldn't know for years if his father had failed. Even Katydid might not notice, but Savannah was different. She was older, wiser. She'd see. She'd know he'd tried to be something he couldn't. She'd know he failed, and the failure would break both their hearts.

I won't fail.

But this time the words didn't matter. Maybe he would fail, he thought tiredly, and maybe he wouldn't. But one thing he knew for sure—had always known—was that not trying was the biggest failure of all.

Enough was enough, he decided. God had given him this chance for a new beginning—given it to all of them. And Jack wouldn't run away this time. He wouldn't be a coward again.

He turned slightly and gave Savannah a bright, love-filled smile. "I'm fine. Now, why don't you two climb on up here and tell me how you made these wonderful boxes."

Savannah and Katie clambered on either side of him, sitting close, and began animatedly talking about flower picking and pressing.

Jack felt as if a thousand-pound weight had been lifted from his back. A warm sensation began in the pit of his stomach and spilled outward, radiating a sense of peace throughout his body. Tentatively he curled an arm around each girl's shoulder. Savannah and Katie immediately snuggled closer.

He laughed at something Katie said and looked up.

Lissa was still standing in the doorway, looking at him. Tears magnified her eyes. He was somehow certain that she knew how hard today had been. And that she was proud of him for making the effort.

Love for her washed through him in an overwhelming wave. "Thanks," he mouthed.

Eyes sparkling, she smiled. Then, plucking up her burr-dotted skirts, she came over and climbed up onto the bed, gently drawing Caleb into her arms. Savannah moved over to make room for her. Katie snuggled closer on Jack's lap.

As his loved ones came closer, clustered around him, Jack felt the most powerful emotion he'd ever felt in his life.

For the first time ever, they were a family.

Chapter Eighteen

That night, Tess sat on the swing, her fingers curled loosely around the rough ropes, and swung very slowly, letting her bare feet drag on the cold, dark earth.

She closed her eyes. The sounds of the night mesmerized her. The distant, echoing whoosh of the sea on the rocks and sand below, the airy cant of an early evening breeze, the shuffling movement of sheep settling down for the night.

She didn't take a single sound for granted; instead she focused on them one at a time, marveling in them all and the miracle it took for her to hear them.

"Lissa?"

Tess snapped upright and saw him standing on the porch, a tall, black shadow against the charcoal gray of the house.

Just looking at him made her heart speed up, her throat go dry. His name slipped from her lips and was lost in the breeze. Her fingers tightened around the scratchy rope.

"I . . ." He moved, his footsteps a quiet thudding across the wooden porch. Then he stopped. "I'm going to bed."

Take me with you. Tess swallowed hard, trying to still her racing heart. "Why are you telling me?"

It took him forever to answer. Tess leaned forward, waiting. *Ask me, Jack. Just hold out your hand to me. . . .*

"I wanted to say good night."

"Oh." Tess's hands unfurled, slid down the ropes, and landed in her lap. "Good night."

He stood there for a while longer. Tess felt his gaze on her and knew he was trying to summon the courage to stay. Perhaps even to come closer.

"Well . . . good night." He turned and disappeared into the house. The door creaked quietly shut behind him.

Tess let out her breath in a disappointed sigh. Standing, she hugged herself and walked idly around the tree. Tiny pebbles clung to her bare feet as she wandered across the dirt road and headed into the grass. Thin, swaying stalks tickled her ankles.

She stared at Haro Strait far below, its shimmering gray-black surface streaked by a single, wobbling finger of blue-white moonlight. Stars danced like fallen diamond chips across the night sky.

She knew what she wanted to do right now, but she was afraid. The realization irritated the hell out of her. Never in her life had she been a coward, and yet now, faced with the greatest opportunity of her life, she was skulking outside like a frightened kitten. Waiting.

It didn't make sense. Adversity had always spurred her to accept greater and greater challenges. When they told her a deaf girl couldn't be a doctor, she proved them wrong; when they told her she might be able to get an education, but she'd never be able to find employment, she proved them wrong again; and when they'd told her cancer didn't have a cure, she'd dedicated her life to changing that.

But somehow all of those challenges paled in comparison to this one. Then, she'd risked being laughed at or, at worst, failing where few had ever succeeded. Here, with Jack, she was risking something greater, something infinitely more precious.

Her chance to belong.

What if he laughed at her, or turned her away? What if all the loving glances and quiet smiles were in her mind, a figment of her own love-starved imagination?

Then you'll get hurt. The answer came as easily as the question. Surprisingly, it calmed her down.

She'd been hurt before, and she'd always survived. If the worst happened tonight and Jack rejected her, she'd get over that, too.

Someone had to take a chance here; that much was obvious. Both she and Jack were desperately afraid of being hurt, and they were both immobilized by that fear.

No more, Tess decided suddenly. She had a chance here—a chance she'd waited for all her life. A chance she'd died to find. And she wasn't going to throw it away because of a few fluttery nerves and old anxieties.

If Jack rejected her, she'd simply wait for another opportunity and try again. And again and again and again.

Jack was her future, her destiny, and she wasn't about to walk away from him.

Jack sat stiff as a board on the sofa, the blanket thrown haphazardly across his knees, his hands coiled in his lap.

The house was still and quiet. Every now and then a breeze rattled the windowpane behind him, but other than that transient noise and the quickened tenor of his breathing, the place was silent. In the kitchen a lone candle sat on the table, its glow splashing across the white tablecloth.

Then he heard it. The doorknob was turning.

Jack's heart picked up speed, thudded in his ears. The door squeaked and whined, then clicked shut.

Lissa picked up the candle and moved toward him. Wreathed in pale, golden candlelight, she looked like an angel. Honey-hued hair curled riotously across her brow and hung in undulating waves along her arms. Her eyes, an even deeper brown in the uncertain light, glowed like pools of promise against the creamy oval of her face. The white eyelet of her stand-up collar looked fragile against the curve of her neck.

"Jack?"

He tensed. "Yeah?"

"I've made a decision."

"Should I ask?"

She came toward him. As she got closer, he could see that she was smiling, a soft, beguiling smile that made his breathing speed up even more. "Probably not."

She set her candle on the table in front of him. The metal holder clanked down hard. Light spilled across the scarred wooden surface and cast the area between them in pale gold. Straightening, she stared down at him. For a second, he thought she was going to come closer.

He tensed. But she didn't move. She just stood there, hair cascading in a golden waterfall around her face, hands clasped at her waist, staring down at him.

His throat felt so dry, it was difficult to speak. "W-What do you want?"

"How long have we been married?"

Confusion made him stutter. "Thirteen y-years or so."

She nodded. "And how long have you been sleeping in another room?"

Jack knew suddenly where this conversation was going. Emotions hurtled through him—fear, excitement, hope. He licked his paper-dry lips and said quietly, "Ever since I got out."

She frowned. Jack saw his mistake instantly. She didn't remember about the hospital or his "injuries."

"Out of where?"

He didn't answer, and after a few silent moments, she asked again. "How long on the couch, Jack?"

"Almost eight years."

She looked down at him again, and the look in her eyes

was infinitely soft and welcoming. Longing twisted his insides into a throbbing knot. "That's a long time."

"Yeah."

"Long enough."

Jack froze, swallowed. "What are you saying?"

She drew in a deep, shaking breath. He could see that she was nervous, perhaps even afraid, but she was going forward anyway. "I'm saying a husband and wife should sleep together."

Jack moved slowly to a sit. "Sleep . . . together?"

"Yes,"

Jack didn't move, didn't even breathe. It was closing in on him, stalking him, turning his every rational thought into a pile of imperceptible rubble. Need. Dark, aching, drenching need.

She reached her hand out. It was pale and trembling in the weak candlelight. "Come to bed, Jack."

He shook his head slowly. "I don't think—"

"Good. Don't."

"Jesus, Lissa." He said her name on a quiet exhalation of breath.

She moved toward him quickly, a flash of white lawn in the candlelight, and dropped to her knees. Jack stared into her eyes and was completely and utterly lost. She was breathtakingly beautiful, so beautiful, it hurt to look at her.

Smiling, she touched his face. Her flesh felt warm and solid and *right* against his cheek. He shivered in response and fell that much further under her spell. "Don't be afraid," she breathed.

Jack sighed and tried to look away, but she wouldn't let him. Her hand held his face firmly in place; her eyes remained fixed on his.

"Please . . ." she murmured.

Jack looked deeply into her eyes, searching for some hint that it was all a lie, but even as he studied her, he knew the truth. This was no act, no game. She wasn't Amarylis anymore. She was Lissa, and she was reaching out to him.

God help him, he couldn't turn his back on her. Not even if someday Lissa vanished as quickly as she'd come. She was his wife, had been for almost half his life. He'd loved her since he was a boy. And he loved her now.

She leaned toward him, so close he could feel the whispering threads of her breath against his lips. His groin swelled, tightened uncomfortably. His throat went bone-dry.

She licked her lower lip slowly, her gaze never leaving his face. "Maybe . . ." She hesitated, blinked, and Jack got the sudden feeling that now it was she who was afraid. She started to look away.

Without thinking, he touched her chin and gently but firmly forced her to look at him. "Maybe what?"

"Maybe we could . . . fall in love again."

Jack didn't know what he'd been expecting her to say, but it sure as hell wasn't that. He'd known her for a long time, since they were both kids running around his daddy's cotton fields, and never—not once—had she ever told him she loved him. Oh, she'd shown him. In the early days, before the horror and the war, she'd shown him all the time. But never had she voiced the words. As a young man, he'd waited, aching inside, to hear the simple sentence. And now here she was blithely wondering if they could fall in love. Again.

He shook his head. "Where would we even start?"

She smiled. "Jack." His name sounded soft, and blurred, and filled with exquisite promise. "We already have."

We already have. Tess said the simple words and held her breath. Fear washed through her, made her heart hammer in her chest. Now, waiting for his response, she felt naked and vulnerable and almost dizzy with longing.

Please, she thought desperately, *please don't turn me away. Please . . .*

"We have to go slow," he said quietly. "I'm not too . . . trustworthy."

A river of relief rushed through Tess. A smile trembled on her lips. "Anything, Jack . . ."

He shook his head, frowning. Regret and shame darkened his eyes. "I've let you and the girls down so many times."

Love poured through Tess, filling every corner of her soul with light. She knew how much that confession had cost him.

"Oh, Jack." She leaned toward him, brushed the hair from his eyes with cold, shaking fingers. "Maybe we've hurt each other."

Their gazes met and held. Beside them, the candle sputtered.

"I need time, Lissa," he said quietly. "I've spent a long time trying to fall out of love with you, and frankly, it scares the shit out of me to think of going back."

"I don't want to go back to another woman's past. I want to go forward . . . into a future that's all ours."

"Christ, Lissa." He squeezed his eyes shut and ran a shaking hand through his hair.

Tess stared at his mouth and felt a sharp, almost painful stab of longing. *Kiss me,* she thought. *Now, before I break my promise . . .*

But he didn't move, didn't seem even to breathe.

God, how she wanted him to kiss her right now. She'd dreamed of it constantly since that day on the schoolhouse steps. Like a child reaching for the forbidden piece of candy on the counter, she strained forward. Wanting, needing.

And still he didn't move.

"Jack . . ." His name was a whispered question, a proposal. "Make love to me, Jack."

"Aw, hell." His voice sounded raw and defeated as he opened his eyes and looked down at her. Slowly his hands slid around her neck and up the sides of her face. His fingers burrowed into the golden mass of her hair and pulled her inexorably toward him.

Their lips touched. The kiss was slow and hesitant, filled with the quiet, desperate longing of a man who'd been in love alone for so long, he couldn't believe in anything else, and a woman who'd never been in love at all.

It seemed to go on forever, until Tess was dizzy and her body tingled all over. The hunger in his kiss, the need, filled Tess to overflowing and stole the breath from her lungs.

Then, slowly, he drew back and looked at her. "God, you're beautiful."

She drew a shaky breath and smiled. "So are you."

His hand glided down her throat, moving slowly, as if he were savoring the velvet-soft feel of her flesh. His fingers slipped under the thin lawn of her nightgown and glided over the swell of her breast. She shivered at the heat of his touch.

"Mama? Are you in there?"

Tess yanked away from Jack with a gasp, clutching her gaping nightgown to her chest. *Katie!*

Heart pounding, Tess staggered to her feet. "Y-Yes, honey?"

"I heard a noise."

Behind her, Jack laughed quietly. "It was probably your breathing."

Tess bit back a smile. "Shh!"

"Who are you talkin' to, Mama? Is Daddy in there?"

"Yeah, honey, your daddy and I were just . . . talking."

Tess crossed the room and kneeled in front of Katie, taking the child in her arms. "Honey, you're trembling."

"I'm scared."

Tess smoothed a sweat-dampened lock of hair from Katie's face. "Would you like a cup of warmed milk or something?"

Katie shook her head.

"Well, what would you like? How about if we—"

"I wanna sleep with you."

Tess's stomach sank. She shot a despairing glance at Jack. She was just about to say no when she turned and looked into Katie's wide, frightened eyes.

This was important, she realized. Katie was asking something of her mommy, and Tess couldn't turn the child away. Katie might never trust her enough to ask again.

"Okay, honey. You go on in; I'll be there in a second."

"I'll wait for you." Katie popped a pudgy pink thumb in her mouth.

Tess tried to smile. Reaching down, she took Katie's hand, and together they headed for the bedroom. At the corner she paused, turned back around. Jack was sitting on the couch, staring at her with an enigmatic smile.

Tess felt a sharp pang of regret. "Sorry," she mouthed.

He nodded, still smiling. "Later."

A thrill raced through Tess at the thought. Then, with a sigh, she turned and went to her room.

The knock, at first, was so quiet, Tess almost missed it.

"Mama?" Katie tugged on her sleeve. "There's someone at the door."

Tess sat up. Her heart was beating so loudly, she was sure Katie could hear. "Jack? Is that you?"

He opened the door and peeked his head around. "Lissa . . . I'm scared."

Tess burst out laughing. Jack grinned.

Katie looked from Tess to Jack and back to Tess again. There was a small, confused frown on her face.

"Well," Tess drawled. "There's plenty of room. You can sleep on the other side of Katie."

Jack climbed, fully clothed, into bed beside Katie.

"Leave the candle on till I go to sleep, okay?" Katie mumbled, her little eyelids already drooping.

Tess smiled down at her. "Sure, honey."

The three of them snuggled under the thick quilt. Katie curled up against her Mama and went to sleep.

When Katie was sleeping soundly, Tess pushed up onto one elbow and looked at Jack. "Tell me something so I know you better tomorrow than I did today."

Humor glinted in Jack's eyes. He opened his mouth to speak, then closed it. The humor in his gaze vanished, and a dark, formless pain filled his eyes. He glanced down at Katie's head. He brought a hand up, as if to stroke her hair, and Tess could see the tremble in his fingers.

Tess stared at his hand, hovering so close above his daughter's head—close, but not close enough—and she felt tears burn behind her eyes. When he began to draw his hand away, she grabbed it. Their eyes met, and in the troubled green depths she saw his indecision, his fear. "It's okay," she whispered. "Don't be afraid."

He licked his dry lips and slowly, so slowly, lowered his hand to Katie's head and began stroking her curly hair. "Katie . . ." His voice thickened, and Tess could see by the pain in his eyes that it was killing him to speak. "My Katydid. No one's ever dried her tears, or rocked her to sleep, or told her she was loved."

Tears burned Tess's eyes, streaked in hot, wavering lines down Tess's cheeks. "Oh, Jack . . ."

He looked up suddenly, and over Katie's small, dark head, their gazes locked. The bleak desperation in his eyes tore ragged slices from her heart. "If you can change anything, Lissa, change that."

Tess's hand moved over the slim hump of Katie's body and found Jack's. Their fingers threaded into a warm knot.

"I can't do it alone, Jack."

He gazed at her for a long time, then slowly, quietly, he spoke. "Okay. We'll do it together."

Smiling, holding hands across the child, they fell asleep.

Chapter Nineteen

Someone banged hard on the back door. "Jack! Are you there?"

Jack came awake with a start.

"What . . . huh? Whaas going on?" Lissa lifted her head and blinked hard, trying to focus.

Jack stared across Katie, who was still asleep, at his wife. She looked unbelievably sexy, with her hair all messed up and her cheeks flushed from sleep. Desire flashed through his body like a bolt of lightning. "There's someone at the door," he said in a husky voice. "I'll be right back."

Thankful now he hadn't undressed last night, Jack hurried through the cold, dark house and opened the back door.

Jim Hannah stood on the porch, dressed in his old work dungarees and straw hat. "I know you didn't expect us till day after tomorrow, Jack, but Clyde Johnson's wife took sick. They had to take her to Victoria to see some special doctor."

Jack squinted into the predawn darkness and saw three men standing out on the dirt road. "Who you got with you?"

"A couple of Indians and Jerry Sikes. We thought we'd do your herd today and tomorrow, then move over to mine."

"Sikes doesn't mind working with me?"

Jim looked uncomfortable. "Well, truth to tell, he's a mite . . . concerned. But I told him you were a friend of mine."

Jack nodded. "Thanks, Jim. I'd been wondering how you and I were going to shear all these sheep alone."

Jim grinned, obviously relieved by Jack's easy acceptance of Sikes's anxiety. "It shouldn't take us more'n a couple days now."

"Great. I'll throw on my work clothes and meet you in the barn in fifteen minutes."

Jack raced back into the bedroom and found Lissa dozing again. Quietly he dressed in his work clothes, then went to the bed and dropped to his knees.

She was turned toward him, her profile like a pale, perfect cameo atop the grayed pillow. Desire shot through him like a molten streak as he stared at her full, parted lips. The quiet whirring of her breath caressed him. God, she was beautiful.

"Lissa?" he whispered, stroking the velvet-soft side of her face. "Wake up."

She blinked awake. At first she looked confused, then she saw Jack and gave him a slow, lazy smile that made him ache to crawl in bed beside her. "Mornin', Jack."

"Mornin', Lissa. Jim Hannah and the men are here to help me shear the sheep."

She brushed a lock of hair from his eyes. "Sounds like hard work."

"It is. Backbreaking."

Disappointment flickered through her eyes. "I guess you'll be tired tonight."

He grinned. "Not that tired."

"Promise?"

He leaned over and gave her a rousing kiss. "I promise."

* * *

McGuffey's First Eclectic Reader lay open on Katie's school desk. She stabbed her forefinger under the letter and stared at the page. Concentration pulled her mouth into a taut frown. The letters danced around and mixed themselves up, but she just took a deep breath like her mama had taught her and tried again.

It was easy to calm herself down now. Being in school didn't cause that horrible panic and fear anymore. Miss Ames had promised not to call on her to read out loud until Katie herself said she was ready, and knowing that she wouldn't be embarrassed freed her to concentrate on the task at hand: learning to read.

B-A-R-N. Barn. Barn! It said barn.

Katie felt like she was gonna float right off the chair. Grinning, she poked Savannah in the side. "It says barn, Vannah. I read it!"

Savannah gasped and threw her arms around Katie, squeezing hard. "Oh, Katie. You done it!"

Miss Ames rapped her stick down on her desk. "What's going on back there, Savannah and Mary Katherine? We're in the middle of reading."

Savannah's arms popped free. She slid back into her own chair and folded her hands on her desk. "Sorry," she mumbled.

"I read 'barn,' Miss Ames," Katie said proudly. "All by myself."

Miss Ames's stern face softened. "That's wonderful." Her voice sounded sort of funny, and she cleared her throat. Snapping her chin up, she sniffled softly and glanced around the room. "You may take your break now. Run along."

Everybody bent down and grabbed their lard tins and beelined for the outside. The sound of running, shuffling feet echoed through the small wooden building.

Katie and Savannah walked to their regular spot beneath the big tree and plopped down onto the short grass. Burrowing through their tins, they pulled out the cornbread and bacon sandwiches Mama had made.

"I think Miss Ames was proud of you," Savannah said with a smile.

Katie grinned back. "I think so, too."

Savannah started to say something else, then stopped. Her gaze fixed on something behind Katie.

Katie turned, following the path of Savannah's trancelike stare. Jeffie Peters was standing by the water pump. He was staring at Savannah with a dumb expression on his face.

Katie frowned and looked back at her sister. Savannah's cheeks were bright pink.

"Why don'tcha go talk to him?"

"What? Huh, Katie, what did you say?"

Katie smiled. "I'll be right back." Setting down her food, she got to her feet and walked, arms swinging, to the water pump. "Hey, Jeffie."

He was startled out of his trance. "Oh. Hi, Katie."

"Why don'tcha go talk to Vannah? Maybe she'd like to go to the shearin' dance next week."

"But your mama—"

"She ain't so strict no more. I think she'd let us all go if we wanted to. My daddy don't like the Fourth o' July none, but the shearin' dance might be all right."

He grinned. "Really? Thanks, Katie, I'll do that." Without a backward glance, he raced over to Savannah. She looked up, shielding her eyes from the sun. Katie yanked up her skirts and ran across the dirt road, skidding beside Savannah just as Jeffie was finishing his question.

". . . Do you think she'd let you go?"

Savannah blushed and stared down at the cornbread in her hands. "I think she might."

"Great! Well . . ." Jeffie looked as if he was trying to think of something else to say.

Tired of the silence, Katie butted in. "Ain't you two gonna talk or somethin'?"

"Hey, Jeffie!" yelled Harvey Hannah. "You gonna play ball or not?"

Jeffie looked relieved. "I gotta go. 'B-Bye!"

"'Bye, Jeffie," Savannah said without looking up.

He flashed Katie a grin and mouthed *thank you*. Then he turned and hightailed it back to the group of boys.

Katie took a bite of cornbread and chewed thoughtfully, staring at her sister's still pink cheeks. "You know, Vannah, you act sort o' . . . fool-headed around Jeffie."

Savannah sighed. "I know. But Mama says it don't mean there's somethin' wrong with me. She says it's normal."

Katie thought about that for a minute. "Yeah, Jeffie acts just as stupid around you."

Savannah gave her a sudden smile. "Thanks for tellin' him to ask me to the dance."

Katie took another bite and mumbled, "Sure" with a full mouth. "Now all you got to do is learn to dance."

Savannah dropped her cornbread. "Oh my gosh, I never thought about that. I'll make a fool of myself."

"Yep, you'd best get Mama to help you."

Jack held the squirming, frightened sheep in an iron grip. Stooping low over the animal, he ran the razor-sharp clippers along the belly. Fleecy yellowed wool fell away from the pink flesh in a thick trail and heaped on the straw-covered floor. Occasionally the sharp blades nicked the sheep's soft belly, sending tiny droplets of blood splattering upward onto Jack's face and neck.

He sheared the sheep in a matter of moments, then jammed the clippers in his belt and let the sheep go. The animal bleated loudly and ran on wobbly legs right into the wall.

Tiredly Jack turned the sheep around, pointing him toward the pasture. Still bleating, the sheep barreled from the lean-to and joined the rest of the already-sheared sheep in the pasture.

Jack straightened. Pushing a fist at the base of his aching back, he swiped the sweat from his brow and let out his breath in an exhausted sigh. Christ, he was tired. And sore. He couldn't remember when he'd been this sore. The constant squeeze-release action of the clippers caused an ache that started in his hand and drove deep into his shoulder, and his back was half-broken from stooping over sheep for twelve hours.

He lifted his heavy head and looked around. Jim was at the front of the lean-to, bent over a squirming sheep. Sikes and the two Indians followed in a straight line. Jack brought up the rear. Beside them, out in the holding corral, there were a good hundred sheep left to be sheared. The last rays of the day's sun slid across the closely bunched animals, turning their fleecy backs into humps of pinkish gold.

Jack shoved the hat off his damp brow. "Come on, boys, how 'bout we call it a night?"

"Whew!" Jerry Sikes yelled back, letting his sheared sheep go. "I thought we'd never quit."

The men finished up the sheep they were working on, then closed the pasture gate behind them. Jack pitchforked some hay to the corralled sheep, and the day's work was done.

Too tired to say much, the men walked back to the barn, where their bedrolls were already laid out on layers of new straw.

"Christ on a crutch, I'm tired," Jerry said, collapsing on

his bedroll. "Every year it seems I forget how damn hard this job is."

Jim laughed. "Ain't that the truth. I shoulda taken the family to Texas and raised cattle."

Jack went to the workbench and lit a lantern. Flames sputtered on the ragged wick, then took hold. Pale golden light seeped through the shadowy barn.

"Holy shit!" Jerry yelled. "What the hell happened to your workbench?"

Jack winced and cast an embarrassed glance at Lissa's handiwork. The huge yellow tulip seemed to dance and throb in the light. He tried not to smile but couldn't help himself. "My wife thought I took things a bit too seriously. Seems she took it in her mind to change that."

The men laughed. All except Jim Hannah, who was strangely silent.

"What you thinkin', Jim?" Jerry asked, stretching out on his bedroll.

Jim eyed the workbench. Plucking up a piece of straw, he stuck it between his teeth. "I dunno. Guess I'm thinking maybe Mrs. Rafferty's right." He looked up at Jack. "A man's mighty lucky to have a woman who cares enough to change things."

Jack caught Jim's knowing smile and thought suddenly: We could be friends. Not just neighbors who occasionally help each other, but honest-to-God friends.

Friendship with another man was something Jack had given up on long ago; he knew that to make a friend, you had to be a friend, and that was a commitment he'd never been able to make before. But now, looking at Jim's smiling, uncondemning face, Jack thought maybe there was a chance.

"You know, Jack," Jerry said casually, "you ain't so bad as everybody says. And you're a damn hard worker."

Before Jack could respond, the barn door creaked open,

drawing every eye. Lissa stood in the doorway, her hands clasped behind her back. Her hair was drawn back in a lopsided knot that hung lamely over one ear. Flyaway strands stuck out in damp corkscrew curls all across her brow. She looked as if she'd been standing in front of a hot stove for hours.

She smiled. "Y'all done for the night?"

The men clambered to their feet and doffed their hats. "Evenin', Miz Rafferty," Jerry said. "That supper was mighty good tonight. Thank you kindly."

Lissa beamed. "Thanks, Mr. Sikes. I appreciate that. Here's a little snack to keep y'all till breakfast." She walked into the barn, placing a full-to-the-brim basket down between Jerry and Jim. "There's some cider and bread and leftover chicken. I hope you like it." She shot a quick smile at Jack. "Don't worry. Savannah cooked it."

"Thanks, Mrs. Rafferty," Jim said.

She nodded and turned to Jack. "Are you coming in tonight?"

The men whooped and chuckled.

Jack gave her a slow smile. "I sure am."

"Good." Lissa looped an arm through his and guided him toward the barn door. The men were still laughing when the door closed behind them.

Outside, the falling night was beautiful, full of spangling stars and gentle breezes, and anticipation. Tantalizing anticipation.

Arm in arm they walked down the dirt road toward the house. There was a spring in their step that had been missing for a long, long time. As if they were both thinking—dreaming—of the kisses to come.

They didn't talk; they didn't need to. But the silence between them was different tonight. Instead of the sharp-edged anger that had marked their union for years, it was a blurry, companionable quiet that settled comfortably between them. They didn't speak because it wasn't necessary. Touching, walking, being together, were enough.

They climbed the porch steps, and Jack held the back door open for Tess. She smiled and swept through.

The kitchen was warm and cozy, scented by the humid, salty leftovers of boiling water and the cinnamon-sweet memory of baked apple pie. In the center was the large copper bathing tin, filled halfway with water. She hurried to the stove and eased a heavy pot of water from the back burner.

Jack surged toward her. "I'll get that."

She laughed. "Jack, I've been filling this tub for a half an hour."

He reached out. His fingers curled around hers. The feel of his flesh against hers sent a bolt of desire shooting through her body. They stood side by side, their fingers interlaced over the pot of boiling water. Steam puffed up, pelted their faces.

"I'll do it," he said quietly.

Tess gazed into his eyes. She saw him swallow convulsively, and knew he'd felt the same burst of desire she had.

She didn't look away. Neither did he. Steam continued to spiral upward, curling in hot strands along their joined hands. Slowly Jack's tongue slid along his lower lip, leaving in its wake a sparkling trail of wetness.

Tess's stomach clenched. She let out a shaky breath. Suddenly she realized what was happening here, what was going to happen. And though she'd looked forward to it all day, waited and ached and longed for it, now that it was here, she felt afraid.

She'd had sex before, but only a few times, and those were mostly awkward, silent fumblings in the night that left her feeling more alone than ever. It had never been like this, never with a man who held her heart in the palm of his hand. With Jack she felt completely vulnerable, and so very innocent.

"Lissa?"

She jumped at the unexpected sound and stared steadfastly at his throat. He touched her chin, tilted her face up. She hesitated, then looked up.

"Lissa, what is it?"

She tried to laugh, but it was a watery failure. "I'm . . . afraid."

"Don't be." Taking her face in his hands, he whispered her name, and kissed her.

At first the kiss was so soft, it felt like the stirring of his breath against her lips. Tess closed her eyes and tilted her head back. She let go of the kettle and brought her hands to his chest, reveling in the strong, hard feel of him, and in her right to touch him.

As the kiss deepened and their tongues twined, Tess felt something inside her break free and float away. The heartache and pain of being unwanted and lonely took on the consistency of smoke and vanished.

Chapter Twenty

Tess pulled slowly back. Smiling up at him, she whispered, "That bath won't be hot much longer."

A slow, lazy grin spread across his face. "Then you'd better undress me." He held up two scraped, bloodied hands. "My hands are too sore to work the buttons."

Tess swallowed thickly. Self-consciousness washed through her in a trembling wave. She'd never done anything like this in her life. It was so . . . intimate.

Tess looked up and met his gaze. The love in his eyes drenched her, swept her hesitation away like dust in the wind. He made her feel beautiful and sexy and wanted.

For the first time in her life, she saw sex as something different, something more. *Making love.* Suddenly she understood the phrase in all its splendor, all its promise and passion.

She wanted to make love with this man, *to* this man. She wanted to show him, in every way, that she loved him.

With shaking fingers she undid his dungarees. The stiff fabric slid down his body and puddled on the floor at his feet. He stepped out of the overalls and kicked them away.

Tess's gaze fell, moved slowly down his muslin-clad legs. The evidence of his desire sent a tiny, flamelike thrill shooting through her. She felt his breathing as a patter of heat against her forehead.

Swallowing thickly, she undid the top button of his

work shirt, then the next, and the next. The tired fabric fell away from his body, exposing the curly black hair that lightly covered his chest. His breathing sped up. Her fingers moved down.

One by one the buttons gave way, the material gaped. She looked up at him, stared at him through eyes filled with a promise. Gently she pushed the shirt off his shoulders and let it fall down his arms. He shrugged slightly, and the shirt fell to the floor.

Her fingertips grazed his flesh. He shivered in response.

So did Tess. At the sight of his bare chest, something deep inside her quivered, sent a flurry of sensation to the pit of her stomach. Her throat went dry.

She pressed her open hands to his chest, marveling in the feel of his skin. Her fingers splayed out, moved slowly upward, memorizing every detail of him. The crispness of his hair, the satin-soft hardness of his muscles, the tiny scar that crossed his collarbone.

"Jesus, Lissa," he growled as her fingers breezed gently across his hardened nipples.

Startled by the throaty sound of his voice, Tess looked up. "Did . . . did I do something wrong?"

He smiled. It was a hot, slow smile that made Tess's pulse quicken. "No," he whispered. His eyes held her captive, promised things she'd never even dreamed of.

Without thinking, just feeling, *needing*, she pressed up onto her toes for a kiss.

He bent toward her, meeting her more than halfway. His mouth formed to hers in a hot, possessive kiss that left her reeling and dizzy. His hands settled in the small of her back, drawing her flush against his half-naked body. "God, you taste good," he whispered, letting his tongue brush lovingly along her full bottom lip.

Tess shivered at the moist warmth of his breath on her parted lips.

A small moan slipped from her mouth as the kiss deepened, became harder and more demanding. His tongue pushed past her lips, exploring, tasting, probing. She curled her arms around his back and clung to him. Desire burned inside her, became a painful ache between her legs.

Tess felt control begin to spiral out of her grasp. She began to tremble. She needed time, just a little time. It was happening too fast. . . .

"Th-The bath . . ." she said lamely.

Pulling backward just a step, he dropped to his knees beside the tub and washed the blood from his hands and face. Then he got to his feet and grinned at her, hair dripping. "Forget the bath," he said, sweeping her into his arms and carrying her to the bedroom. He shoved the door open with his elbow and kicked it shut behind him.

He laid her out on the bed and kneeled beside her. The bed planks creaked beneath their weight. His gaze lingered on her face for a long, breathless moment, then moved slowly to the muslin-clad mound of her breasts.

Anticipation shuddered through Tess's body and left her breathless. Everywhere his gaze landed, she felt singed. Inside her, deep, a fire started, coiled through her vitals. She wanted so desperately to be everything he wanted, but she didn't know how to be good in bed. Confusion chilled the mounting heat of desire, left her once again feeling shy and afraid.

"Jack . . ." She tried to reach for him, but he gently pushed her back into the pile of pillows.

"Not yet." He smiled. "Turnabout is fair play."

"But—"

"Relax, Lissa."

Tess swallowed hard. He didn't want her to touch him . . . not yet. He wanted her to relax. *Relax, Tess. Relax.* She drew a deep breath and tried to do as he'd asked.

It was impossible. Stretched out on the bed, she lay like

a butterfly pinned to a bed of soft velvet. She lay perfectly still, waiting. *Waiting* . . .

He leaned down and pressed a hot, moist kiss on the curve of her throat. Tess shuddered at the contact. Her eyes fluttered shut. He moved with tantalizing slowness, planting a trail of openmouthed kisses down her throat.

The gourd-seed buttons on her half gown seemed to magically dissolve beneath his fingers. She felt the thin fabric pull away from her body and fall to the floor. Tess tensed. A small, mouselike sound squeaked past her trembling lips. She felt achingly vulnerable. It was all she could do not to cover herself.

"Lissa?"

She opened her eyes and looked up at him. His gaze locked with hers, and in his eyes was a restless longing, a need, that mirrored her own. Then slowly—so slowly— he unlaced her corset and pushed the utilitarian contraption away from her skin. Cool air breezed across her flesh, hardened her nipples.

Candlelight bathed the creamy softness of her breasts, undulated across her stomach in golden waves. Her hair, spread out across the grayed pillows, glittered like gold dust.

He traced the pale outline of her breasts with his hands and leaned down to kiss the full swell above her nipple. "Jesus, you're beautiful," he whispered.

With those simple words, Jack freed her.

His hot breath wafted across her nipples and set off another flurry of goose bumps. Need coursed through her body, melted her insides, and suddenly she had to be closer, had to feel the heat of his skin against hers.

She pressed up on her elbows; he bent down. Their mouths came together in a hungry kiss. Tess wound her arms around his neck and clung to him. His chest was hot and damp against her nipples. The tingle between her legs deepened into an almost painful throbbing.

As they kissed, his hand roamed down her quivering stomach and slid across the throbbing center of her desire. She shuddered and strained up for his touch. But the brief caress was a tease and nothing more. His hand moved downward, along her thigh to her ankle. With strong, sure hands, he shoved her skirt up to her waist. Once again she felt the coolness of the night air against her hot flesh.

The skirt and drawers seemed to melt off her body. His gaze turned to liquid fire and slid down her naked body. She lay still and trembling beneath his perusal, her hair fanned out in a tangle around her face, her breasts shuddering in shallow, expectant breaths.

His hand curled around her throat, moving slowly downward, as if he were savoring the velvet-soft feel of her flesh. Her pulse thrummed and beat beneath his fingertips.

She swallowed thickly, nervously, trying not to be frightened by the intensity of her need. She'd never wanted anything, anyone, as much as she wanted him right now.

"Jack." His name slipped past her lips in a whisper of longing.

"Touch me," he said in a harsh, ragged voice that matched her own. She knew then that it wasn't just her. He was also out of control.

The realization gave her confidence. She took a deep, shuddering breath and let go of her fear.

The moment she made the decision, her inhibitions melted away. Without them, she was left ragged and aching for his touch, desperate for the feel of his flesh against hers.

With trembling fingers, she grabbed the waistband of

his drawers and dragged the fabric down the length of his body.

Naked, breathless, they came together. Their bodies fused into a hot, throbbing whole. The drawers slipped through Tess's shaking fingers and fell to the floor.

He kissed her again, and this one seemed to go on forever. She clung to him, feeling the shifting of his muscles beneath her fingertips. The masculine scent of him filled her nostrils. Sweat sheened his back, turned it slick. Her hands clutched at him, nails raking his back. "Oh, God," she whispered throatily. She'd never known she could feel this way, never even imagined it.

He rolled her on top of him. Tess pressed her fists into the pillow and looked down at him. Her hair cascaded around them, creating a shimmering curtain of golden silk.

He gazed up at her through eyes that looked like burning emeralds in the half-light. His lips parted slowly; his tongue slid out to wet them. Tess stared at the moist pink tip and felt something deep inside her clench. His breath caressed her nipples in hot, ragged spurts.

His hands curled around her body and clutched her buttocks, dragging her against him. His hardness slid against the curly thatch of her hair and touched the core of her desire.

Tess shuddered at the contact. Longing pulsated through her body in fire-hot waves. Need made her bold and wanton. She straddled him. The feel of him against her, hot and ready, made her whole body shake.

His name slipped past her lips in a breath of wonder. His hands slid up her back and anchored behind her neck, pulling her down for a dark, desperate kiss. As they kissed, she ground her hips against his in a slow, tantalizing circle.

He groaned and pushed her away gently. Quivering,

breathing hard, she stared down at him in confusion. "Did
I do something wrong?"

"God, no," he rasped. "It's just so . . . different."

Tess felt a cold stab of fear. She should have known,
should have prepared for it. This was the one change a
husband would notice for sure. "Oh. I . . ."

He looked up at her, and in his eyes she saw all the love
she could ever want, and more. "It's better," he said quietly.

He cupped her breasts in his hands and pushed the
heavy mounds together. At his touch, desire blasted
through her in a dizzying wave. Blood pounded in her ears
until she couldn't hear anything except the thudding beat
of her own heart. "Yes," she moaned. "Oh, yes."

His tongue breezed across one nipple, wetting it, and
then was gone.

She moaned, arched her back. And he was there again,
sucking gently on one nipple, then the other, until her
body was shaking so badly, she couldn't control it. She
couldn't catch her breath. She pressed downward, rubbed
herself against his hardness until she was light-headed
with need.

"Jack . . ." His name was a breathless moan.
"Please . . ."

His hands slid around to her back and moved to her buttocks. Clutching her with fingers of fire, he drew her
downward as he thrust up. She spread her thighs farther
and let him guide her onto him.

He pushed inside her, filled her. A whimper escaped her
mouth at the unexpected pleasure of it.

He stilled. "Does that hurt?"

She shook her head. Sweat-dampened hair whipped
across her face. "No. God, no. Don't stop."

He held her firmly against him and started to move.
Slowly at first, then faster. With each upward thrust of his

body, Tess gripped the pillows tighter, clenching her fingers around the puffy softness. Her hips ground against his. The pressure between her legs quivered, thrummed, grew so hot and throbbing, she felt tears prick her eyes.

She whimpered, moaned, tossed her head, but nothing helped.

"Oh, God, Jack . . ." She writhed atop him, desperate for release.

He pulled her toward him and buried his face in her breasts. She felt his tongue on her nipples, felt him take a hardened peak in his mouth. The sensation sent her into a tailspin of desire. She clutched his head in her shaking hands, holding him where he was. Her breath came in lung-searing gasps.

His hands moved urgently, almost roughly, across her breasts and along her flushed flesh. Tess squeezed her eyes shut and strained forward, panting, aching. "Oh, God, oh, God, oh, *God*!"

It burst upon her so suddenly, Tess screamed out. Wave after wave of intense pleasure went through her body. Tears stung her eyes, blurred her vision.

Jack thrust into her one last time, deep and hard. He clung to her, his breathing ragged, whispering her name against the crook of her neck.

Tess collapsed on top of him like a rag doll. Her body felt boneless, sapped of all strength, and there was a tremble in her legs she couldn't quell.

They lay there for a long time, panting, shaking with the aftermath of their passion. Jack held her close, stroked her hair. Tess curled lovingly against him, amazed at how comfortable it felt to be in his arms, how *right*.

He turned slowly toward her and pushed up on one elbow. "Lissa?"

She looked up into his eyes and felt a rush of love. Idly

she brushed a sweat-dampened lock of hair from his eyes and smiled. "Uh-huh?"

He leaned down and kissed her. It was a soft, gentle kiss that spoke not of passion sated, but of promises made. Of futures and the kind of love that lasts. "I've loved you ever since I was in a kid in short pants, Lissa. But I have never, ever loved you as much as I do right now."

Hot, stinging tears filled Tess's eyes. A huge lump of emotion swelled in her throat, made it difficult to breathe. She knew she should simply say nothing at all, but she couldn't. There was something she had to say—she, Tess Gregory, not Amarylis Rafferty. If it caused problems, or required explanations, or screwed up the damn time-space continuum, she'd deal with that later. Right now she had to utter the words she'd waited all her life to say.

She touched his face, and wasn't surprised to find that her fingers were trembling. "When I was little, I used to dream of someone who would be all mine, someone who would hold my hand and check under the bed, and tell me the world was a safe place. Every night I wished on the moon and waited." She kissed him, tasting the salty tang of her own tears against his lips. "I love you, Jack Rafferty. I have ever since I was a little girl."

As she spoke the words, Tess realized the truth of them. She *had* loved Jack Rafferty since she was a child. She hadn't known what he'd look like, or where—or when—he'd live, but those were only details. All her life she'd waited for this moment, this man. He was the somebody she'd always prayed for and never really let herself believe in.

"Thanks, Carol," she breathed.

"What was that?" Jack asked.

Tess stifled a smile. "Nothing. Now, put those strong arms to good use and give me a hug."

Jack grinned. "I'd be happy to."
And he did.

The next week passed in a rosy-colored blur. Jack spent
the days working hard, shearing sheep, and the nights
camped out in neighboring barns. Tess spent her days
cleaning the house, caring for Caleb, and playing with the
girls. It didn't bother her much that Jack was gone during
the day; her time was too full with the everyday chores of
running a sheep ranch to miss him. But the nights were
different. Longer.

After the dishes were cleaned and put away and Katie
was done with her reading lessons, the night stretched out
forever, dark and lonely and filled with subtle noises. She
lay in her bed, thinking of Jack, dreaming of Jack, aching
for Jack.

He heard Jim talking to him, but the words sounded a
million miles away.

Jack rested his elbows on the canoe's thick rim and
leaned slightly back, careful not to rock the boat. The hot
spring sun beat down on his face and warmed his body,
bringing a sheen of sweat to his brow. His hair hung
heavily along the sides of his face.

He closed his eyes, reveling in the warmth of the sun.
Tomorrow night he'd be coming home to his wife. Finally,
after more than a week's worth of sleeping in barns and
eating self-consciously at other people's tables, he'd be
home. *Home.*

The word conjured a dozen welcome images: Lissa
leading mealtime prayers, Katie reading slowly from her
primer, Savannah offering her daddy a cautious, heartfelt
smile, Lissa feeding chickens, Lissa in the bath, Lissa in
their bed.

Lissa.

He sighed, listening to the water slapping against the canoe. He couldn't remember when in his life he'd felt this good, this full of hope. For the first time in years, he was beginning to believe in himself again, and damn, it felt good.

"Jack? Jack?"

Jack came out of the pleasant daydream with a snap. "Uh, sorry, Jim. What were you saying?"

Jim brought the dripping paddle out of the water and laid it across the canoe in front of him. Letting out a tired breath, he shoved his hat back and grinned at Jack. "I said, it's your turn."

Jack reached across the bundles of yellowed fleece that represented most of his yearly income and grabbed the paddle. Straightening, he plunged the paddle in the water and maneuvered the canoe around, following Jim's course for the huge green hump of land in the distance, the island called Vancouver, where they'd sell their goods for winter supplies.

"You know, Jack, I'm not one for jabberin' a whole lot, but I've got to say, you've changed lately."

Jack squinted into the sun and drew his hat lower on his forehead. "Yeah, I s'pose I have."

Jack could tell that Jim was waiting for an explanation. He knew, too, that Jim would never ask.

Normally that would have been the end of it right there. Jack had spent years closing himself off from all human contact. With each year since the horror, he'd moved further and further into his shell, hoping that if he went deep enough, he couldn't hurt anybody, couldn't let anybody down.

But his efforts to protect his children had only hurt them more. The girls he loved more than life itself had never heard the words "I love you" from their own father.

He thought about the smile Savannah had given him

when he'd complimented her painted curtain. It had been bright enough to blind him.

So much joy he'd given her, with so little effort. It pained him to think about it, to realize how little his children needed to be happy. And fool that he was, he had given them even less.

No more, he decided. No more lying and hiding and pretending not to care. He didn't want to live like that anymore. That day in the church he'd vowed to make a new start, and not only in his marriage. He'd vowed to begin again with his children, himself, his neighbors. To become the man he should have been for years.

He took a deep breath and dove into the cold, frightening waters of communication. "Lissa and I have had our problems in the past. . . ." The surprise on Jim's face made Jack laugh out loud. His anxiety over talking disappeared. "Didn't expect me to say anything else, huh, Jim?"

"I've known you a long time, Jack, and frankly, it surprises me when you speak at all."

Jack nodded. "Yeah, I guess it would. Anyway, everything's going well with Lissa and me now."

Jim pulled a toothpick out of his pocket and wedged it between his teeth, moving it back and forth thoughtfully. "Nothin' like love to make a man smile."

"Yeah. I . . . I missed her this week."

"Yep. Too bad we'll be gettin' back just in time for the first shearin' dance. I wouldn't mind spendin' the night curled up in bed with my wife."

Fear cut through Jack's new resolve. He stared out at the choppy blue waves, their peaks gilded by the bright sun. "I forgot about the dance."

"You gonna go this time?"

"I don't 'spose I'd be too welcome after the Fourth of July dance."

"Aw, hell, Jack, that was almost a year ago. 'Sides, you

put too much store in that one time. So you went a little
bit crazy. So what? Hector Jones has done a hell of a lot
worse after a little too much whiskey. Give yourself a
chance."

Give yourself a chance.

Jack's fingers tightened around the paddle. The wood
felt warm and slick; the whooshing slap of the waves
against the sides of the boat seemed thunderous in his ears.

"Lissa and the girls would sure like to go." He said the
thought aloud, testing it.

Jim leaned back, dangling his arms over the side of the
canoe. "I'm sure they would. Hell, Minerva and Lissa are
probably figurin' out what to wear right now."

Jack imagined the look on Lissa's face when he told her
they were going to the dance. An anticipatory smile pulled
at his lips.

A new start was a new start.

Tess shifted her weight, moving Katie slightly to the left
on her lap. In front of them, on the kitchen table,
McGuffey's First Eclectic Reader lay open. Pale, throbbing
candlelight splashed across its yellowed pages.

"What's that letter, Katie?" Tess murmured tiredly,
pointing to the first letter of the sentence.

Katie plopped her elbows on the table and cradled her
chin in one hand. "I think it's a-b. Or a-d."

Tess smoothed the back of her hair. "Here, watch."
Carefully she drew a big picture of a B in the air.

Katie watched intently, frowning. "Is it a B?"

"Very good. Now, what's next?"

Tess lifted her now blurry gaze from the reader and
glanced into the living room. Savannah was sitting on the
sofa, hunched over her old linsey-woolsey dress.

"How's it coming, Savannah?" she asked quietly.

Savannah lifted her head. Even from this distance, Tess

could tell that the girl's eyes were bloodshot. "Not so good. This dress ain't—"

"Isn't," Tess corrected automatically.

Savannah sighed. "This dress *isn't* ever gonna look good."

Tess felt a pang of empathy. She knew how important it was for a young girl to look good at her first dance, but there was nothing Tess could do. She couldn't sew a stitch, and besides, there wasn't any fabric or any time. They didn't even know for sure if Jack would let them attend the dance.

"I wish there was something I could do to help. . . ."

Savannah's hand fell in her lap. She looked across the room at Tess. "You . . . you really think Daddy's gonna let us go?"

Tess licked her lips nervously. "I hope so, Savannah. But there's something . . . different about how your daddy feels about this. I think he's scared, and I don't want to push him too hard."

Savannah's mouth turned down in a pitiful frown. "Yeah, I know."

Tess tried to force a bright smile. "But you never know, kiddo. Strange goings-on have been happening around here."

Savannah gave a forlorn sigh and went back to her sewing. "I don't know how to dance anyhow. Probably make a fool of myself."

Tess stared at Savannah. She was working so hard on her dress, trying desperately to make it ready in time, and yet she had no hope that they were even going. No hope at all.

Please, Jack, Tess prayed, *don't let her down. Please . . .*

The next evening, Jack returned to the island, his pockets filled with money, and Jim Hannah's barn filled with the supplies they'd traded for the fleece.

From the road, he stared down at the house. It lay like a perfect white pearl amidst the darkening twilight.

He clutched the packages to his chest and began to run. His bootheels crunched through the rock and dirt road, his breathing sped up. That ridiculous smile came back to his face, and he couldn't—didn't want to—shake it free.

Panting and out of breath, he rounded the last corner and sprinted toward the house, bounding up the sagging slatted steps and bursting into the warm, golden kitchen.

"Jack!" Lissa whirled around at his entrance. Her face revealed first shock, then a joy that matched his own. She picked up her skirts and ran for him, throwing herself into his arms.

It was the greeting Jack had waited for all his life. He dropped his packages and bear-hugged her, twirling her around and around in the warm, mutton-and-potato-scented kitchen.

"Oh, Jack," she whispered, gazing up into his eyes, "I missed you."

He kissed her full, pink lips, and when he did, he felt as if a very special, very important part of him had just been given life. "I missed you, too."

"Daddy!" Katie came running into the room, her skirts hiked up to her knees. She flung herself into the hug, and the three of them whirled around, laughing.

Jack smoothed the tangled hair from Katie's face and planted a kiss on her flushed cheek. "Hi, little Katydid. I missed you."

She gave him a bright, gap-toothed grin that twisted his heart. "I missed you, too, Daddy. Know what?"

"What?"

"Mama burnt supper tonight." Her voice dropped to a giggly whisper. "Really bad."

Jack tried valiantly to remain serious. His mouth

twitched traitorously. "Really? Well, we'll have to do something about that."

Lissa looked up at him. There was a fire in her eyes that made his blood turn searingly hot. She pressed a hand to his shoulder. "What sort of . . . thing did you have in mind?"

He licked his lips. His eyes glittered with promise. "I don't know. We'll have to think of something . . . fitting. Something that teaches you how to put out a fire."

She smiled. Her hand slid down from his shoulder and moved dangerously close to his groin. "I'll have to build one first."

He laughed. "Shouldn't be any problem there."

Lissa laughed and slipped her hand in his. He loosened his hold on Katie and let her glide down his body to the floor. Her feet hit with a click of heels.

Savannah came around the corner, her schoolbooks clutched to her chest. "Mama, I—" She saw Jack and froze. The smile slid from her face. "Daddy." She started to come toward him, then paused. The hands around her books curled into taut fists.

Jack felt her hesitation like a blow. Savannah, of all of them, would be the most difficult. She'd seen so many of his little failures, so much of his weakness. She'd been afraid of him for most of her life.

The realization was like a burning coal in the pit of his stomach. How the hell did a man say *I'm sorry* to an innocent child? And was an apology enough? Could years of neglect be simply forgiven?

Jack swallowed thickly, wishing he were the kind of man who could make glib statements of sentiment. He wanted to say, ached to say, *Hi, Savannah, I missed you.* But the words were a lump of regret in his throat. He knew they wouldn't be enough; not for Savannah, whose youthful eyes had seen too much, whose young heart he had broken. He had to show her, every day, in every way, that he was sorry. And most of all, that he loved her with all his heart.

"Hi, Vannah," he said quietly, using the pet name he hadn't used since she was a toddler.

She blinked in surprise. Her hold on the schoolbooks relaxed a little. "H-Hi, Daddy."

"I brought presents," he said lamely.

"You did?" three feminine voices said at once.

Jack stooped down and picked up the three brown-paper-wrapped packages. He handed little ones to Katie and Lissa, and a big one to Savannah.

All three of them hurried to the kitchen table and began ripping at the twine bows. The crinkling sound of folding paper and giggling girls filled the kitchen.

Katie sidled alongside Lissa in a wordless bond that caused a small ache to form in Jack's chest. The child's pudgy pink fingers worked feverishly on the thin twine bow and then yanked back the brown wrapping paper. Three bright red grosgrain ribbons lay tangled alongside a beautiful doll.

Katie squealed in delight and clutched the treasure to her chest. She hopped excitedly for a second, then twirled and threw herself into Jack's arms.

"Thank you, Daddy, oh, *thank you.*"

Jack coiled his arms around her in a fierce, loving hug. "You're welcome, baby," he said in a thick voice.

"Jack!"

At Lissa's awed whisper, he brought his head up and looked at his wife.

Lissa eased the beautiful silver and pearl necklace from the paper and held it up into the candlelight. "Oh, Jack, it's beautiful."

He smiled at her, then glanced nervously at Savannah. His eldest daughter was chewing on her lower lip and carefully unwrapping the package. She moved slowly, as if she were afraid of what lay beneath the thin paper.

She peeled the brown paper back, and immediately looked up at him.

Jack smiled at her, nodding.

A slow, excited smile tugged at her mouth. She bit down harder on her lower lip, as if she were afraid to show how much the simple frock meant to her. But she couldn't keep the emotion from her eyes. "Oh, Daddy," she breathed, holding up the short-sleeved muslin gown sprigged with tiny pink flowers. "It's beautiful."

"I thought you ladies might need something special for the dance tomorrow night."

Savannah gasped. "Really?" she said. "We can go?"

Jack knew then that he'd made the right decision. "Yeah," he said quietly. "We can go."

Chapter Twenty-one

That night, Tess dried the last supper plate and put it carefully away. As she was turning to leave, a shadow of movement caught her eye.

Intrigued, she went to the window and saw Savannah sitting on the tree swing. Just sitting there, head bowed, hands in her lap. Alone.

Tess tossed her damp rag on the riddle board and went outside.

"Savannah?" she said quietly, making her way cautiously down the shadowy steps.

Savannah sighed unhappily. "Hi, Mama."

Tess picked her way across the yard and kneeled in the cold, damp grass in front of Savannah. "What's the matter?"

"Oh, Mama, that dress ain't—*isn't*—gonna help me. I'm gonna make a fool of myself at the dance tomorrow night."

"You don't know how to dance?"

She shook her head.

Tess pushed to her feet. "Well, that's nothing to worry about. I'll have you dancing in no time. You go run on into the barn. I'll get . . . a few things and meet you there."

"Really?" Savannah whispered. "You'll teach me?"

Tess forced a smile. "Sure. Now, run along. I'll be right there."

Savannah was up like a shot. "Thanks, Mama," she called out, already skipping along the dirt road toward the barn.

Tess crossed her arms, the false smile on her face turning downward. She had no idea how to dance, of course. It was not something she'd done a great deal of in her life, for though she had always been able to feel the beat of the music, she'd felt too self-conscious to actually get out on a dance floor.

Then again, she *had* learned the steps to a dance back in the seventies, during college. She grinned at the thought of teaching *the hustle* to Savannah.

Remembering to hike her skirts like a good little pioneer gal, she walked back into the house. There was only one thing to do. And it was a damn good plan, if she did say so herself.

Jack stared at her in horror. "I can't teach Savannah to dance."

Tess frowned. "Don't you know how?"

He shoved a hand through his hair. "Of course I know how. We were raised in the South, for Christ's sake. Dancing's like breathing."

"Then what's the problem? You know how, she doesn't. Seems like a perfect fit to me."

He looked away. Tess moved toward him, placed a hand on his arm. "Jack? What is it?"

Slowly he looked down at her. "What if she won't let me?"

The quiet question wrenched her heart. Tess smoothed the unruly hair from his face. "Jack, she's been waiting for you all her life. She won't turn you away."

"Okay," he murmured. "I'll give it a try."

"No, Jack. Don't try. *Do*."

He almost smiled. "You're an authoritative wench, you know that?"

She pressed onto her tiptoes and kissed him. "So I've been told. Now, hurry up."

He curled an arm possessively around her waist and drew her up for a longer, more intimate kiss. Then he opened the door and stepped out into the night.

He stood on the porch, staring down at the blackness of the Straits. A thick gray cloud let go its anchor and scudded past the half moon. Pale, blue-white light immediately slithered across the water in undulating waves. Stars poked their faces through the velvet sky.

He felt a small foot on his butt. "Go, Jack."

"Yeah, yeah." Dropping his chin, he moved woodenly down the steps and headed toward the barn. With every crunching step of his bootheel in the dirt, he winced. His mind was chock-full of images—times Savannah had looked at him with mistrust or not looked at him at all; times she'd almost come toward him and then stopped, her eyes wide with fear; times he'd wanted to reach out to her and been too damned afraid of his own darkness to even try.

Please God, don't let me screw up.

Savannah paced back and forth, her small, boots clicking on the hard-packed dirt floor. Her stomach felt like a butterfly nest, all fluttery and full. She let out her breath in an anxious sigh. *Calm down, Savannah. It ain't—isn't—that hard. Mama'll teach you, 'n' everything'll be fine.*

Tiny teeth nipped at her self-confidence. Maybe this wasn't such a good idea after all. She was gonna make a fool of herself at the dance for sure.

"Savannah?"

She froze at the sound of her daddy's voice, then spun around. He was standing in the doorway, a broad-shouldered shadow against the midnight blue of the night behind him. A few stars twinkled in the sky beyond. There was only the barest light from the moon behind him, and yet even in the semidarkness, he was so handsome, he took her breath away.

"There's a rumor my little girl can't dance."

Yearning wrenched through Savannah. Tears lurched into her throat and stung her eyes. Her mouth wobbled dangerously. But she did her level best not to cry.

She wanted to say something that sounded grown-up, but all of a sudden she felt like a little kid, scared and lonely. She'd wanted him to notice her for so long, had waited and ached and prayed for it. But now that it was here, *he* was here, she didn't know what to do. Her knees felt like unset pudding.

She didn't move. She just stood there, her heart beating too fast and her throat as dry as toast, staring at her daddy. She was scared to death she'd burst into tears and he'd run away again. Standing still, she tried desperately to be a perfect little lady so he'd be proud of her.

"Come here, Vannah."

Vannah. The nickname almost did her in. She squeezed her eyes shut. *Don't be a crybaby. Don't do somethin' stupid and make him leave again.*

She tried to clear her mind, but it was impossible. Her head was full of the cherished, oft-remembered memories of long ago, from before she should even be able to remember, when she used to wake in the middle of the night to the sound of crying. It had happened so often back then. So often . . .

When she woke up, she'd see him through the slats in her crib. He was standing there, reaching for her, whispering her name, *Vannah,* over and over again.

Somehow, even as a child, she'd sensed that he didn't want her to say anything. But once she hadn't been able to help herself. The word "Daddy?" had slipped from her small mouth.

He'd jerked his hand back and stumbled away from her. He'd never come back.

The memory burned in Savannah's chest, brought more stupid, stinging tears. She'd done something wrong that night. Something bad to make him run. Ever since, she'd tried to be so good, so quiet. But it didn't seem to matter.

Now he was giving her another chance, and she didn't want to do something wrong.

He held his hand out. "Come here, Vannah."

She stared at his outstretched hand until it became a flesh-colored smear. She blinked, swiped at the babyish tears.

"I'll wait here all night, Vannah," he whispered. "I'm not going anywhere this time."

"I don't understand. . . ." she said for lack of anything better to say, but it wasn't true, and she knew that even as the words slipped from her lips. She was afraid to understand, afraid she was wrong.

"It's simple, Vannah I just want to teach my little girl to dance."

A tiny sob escaped her. This time there was no force on earth or within her soul that could have kept Savannah back. With a hiccuping squeak, she snatched up her skirts and ran for him. His strong arms closed around her, squeezing so hard, she had to gasp for breath as he lifted her up.

She didn't care a bit. She drew in a shuddering, watery breath and buried her face against his shoulder. He held her tightly against his chest, and this time there was no holding back the tears. They burst from the small, dark box in her heart in which she'd buried them long ago, surging through her dry soul in streaks of life-giving moisture.

Daddy smoothed the hair from her cheek and kissed her forehead. "Vannah," he murmured against her moist temple, "I'm so sorry. Can you forgive me?"

Savannah tilted her face to look up at him. Moonlight illuminated half his face, casting shadows through his lashes and across his high, sharp cheekbones. He gazed down at her through eyes that were overbright, as if he, too, were holding back tears.

"Oh, Daddy." The words slipped out in a watery blur. She wanted to say more, but her throat was thick with tears, so she simply nodded.

He gave her a smile so warm, it heated all the places in her heart that had long been cold and dark. "I love you, Vannah."

Savannah's breath caught. Happy tears rolled down her cheeks and plopped on his flannel shirt. "I . . . I love you, too, Daddy."

After that, the night took on a magical quality. Savannah knew it was a time she'd remember all her life. They hugged for a long time, forever, and then, gently, he let her down.

"Come on," he said, cocking his head toward the center of the barn. "We've got dancing to do."

Savannah followed him to the middle of the barn. They stood there, arm's length apart, staring at each other. Neither seemed to know what to say, or how to begin. Beside them, on the workbench, the lamp sputtered, sending plumes of gold into the darkness and creating a magical circle of light. From the stalls came the quiet rumbling of hooves on hard-packed dirt. The barn-smell of fresh hay, old wood, and dust filled the air.

Daddy reached for her. "Take my hand."

Savannah shuffled into the circle of light, and took his hand. His other hand moved to the curve of her back and drew her close. In his arms, she felt small and warm and infinitely safe—it was a feeling she'd never had before, and it filled her with a giddy sense of happiness. She grinned up at him.

He smiled. "We'll start with a waltz." Humming a quiet tune, he began to move. He went slowly, accommodating her clumsy, awkward movements. Her feet seemed suddenly to swell to elephant size and she stumbled gracelessly in his arms.

Shameful heat crawled up her throat and fanned across her cheeks. "Daddy, I can't do—"

"Shhh," he murmured. "Just relax. One, two three. One, two, three."

Savannah closed her eyes and accidentally slipped into the timeless rhythm. The soft, lilting rain of his humming soared in her senses like a symphony, merging with the creaking floorboard and sputtering lamp to create a full, rich sound. Smiling, moving easily in his arms, Savannah joined her voice to his, and together they made the dusty old barn swell with music.

The night was more than half gone by the time Jack and Savannah finished dancing. They'd laughed and danced and talked for hours, forging the strong, solid bonds of a new relationship.

But finally Savannah's eyelids had begun to droop, and Jack had known this special night must come to an end. So, still talking and hand in hand, they walked back to the house. A lazy breeze chattered through the leaves overhead and whistled through the grass as they climbed the creaking steps.

The house was cold and dark inside. On the kitchen table lay a puddle of wax where a stubby candle had been.

"Uh-oh," Savannah said, smothering a giggle. "I guess we stayed a bit too long."

Jack gave her hand a squeeze. "I could've danced all

night with you, pumpkin. It was like dancin' with air, you were so light on your feet."

She blinked up at him. "Really? You think Jeffie'll think I'm a good dancer?"

Jack's heart tugged hard at the thought of his Savannah, his baby girl, dancing with a boy. He gave her a bittersweet smile that was the best he could do. "Yeah," he choked out. "He'll think you're great."

She grinned. "Thanks, Daddy." She reached up on her toes and planted a kiss on his cheek. "Good night."

He kissed her. "Night."

Before he could say anything else, she scampered down the hallway and disappeared in her room. The door squeaked shut behind her.

Jack stared at the door long after it had closed. A strange mixture of emotions was swirling through him: joy that he'd finally kissed his daughter, sadness that he'd waited so long, and regret for the thousands of moments he'd missed. He felt all these things and more, much more.

For the first time in years, he felt good about himself, about the decision he'd made.

Amazingly, it wasn't as hard as he'd thought. He'd reached out just a little, and his hand hadn't been smacked as he'd feared. Instead, it had been grabbed, held firmly.

And he hadn't failed her. He thought about how it had felt in the barn, swirling on the straw-strewn floor with his daughter in his arms. About how she'd looked, her face all flushed with happiness, her eyes glittering with tears.

I love you, too, Daddy.

They were words he'd remember all his life. Smiling, Jack headed for his wife's—no, he reminded himself, *their*—bedroom. He found her sleeping, curled up beneath the heavy coverlet. Her deep, even breaths filled the darkened chamber.

Jack quickly peeled down to his long johns and climbed

into bed beside her. The tired old bed planks creaked beneath his weight. He thought briefly about waking her, loving her, but decided it was too late. Tomorrow was a big day that started early, and they'd have plenty of time for lovemaking tomorrow night.

He smiled and drew her into his arms. Holding her tight, breathing the unique wildflower and lavender scent of her, he went to sleep.

Sunlight streamed through the open kitchen window, bringing with it the smell of new roses and the singsongy chatter of nesting birds. Tess opened the stove door and bent down, peering into the oven. Hot, dry heat hit her in the face, bringing with it the cinnamon-spicy scent of baking apple cake. Certain that it was browning nicely, she closed the heavy metal door and straightened slowly.

Pushing a sweaty lock of hair from her eyes, she glanced around. The kitchen table was heaped with bags of flour and sugar. Beside the huge crockery bowl of batter lay a dozen or so cored apples and a pile of precious walnuts. Five cakes were cooling along the edge of the table, and a big pan of chicken pieces was frying on the back burner. Minerva Hannah was standing at the kitchen table, elbow deep in cake fixings.

"Thanks for coming over, Minerva," Tess said, feeling a rush of affection for the woman who'd shown up at ten o'clock with her sleeves rolled up and a wagonload of baking supplies. "I don't know what I would have done without you."

Minerva waved a floury hand. "I was glad to come. Nothing makes a big job seem small like a friend's help."

Smiling, Tess poured two cups of coffee and went to the table.

"Just put mine down," Minerva said. "I'm almost done." Before the words were even out of her mouth, she thwacked a big glob of lard into the blackened cast-iron pan and started smearing the goo around.

Tess looked the other way. Lard was one of those foods a twentieth-century woman had trouble with. Sitting down across from Minerva, Tess curled her fingers around the warm tin. "So, how many of these cakes do we need to make?"

Minerva expertly poured the last of the batter into the greased pan and carefully smoothed it out with a wooden spoon. "Three per family is usual. When we get to the dance, we layer the cakes with applesauce and whipped cream and have plenty for everyone. And no two cakes taste the same."

Tess smiled at the quaint custom. "I'm really looking forward to the dance."

Minerva pushed the pan aside and sat down. With a tired sigh, she took a sip of coffee. "Hey, this is better than the last batch. You're catching on."

"Thank God. I was about ready to chew the beans."

Minerva laughed easily. "Don't forget: Tonight you'll want to pack enough meat and fixin's for your own family. At the hall, they'll have a big table set out for food. You just put yours in with everybody else's and eat whatever you want. It's a real treat."

"Not for the poor soul who picks my cooking."

Minerva clucked her tongue in disapproval. "Now, Lissa, that recipe I gave you is so simple, a child could make it."

"It's a good thing," Tess laughed, " 'cause I'm going to give it to Savannah."

Minerva laughed with her. Deftly moving a bag of flour from the table in front of her, she plopped her elbows on the table and stared at Tess. "You've really changed, you know that?"

Tess smiled softly. "Minerva, you don't know the half of it."

They sat there a long time, sipping coffee and chatting. They talked of many things, of children and diapers and husbands. Of big things and small, of the myriad day-to-day challenges facing pioneer women trying to forge a new life in a rugged land. The morning slid into noontime, then drifted into early afternoon.

By the time Minerva left, Tess felt as if she'd really, truly made a friend.

Chapter Twenty-two

Tess was sweating like a pig by the time she finished lacing, buttoning, hook-and-eyeing, and smoothing her dress. Panting for air, blinking against dizziness, she took a cautious step backward. The distance helped. She could see more of herself in the wide, U-shaped mirror on the washstand.

What little breath she had disappeared. Her mouth rounded in surprise.

She looked beautiful. Not just pretty; pretty was a dime a dozen. She was drop-dead gorgeous. Savannah had pulled the pale, honey-hued hair away from Tess's face and braided it, then curled the wrist-thick weave into a coronet that sat on her head like a fragile golden crown. Wisps of curly blond hair fell in disarray across her brow and temples, giving her a soft, almost ethereal look. The beautiful silver lavaliere Jack had brought her hung just below the hollow of her throat.

Her long-sleeved gown was the most beautiful sea blue silk Tess had ever seen. The bodice had a three-inch-wide band that began off the shoulder and veed down to reveal a modest swell of breast. Elegant sapphire threads zigzagged the band and cuffs, and ran in dual lines down the front of the skirt.

The dress formed smoothly across her bust and tapered down to her artificially wasped waist, then flowed like a waterfall over her horsehair-crinoline underskirt to the floor.

Tess swirled around and came to a breathless stop. The silk shirt rustled at the movement and belled out before it settled back into place.

The bedroom door creaked open. "Are you ready, Mama?" Katie stood in the doorway in a ruffled red and white polka dot dress. Baggy lace pantalets peeked out from underneath her hem. The bright red grosgrain ribbons her father had brought her dangled from the ends of her long braids as she skipped into the room.

Tess bent down and kissed her puffy little cheek. "You look pretty as a picture."

"We'd best get goin'," Katie said matter-of-factly. "Savannah's . . . sort o' . . . "

"Snappy?"

Katie nodded solemnly. "She's been yellin' at me to hurry since dawn."

Tess bit back a smile and slipped a sapphire blue shawl over her shoulders. "She's a bit nervous, that's all." She went to the cradle and picked up Caleb. After a quick check of his diapers, she folded him in a warm homespun blanket, took Katie's hand, and headed for the porch.

The team was hitched and waiting outside the house. Jack was standing at Red's head, checking something on the bridle. He looked incredibly handsome in black twill pants, white shirt with gold buttons, and black vest.

"Hi, Jack," she called out.

He turned toward her, already smiling. "Hi, Li—" His greeting melted away. The smile slid off his face.

Tess nervously smoothed her skirt. "Do I have it on backwards or something?"

His smile came back full force. He let go of the bridle and ran toward them, bounding up the porch steps.

Their eyes met and held. Tess felt the promise of magic glitter around them. He touched her cheek and leaned close, whispering, "You take my breath away."

Tess shivered at the heat of his breath on her throat. "I can't breathe too well myself," she murmured.

Smiling, Jack turned to Katie and dropped down on one knee. "Little Katydid, you look beautiful."

A grin erupted on her tiny face. "Thanks, Daddy."

Jack helped them both onto the wagon, Tess up front with Caleb in her lap, and Katie back with the baskets of food.

They waited for Savannah. First patiently. Then not so patiently.

"Daddy, we're gonna be late, an' all the good food will be gone. Miz Hannah makes the very best fried chicken, 'n' I don't wanna miss it."

Jack threw a frowning glance at the house. "What the hell's taking her so long?"

Tess remembered her first date with a bittersweet smile. She'd spent hours in front of the mirror, trying to get everything just right. She'd bought a new dress and even had a manicure. Unfortunately, Harry Spitz hadn't shown up.

Tess was surprised to realize that the memory didn't hurt anymore. For years she'd carried around a silent, rock-heavy weight in her stomach. She'd never really trusted dating after that, hadn't really tried it again until college. And even then she'd never tried really hard. But now the memory of Harry Spitz was just that: a faintly poignant remembrance that might have happened to someone else.

She patted Jack's hand. "This is an important night for her, you know. Be patient."

"But—"

Just then the door creaked open. Savannah moved stiffly

onto the porch, her hands clasped together at her waist, her newly curving body accentuated by the short-sleeved, rose-sprigged white muslin gown. She'd combed her hair away from her face and coiled it in a loose, romantic knot at the top of her head. In the pale light of twilight, her skin glowed like fresh cream. "I'm ready."

Jack did a double take. "Savannah?"

She met his gaze. In her huge blue eyes was a single, frightened question that only her daddy could answer.

Jack jumped down from the wagon and hurried toward her. Vaulting up the steps, he took her hands in his. "Let me look at you, Vannah."

Shyly she let go of his hands and stepped back.

"You're the prettiest woman I've ever seen." He shot a glance back at the wagon and grinned. "But don't tell your mama."

A slow smile spread across her face, keeping pace with the blush that pinkened her cheeks.

He held out his arm for her. "Shall we go, m'lady?"

Grinning, she looped her arm through her daddy's and let him guide her to the wagon. She plucked up her skirt and climbed slowly—every inch the lady—into the planked bed and sat cautiously beside Katie.

"Gosh, Vannah, what took you so long?"

Savannah smiled serenely. "It takes a woman longer to get ready. Right, Mama?"

Tess battled a smile. "That's right."

Jack tried to concentrate on the familiar feel of the leather between his fingers, but couldn't quite manage it. He stiffened and leaned forward in his seat, wishing he had a hat to pull low on his head. Anything to shield his eyes from the wary looks he'd get from the islanders.

The wagon crunched along, bouncing its occupants with each rut in the dirty, rock-studded road. Night was just beginning to claim the day, throwing a purplish blanket across the Straits and silhouetting the trees against a midnight blue sky. Charcoal gray clouds scudded overhead.

They turned the last corner and started down the road toward the hall. Jack tensed. His fingers tightened uncomfortably around the flat leather reins. Behind him, he could hear the girls' excited chatter and an occasional giggle. He thought vaguely that one of them might have spoken to him, but the words were a dull buzzing inside his head.

It took him a moment to notice that Lissa had taken his hand. Her fingers were curled protectively around his right hand, a silent offer of comfort and caring.

He let his pent-up breath out in a shuddering sigh and tried to give her a bright smile. It was hopelessly false.

"It's okay," she murmured, leaning against his shoulder. "We're together."

Together.

The word calmed him somewhat, offered a grain of hope. This year, he told himself, it wouldn't be so bad. He was better than he'd been in years. Stronger. More in control. With Lissa by his side, nothing horrible and embarrassing could happen.

Like last year . . .

He tried to forget about last year's Fourth of July dance, and focused instead on the warm feel of his wife, pressed so lovingly against him. A shearing dance wouldn't provide the same . . . trigger as a Fourth of July dance. He'd be fine.

Besides, the past was past. Forgotten. He was better now. More healthy. Nothing bad could happen to him now.

He wanted desperately to believe it.

Pale light spilled from the hall's windows and doors, casting a golden net around the big log building. Smoke spiraled up from the pipe chimney and lay in a motionless haze along the roof. A full moon hung in the gunmetal gray night sky like a perfect pearl.

Tess heard the first vague stirring of music. At first she thought she'd imagined the heartbreakingly beautiful sound.

Her fingers tightened around Jack's. Her breath caught.

"Music." She said the word reverently. Emotion coiled around her throat, brought the sharp sting of tears. All her life she'd tried to imagine what music sounded like. She'd tried to remember, but she'd been so young when she'd lost her hearing. Too young to remember.

She'd spent years *feeling* music as a rumbling beat beneath her feet and watching its effect on people. And wishing—just for a second—to truly hear its magic.

Now here it was, seeping through the open windows and floating gracefully on the cool night air. The music swelled in her soul like a symphony.

"Oh, Jack," she sighed, "it's beautiful. . . ."

He gave her a stiff-lipped smile and brought the wagon to a stop.

Excitement coursed through Tess. She jumped down from the wagon and quickly organized the unloading. Giving Jack the box of stack cakes, Savannah the basket of chicken, and Katie the cold potato pie, Tess wrapped Caleb in her arms and they were off.

Jack moved slowly, as if each step were fraught with danger. She ribbed him gently in the side. "Lighten up," she said with a grin. "We're going to have fun."

He gave her a wan smile.

They walked up the creaking wooden steps and stopped just inside the open doorway. The hall was ablaze with lights and filled with laughing, talking, dancing people.

Tess stared in awe. She knew it was just a nothing old

log building with a few candles on the tables and straw on the floor, but to her, listening to the gay sound of the fiddle music, it was the most sumptuous, magical ballroom she'd ever seen.

Candles and lamps were everywhere, creating pockets of golden, shimmering light that melded into one another. People whirled across the makeshift dance floor amid the rustle of silk and the stomping of heels. The scents of burning wood, fresh-baked foods, cinnamon, and sweat clamored for dominance in the crowded room.

The fiddler stood apart from the crowd, barricaded behind a row of whiskey barrels. Sweat shone from his balding head and slid down his flushed, fleshy cheeks as he played.

He looked up suddenly and saw Jack. The fiddle squeaked loudly and struck a sour note, then went quiet.

The dancers shuddered to a stomping, uncertain halt and turned toward the door. Conversations ground to a halt, laughter died stillborn in a dozen throats.

The silence turned thick, wary. Somewhere a candle sputtered, but it was the only sound in a room filled with people.

Then Minerva Hannah broke from the crowd and came rushing toward Lissa. "There you are," she said loudly enough for all to hear. "We've been waiting for you."

Her greeting severed the unnatural silence. Jim followed on his wife's heels, his hand outstretched to shake Jack's hand. "Hi, Jack. Glad you could make it."

Jack lifted an eyebrow derisively. "A feeling shared by all, I see."

"Give 'em time, Jack," Jim said. "They'll forget."

If you don't do it again.

Jack heard the words as surely as if they'd been spoken aloud. He stiffened, nodded curtly. "Yeah, sure."

"Forget what?" Tess looked in confusion from Jim to Jack.

Jack's gaze skittered away. "Nothing. Come on," he said, already heading toward the food tables that lined the far wall.

Frowning, Tess hurried to keep up.

Savannah remained in the doorway. She stood frozen, paralyzed by self-consciousness.

Jeffie was across the hall. Their gazes met across the crowd. Her heart seemed to stop beating. She twisted her hands together to keep them from shaking.

He pushed through the people and came to a stop in front of her. "Hi, Vannah." Her name was a high-pitched squeak. "Uh. Sorry." He cleared his throat. "H-How are you?"

Savannah swallowed thickly. "Fine."

He cleared his throat again. "You look . . . pretty."

"I do?"

His voice fell to an earnest whisper. "I never seen anyone so pretty. You wanna dance?"

She nodded. "Yeah. I . . . I mean yes, I would."

He reached for her hand. She hesitated only a heartbeat, then slipped her hand in his. It felt warm and nice.

He led her to the middle of the dance floor. All around them people were stomping, laughing, and dancing, but neither of them noticed. They stood there, staring at each other.

Jeffie cleared his throat. "I . . . I'm gonna put my hand here . . . on your back."

"Okay."

As he pulled her into his arms, Savannah cautiously moved her hand to the center of his back, just as her daddy had taught her. The flannel of his shirt felt soft and slightly fuzzy against her damp palm.

They moved stiffly at first, each mentally counting.

One, two, three. One, two, three. Gradually they became more comfortable together. They picked up their pace, swirling in a huge clover pattern across the wooden floor.

Savannah felt giddy and trembling as he twirled her around the floor. The room blurred, became a hazy world of golden light and shifting shapes. She felt like a fairy princess.

All too soon the dance ended. Savannah and Jeffie stopped dancing. She looked up; he looked down. His fingers tightened around hers; his gaze narrowed and slid down to her lips.

He's gonna kiss me. Right here in front of everyone!

Savannah's breathing quickened. Her heart pounded so loudly, she thought for sure he could hear it. Anticipation made her lean ever so slightly toward him.

He bent his head.

She tilted hers just a little.

His lips touched hers in a feather-stroke.

She drew in a shaky breath and kissed him back. When they drew back, they were both grinning.

Tess watched Savannah and Jeffie twirl awkwardly around the dance floor. A mother's pride filled her heart to overflowing. She smiled, fighting back tears.

Jack moved closer. She felt the heat of his body alongside hers. Gently he withdrew Caleb from her arms and handed the baby to Minerva. "Let's dance," he whispered in Tess's ear.

Her heart tripped hard. Emotions hurtled through her with breathtaking velocity. Excitement. Happiness. Fear. This was a moment she'd dreamed of all her life. Since junior high when she'd stood pinned to the wall with the other special ed kids, watching the dancers move. The beat

of the music had vibrated in her mind like a teasing flash
of memory.

And now, finally, she could hear the music and she was
being asked to dance. But she didn't know how. What if
she made an idiot of herself, what if—

Jack took her in his arms. She melted against him, reveling
in the familiar, masculine scent of him.

He touched her chin, tilted her face up. "Hey, you're
trembling."

She looked up into his loving, concerned eyes and almost
burst into tears. Emotion swelled in her throat. Suddenly
it didn't matter if she tripped all over his feet and
made a spectacle of herself. For now, tonight, she was going
to dance.

She nodded. "I'd love to," she breathed.

He took her hand and led her onto the dance floor. All
around them, dancers whirled and stomped. Color flashed
by her eyes in a dizzying rainbow.

She closed her eyes, listening to the glorious sounds.
Dreamily she swayed with the music.

"Come on, Lissa," he murmured, drawing her close.
The warm, brandy-soft tenor of his voice washed over her
in a tingle-inducing wave. His hand settled possessively in
the small of her back.

He took her in his arms and began to move. Tess
gripped his hand and stumbled along with him.

"You're leading," he whispered.

She cast him an apologetic glance. "It's a character
flaw."

He laughed and held her tighter. "You've forgotten how
to dance, I take it."

She nodded. "Maybe we could—"

"Come closer. Put your cheek against my chest."

She did. His arms curled around her, held her lovingly.

"Okay," he said softly, and she could feel his breath against her forehead, "now, *feel* the music."

She looked up at him. "No. I've done that enough in my life. I want to *hear* it."

"Close your eyes."

She sighed. "Jack—"

"You've forgotten how to dance. I remember. So close your eyes."

Reluctantly she did.

"Now, *feel* the music," he murmured. "Let it speak to your soul."

She pressed tighter against him. His heartbeat thudded against her ear. The whiny twang of the fiddle became louder, soaring above the sound of shuffling feet and rustling skirts. Eyes closed, moving within the warm, protective circle of his arms, she lapsed into a whimsical, relaxed state. The hay and woodsmoke and musk scent of the hall wreathed her, took her to a magical, music-filled world that was hers alone.

The music coiled around her heart. She felt its vibration, and more than that, its emotion, in her soul. She looked up at Jack in wonder. "My God," she breathed. "I can feel it."

He laughed and twirled her around. She clung to him as he spiraled around the crowded floor. Laughing, they swept past the fiddler. Tess saw the whiskey barrels in a blur of brown and black. Another wave of amazement passed through her in a shiver. She was dancing. *Dancing*.

They moved around the floor in a colorful swirl. The other dancers twirled around them, feet stomping to the fast beat, hands clapping. But Tess and Jack continued to waltz.

Tess looked up at him. Her eyes were shining with all the love in her heart. "I could dance with you forever."

"You will, Lissa."
"Promise?" she breathed.
He smiled. "I promise."

Chapter Twenty-three

Savannah gripped Jeffie's hand and ran beside him through the copse of trees. Moonlight glittered through the dense leaves overhead and illuminated the trampled-down path with eerie blue-white light.

"Hurry up, Peters!" Joey Schmidt yelled from somewhere up ahead. "We don't got all night. It's almost time for the supper break."

Jeffie tightened his hold on Savannah's hand and ran faster. When they reached the small clearing, Savannah let go of Jeffie's hand and clutched her aching side, bending over in an attempt to catch her breath.

"Jeez," Jeffie murmured. "They're great. Where'd you get 'em, Joey?"

"One o' the soldiers from the English Camp gave 'em to me. Too bad they had to leave. Them British had all kinds of good stuff."

Savannah's breathing normalized. Straightening, she stared down at the group of boys huddled in the center of the clearing. "What you guys got there?" she said, moving toward them.

The boys pushed to their feet. Grinning, Joey showed her his treasures. In one hand was a long metal sparkler, and in the other was a small burlap sack.

"This one's called a Brilliant Star," he said, thrusting

the sparkler toward her. "And I got tons of other fireworks in the bag."

Fear spilled through Savannah in an ice-cold wave. The world seemed suddenly to tilt and throw her off balance. Her stomach lurched sickeningly.

She brought a hand to her mouth to stifle the scream that crept up her throat.

"Oh, God." The words came out in a strangled-sounding gasp. "No," she said, shaking her head. "You can't—"

"Come on, Vannah. Don't be such a girl." Laughing, the boys pushed past her and ran back down the path.

Toward the hall.

Savannah's inertia snapped. The hall!

She snatched up her skirts in shaking hands. Crying, desperate, she ran after them.

The last echoing notes of a waltz hung in the air. Jack and Tess came to a reluctant stop. She stared up at him, smiling broadly. She was just about to say, "I love you" when the world exploded with sound.

Tess leapt out of Jack's arms and looked wildly around. Streamers of light shot across the open doorway on their way into the sky. Red-gold sparkles glittered against the darkness in a flickering spray.

She let out her breath in a relieved sigh. "Fireworks," she said, smiling. "I never knew they were so loud."

Jack let out a bloodcurdling scream.

She spun around. Jack was standing about two feet away from her, his legs braced apart, his hands plastered to his ears. There was no color in his cheeks.

"Noooo!" he screamed.

The islanders began to slowly back away, muttering quietly among themselves and shaking their heads.

Fear coursed through Tess. "Get them to stop the fire-works," she yelled frantically. When no one moved, she grabbed hold of the nearest sleeve and whipped a frightened-looking woman around. "Please," Tess begged. *"Please . . ."*

The woman's eyes bulged. "O-Okay." She turned to the man beside her. "Go stop that racket, Frank."

Jack screamed again and started to run. He shoved through the silent crowd as if he didn't see them at all.

Tess stared dumbly at him for a heartbeat. Her bones felt as if they'd been pulverized. Ice-cold fear rushed through her blood. What was happening? She brought a trembling hand to her mouth. Oh, God, what was happening?

Jack pushed through the doors and disappeared.

Screaming, she ran after him. "Jack! Wait!"

He stumbled across the threshold and half fell down the sagging steps. Righting himself, he kept running through the knee-high grass and disappeared into a stand of maple trees.

Tess ran faster, her arms pumping hard at her sides, her breath coming in hot, painful spurts.

Up ahead, there was a *thunk*, then a crash.

Tess burst into the trees and came to a shuddering halt. She was alone.

"Oh, God," she whimpered. "Jack?"

She heard a groan.

Tess yanked up her skirts and dove for him. He wrenched out of her grasp and started to stumble away.

Tess surged toward him and grabbed his wrist, hanging on with both hands. "Jack?" She tried to scream his name at the top of her lungs, but it issued past her lips as a frightened, trembling whisper.

He didn't seem to hear her.

Tess stared at him in mounting terror. He didn't even know she was there. He was stiff as a board, and breathing hard. His eyes were glassy and unfocused, and his skin was pale as death. He appeared to be having a psychotic episode.

Fear twisted her insides into a quivering knot. She'd seen breakdowns in psychiatric wards of hospitals, and they'd always terrified her. "Jack?" she whispered. "What is it? What's happening?"

He didn't even look at her.

She stared up into his chalky face and felt a stab of fear so sharp, she cried out. A sob burst from her throat. "Oh, God, Jack . . . what's happening?"

He screamed again, another bloodcurdling shriek of pure, primal terror. He turned, tried to run.

Tess clung to his wrist. He dragged her through the damp grass. "No, Jack," she cried, the words broken by tears. "Please . . ."

He screamed again and dropped to his knees. "Johnny . . ." The name was a twisted, rasping fragment.

Tess took a deep, shuddering breath and clung to his hand. The warm, solid feel of him calmed her down, reminded her that he was here, beside her, and as long as they were together, there was hope.

She grabbed him by the shoulders and tried to will him to look at her. He stiffened and stared past her, his eyes still glassy and unfocused.

"Jack, I know you can hear me. Please . . ." She said the words over and over again, until her throat ached. With each repetition she felt him drifting that much further away from her.

Desperation slid into her fear, giving it a razor-sharp edge.

"Please, Jack, look at me. *See* me. Please . . ." A sob shook her body, slipped past her parched lips as a silent hiccup. Her fingers dug into the soft chambray of his shirt. She squeezed her eyes shut. Memories twirled through her mind. *The next time we kiss, Jack Rafferty, you'll be the one to start it. . . .*

My Katydid. No one's ever dried her tears, or stroked her hair, or told her she was loved. If you can change anything, Lissa, change that. . . .

I love you, Lissa.

Love you, love you, love you. The words circled through her brain in a kaleidoscope of agony. He was leaving her; after everything they'd done and not done, after all the promises of love, he was leaving her. . . .

"*No!*" She screamed the word, suddenly angrier than she'd ever been in her life. "No, goddamn it," she yelled, shaking him hard. "I won't let you do this. You promised." The word broke in half. Pain ripped through her. Clinging to him, she bowed her head and cried. The fight whooshed out of her, leaving in its place an aching, pain-filled void.

"You promised, Jack," she said between sobs. "You said we'd dance forever. . . ."

Tess had no idea how long they sat there, clutched together, Tess crying quietly, Jack staring straight ahead. Cloud after cloud swept past the nearly full moon, plunging them now and again into the utter blackness, then tingeing the clearing in blue-white light.

"Lissa?"

The word was spoken so quietly that at first Tess thought she'd imagined it. Willed it. Tiredly she lifted her head.

"Lissa?"

She clamped a hand over her mouth. Relief spun through her in a dizzying wave.

He blinked down at her.

Tess threw her arms around him and clung to him, crying out with relief and joy. "I'm here, Jack," she crooned, rocking back and forth, "I'm here. You're safe."

He pulled back and looked down at her. There was a

bleakness in his eyes that shredded Tess's heart and brought more tears to her eyes. "I'll never be safe, Lissa." He closed his eyes. "Never."

"Don't say that. Please. We can work through this together. I know we can."

He shook his head slowly, with infinite sorrow. "I thought . . . with you . . . with things the way they were . . . I thought I was getting better." The words were spoken with no emotion whatsoever.

Tess swallowed convulsively. "Don't you do that, Jackson Rafferty. Don't you dare."

He stared through unfocused eyes at the shadowy grass. "Do what?"

"Don't you dare give up." She took him by the shoulders and shook him hard. "I love you." Her voice cracked with emotion, with all the desperation of a woman who'd found love too late and saw it slipping between her fingers. "I won't let you give up. We're a family, goddamn it, and we need you. *I* need you."

He flinched at every word. "You don't need anyone. You never did."

Hot, aching tears burned her eyes and slid down her cheeks. Once again she felt it all slipping away, slipping through her fingers. She tried to close her hand, tried to fist it tight, but the harder she tried, the faster it fell away.

"You're wrong," she whispered desperately. "Before you, I was always alone, always afraid. I've waited for you all my life."

"Lissa . . ."

Her name was a sigh of defeat. Tess felt the softly spoken word like a fist to the throat. Tears streamed down her face and burrowed onto her tongue. They tasted like all the things she'd reached for in her life and never quite attained, all the missed opportunities and forgotten dreams. "Please, Jack," she said brokenly, "don't shut me out."

It was a long time before he spoke. When he finally did, his voice was shaky and weak. "I don't want to."

Tess felt a rush of relief so strong, her knees buckled. She wiped the tears from her eyes and stared up at him. "Promise you'll always stay with me." Her voice broke. "Promise me you won't give up."

He looked at her then, and in his eyes she saw how fiercely he loved her. Her throat constricted so tightly, she couldn't talk. *Please Jack, just say it. Such a tiny, nothing little word . . .*

"I can't." The words sounded ragged and ripped from his soul.

Tess felt as if she'd been struck. She wanted to shake him or rattle him or something—*anything*. Just something to break through the distance he'd encased himself in.

But there was nothing she could do. He was sitting right beside her, touching her, and it felt as if he were a million miles away. *Oh, God . . .*

He took her into his arms, holding her so tightly, she couldn't breathe. She clung to him. Their tear-streaked faces were cheek to cheek, and then, slowly, they drew apart just far enough to gaze into each other's eyes.

The kiss he gave her was desperate and frightened and tasted of their tears.

That night, Jack stood at the bedroom window and stared at the shadowy farm. His body felt taut, as if his skin were stretched to the breaking point. Frustration lay like a thick, angry fog in his mind. He'd been so close. So goddamn close to having it all.

For a few precious moments, he'd forgotten his past.

He let out his breath in a ragged sigh that clouded the windowpane.

"Come to bed, Jack."

He stiffened. Behind him, the bed planks creaked beneath Lissa's weight. *Please don't come over here,* he prayed desperately. He knew that if he touched her, even once, he'd be lost. He'd never have the strength to turn away. To protect her from the darkness in himself.

"I . . . I'm not tired. I think I'll just—"

"Come to bed."

He didn't move. She did.

Jack tensed, feeling her every step like a blow to the gut.

Behind him, she stopped. He could feel the whisper-softness of her breath at the back of his neck.

He stood stock-still, afraid even to breathe.

She whispered his name and touched him at the same time. Her arms curled around his waist and locked. He felt the soft, rounded mounds of her breasts against his back, and he groaned. A yearning ache settled in his heart. Sweet Christ, how he wanted to turn around, take her in his arms, and forget about everything. . . .

"Jack . . ." His name slipped from her lips. "Come to bed."

He shook his head, not trusting himself to speak. If he tried, the words would come out mangled and rasping, and she'd know how scared he was. How terrified. And if she knew that, it would start again. She'd remember why she'd hated him for so many years, what he'd done to ruin their lives. She'd remember that he was a coward who couldn't forget what he'd done. And not done.

The fantasy they'd been living in for the last few weeks would vanish. And again he'd be an outcast, alone and lonely and achingly afraid.

Her hands flattened against his stomach and smoothed slowly upward. Her thumbs hooked his suspenders and flicked them away. They swung alongside his arms in useless black loops.

"W-What are you doing?" he managed to ask.

Her hands glided downward again, passed the thin wooden buttons one by one, until she reached the waist-band of his pants. There she paused for a single, heart-stopping moment, then she flicked the top button open. Then the second.

Jack drew in a ragged breath. The thick twill fabric of his pants gaped open. "Lissa, don't . . ." The words came out as he'd feared: rasping and weak.

The third button popped free.

"Lissa, don't. I can't . . ."

Her hand pushed the gaped fabric aside and slid beneath the thin linen of his drawers. Her palm felt hot and damp against his flesh. He shivered in response.

Her hand moved downward.

Jack's throat went dry. He tried to swallow but couldn't form enough saliva to do it. Instead he pursed his lips together and tried to remain still.

Her hand eased through the crisp hair and crept down-ward, closing around his hardness. Jack gasped, shud-dering at the intimacy of her touch.

She pressed up onto her toes. Her breath was hot and inviting against his ear. "I think you can, Jack."

She slid back down. Her heels hit the floor with a muf-fled thump. Her hand began to move slowly up and down. Each finger felt like a curl of fire around him.

"Ah, Christ." He spun around and grabbed her shoul-ders, jerking her toward him. "Don't do this, Lissa. Don't you know I'm dangerous?"

"Not to me."

Her answer defeated him. Longing spilled through him again, taunted him with how good it would feel to just give in. "How can you be so sure?"

"I trust you."

The simple sentence, one he'd waited half his life to hear, ripped through the rest of his resistance. Groaning, he pulled her close and kissed her, a hot, hard, demanding kiss that was filled with dark, desperate need. He clung to her like a drowning man, planting kisses on her cheeks, her nose, her eyelids. "God, I love you," he murmured against her hair.

She looked up at him through moist eyes. "I love you, too, Jack. Now, come to bed. In case you haven't noticed, I'm trying to seduce you." She gave him a trembling smile that betrayed her own need.

She took his hand and led him to the bed. Candlelight turned the faded, gray sheets into a magical bower of rumpled gold. The huge coverlet hugged the back of the bed in a series of welcome shadows. They stood silently by the bedside, staring at each other. Slowly Tess began unhooking her dress.

"Let me," he said.

Tess felt his every breath like a caress across her bare shoulders. Shivering, she turned around, presenting her back to him. He moved closer.

His hands curled gently around her neck, his thumbs stroked the sensitive flesh of her nape. The warmth of his touch set off a flurry of goose bumps. Slowly his hands glided down her bare back and onto the textured silk of her gown. One by one the hooks and buttons gave way. The gown fell open.

He eased the sleeves downward, freeing her arms. The dress dropped to the floor in a whoosh of pale blue silk. Her undergarments followed until, in no time, she was naked.

She started to turn around, but he wouldn't let her. Moving closer, he let his hands roam gently across her weighty breasts, toying at her nipples until they hardened. She brought her hands up and locked them behind his neck. The roughened pads of his fingertips breezed across her flesh, lingered on her nipples. He kissed her bare throat and shoulders.

Tess shivered at the heat building slowly inside her. She moaned quietly and turned around to face him.

He was bathed in the shimmering glow of candlelight. As she stared up into his handsome, life-hardened face, Tess felt something huge and achingly hard settle in her heart.

Love. For the first time in her life, she understood the magnitude of the simple word. It was more than she'd ever thought it could be. She couldn't imagine how she'd lived without it, and yet, even now, in the midst of its grip, she could see its darker underside. The heartbreak and pain that shimmered beneath its surface like hidden evil beneath a smooth, calm lake.

"What is it, Lissa?" he asked quietly.

She shook her head, unable to force anything past the lump in her throat. How could she tell him? Even if he was able to understand what this moment meant to her, what *he* meant to her, how would he ever understand the newness of her emotion?

She loved him so damn much. Yesterday it had seemed as if they had everything, that love was everything. Now, suddenly, their love seemed fragile, a bond too easily broken.

Fear brought a tremble to her parted lips, and for the first time she wished she'd come to this century without her memories intact. Right now she wanted desperately to be Lissa, only Lissa. She wanted a lifetime's worth of happiness to bind them. They hadn't had enough time together. They needed more. So much more.

"Love me, Jack," she said brokenly. "Love *me.*"

He swept her into his arms and eased her onto the bed. Quickly stripping out of his clothes, he stretched out beside her.

Tess lay naked next to him, feeling the minuscule distance between them swell into a huge, icy chasm. She looked at him, saw that even now, in the midst of a burgeoning passion, there was sadness in his eyes. It ripped at her heart.

Something bad was going to happen. She suppressed a shudder of apprehension.

She slipped her arms around him and huddled close. Their bodies fused, creating a heat that banished the last icy tendrils of fear. Desire and need and desperation coiled together and washed through Tess in an electrifying wave. Suddenly she had a deep, primal urge to mate with him, to merge their bodies and souls into a single, unified whole that could never be ripped apart. She wanted to use her body to drive away his fear. For now, she wanted him to think about her. Not secrets or nightmares or even Amarylis. Just her.

"Lissa?" he whispered against her ear, and there was a world of silent fear in his voice.

She pulled back and looked up at him. "No more being afraid, Jack," she said earnestly.

"It's not that e—"

She kissed him. He held back for a heartbeat, then shuddered hard and held her tightly. Their tongues met, mated, twined in a moist, fervent dance.

The kiss went on forever and beyond. Tess closed her eyes and gave in to the sensations swirling through her. As they kissed, his hand roved down her naked back. Tiny spasms rippled across her flesh at his too gentle touch. Deep inside her, something twisted and began a slow, tantalizing burn.

His mouth moved from hers, trailing hot, openmouthed kisses along her jawline and down her exposed throat. He licked the tiny hollow where her pulse beat too fast.

He pulled away. Cool night air rushed in, skipping

along her naked flesh. She shivered, moaned softly. At the
sound, he looked up. Her gaze caught his, held it fast, and
in the green depths of his eyes she saw a restless longing,
a dark-edged need that matched her own. He felt it, too,
she realized. That desperate need to obliterate the world
beyond this bed.

His head lowered. She felt his tongue like a lick of fire
against her nipple. His hand moved downward even farther. The curly thatch of light brown hair parted easily as
his fingers explored her moist flesh. He cupped her with
his hand, his sweat-dampened palm forming against the
pulsating center of her body.

Tess let out a tiny sound of pleasure. Desire throbbed
between her legs, sending red-hot tentacles shooting
through her blood. His hand pressed against her flesh,
moving, grinding. Slowly at first, and then faster. Harder.

Tess's breath caught. His mouth teased her hardened
nipple. Desire melted into need and became a painful
throbbing. She writhed beneath his touch, aching. . . .

"Now, Jack. Please . . ."

The soft, strangled sound of her voice pushed Jack almost over the edge. Groaning softly with the effort of restraint, he buried his face in the softness of her breasts.
His hand slipped lower, feeling the hot moisture of her response.

"God," he whispered brokenly, "you're so ready."

She clutched him with frantic fingers, drew him close.
"I know."

A sound that was part laugh, part groan pushed up his
throat. Murmuring her name, he curled his arms around
her and rolled her beneath him. Her legs slid apart, her
hand closed around his hardness and guided him in.

Slowly he entered her.

She gasped, shivered. Her arms coiled around his body

and squeezed hard. She stared up at him through dreamy, unfocused eyes.

In that gaze Jack saw everything he'd ever dreamed of seeing and more. So much more. An aching tenderness unfolded within him, wrapping him in layers of soothing warmth. He'd loved this woman for more than half his life, but never had he loved her as much as he did right now.

She grabbed his buttocks in shaking, desperate fingers. "Now, Jack," she said urgently. "Now."

Need coursed through his body at her passionate plea. With a bitten-off groan, he thrust into the welcoming tightness of her body.

"Yes, Jack. *Yes* . . ."

He plunged deep within her, then withdrew. She quivered, staring up at him. Passion turned her eyes into dark brown pools. Her legs wrapped around his body. Slowly, so slowly, he entered her again.

She thrust up to meet him. Her fingernails raked his sweat-dampened back, her head lolled into the pile of pillows.

He made long, exquisite love to her, bringing her time and again to the point of release, then slowly drawing away. She clung to him, whimpering his name and dozens of unintelligible words of passion and love. Her legs locked behind him, her feet pressed hard against his buttocks.

He kissed her mouth, her throat, her nipples, kissed her and thrust against her until they were both desperate and aching.

"Oh, God, Jack," she moaned, writhing beneath him. "Now."

He squeezed his eyes shut and plunged inside her, deep and hard. She gasped, planting her legs and thrusting up to meet him.

He felt it first as a whoosh of breath across his cheek. Then he felt the pulsations rippling inside her. The last shred of Jack's restraint snapped. He pressed his fists into the tired cotton sheets and arched his back, driving into her body.

Bolt after bolt of white-hot pleasure erupted through his body. Afterward he rolled onto his back and slid his arm beneath her, drawing her beside him. She stretched out alongside him, one leg thrown casually across his thighs.

Tess floated slowly back to earth. And hit with a bang.

She had about fifteen seconds of blissful oblivion, then reality drifted back into her consciousness, and try as she might, she couldn't dislodge it. Not even for a moment.

His arms curled around her, held her tightly against his sweat-slicked flesh. But it wasn't enough. Tess fought a wave of sadness. She was right next to him, almost on top of him, and yet she wasn't close enough.

It—whatever *it* was—lay between them like a living, breathing presence.

She rolled half on top of him, resting her chin on the hard wall of his chest. The sweet, cloying scent of fresh passion and sweaty flesh filled her nostrils, reminding her with every breath that they loved each other. Desperately, completely.

He wedged up on his elbows and looked at her. A damp lock of black hair fell across his eyes. He smiled, but it was a pale imitation of the real thing, and Tess felt the falseness of it like a raw wound on her heart.

They both knew the truth, could feel it like a cold wind blowing across their love. They were close, but not close enough.

Tess touched his cheek in a bittersweet caress. She thought of all the times she'd dreamed of him, back when he was a faceless, restless shadow not remembered with the light of dawn. All the nights she'd lain awake, aching for someone to hold her and kiss her and whisper quiet words of love.

Now she had all that and more.

And yet, with his secret between them, inside him, eating like a cancer through his heart and soul, she wondered if she really had anything at all.

His finger breezed across her trembling lower lip. "What's the matter?"

Tess squeezed her eyes shut. There were so many questions she wanted to ask him; they hung heavy and demanding on the tip of her tongue. But if she probed too deeply, or too soon, she'd scare him away. One wrong question and he'd retreat back into that small, silent place inside himself, and she would be left alone. Worse than alone.

"Lissa?"

She gazed at him through a watery blur of tears. It took every ounce of strength she possessed to shake her head.

He stared at her for a long time. "You want to ask me questions, don't you?" he said quietly.

Her breath caught. Hope spilled through her in an unwanted rush. "N-No. You have to want to tell me."

"Tell you what?"

She felt as if she were walking out on a very thin ledge below which was a hell of a fall. She moved cautiously. "You're afraid of something. Maybe . . . maybe if you talked about it, the fear would go away."

Jack paled. "I . . . I can't. . . ."

Tess knew she'd pushed too hard. She pressed a finger to his lips. "Shh, don't. We have all the time in the world. It doesn't have to happen tonight."

He tried to look away. She took his face in her hands and gently forced him to meet her gaze. "I mean it, Jack.

Whenever you want to talk, I'll listen. I'll listen every night for sixty years if I have to, and I'll never judge you. I promise."

"Why?" The word sounded strangled and far away.

"Because I love you."

He deflated. The fear in his eyes melted into despair and tore a ragged hole in her heart. "The doctors said . . ." He squeezed his eyes shut in shame. "I can't talk about it."

Sadness seeped through Tess. She tried to understand, telling herself it was normal. But still she felt betrayed and rejected. She broke eye contact and stared at the bedpost through a blur of tears.

"Lissa?"

She squeezed her eyes shut. Defeat, she reminded herself, was something she knew how to deal with. She knew better than to let a setback get her down. She loved Jack, and she'd never stop trying to reach him. Never.

She opened her eyes and gazed down at him, trying desperately not to feel the tiny, serrated crack in her heart. He needed her now, needed her strong and patient and loving. And that's what she'd be. Every day, in every way, she'd let him know that, secret or no secret, he was loved. And maybe, when he really believed it, he'd be ready to trust her.

"We'll get through this, Jack. I promise."

Chapter Twenty-four

The storm waited until midnight, then struck hard.

Jack writhed restlessly. Sweat crawled across his forehead, and a low, frightened moan escaped his lips.

"No." The word was a dry, hopeless whisper. He whipped his head from side to side, fighting to wake up. "No . . ."

The nightmare sank its teeth into his soft flesh and pulled him downward, into the whirling, terrifying blackness lodged in his soul.

The clearing smelled of gunpowder and fire and death. Jack stood frozen with fear.

Gun and cannon fire exploded around him. Smoke filled the clearing and stung his eyes. Rain slashed at his head and ran in cold, gushing streaks down his face. The endless, hammering thunk of each droplet echoed the pounding of his heart.

"Jacko!" Johnny yelled from up ahead. "Come on."

Woodenly Jack started to run. The winter-hard ground sliced his bare feet and sent shafts of pain up his legs with every step. His rifle thudded against his back. Smoke stung his eyes and blurred his vision.

"Johnny, where are you?" He stumbled to a stop and desperately scanned the hazy battlefield. His gaze darted through the fallen and the dead. Fear clawed up his throat. "Johnny!"

Suddenly something hurled out of the foggy haze and landed in his arms. Warm blood splatted across his face. Jack looked down at what he held and screamed. "Noooo . . ."

He kept screaming until his voice was rasping and weak.

He sank to his knees in the wet dirt. The smell of blood and gore clogged his throat and nose, and tears stung his eyes until he couldn't see anything at all. Not even his brother's cold, dead eyes.

"Jack . . . you're hurting me. Let go of my wrist."

Jack thought he heard something. He opened his eyes. They felt painfully dry and unfocused. A headache pounded through his head.

He was looking at a face. Frightened brown eyes peered up at him through a maze of spun-gold hair. "Jack, please . . ."

He blinked hard, trying to focus. The eyes changed subtly, blurred into glassy, dead gray orbs that stared at him accusingly. *Johnny.*

Fear chilled him to the bone. Wildly he looked around, but the world was cold and dark.

"Jack, honey, I'm right here. You're okay. You're safe."

The night exploded with thunder. Jack came awake with a start. Terror tingled in icy shards through his body, turned his stomach into a twisted knot. He lurched out of the wet grass—or was it his bed?—and stumbled to his feet.

He stood rooted to the spot, his heart pumping in his ears. Rain slashed against a familiar window. Wind rattled the glass.

The bedroom, he realized. He was in the bedroom. With a sigh of relief, he yanked his long johns off the bedpost and got dressed.

Lightning flashed twice in rapid succession, transforming the window into an eerie mirror. For a split second Jack stared into his own haunted, frightened face. Then the image changed slightly, and he was staring into Johnny's dead, lifeless eyes.

It was happening again.

The darkness was coming. He could feel it creeping up on him, inexorably padding through the shadowy blackness of his mind. It was coming to take him away.

He turned for the door and ran down the hallway, through the menacing shadows of the house. As he rounded the kitchen table, thunder reverberated. The dishes in the dresser clattered together, the table creaked.

He skidded to a stop. Lightning flashed, and in the momentary light, he saw Johnny's face again in the window. Pale. Dead. Accusing. *Jacko, where were you? I needed you, needed you, needed you. . . .*

Fear devoured Jack. His heartbeat turned into a deafening roar in his ears.

He had to get out of here. Now, before the darkness came. Before he hurt someone. Shaking, breathing hard, he reached for the door.

Something grabbed his arm. "Jack, please . . ."

He flinched at the sound of his wife's voice. Longing spilled through him in hot, desperate waves. He swallowed thickly. If only he could turn and take her in his arms and hold her until the danger was past, until she made it go away.

Maybe if you talked about it. Her words pushed their way into his foggy brain, bringing with them a need so strong, he almost sank to his knees. He squeezed his eyes shut, curled his hands into shaking fists. God, if only it were that simple.

He wanted to talk to her, *ached* to talk with her. The need to try was like a hard, dry knot in his chest. *If only.*

But he'd tried that before.

The memory hit him like a splash of cold water. He couldn't talk about his past, couldn't reopen wounds that were held together with unraveling threads of fear. If he told her the truth about himself, this fantasy love affair would end. Either she'd remember why she'd hated him before, or she'd start fresh from today. At the end of his horrible confession, she'd look at him through new, narrowed eyes. She'd see his failure, his shame, and she'd never be able to love him again.

He couldn't do it, couldn't watch the love in her eyes shrivel and die. Couldn't bear the thought that the warmth of her touch would turn icy cold again.

He looked down at her, feeling old and tired. Their gazes met. Her dark eyes were sad—so sad, it shamed him to the depths of his soul.

"Stay," she whispered, clutching his arm. "Please . . ."

"I can't." His voice was ragged and torn.

"But, Jack—"

He grabbed her by the shoulders, holding her at arm's length. "Don't you understand? I could *hurt* you. Jesus, I could—" He looked away. "Go back to bed," he said in a voice so frayed, he didn't even recognize it. "Please . . ."

Then, cursing thickly, he flung the door open. It hit the side of the house with a crack.

She lurched toward him. "Don't go, please, we can—"

He gave her one last, longing look, then he grabbed his boots and coat and ran from the house.

Tess ran after him onto the rain-slicked porch. Fear suffocated her, settled in her lungs like a dull, throbbing ache.

Rain slashed at her naked breasts and ran in rivulets down her stomach. Drumrolls of thunder pulsated through the night. Gray-black rain clouds boiled ominously overhead. Far below, angry waves churned and crashed against invisible boulders.

"Jack!" she screamed, but the wind dashed her voice into nothing.

A series of lightning bolts shot from the heavens and illuminated the farm. In the flash of unearthly light, she saw him, a shadowy, hunched-over figure running past the barn and down the hill.

"Don't go . . ." This time the words were no more than a whispered prayer she knew he couldn't hear.

The lightning flashed again, and he was gone.

Tess stood rooted to the spot, naked and shivering. Terror, colder and more debilitating than anything she'd ever known, washed through her in wave after ice-cold wave. Her body trembled with it, her eyes burned.

He wasn't coming back.

At the realization, Tess's legs gave out. She sank to her knees on the hard, wet floor. Her breathing was rapid and shallow, and every breath hurt.

He didn't trust her. Even now, after everything, he didn't trust her. Maybe he never would.

"Please." The word was a broken thought, a formless longing. "Please . . ."

She brought her hands to her lap and stared down at the shaking, frozen fists. Tears squeezed past her lashes and blurred her vision. It was slipping through her fingers, slipping so fast, she couldn't get a hold. Everything she'd ever wanted or needed or ached for was here, in this house, and she couldn't hold on. He wouldn't let her.

A sob broke free and spilled from her trembling lips.

"Come back, Jack," she whispered, tasting the mingled moisture of her tears and the rain. "Please come back . . ."

Tess stumbled back into her bedroom and collapsed on the bed. She lay there for a long time, curled in the fetal position, shivering and praying, *Please, God, just bring him back safe. Please . . .*

Someone knocked at the door.

For a heart-stopping moment, she thought it was Jack, then she realized he wouldn't knock. She let her breath out in a defeated sigh and slipped into her lawn nightgown.

"Come in," she called out wearily.

The door opened. Savannah and Katie stood in the doorway, their faces pale with uncertainty.

Tess tried to smile but couldn't quite manage it.

Savannah twisted her fingers together. "Is Daddy gone again?"

Sadness wrenched through Tess. The heart she thought she'd lost twisted hard. The girls—her girls—were trying so hard to be brave, not to cry. The realization reminded Tess that they were a family now. A family. None of them had to suffer alone; they had one another.

"Come on over," she said, patting the bed next to her.

They were beside her in a second, clambering up onto the big bed. Katie snuggled alongside her mother and tilted her small face up. "Will he be back?"

Tess swallowed a lump of fear. She wished she could lie. *Yes, girls, I'm sure your father is fine. He knows how to take care of himself.* No doubt it was the parental thing to do—say anything to ease their minds.

But as she stared down into Katie's earnest, frightened eyes, she knew she couldn't do that. They were a family now, and they'd weather their storms together. "I don't know. I wish I did."

They lapsed into silence, each lost in her own fears, her own thoughts. Tess tried to calm herself down, tried to call upon the rational scientist she'd been all her life, but she couldn't quite manage it. She was so afraid. . . .

Focus. Concentrate.

She took a deep, ragged breath and counted silently to ten. She had to be strong now. For Jack, for the children. He was in trouble, real trouble, and he needed her. She needed to look at this situation with a clear head and figure out what the hell to do. How to help him.

She felt herself calm down. She was on familiar ground now. The beginning of any project was always the same. Gather data and find facts. As a scientist, she'd learned to take a particularly thorny project slowly, studying it from every angle before she began. One misstep, one rushed diagnosis, could botch the whole experiment.

She glanced down at her wrist. Tiny blue marks were just beginning to form against her pale flesh. It was tender where his fingers had squeezed. He hadn't known he was hurting her; she was almost certain. She didn't think he even knew he was touching her. Or even that she was there beside him.

When she'd called out his name, he'd looked confused and disoriented. And desperately afraid.

Fear was the key; she was sure of it.

"What are you so afraid of, Jack?" she murmured, unaware that she'd voiced the question aloud until Savannah answered her.

"Loud noises, I think."

Tess's trancelike concentration snapped. "Huh?"

"I think loud noises make him leave," Savannah said quietly. "You know, like thunder, firecrackers, rain on the roof, gunshots. When he hears noises like that, he goes . . . crazy."

Tess frowned in thought, trying to analyze the information. Loud noises made him run. And then what?

How long have I been gone?

Tess's heartbeat quickened. Loud noises made him run away, and afterward, he didn't remember what he'd done or how long he'd been gone. *Blackout.*

She was getting closer.

Loud noises. Nighttime. Temporary amnesia. What was the connection?

"What's a coward?" Katie asked.

The question caught Tess completely off guard. Reluctant to let go of the puzzle, she glanced down at Katie. "Why do you ask?"

"You always say Daddy's a coward, and that's why Johnny's dead."

Tess gasped at the cruelty of the remark. It took a moment to compose herself enough to answer. She curled her arms more tightly around both girls, feeling the slight trembling of their bodies. "Your daddy's not a coward."

"How do you know?" Savannah asked.

Tess smiled grimly. "Because he stayed with me all these years. And from what I can tell, that takes courage of the purest kind."

Katie smiled and leaned against Tess again.

Absently Tess smoothed the child's hair. Again they lapsed into silence. It was a few seconds before Katie's innocent question hit home.

Johnny.

You always say Daddy's a coward, and that's why Johnny's dead.

Tess straightened. "Savannah, who's Johnny?"

"Daddy's brother. He died in the war. You know that."

The war. The word landed in Tess's lap like a gift from God. Excitement made her heart race. She knew better than to jump to conclusions, but she couldn't help herself. Her next question came eagerly. "Was your daddy in the war, too?"

"Yeah."

Tess sagged with relief. The puzzle pieces fell into place. Gunshots, firecrackers, loud noises; they were all triggers.

Something had happened to Jack in the war. Something so terrible, he couldn't deal with it; so painful, his conscious mind worked to keep it covered and out of sight.

Whatever it was, he'd run from it then, and he was running from it now.

Tess leaned back into the pile of pillows. Hope surged through her. Now his fear had a name. A reason. It wasn't that he didn't trust her. It was that he didn't trust himself.

Tess's breath released in a relieved sigh. This was something they could work through.

"Hey," she said quietly, "do y'all want to sleep with me?"

Both girls nodded at once.

Tess leaned over and blew out the lamp. Then, curling tightly together under the heavy coverlet, they all fell asleep.

Outside, the storm raged on.

The next morning dawned bright and beautiful, without a trace of the torrent that had ravaged the land the night before. Tess stood on the porch with Caleb in her arms, waving good-bye to the girls as they left for school. Beside her, the oak's leaves glistened in the pale sunlight.

In her arms, Caleb gurgled playfully. Rocking gently side to side, Tess stared across the rolling pasture and thought about last night.

Post traumatic stress disorder.

She'd studied the disorder in a few of her graduate-level psych courses. From what she could remember, it was a condition suffered by a wide range of people—accident survivors, rape and child abuse victims, wartime soldiers. Anytime a trauma was too intense or too severe to be handled, the mind simply shut it out in self-defense. Amnesia, blackouts, insomnia, anger, and depression were all completely normal responses.

In class, they hadn't specifically discussed the Civil War, but she knew it had to have been the most psychologically devastating of any war. Brothers, fathers, uncles, friends, all fighting one another, face-to-face. Killing one another.

Tess shivered at the thought. No wonder Jack had nightmares and couldn't sleep. He was grappling with a disorder that wouldn't be understood for another one hundred years. He probably thought he was insane.

Suddenly the haunted eyes made sense. So did the anger and the anxiety and the shield of silence. And the fear that he would hurt someone. They were all ways to deal with sanity that occasionally seemed to slip, with nights that wound their way through hell before coming to the light of morning.

That's why I'm here. The realization hit her hard. No one from this century could help Jack. It was up to someone with the knowledge of the future. It was up to Tess.

"I can help you, Jack," she murmured. "Just come home and let me try."

Tears burned her eyes. Her voice cracked with emotion. "Just come home."

Jack drifted in and out of consciousness. Finally he blinked awake, feeling groggy and disoriented.

Fear started as a queasy feeling in the pit of his stomach and graduated into a suffocating presence. His heart started beating faster, harder, thudding painfully in his rib cage.

He eased his eyes open and immediately regretted it. Late afternoon sunlight stabbed deep in his skull. He winced, knowing what would come next; what *always* came next.

The migraine began as a low, thudding pulse in the back of his head. With every heartbeat it expanded, seeping through his brain and drilling hard behind his eyes. Nausea churned in his gut, its vile, bitter taste invading his mouth.

Where the hell was he?

Frantically he searched for landmarks, and found none.

He was sitting beneath a tall cedar tree in the middle of a huge field. It could be any field, anywhere on the island. The only thing he knew for sure was that it wasn't his field.

Trembling, nauseous, he tried to stand, but his legs were too weak to support his weight. Halfway up, he wobbled, reached blindly for the tree. Rough bark scraped his knuckles and bit deeply into the back of his hand. He yanked his hand back and pinned it protectively to his chest. Warm blood seeped into the dirty fabric of his long johns.

Staggering sideways, he hit the tree hard. Pain ricocheted through his shoulder and shot down his arm. Panting hard, he leaned heavily against the thick trunk.

Panic and despair choked him as he tried to remember. Something, he thought, desperately, please let there be *something*. . . .

But there was nothing. No memory; no hint of memory. His mind was chillingly, terrifyingly blank.

He banged his head back against the tree and squeezed his eyes shut. He started to fist his gun hand and felt a red-hot stab of pain.

He glanced down. His hand was a scraped, wood-infested blur of dripping blood and ripped flesh.

The image hurled him back in time. Bloody fingers, a bloody arm. Blood and dirt, blood and dirt, blood and— *Johnny.*

Jack moaned softly as image after image spiraled through his mind. The rain, the thunder, the image of Johnny's dead face in the window. The nightmare.

He remembered what he always remembered: the beginning and the end. It always started with the nightmare and ended with the darkness.

Self-loathing washed through him in a dizzying, nauseating wave. He ignored the pain and curled his injured hand into a bloody, shaking fist.

The war was over, goddamn it. Why couldn't he forget? *Why?*

He'd tried so hard. He'd done everything the doctors had told him to do; he'd told himself he'd done the manly thing, the *normal* thing; he'd sealed his lips and never once spoken of the bloody battlefield at Antietam or the day Johnny had died.

And yet the memories persisted, thrived in the dark, twisted recesses of his mind.

Once he'd thought that talking about it might help. After so many years alone, sitting in that lightless, airless hospital room, with nothing to do but think about—dwell on—the horror, he'd thought all he had to do was share his memories and they would go away.

Except there had been no one with whom to share them. No one who would listen. He still remembered the day he'd finally made it home. The endless, aching months on the road between the hospital and home had dissolved the instant he'd seen the tall, graceful mansion. On bare feet that had walked hundreds of miles over rocky, dirty roads, he'd run to the front door.

He told himself it didn't matter that there was no one to greet him. They didn't know he was coming home, after all. They hadn't even known he'd been in the hospital. They knew only that the war had been over for months, and neither of their sons had returned.

At first the welcome had been everything he'd hoped for. His father and mother and Amarylis and Savannah had crowded around him, hugging, laughing, weeping, welcoming. He and Amarylis had shared a wonderful, magical night of love. A night that had given Jack his wonderful Katie.

In the morning, though, everything changed. All it had taken was a single, casually spoken word. "Hospital."

We thought you were a prisoner of war, son.

Jack cringed even now, remembering the gut-wrenching shame he'd experienced at his father's quiet words.

No, I was in a hospital.

Where were you hurt? His mother's words, filled with concern.

That had been the hardest question of all to answer. He had no physical scars, no limp, no missing limbs; no injuries of the kind they could understand and accept.

He didn't blame them—or at least, he tried not to. Hell, he'd lived through it, and he couldn't understand.

He'd tried his best to explain. *I don't know what happened, Dad. . . . They shouted the order to attack. But I . . . I couldn't move. Then Johnny yelled to me, and I ran after him, but it was too . . . late. He was dead. After that, I woke up in the hospital—*

You froze like some two-bit coward because things got a little bloody? His father turned away from him in disgust. His voice had been full of quiet condemnation. *You're no son of mine.*

Jack said nothing more. He realized then, when he looked into his father's cold, disgusted gaze, that the doctors had been right. He should have sealed his lips and borne his heartache and guilt like a man. In silence.

He'd disgraced them, and to his father, a third-generation Georgia gentleman, there was no greater crime.

He and Amarylis had been asked to leave. His wife hadn't wanted to go—she'd made that more than plain—but there was Savannah to worry about, and Amarylis had no money and no family. That's why she'd married Jack in the first place.

Then the hatred began. Not a little bit at a time, day by day like some marriages, but *bang!* all at once. One day she loved him, the next day she despised him. And Jack understood her contempt. She'd married him for security and respectability, and in one miserable sentence, he'd stripped her of both.

Together and yet horribly separate, they left Rafferty Farms, left Georgia, left the South. Jack hadn't known then where they were headed; he knew only that he had to be as far from the South as possible, as far from other men as he could be.

By the time they'd reached North Dakota, Amarylis had started to show with Katie. Every new inch on her waistline added to her hatred for Jack and their unborn child. Even Savannah, who had once been the apple of her mother's eye, became just another tainted fruit from the poison tree.

He understood her contempt and almost respected it. It mirrored so closely how he felt about himself.

The gun. The thought burrowed in his mind and grew. This time he could do it. This time he wouldn't let fear stop him. This time he could pull the trigger for sure. This time—

Lissa.

Memories of her spilled through him, warming the cold, dark spots in his soul. All thoughts of suicide and failure vanished.

We'll get through this together, Jack. I promise.

A broken sob escaped him. He clamped a bloody hand over his mouth. God, it sounded good. Jesus . . .

He closed his eyes, remembering the strength of her arms as she'd held him, the taste of her tears as she'd begged him never to leave her. Then he remembered the night he'd left. She'd reached for him, held him in shaking, desperate fingers, tried to keep him from running.

Together, Jack. Together.

Suddenly he ached to hear those comforting words

again, trembled with the need to feel the softness of her skin and smell the lavender-scented sweetness of her hair.

He moved away from the tree and started walking through the tall, swaying, golden grass toward home.

Toward Lissa.

Chapter Twenty-five

It took Jack hours to find his way to the house. He paused by the side of the barn. The last, fading rays of sunlight cast the farm in a cozy glow. The house seemed almost iridescent, its ordinary whitewashed boards transformed into pearlized planks by the setting sun.

He felt a stab of longing so powerful and unexpected, he almost staggered from the force of it. For years he'd dreamed of living in a place like this. An honest-to-God home. A place filled with dreams and laughter and light. And here it was at last.

He started to take a step toward it when a sound caught his attention. He paused, turned toward the barn door. From inside came the clanging thunk of metal on metal. Frowning, he eased the big wooden door open and slipped quietly inside.

Lissa was standing with her back to him, carefully reorganizing his tools. She'd cleaned his pitchfork and put it back where it belonged. The huge red ribbon around the tool barrel was gone. The only thing out of place was his old Winchester shotgun. For some reason, the weapon was propped in the corner of the barn. It stood at an odd angle, almost as if it had been thrown there and then forgotten.

"Lissa." He said her name quietly, half expecting her to vanish at the sound.

She gasped and spun around. The hoe she was holding slipped from her hand and thudded to the ground. "Jack!"

She snatched up her skirts and ran for him, throwing herself into his arms.

At her touch, Jack swayed with relief. The warmth of her body against his was a soothing balm on his soul. "God, you feel good," he murmured against her hair.

She clung to him. "I missed you so much. I was so afraid."

"I always come back," he whispered, feeling the moisture of her tears seeping through the flannel of his long johns and dampening his chest.

She pulled away suddenly and stared up at him through glazed eyes. He realized then, looking in her eyes, how much he'd hurt her by leaving. How afraid she'd been that he wouldn't return. The knowledge that he'd hurt her was like a dull, aching sore in his heart.

He wrapped her in his arms and held her tightly. He wanted to share with her, wanted to tell her everything, but he was afraid. So goddamn afraid. The doctors told him never to speak of it, never even to think about it. What if he opened his mouth and instead of words coming out, he screamed? He was afraid that if he screamed once, he'd never be able to stop, and one day he'd wake up again, nameless and alone, in a dirty hospital bed.

He shivered at the thought, remembering the countless months he'd spent in that sagging cot, unable to think or speak. Staring sightlessly at the blood-splattered ceiling.

"Jack?" she whispered, touching his cheek.

He looked down at her. He could see the question in her eyes, see how desperately she wanted to understand where he'd been and why he'd gone. But she didn't ask.

"Why?" The word slipped out unexpectedly.

"Why what?"

"Why don't you ask?"

She blinked in surprise. "I want to know, but ... I trust you, Jack. That's the most important thing. You'll tell me when you're ready."

Jack stared down into her trusting, loving gaze and felt something inside him begin to crumble. He'd told himself he was making a new start. He'd promised God, and yet he hadn't begun again. Not really. There would be no beginning, no new start, until he trusted his wife. Trusted her with his heart and his soul and his secret.

Jack's heart felt as if it were being twisted out of his chest. This was the moment, he knew. If he didn't trust her now, didn't hand her his soul on a silver platter, she would never look at him this way again.

But if he told her, the love in her eyes might congeal, turn into something cold and ugly, as it did before.

Or it might not.

He looked down at her, raking her face with his eyes, memorizing it, loving it. She was all he'd ever wanted in his life, all he'd ever needed. Here on this tired old sheep ranch, with her and the children, he'd finally found the home, the place, he'd searched for all his life.

And now, to keep it, to find out if it was real, he had to risk it all.

Don't be a coward for once in your life. Just open your mouth and spill your guts. She might leave—hell, she'll probably leave. But she might stay. She might take you in her arms and kiss you softly and tell you she loves you anyway.

At the thought, he groaned aloud.

"Jack?"

"All right." He shoved the words up his throat. "We'd better sit down. This'll take a while."

A quiet gasp escaped her. She stared up at him earnestly. "Are you sure?"

Unable to speak, he nodded. He took her hand and

grabbed the lamp, leading her up the ladder into the hay-loft. Together they sat against the back wall. Jack focused for a moment on the feel of her fingers twined through his, and prayed that when it was over, she'd still want to touch him.

"It's all about Johnny." His voice softened as he spoke his brother's name. "He was strong and funny and not afraid of anything." A bittersweet smile came with the memory. "I was . . . small and weak and afraid of every-thing. Except when I was with Johnny. He always made me forget how scared I was of things.

"Like the war." He shuddered. "Johnny just had to go in the first wave. Me, I didn't want to go at all. I thought it was wrong, and besides, you were just starting to show with Savannah, but . . . I couldn't let him go alone."

Jack let his gaze wander to the back wall, where the hay lay piled in heaps. The sweet scent of it filled the air, but Jack didn't notice. All he could smell was blood and sweat and fear.

"So we went." His eyes narrowed, he stared at the planked wall, dancing with dust motes. Bitterness churned through him, leaving an acidic taste in his mouth. "It didn't take long to realize how undersupplied and un-trained we were. We marched and marched and marched. After a while our boots gave out, and there were no more, then our food gave out, and there was nothing but rotten apples and stolen corn. We were tired and hungry and sick.

"Our company fought a few little skirmishes here and there, but nothing much. Nothing really dangerous. Our biggest enemies were disease and boredom.

"Then . . ." His voice cracked, gave out. Memories and images shot through his mind. He winced and squeezed his eyes shut.

"I'm right here, Jack. You're safe. It's okay."

She said the words over and over again. Jack concentrated on the gentle drawl of her voice until the rawness of his emotions melted into something more manageable. "Then came Antietam." He shivered at the name. It had been forever since he'd uttered it out loud, and even now, years later, it made his stomach seize up with fear and shame.

He tried to detach himself from the horror. He stiffened and stared straight ahead. Images filled his mind in a sickening array of blood and death. The warm, cozy barn blurred, became the mist-shrouded cornfield. "The rain had started again by morning, and ground fog hugged the hollows and trenches. It was nothing but mud—so much mud. . . .

"All of a sudden all hell broke loose. Guns and cannon fired into the mist from a dozen directions. The call came to charge. I . . . I took a step. But it was so muddy, I couldn't move—I didn't move. I was so goddamn scared."

Shame pulled the strength from his voice. "Then a canister exploded in front of me. An arm flew past my face—

"I saw Billy Walker standing in front of me, clutching a bloody stump. 'My arm,' he kept saying. 'My arm.' "

Jack felt battered by the tide of memories he'd kept suppressed for so long. "I couldn't move. I heard Johnny yell at me from somewhere up ahead."

Come on, Jacko. We need you!

The memory seized him by the throat. An eerie coldness crept through his body, chilling him to the bone. He shivered, squeezed his burning eyes shut. "I ran as fast as I could, screaming Johnny's name over and over again. I knew he was in trouble, but I didn't know . . ." His words trailed off.

"Jack?"

He shook his head. Shame wedged so tightly in his throat, he couldn't talk, couldn't breathe. Tears burned his eyes and blurred his vision. He clamped a hand over his mouth to keep from crying.

Lissa eased the hand from his mouth and held it tightly. "It's okay, Jack. It's okay."

A racking sob shook his body, but he held it back, shaking with the effort it took to remain motionless. "The doctors told me to forget about it," he rasped.

"They were wrong," she said quietly. "You know they were. Have you ever been able to follow their advice?"

Full of shame, he shook his head. A hot tear slid down his cheek. "No."

Lissa touched his chin and turned his face. "You have to let it out, Jack. It's eating you up inside. If we have to talk about this every night for ten years, we will."

He blinked back the scalding tears and stared into her earnest eyes. In their depths he found a place of comfort, of hope and belonging. The safe harbor he'd searched for all his life. All she was asking was that he try. *Try.*

"His ... head ... it ... hit me." Tears ripped from him and turned into hot, aching sobs that rocked him to the core of his being. He squeezed his eyes shut, rocking back and forth as he pushed the hated words out. "I was running, and there it was. Johnny's head hit me in the gut. I ... I grabbed it."

"Oh, God, Jack ..."

"There was blood. So much blood. I felt it seeping through my fingers, and all I kept thinking was, 'It's Johnny's blood. He needs it.'

"I couldn't let go of it. . . ."

Where were you, Jacko?

"I ... killed him."

Lissa touched his shoulder. "No, you didn't. Someone else killed him."

He turned to her. It felt as if his soul were being slowly

twisted inside out. "Don't you see? I waited. I *froze*. During the battle. I was a coward, and it killed my brother."

"How old were you?"

"Old enough to know better." He looked away, stared hard at the candle's golden flame.

"Okay," she said quietly.

He frowned, turned to look at her. "Okay what?"

"Okay, you waited thirty seconds. Maybe you were even a coward. But you didn't kill your brother."

"But ... but I didn't save him, either."

Lissa clambered around and sat on his lap, bunching her skirts up around her legs. Her fingers curled tightly around his shoulders. "You didn't save him. Can you see how far that is from killing him?"

"It's splitting hairs, I—"

She shook him, stared deeply into his eyes. "It's not splitting hairs."

He got a glimmer of what she was talking about. It was no more than that, just a shimmering reflection of something, but for a heartbeat, he felt ... *maybe*.

She saw the fleeting hope in his eyes and nodded. "That's right. Think about it."

He let his breath out in a tired sigh. He'd believed the worst of himself for so long, he couldn't imagine seeing things any other way. "I don't know. . . ."

"Okay," she said softly, "there's lots of time for you to think." She slid off him and plunked onto the floor beside him, curling close. Her cheek was a warm pressure against his arm.

The truth washed over Jack in a wave. She was still here, smiling at him, touching him, loving him. He'd told her the truth, and she was still here. A joy unlike anything he'd ever experienced rushed through him, filled his soul.

He sagged against the wall in relief and closed his eyes. Curling an arm around her, he drew her close—so close, he couldn't tell where he ended and she began. Their quiet, soft breathing mingled, gave the musty old barn a stirring of life.

Jack felt the fear that had cramped his spirit for so long begin to slip away. The first sparkling threads of hope wound through him. She was right. It *had* helped to talk about it. For the first time since waking in that horrible, dingy hospital room, Jack wondered if maybe he *could* help himself. Maybe even heal himself.

He stroked her hair softly. Before he knew it, he was talking again, sharing with her what he'd never shared with another soul. "After that, I . . . woke up in some sort of hospital for crazies and cowards. They told me I'd been there for years, just staring at the ceiling and screaming. Then one day I woke up. The doctors told me not to think about what I'd seen at Antietam, and kept plugging laudanum down me until I wasn't even human anymore.

"When the war ended, they opened the doors and let us go. I wandered for months until I finally found home. My folks . . . and you . . . thought I was just another coward."

Lissa turned and took his face in her hands, touching him as if he were made of the finest china. "We were wrong, Jack. And if you believe it, you're wrong, too."

At her words, spoken so softly and thickened with the threat of tears, Jack felt something inside him, something gnarled and ugly and afraid, begin to melt away. And in that moment, in the hay-scented half-light of a musty old barn, Jack knew he'd been given another chance.

"I love you, Lissa."

The next morning, Tess and Jack slept in late. They were wakened by a knock on the door.

"Mama?" Savannah said. "Are you awake?"

Tess smiled lazily and snuggled closer to Jack. "Are we?"

He curled an arm around her shoulders and drew her closer, planting a slow, loving kiss on her lips. "I'm afraid we are."

"Come on in, girls," she called out.

The door opened. Savannah and Katie lurched into the room then stopped dead. Two little mouths dropped open. "Daddy!"

Jack scooted to a sit and grinned at them, shoving a dirty lock of hair out of his face. "Hi, girls."

Katie ran pell-mell for the bed and threw herself in her daddy's arms.

Savannah stood hesitantly, her hands twisting together at her midsection. "We missed you yesterday. Are you . . . all right?"

He gave her a smile. "There's only one thing that could make me better."

"What's that?"

"A good-morning kiss from my favorite girl."

Savannah grinned and ran to the bed. Jack swept her lithe body into his arms and plopped her on his lap. The four of them sat there, huddled and happy in the middle of the big bed, laughing, talking, chattering away. Thinking that nothing could ever go wrong again.

Tess went out to the porch to call everyone in for lunch.

But what she saw outside made the words catch in her throat. Smiling softly, she leaned against the railing. Beside her, the white post was covered with twining roses, their small, pink buds just beginning to open. Their scent mingled with the aroma of baking bread and sea air and reminded Tess that she was home.

"Mama's gonna love these roses, ain't she, Daddy?"

"She sure is, Katydid."

Tess's gaze slid lovingly along her new family. Love swelled in her heart. Jack was squatted beneath the oak tree, digging a flower bed. Beside him, Caleb lay sprawled on a huge blanket, busily batting his fists in the air.

Savannah and Katie were crouched on either side of the path, planting more roses.

Tess reached up and rang the supper bell. The clanging, metallic sound vibrated on the air. "Come on, y'all. It's time for supper."

Jack looked up and gave her a smile. "Thank God." He waved her over. "Come here."

Katie popped to her feet. "Look at what we did!"

Tess smiled happily and moved down the steps. "It's perfect. I love it."

"Come here," Jack said, pushing to his feet. "I have something for you."

Tess stopped in front of him. "What is it?"

"Close your eyes."

"Okay."

Something airy and nearly weightless settled on the top of her head.

"Aw, shit," he cursed. "Don't move."

Tess smothered a laugh.

"You can open your eyes now."

Tess blinked up at him. "What is it?"

"A dandelion crown. I made it myself."

Tess felt as if she'd been given the crown jewels of England. She smiled up at him.

Jack leaned down to give her a kiss.

"Look, Daddy!" Katie yelled. "Miz Hannah's runnin' over here."

Jack pulled back. Turning, he saw Minerva run through the fields toward them. As he watched her, a chilling sense of apprehension skittered up his spine. He tensed, breathing heavily, his hands coiled into fists at his side. Something was wrong.

By the time Minerva Hannah reached them, she was

pale and out of breath. "Thank ... God ... you're ... here," she panted, clutching her side.

"What is it?" Jack asked.

"Henry and Selina Dwyer have been murdered. The Terrells found their bodies this morning, but it looks like they've been dead since yesterday."

Yesterday. The word hit Jack like a punch to the lungs. Horror crept through his body in an ice-cold river.

Yesterday. Exactly when he'd been wandering the island in a blackout.

The sickness in his stomach intensified, turned his insides into a burning, twisting coil of terror. Where had he been? *Where the hell had he been? And what in God's name had he done?*

"I must go now," Minerva said shakily. "There's a meeting down at the schoolhouse to discuss it. I figured you'd want to go."

Lissa gave her a quick hug. "I understand. We'll see you there."

Tears glistened in Minerva's eyes as she nodded. "Thanks." Then she turned and hurried back toward her farm.

There was a moment of stunned silence, then Lissa said his name. He heard the quiet fear in her voice and felt a stab of regret so strong and sharp, he almost cried out in pain. The hope he'd felt only moments ago shattered like glass, sending thousands of clear, invisible shards scattering around his feet.

With a certainty that sickened and shamed him, he knew he'd killed those people. He knew without a doubt that he hadn't *meant* to hurt them, but somehow he had. And to them, dead now and in the ground, his intentions and his sickness didn't mean shit.

The memory of that night washed over him in a cold wave. The excessive amount of blood on his long johns—

had he really been naive enough to believe it was from his scraped hand? The marks he'd left on his wife's pale, fragile wrists that night came back to him suddenly, burning through his brain. He remembered the Winchester shotgun, propped in the corner of the barn. So out of place, so forgotten. The nightmare had gripped so hard that night, and so fast, with icy-cold fingers that seemed to suffocate him. He hadn't been thinking right—only feeling, acting on impulse. During a blackout his mind turned into a morass of fear and darkness and desperation. Maybe he'd taken the gun, thinking he was shooting Johnny's killer. Who the hell knew what had gone on in his mind?

Who the hell knew? He knew only that he'd been right to believe the worst of himself all those years.

He squeezed his eyes shut, battling a near-crippling flood of remorse and grief for the Dwyer family and what he'd done to them. *God, forgive me. I never meant to hurt anyone.*

Lissa came up beside him, touched his arm. "Jack, are you all right?"

He didn't dare look at her. He was afraid it would all be revealed in his eyes—the fear, the dread, the ache. Even some tiny, regret-filled remnant of hope. The only voice he could find was flat and lifeless, like the scratchy rustling of long-dead leaves. "No."

He pulled his arm free of her hold and turned to go.

"Wait, Jack—"

He didn't slow down. "I'll get the wagon hitched. We'll leave in fifteen minutes."

Jack strode into the barn, every step reverberating up his spine like a hammerblow. His breathing was fast and shallow, the ragged cant of a man on the verge of exploding.

He moved into the cool darkness of the barn with a relieved sigh and slammed the door shut behind him. Alone, he sank to his knees on the hard-packed dirt floor.

"Oh, God." The words slipped past his mouth in a desperate sigh.

He closed his eyes to pray, but couldn't find the strength. Slowly opening his eyes, he saw a wadded pile of red in the corner by his workbench. Fear brought him to a stumbling stand. *His long johns.* Trembling, he made his way to the rag box and pulled out the torn, dirty garment.

The wrinkled cotton fabric dipped and swayed in his shaking grip. The dried black splotch seeped for one dizzying moment into the sea of red. He blinked hard, clutched his long johns more tightly. Gradually his vision slipped back into focus, and the black blotch became once again a crust of dried blood easily distinguished from the rest of the red.

Whose blood is it?

The terrifying question catapulted into his thoughts again, bringing with it a wave of helplessness and fear so strong, his knees buckled. His hands shook harder. An icy chill crept down his spine and spilled through his blood. *Whose?*

When he'd first come out of the blackout, he'd assumed it was his blood. He glanced down at the scraped, bruised back of his hand. Scabs streaked from his knuckles to his wrist in intermittent dots and dashes. It had bled. It *had*. And he'd pinned it protectively to his chest. Exactly where the blood was on the underwear.

But he didn't believe it. Deep down he knew what he'd always known about himself. He was capable of violence, even murder. The coincidence was too strong to deny: He'd been blacked out the day of the murder, and he'd come home with blood on his clothing. Everything Lissa had told him meant nothing, less than nothing. It had given him a night, a glorious, laughter-tinged night he'd remember all his life, but no more.

A crazy killer like himself didn't deserve even that. All that mattered now was protecting his family, keeping his wife and children safe from the terrifyingly dark side of himself. He thought again about the bruises on Lissa's wrists—pale, bluish-yellow marks on the softness of her flesh. More pressure, just a bit more, and he might have broken her bone. Or worse.

He swallowed thickly. Nausea tasted sharp and bitter on his tongue. He could have hurt her; he could have hurt them all. Could hurt them still. The blackouts would return, creeping in when he didn't expect and ripping him from the caring circle of his family without a backward glance.

He had to leave them; if he didn't, he ran the risk of hurting the people he loved more than life itself. Maybe next time he wouldn't be so lucky as to grab Lissa's wrist in his sleep; maybe next time it would be her throat.

A shudder wrenched through him at the thought. If only he could believe—even for a moment—that he was innocent. But he couldn't. The evidence pointed to him, but that wasn't what convinced him. The evidence was simply that: evidence. Jack had something stronger to go on. He knew himself, knew the dark, twisted torment that was his mind, knew the violence he was capable of inflicting without even a hint of memory to mark its passing.

Tomorrow he'd ask Ed Warbass to arrest him. Cage him. It wasn't much, he knew; he deserved something colder and infinitely worse. But it was all he could do, the only way he could keep his loved ones safe. The only way he could atone for the atrocity he'd committed on that poor, innocent family.

He sank again to his knees, barely feeling the cold

dampness of the floor. His chest ached with the need to cry, but his eyes remained painfully dry.

I'm sorry, Lissa. The words churned through his mind in a litany of agonizingly sharp regret. With each repetition he was reminded of how meaningless and stupid the apology sounded, how hollow. In the past weeks, Lissa had given him things he'd thought long gone. He'd even started to think he wasn't such a failure.

Memories and moments crystallized in his mind, lodged like shards of glass in his soul. Lissa, soothing the sweat-dampened hair from his eyes and touching his cheek, guiding him through the pain-filled darkness of the near blackout; Lissa sitting in the big rocker on the porch, with Katie curled in her lap, drawing pictures of letters in the cool night air; Lissa naked, astride him, bending down for a slow, lingering kiss.

Regret and shame coiled together, tasting acrid and bitter in the back of his throat.

Christ, it had felt good to finally be a father. A husband. It was better than he'd ever imagined it could be, and he'd spent a lifetime imagining it. So many nights he'd lain on his lonely couch bed, staring at the darkened ceiling, breathing hard, aching to be invited into a loving circle that existed only in his mind.

Until Lissa had made that circle a reality. She'd brought the children together and formed a strong, lasting bond of love. And, miracles of miracles, she'd held her hand out to him.

Fool that he was, he'd taken it, clung to it, held it to his heart and let himself believe. . . .

The selfish act had hurt them all. He'd let the girls, and Lissa, believe in the circle, and then he'd ripped the shit out of it and stomped on all their hearts. With each breath he took now, he saw his dream—their dream—slipping beyond his grasp, slipping through fingers too numb and use-less to know how to hang on.

He never should have tried to be a father and husband. He had failed, and the failure had caused the horror he'd always known it would. That and so much more. His fail-ure was worse than not trying. He'd let them all down and left them with the most painful memory of all. Happiness.

Chapter Twenty-six

The schoolhouse bell clanged in a slow, melancholy march. Tess pulled the heavy shawl more tightly around her shoulders and glanced uneasily around.

Low-slung clouds slid through the robin's-egg blue sky, casting dark, sinister shadows on the ground. On either side of the dirt road, giant cedar trees reached toward the heavens, their deep green coats rustling softly in the breeze.

The horses plodded methodically onward, their hooves striking the hard-packed earth in a muted march that accentuated the throbbing echo of the bell. With every rumbling, clanking turn of the huge metal wheels, Tess's anxiety increased. She couldn't put her finger on what was wrong. She tried to tell herself it was just the horror of the crime, but she couldn't make herself believe it. There was something else, something dark and dangerous eddying around her family. Something that scared her to death.

The schoolyard was crowded and silent when they finally arrived. Jack expertly maneuvered the wagon amidst the mass of people and horses, and pulled up alongside the fence. Many faces turned their way. None of them called out a greeting or waved hello.

Tess glanced sideways at Jack. He was sitting as straight as a bowstring, staring dead ahead. The battered Stetson was drawn low on his brow, as if to shield his face from the townspeople. On the reins, his hands were tight, white fists. His mouth was a tense, colorless line.

He looked like a man on the verge of exploding.

She reached out for him. "Jack, are you—"

He turned to look at her. Tess gasped at the raw, unmasked pain in his eyes, and for a moment she was left breathless. It was more than loss, more even than grief. Something darker, deeper, more akin to terror than mourning.

He started to speak, then changed his mind and jumped down from the wagon. The girls followed.

Tess got down from the wagon and stood beside Jack. Holding Caleb close, she stared up at her husband, feeling a strange sense of foreboding. Something was wrong. Something different and infinitely more dangerous than a murder.

"Jack, I—"

He pushed past her and headed for the schoolhouse, head held high, shoulders stiff.

Katie gave her a tiny shrug, then scurried to keep up with Savannah and Jack. Tess had no choice but to hurry along behind.

The family came together in a military straight line at the schoolhouse steps. They closed ranks, taking strength from one another's presence as they sidled wordlessly together. A silent "chin up" glance passed between the girls.

Jack looked at no one. His gaze was pinned on the closed door, and there was no trace of emotion on his face.

They climbed the stairs and entered the school. The room was filled to overflowing with gesturing, chattering people. Phrases and snippets of conversation rose above the din, leaving no doubt what everyone was talking about.

"What do you think—"

"It's horrible, I heard—"

"Indians—"

Suddenly voices sputtered and stopped. The din melted into a buzz, and then became nothing at all.

One by one the townspeople turned toward them. Faces paled. Mouths compressed. Eyes narrowed into suspicious slits as they watched Jack.

Realization spilled like ice water through Tess. *They think he killed those people.* She glanced up at Jack's stern, emotionless profile and knew that he knew it as well. But there was something else in his eyes, something that scared her so badly, she couldn't speak. Guilt.

Yesterday. The memory of Minerva's word flashed like lightning through her mind, rooting her to the spot. Minerva said the murder had taken place yesterday or the day before. Yesterday Jack had been wandering the island alone, with no memory of what he'd done.

Tess felt a numbing rush of fear. The townspeople be damned. *Jack* thought he'd killed those innocent people.

She clamped a hand over her mouth to stifle a quiet sob. She wanted to say something, anything, to relieve the stark, unrelenting hardness in his face, but no words came to her. There was nothing she could say. He wouldn't listen.

It would never be enough, she realized with an unfamiliar surge of anger. She could believe in him forever, love him for all time, and it would never be enough. Not if he didn't believe in himself.

"Okay, folks, let's get started," called out a voice from the front of the room.

"What'dya know, Ed?" yelled someone.

The man at the front of the room held out his hands for silence. "Not much yet, Charlie. As you all heard, Henry and Selina Dwyer were found murdered today. Judging by the evidence, we think they were killed early yesterday. Maybe the day before."

"Who done it?" another angry voice demanded.

Ed shrugged. "We don't know that yet, Will. All we know for sure is that the murderer wore size-seven shoes with seven rows of nails in the sole. I also found an interesting bit of evidence in the Dwyers' root cellar. I've dispatched a letter to Victoria asking for a special officer to help us investigate."

"Well, what can we do?"

"If any of you saw or heard anything out of the ordinary, I'd be much obliged to hear it. Try to think back on anything unusual that happened after that storm. For the rest of you, just go home and stay home. And keep your houses locked tight. There's a murderer on the loose—and he might be one of us."

The drive home seemed endlessly long. The family sat in utter silence. Dark undercurrents swirled around them, shrouding them with a sense of impending doom.

Tess sat stiff as a new nail, her hands coiled in a bloodless ball in her lap. Every now and then she cast a sideways glance at Jack, but every one was like a stab to the heart. He sat perfectly straight, his eyes focused dead ahead. Sorrow formed a network of lines around his mouth and eyes, adding a dozen years to his face.

When they got home, Tess put Caleb to bed, then herded the girls together and led them to their room. When she looked into their frightened eyes, she felt a surge of anger so strong, she wanted to scream at the top of her lungs. But she said nothing. There was nothing yet to say until she talked to Jack.

"Night, Mama," Savannah said tonelessly.

"Yeah," Katie murmured.

Tess drew them both into her arms for a long hug, then kissed them good night and watched them crawl into bed together.

"Are we gonna say prayers tonight?" Katie asked quietly.

Tess forced a comforting smile. "Not tonight, sweetie. I need to ... talk to your daddy."

"T-Tell him we love him," Savannah whispered.

The softly spoken words, whispered by a child but filled with adult fear, was almost more than Tess could bear. It was all she could do to nod.

"Good night, girls."

Turning away, she closed the door behind her and headed toward the barn. It took her a moment to regroup, then she strode purposefully down the dirt road, her chin forced up.

She wouldn't let Jack retreat again. They'd come too far to go back now.

But her good intentions wavered as she neared the barn. Indecision slowed her step. At the door, she paused. Light slid through the darkened slit of the partially open door, crossing her skirt in a snakelike golden streak. From inside came the ragged strains of Jack's labored breathing.

The sound cut through her indecision and revitalized her. Jack was in there, alone, and he was hurting. Tilting her chin again, she slipped inside.

"Help me, God." Jack's prayer was a harsh, anguished moan. "Please ..."

Sadness settled like a hard lump in Tess's heart. He looked so sad and lonely and afraid, standing there at the workbench. His back was to her, but she didn't need to see his face to see the fear in his eyes. The emotion was in every muscle and fiber of his body, in the rigid way he stood, and the thickened rasp of his voice. Even from this distance, she could see the wrinkled red fabric stretched out in front of him. The dried blood was a black splotch across the buttons. Next to the long johns was a muddy pair of work boots. Tess knew they were size seven.

Jack had gathered the evidence, thin as it was, and convicted himself.

"Please," he whispered again. *"Please ..."*

Tess's heart twisted painfully in her chest. Tears stung her eyes.

She understood the formless, aching prayer so well, remembered the tone of voice—harsh with need and low with longing. She'd said the words a thousand times herself, only no one had ever heard them. To the rest of the world, Tess's prayer had been nothing more than the futile movements of a deaf girl's lips. No one had ever heard. No one except God.

She knew how Jack felt, knew it with a certainty that no longer surprised her. Somehow they were linked, she and Jack, and she knew parts of him as well as she knew herself. She knew and understood. He was scared, desperate, lonely.

Loneliness, she knew, was the worst. It made everything more terrifying and overwhelming. She came up beside him without making a sound and touched his arm. "Jack?"

He straightened suddenly, spinning away from her. "What in the hell are you doing here?"

Tess looked in his eyes and saw her worst fear. He was ready to throw it all away again. Ready to run. "Damn it, Jack, don't do this. Don't go backwards again. We've come so far."

He paled. "Go away."

"Jack, you can't shut me out again. I won't let—"

He grabbed her by the shoulders and yanked her toward him. She slammed into his chest so hard, the breath blasted from her lungs in a painful wheeze. Her head snapped back. Gasping, she stared up at him.

"It's over, Lissa." Pain glazed his eyes and turned his voice into something scratchy and harsh. "Let it go."

Tess stared at him in horror. The inevitability of this

moment slipped around her neck like a noose, tightening slowly. Irrevocably. "No," she said in a shaking, desperate voice she hardly recognized. "I won't let you do this."

"You don't have any choice."

Tears blurred her eyes at his calm, quiet words. She squeezed her eyes shut, refusing to cry. "I love you, Jack."

"And I love you." His words were spoken quietly, and with such an aching sadness, Tess felt as if she'd been punched in the stomach.

She knew then that for Jack, it wasn't enough.

The next morning Tess stood at the kitchen table, crushing salt. She stared at the white pile so hard, it melted in and out of focus, became a mountainous smear. She saw her fingers curl around the smooth wood of the rolling pin, but it might have been another woman's hands for all the connection Tess felt to her body.

She felt ... disembodied, as if her spirit were tagging behind her form. She was scared, terribly, desperately scared, and it took every ounce of her self-control to keep from bursting into tears or screaming at the top of her lungs.

Last night, after the barn, Jack had been so distant and cold. His silence stabbed through her soul and twisted hard.

They'd lain in bed, side by side, touching and yet not melding, their slow, mingled breathing a melancholy march in the strained quiet of the room. She'd waited for him to kiss her, but when he finally did, she wished he hadn't. The kiss was bleak and bittersweet. Then he'd taken her in his arms and held her close. But even then, wrapped in his arms, she'd felt desolate and alone and filled with trembling fear.

He'd whispered, "Good night," then closed his eyes and

pretended to sleep. But all Tess had heard was "Good-bye."

But she refused to give up. They had time, thank God, to recapture their love and banish Jack's fear. She felt a stirring of hope. Maybe today was a good day for miracles.

The rumbling creak of a poorly sprung wagon slipped through the open kitchen window and wrenched Tess out of her thoughts. Setting down the ridged rolling pin, she wiped her gritty hands on her apron and went outside.

Savannah was pushing Katie on the tree swing. The high, clear sound of their laughter rode on the light spring breeze.

Tess looked around for Jack. He was standing across the road, with one boot hooked casually on the fence's bottom rail. His hat was drawn low across his eyes, as though to shield a too bright sun, but the day was cloudy and cold.

Apprehension stirred in Tess's stomach. Something was wrong. Jack never stood around in the middle of the day. Absently she shoved a lock of fallen hair back into the bun at her nape and moved closer to the porch rail, craning her neck to see who was coming.

The wagon rumbled down the dirt road toward them, churning up a moving cloud of dust that obscured the driver.

"Someone's comin'!" Katie yelled, leaping off the swing. She and Savannah raced across the yard and bounded up the steps, sidling close to Tess.

"Who do you think it is?" Savannah asked.

Tess couldn't answer. Absently she shook her head and shrugged, her eyes still pinned on the rolling cloud of dust. With each crunching turn of the wagon wheels, her anxiety jerked up a notch.

Her gaze cut to Jack. His face was a chalky mask. There

was no question in his eyes, no apprehension or confusion. He knew exactly who was in that wagon.

Fear rushed through her, chilled her to the bone. She brought a hand to her mouth. *Oh, God, Jack, what have you done?*

The wagon turned the corner and came into view. Justice of the Peace Ed Warbass was driving.

Tess felt her knees give way. Clamping the hand more tightly atop her mouth, she shot a terrified look at Jack.

Their eyes locked. His gaze was sad and filled with regret. *I'm sorry,* he mouthed.

It crashed in on her in a suffocating wave. Consciousness tried to slip away, but she held on to it with desperate, clawing fingers.

Jack had turned himself in for the murders.

"No!" she screamed. Wrenching the tired old linsey-woolsey of her skirt, she dashed down the steps and ran across the road, flinging herself into Jack's arms.

"Tell me you didn't turn yourself in," she whispered urgently.

When he didn't answer, she yanked out of his arms and stared up at him. "Tell me," she yelled.

He flinched. Sadness twisted his features, made him look infinitely old and tired. "Yesterday after the town meeting I told Ed Warbass to arrest me."

"Damn you, Jack Rafferty," she hissed.

He tried to smile, and failed. "There's no doubt about that, Lissa."

She smacked him, a hard, stinging crack across the face that surprised them both. "Don't you dare be flip." Her voice cracked, frayed. Tears flooded her eyes and clogged her throat. "Don't you dare. . . ."

Tess squeezed her eyes shut and fought for a shred of self-control. She had to be cool and composed, had to calmly and rationally convince Jack—and Ed—that this was all a horrible mistake.

She tried to find the scientific detachment that had always come so naturally, but it was gone now, buried beneath an avalanche of terror. She pressed a shaking, ice-cold hand to her throat. She couldn't find it within herself to be rational. It felt as if her insides were melting, crumbling away. Everything she'd ever wanted, ever dreamed of, was here, standing in front of her, close enough to kiss. And it was slipping beyond her grasp like an elusive fog.

The wagon pulled up in front of them. "Whoa, boy," Ed Warbass said, reining the horse to a stop.

Jack looked up. "Hi, Ed."

Ed pulled the hat off his head and crushed it in his lap. "Hi, Jack." He nodded at Tess. "Miz Rafferty."

She ran up to the wagon, clutching at the splintery wooden side. "He didn't do it, Ed. I swear he didn't do it."

Ed glanced uncomfortably at Jack. "He says different," he answered quietly.

Tess spun around, running back to Jack. "Don't do this, Jack, please. Please."

He didn't look at her, and somehow that hurt more than any slap she could imagine.

Anger revitalized her. "No, goddamn it!" She turned to Warbass. "He didn't do it. Don't listen to him, he's—"

"Crazy," Jack said flatly.

Tess reeled back around. "Damn it, Jack, you're not crazy. You're just . . . afraid."

"Good-bye, Lissa."

The ground seemed to tilt suddenly. Tess swayed unsteadily. The knot of fear unwound, spilling through her blood in an icy stream. Her insides felt hot and shaky. "Oh, Jack . . ."

He turned to her then, and the movement was slow and

wooden. His face was a cold, emotionless mask, without smile or frown. To someone who didn't know him, he looked like a cold-blooded killer.

Except for his eyes. In the green depths was a pain so raw and consuming, Tess knew it was taking all of his self-control not to crack. His mouth trembled slightly, then drew back into a taut line.

"Why?" she whispered.

"I have to protect my family."

Tess swallowed thickly. "We're safe with you, Jack. Not without you." She took a step toward him, rested her hand on his chest. "Never without you."

He leaned down and kissed her. It was a short, bittersweet kiss that ended all too soon. "I love you," he whispered against her forehead when finally he pulled away.

Tess threw her arms around him and clung to him. Huge, desperate sobs racked her body and scalded her eyes. Her heart was an empty, aching lump in her throat. "Please, don't do this. Please, oh, please, oh, please."

Gently he pushed her away. "I have to, Lissa." His voice thickened and cracked. "I have to."

Tess sagged and almost fell. It felt as if every bone in her body were being slowly, painfully crushed. Her tears turned him into a tall, black-haired blur against a solemn gray sky.

"Good-bye, Lissa."

"No, Daddy, don't go!" Savannah flew down the steps and barreled across the road, throwing herself into Jack's arms. "Don't go, Daddy."

Katie was right behind her. Jack hugged them all for a long time, smoothing the tear-dampened hair from their faces. Then he pushed them away, too.

"I have to go."

Katie looked up at Warbass. Her little body was heaving with quiet sobs. "D-Don't tuh-ake my daddy."

Warbass tugged on his collar and looked away. "I'm sorry, missy."

Jack reached down and grabbed a satchel from the other side of the fence. Tess saw the bag and felt a surge of anger and betrayal so strong, it obliterated her sorrow for a heartbeat. "Why didn't you tell me last night?"

He turned and looked down at her. His finger breezed across her jawline in a feather-stroke. "I couldn't. You might have talked me out of it."

"He'll be in the jail in Victoria, Miz Rafferty. You can visit anytime before the trial."

Without another glance, Jack climbed up onto the wagon.

Tess clamped a hand over her mouth to keep from screaming. Tears blurred her vision and formed a huge, aching lump in her throat. She couldn't breathe. Her knees went weak and she collapsed in a crumpled, desperate heap on the dirt road. Dust spewed from the wagon's metal wheels and clogged her nose and eyes, turning her tears into muddy, clammy streaks.

"Come back," she whispered brokenly, tasting the gritty paste of dirt on her tongue.

The wagon rumbled on.

Tess had no idea how long she sat there, crumpled in the middle of the dirt road, her cheeks streaked with muddy tears. She stared through gritty eyes at the road, waiting, desperately waiting for the wagon to reappear, for Ed to come walking up and say, *I'm sorry, Miz Rafferty, it's all been a horrible mistake. . . .*

A small, strangled sob escaped her. The rock-strewn dirt road blurred before her eyes.

"Mama?" Katie shuffled toward her and dropped to her knees. "What are we gonna do?"

"There ain't nothin' we can do," Savannah answered in a tired voice. "Daddy's goin' to jail."

Tess straightened slowly. *The kids.* She couldn't fall apart now. Not here in front of the children. They needed her to be strong.

Sniffling, she backhanded the tears from her eyes and glanced over at Savannah, who was standing stiff as a knife blade, her face colorless and streaked with tears.

"Come over here, Vannah," she said quietly.

Savannah moved to Tess's side and kneeled on the hard dirt beside her. Tess put an arm around each girl and drew them close.

"He didn't do it," Tess said softly, her eyes blurring with new tears at the thought.

"I know that," Savannah said.

"Then why'd he say he done it?" Katie asked in a small, miserable voice that made Tess want to cry all over again.

"Well, honey, that's a hard question to answer. Basically your daddy doesn't think he's a very nice person. And when you don't believe there's good inside you, you're all too willing to believe there's bad."

"Oh," Katie said quietly.

"Right now your daddy can't believe in himself, so he needs us to do it for him. We're his family, and families stick together through everything."

"Maybe God will help him," Katie said.

"I'm sure He will, honey, but God helps those who help themselves."

"What does that mean, Mama?"

Tess hugged the girls fiercely. "It means I've waited all my life for someone to love, and someone to love me." She stroked the girls' hair. "I used to dream about you guys. About being part of a family. And now that I have it, I'll be damned if I'll let it go without a fight."

"I love you, Mama," Savannah whispered.

"I love you both, too," Tess murmured in a throaty voice. "So much, it hurts. Now, let's put our heads together and figure out a plan to help your father."

After breakfast, Tess sent Savannah and Katie in search of wildflowers. She needed some time to be alone, some time to think. She walked across the porch, listening with half an ear to the whining creak of the floorboards beneath her feet.

She went down the steps and crossed to the swing, sitting on its familiar seat. Leaning back, she closed her eyes and let the soft, gentle rocking motion soothe her battered soul. As she sat there, it began to rain. Cold droplets knifed past the tree's leaves and plunked on Tess's upturned face. The quiet, ceaseless patter of the raindrops on the grass matched the beating of her heart.

A particularly large drop landed in her eye. She wiped the wetness away with her sleeve and blinked.

A flash of yellow winked at her from the grass. Sliding off the swing, she plopped onto the ground and crawled through the wet grass.

The wilted, broken dandelion crown lay forgotten in the weeds.

She picked up the linked flowers in cold, shaking hands. The bright yellow blurred before her tear-filled eyes. She held it to her chest, smelling the strong, familiar scent of dandelions and grass and rain.

She tried to be brave and strong for the girls and Caleb and Jack, tried to swallow her tears and force her mind away from the pain. But she couldn't do it. Not this time.

And so, kneeling in the wet grass, alone, with a bunch of silly, wilted flowers plastered to her breast, Tess let herself cry. She cried until her throat was raw and her eyes burned, until her chest ached and her legs were icy cold.

She cried until she had no more tears to cry. Then, sniffling hard, wiping her bloodshot eyes, she clambered to her feet and walked slowly into the house.

She felt better then. Stronger. Ready to figure out a way to get Jack out of jail.

Chapter Twenty-seven

Tess was out of breath by the time she reached the Hannah farm. She skidded to a halt and concentrated on breathing normally as she walked toward the small house. Rain drizzled from the clouds overhead, sliding down the pitched roof and plunking on the weathered planks of the porch.

Be calm, Tess. Be calm.

Grasping her linsey-woolsey skirt, she climbed the wooden steps and rapped sharply on the front door. There was a rush of shuffling feet from inside the house, then suddenly the door was whisked open. Minerva stood in the doorway.

She smiled immediately. "Why, Lissa, what a pleasant surprise."

Tess tried to keep her voice from trembling. "Not so pleasant, Minerva."

Minerva frowned. "Come in."

"Thanks." Tess swept into the small, neat kitchen and sat down at the table.

Minerva went directly to the stove, poured two cups of coffee, and set one down in front of Tess, then took a seat herself. "So, what's the matter?"

For a minute Tess couldn't talk. She curled her fingers around the dented tin cup and took a deep breath.

"Jack . . ." She glanced away, unable to say anything.

Minerva reached across the table and laid her hand on Tess's. "Jack what?"

She swallowed thickly, tasting bitter, unshed tears. "He thinks he killed the Dwyers."

Minerva gasped quietly, but didn't withdraw her hand.

"He didn't do it, of course, but he's so afraid. . . ."

Minerva set her coffee cup down with a clank. "Of what?"

Tess forced her gaze up. "He had a . . . bad experience in the war, and he can't forget it. That's why the fireworks set him off. The sound makes him remember things he'd rather forget, and he goes a little . . . crazy. But he'd never hurt anyone."

Minerva studied Tess for a long, thoughtful moment. Tess shifted uncomfortably under the scrutiny. Suddenly she remembered Jack's words: *Be nice to them.* She thought of all the times Amarylis had undoubtedly been rude to this nice woman, and Tess winced. *Please don't hold her against me. Not now. I need a friend so much. . . .*

"No," Minerva said quietly. "I don't believe he would either." Minerva forced a lackluster smile. "Not that that'll help you much."

Tess sighed. "I don't even know why I'm here. I guess I thought you could help me think of something to do. Anything. I can't just sit around that house and do nothing while he rots in jail for a crime he didn't commit."

Minerva's gaze dropped. She stared thoughtfully at her coffee for a long time. Slowly she looked up. "I'm sorry, Lissa."

Tess bit her lower lip to keep it from trembling. Tiredly she pushed to her feet. "Well—" Her voice sounded thick with tears, so she cleared her throat. "Well, if you think of anything, I'll be at home."

Minerva got to her feet. "I'm sure he'll realize he didn't do it and tell Ed the truth."

Tess nodded stiffly. "I'm sure you're right."

But as she gazed into Minerva's caring blue-gray eyes, Tess faltered. The words were a lie. Jack would never recant.

Minerva opened her arms. Squeezing her eyes shut, Tess stumbled forward, letting herself be enfolded in the comforting warmth of her friend's embrace.

The next morning Tess was wakened by someone banging hard on the front door.

"Lissa! Open the door. Lissa!"

Tess stumbled out of bed and threw on her wrapper. The wooden floor felt icy cold beneath her bare feet as she staggered through the house.

The banging came again. Harder. *Thud. Thud.* "Lissa!"

"I'm coming." The words eked from her mouth in a mangled, morning-harsh slur. At the door, she paused to rub her tired, aching eyes, knowing they were still puffy and red from a restless night. Plastering a smile on her face, she opened the door.

Minerva, Jim, and Ed Warbass were standing on her porch.

Tess gasped. *It was all a mistake.* She had a flash of hope so strong it left her breathless. Then she looked in Ed's solemn eyes, and the hope vanished.

Minerva thrust a shotgun at Tess. "I found this in the barn last night."

Tess shoved a tangled lock of hair from her eyes. "Oh." She eyed the long, ugly weapon. "Nice."

"It's Benjamin and Harvey's gun—"

"Our boys," Jim interjected.

Tess looked back and forth between Minerva and Jim. She could tell something was going on—something important—but frankly she was tired as hell and she'd cried half the night and she didn't feel like hearing about the boys' gun. "Look, Minerva, I—"

Minerva dismissed her protests with an impatient wave. "After you left yesterday, I kept thinking about how much you'd changed lately, about how Jack and even the girls had changed, and I wanted to help. Long after everyone else had gone to bed, I lay awake, tossing and turning. I kept thinking I knew something, something important, but I couldn't put my finger on it. I'd just about given up when it came to me.

"I remembered that the boys had loaned a gun to Joe and Kie Nuanna. For some reason that stuck with me. I kept thinking, *the gun, the gun.* I got up and put on my robe and wandered through the dark house. Before I knew it, I was in the barn, looking for that darn gun. When I found it—and saw the blotches on the stock—everything slipped into place, and I remembered the missing shot pouch."

Minerva sidled past Tess and took a seat at the kitchen table. Ed and Jim followed. Then they all stared up at her as if waiting for her reaction to the startling bit of information that a shot pouch was missing.

Minerva set the gun on the table, then looked up at Tess. "I can tell you're trying to figure out why we're here, babbling about a lost pouch. It took me awhile to make sense of all the pieces, too. But just bear with me, okay? I want you to really understand everything."

Tess nodded. "Okay."

"Joe and Kie had borrowed our gun before; it was nothing particularly noteworthy. That's why I didn't think of it before. Once or twice they'd even brought us back some game. They knew I'd made that pouch for the boys for Christmas. The more I thought about it, the stranger it seemed that they didn't apologize for losing it. Then I figured out the reason." She gave Tess a meaningful look.

"They didn't want to admit they'd lost it, because they knew *where* they'd lost it. The minute I realized that, I sent for Ed, and sure enough, he said I was onto something. Especially after he saw the gun."

Tess looked at the gun again, only this time she really looked. Ugly blackish splotches covered the wooden stock. A tingling thread of anticipation crept through her body.

"It's blood," Jim said quietly. "The only way you'd get blood on the stock is if you used the gun as a . . . club."

Suddenly it all made sense. Tess's heart lurched against her ribcage and pounded. She lowered herself slowly onto a chair. In her lap, her hands started to shake with excitement. "When did the boys borrow the gun?"

Minerva looked steadily into her eyes. "Wednesday. The day the Dwyers were killed."

"Oh my God."

Ed scooted closer to the table. His elbows thumped on the tabletop. "I can't tell if it's human blood on the gun, but I'll bet it is. I'll have to send it over to a chemist in Victoria."

Tess understood instantly why the missing shot pouch was so important. She looked up into Ed's earnest eyes and asked quietly, "Did you find the pouch?"

"I can't comment on the evidence in an ongoing investigation." A shadow of a smile moved across his face. "But I will say I found some mighty interesting things in the Dwyers' root cellar."

Tess sagged with relief. "Will you let Jack go now?"

Ed gave her an apologetic smile. "It isn't that easy, Miz Rafferty. He doesn't want to get out. He thinks he did it, and he's scared to death he's gonna hurt someone else."

"He didn't do it."

Ed laid a hand on her shoulder, squeezing gently. "That's a stubborn man you married. He isn't going anywhere until he's damn certain he isn't a murderer."

"So what do we do?" Tess asked.

Ed frowned. "Well, I'll run on down to the Kanaka camp and see if Joe and Kie are around. If they are, I'll arrest them. Maybe that'll snap Jack out of it."

"Why would the boys kill them folks?" Jim asked. "Was it just a robbery that got out of hand?"

"That's the saddest part of all," Ed said solemnly. "The things stolen didn't add up to spit moneywise. Somebody killed those good people for a pocketwatch that Henry would have given away without a second thought."

"What can we do?" Tess asked.

"Well, another meeting wouldn't hurt. Now we can give folks something specific to go on. Maybe someone saw Joe or Kie on Wednesday and didn't think a thing about it."

"I could talk to the townspeople," Tess said. "Make a personal appeal for help from one neighbor to another."

A pained expression crossed Ed's face. "That might not be such a good idea. The islanders don't trust him . . . or you." He winced, as if every word was painful. "They may not be too eager to help you get Jack out of jail."

Tess frowned. Ed was right, of course. Joe and Kie were more trusted on the island than Jack Rafferty. But she'd be damned if she'd let small town prejudices stop her. She looked right at Ed. "I'll convince them to help us."

Ed gave her a slow, grudging smile. "Why do I get the feeling the islanders don't have a chance?"

Tess grinned for the first time since Jack left. God, it felt good to do something besides sit around and wait. "Because they don't."

The walls were closing in on him. Jack's breathing echoed jarringly in the darkened cell. He felt like an animal, caged and alone.

Think, damn it. Remember!

He paced back and forth, counting the steps from one

end of the cell to the other. Behind his back, his hands were clasped in a sweaty knot. The clicking of his boot-heels on the dirty wooden floor sounded obscenely loud in the otherwise deadly silence.

Nothing. His mind was a huge, aching blank. He had no idea where he'd gone during the blackout, what he'd done. Images and thoughts spiraled through his mind. The blood on his shirt, the size of his boots, the number of nails in the sole. Johnny's dead, accusing eyes. The nearest he could tell, he'd been blacked out for nearly ten hours, maybe more. Long enough.

He went to the tiny window and clutched the iron bars. His whole body was trembling with the effort it took to try to remember. Leaning forward, he closed his eyes and rested his forehead on the cool metal.

Lissa. Her name came to him like a cool taste of water on a hot summer's day. His breath released in a tired sigh. Sweet Christ, he missed her.

You deserve to miss her. Turning wearily away from the bars, he started pacing again.

"Hey, mate. You okay?"

Jack turned, surprised by the jolt of relief he felt at hearing a human voice. He tried to smile at the jailer, and failed. "I'm fine. Thanks."

The man pushed the military-style cap higher on his head. "You want anything?"

A crushing wave of despair coursed through Jack at the casual question. Yeah, he wanted something, wanted it so goddamn desperately, he couldn't take a breath without aching for the loss. He wanted his life back. His wife, his family.

"No," he muttered.

"Suit yourself."

Jack watched the man go, suppressing a stupid desire to call him back—if for no other reason than to hear him talk. Anything, anyone, so Jack didn't feel so goddamn alone. The empty hallway mocked him.

He grabbed the rusted bars in shaking hands and banged his forehead against the cold metal. *Help me, God. Let me remember. Then at least I'll know for sure. Please . . .*

Heels shuffled toward the jail cell again.

Wearily Jack opened his eyes. The jailer stood outside, arms crossed. "You shouldn't be banging your head like that. We don't have a doctor."

Reluctantly Jack lifted his head. "Sorry."

The man turned to go, then he paused and turned back around. "How'dya like some paper and a pen, mate? Give you something to do."

The doctors were wrong, Jack. You can't make it go away by forgetting about it. Only remembering will help you. . . .

Fear settled in Jack's stomach as a cold, hard lump.

"Well?" the jailer demanded. "You want to try it?"

Just try, Jack. That's all I'm asking. Just try.

Jack's fingers tightened around the bars. Tiny flecks of rust stuck to his damp palms. "Yeah," he said quietly. "I'll give it a try."

"Good." The jailer hurried to his office, then returned with a candle, writing paper, a pen and ink. "Here you go," he said, shoving them through the bars.

Jack took them in trembling hands. "Thanks."

When the jailer had left again, Jack set the candle on the uneven floor. The fecund scent of cold, damp earth filled his nostrils. Sitting cross-legged beside the light, he rested the Bible he'd been given on his lap and smoothed the paper on top of it. Then, carefully, he dipped the quill in the ink and brought the tip to the paper.

His hand didn't move. The ink-heavy tip remained poised.

He sighed. He couldn't do it.

Yes, you can, Jack. He heard Lissa's voice as clearly as if she were in the room with him. He closed his eyes, and for a heartbeat, felt the warmth of her body beside him, heard the quiet sounds of her breathing.

He touched the pen to the paper and began, very slowly, to write. *I knew I shouldn't be there. I didn't believe in the war. . . .*

The words came to him, some easier than others, some he had to skip entirely. But they came. He wrote and wrote and wrote. All the memories and thoughts and emotions he'd hoarded in the darkness of his soul for so many years came pouring through the quill's pointed tip.

He wrote until the candle was sputtering and burning low, and tears were streaming down his face, until the darkness was all around him, and shadows made the words blur before his eyes.

And still he kept on writing.

The next day dawned just as gray and dismal as the one before it, with thick, low-hanging clouds anchored to the metal-hued sky. Rain splattered the dirt road in huge, plunking drops and formed muddy puddles.

In the distance, the school bell pealed. Its melancholy clang echoed through the moist air. Tess sat stiffly in the front of the wagon, her hands curled in a tight, nervous ball in her lap.

At the schoolhouse, Jim maneuvered the wagon through the crowded yard to a spot alongside the rickety fence.

Tess swallowed hard, steeling herself for the ordeal that lay ahead. Everything depended on her. Jack's life, their future, the children's future. Everything.

Today—now—she had to be what she'd never been in her life. She had to force her chin up, smile, and walk to the goddamn podium. She had to be easygoing and pleasant and persuasive.

Her self-confidence slipped. She wasn't sure she could do it. All her life she'd been quiet and isolated and alone. A wallflower.

Don't think about that. It was the past. She was no longer the Tess Gregory who melted into the background. Now she was Lissa Rafferty. Jack's wife. And she had no choice but to succeed. Jack's life depended on it.

"Lissa?" Jim's voice broke into her thoughts. "They're waiting for you."

Tess forced her chin up and tried to smile. "Thanks, Jim." Scooting across the splintery plank seat, she took his hand and got down. When her feet hit the solid ground, her knees almost buckled.

Jim grabbed her elbow and steadied her. "Are you all right?"

She nodded stiffly. "Fine. Let's go."

Together they wove their way through the wagons and horses that cluttered the grassy yard. With every step, Tess felt her stomach tighten.

They climbed the steps slowly. At the creaking of the boards, the hushed conversations in the schoolhouse died away. A silence fell across the small room as people turned, one by one, to gaze at Tess.

She stood in the door, feeling as conspicuous and out of place as a weed in a rose garden. "H-Hello." She winced at the breathy, hesitant sound of her voice and cleared her throat. Nodding a silent thanks to Jim and Minerva, she walked down the aisle, her heels clicking matter-of-factly on the wooden floor.

At the front of the room, she turned and faced the mass of unfriendly faces. "Hello," she said again. "I'm Lissa Rafferty. I know most of you don't know me well, and have no reason to trust me, but I've come to ask for your help."

A buzzing of dissent swept the crowd.

Ed Warbass stepped out of the throng of people and made his way up the aisle to stand beside Lissa. "This little lady is here at my request. I expect you to treat her with some respect."

The crowd quieted. Once again Tess felt every eye in the room on her. Her heart was beating so fast, she felt dizzy.

She fought the urge to turn and run. "As many of you know, my husband, Jack, has turned himself in to Ed and is in jail in Victoria."

"It's where he should be!" someone yelled.

Tess winced. "It's where the *murderer* should be," she said quietly, so quietly the crowd had to strain forward to hear her. "But what if Jack's not the murderer?" She waited, allowing the pregnant silence to expand. Then, softly, she said, "If he's innocent, we're all still in danger."

Her gaze cut to a portly man standing in the front row. "If Jack's not the murderer, your children are in danger. So is your wife."

The portly man flushed and looked uncomfortable. "B-But why would he say he done it if he dint?"

Tess let her gaze drift over the rest of the crowd. "Did any of you, or your relatives, fight in the war?"

There was a heartbeat's pause, then slowly, almost reluctantly, a few hands went up.

Tess focused on one of the men, a straggly, hollow-cheeked man in dungarees. "Do you have . . . nightmares about it?"

The man paled and looked away. Staring at the side wall, he jerked his chin in a quick nod.

Tess glanced around again, her gaze sweeping the crowd. "The soldiers in that war saw horrors we can't imagine. And sometimes they can't . . . let go. That's

Jack's problem. When he hears loud noises, it reminds him of gunfire. Sometimes it scares him so badly, he panics."

She watched the room, allowing her gaze to soften. "I know most of you can't understand a thing like that. I have trouble with it myself. The point is, Jack isn't a murderer. He's just a scared, lonely man who has been afraid to talk to most of you. He's . . . different. But that doesn't make him crazy. And it doesn't make him a murderer."

"But he said he done it," someone said from the middle of the crowd.

Ed Warbass stepped forward. "No, that isn't exactly what he said. He said he figured he done it. He can't remember."

"Sometimes Jack blacks out. He can't remember where he's been." Tess moved toward the crowd, and this time she couldn't keep her hands from coiling together. Her gaze landed on a friendly-looking older woman in the front row.

"He's just like your husband," she said softly. "Or your son. He's not a crazy man, or a murderer. He's an ordinary man who's faced extraordinary circumstances in his life. And he needs some help from his neighbors."

The woman shot a nervous sideways glance at her husband. "Wh-What can we do to help?"

"I don't know, Miriam. . . ." the man beside her complained.

Tess looked sharply at the man. "Would a murderer turn himself in? Would a murderer, someone who would kill a pregnant woman in cold blood, *ask* to be locked up?"

The man frowned. "Well—" he drew the word out—"I reckon not. But if he didn't do it, who did?"

Ed strode forward again. "I got some information that might help us there. On my request, the Canadian authorities arrested Joe and Kie Nuanna a few hours ago in Victoria. A shot pouch they'd borrowed from the Hannahs was found in the victims' root cellar."

"Joe and Kie . . . no shit? They're just boys," someone said.

"Poor boys," someone else added in a meaningful whisper.

"They won't talk to the authorities," Ed said, "so we don't know for sure if they did it, but the evidence is pretty strong against them."

Jerry Sikes pushed his way through the crowd and stood by Tess. "I talked to Jack some durin' shearin' season. He wasn't half-bad. As for me, I don't think he done it. Never did."

Tess gave him a grateful smile.

Deep in the crowd, a man tugged a tired old hat from his head and crushed it to his chest. Awkwardly he moved to the front of the crowd. "I'm Charlie MacKay. I know the boys pretty well, and I wouldn't mind talkin' to 'em. Maybe there's a slipup in their stories, but—"

"That's wonderful—"

"Let me finish, ma'am. I . . . I reckon any man'd be proud to have a woman fightin' so hard to prove he's innocent. But, well, what if he ain't? I don't want to get involved unless I'm damn sure your man didn't do it."

Tess battled a crushing wave of disappointment. "I understand, Mr. MacKay, but Jack's a stubborn man. He won't say he's innocent."

"But I couldn't sleep at night if I helped him get outta jail and he . . . you know . . . killed someone."

Tess winced at the ugly words and fought to maintain her composure. She couldn't lose it now, when she was so close. So damn close.

Think, damn it. That's what you're good at. Think.

She had to convince Charlie, just this one man, that Jack was innocent. But how? How?

Only one thing came to her mind, and it was a weak, feeble thing. An almost certain failure. Still, it was all she had. . . .

She licked her lower lip, which felt scratchy and dry. "What if I talked to Jack, and got him to admit that *maybe* he was innocent? Would that be enough, Mr. MacKay?"

Charlie pulled a wooden pipe from his shirt pocket and wedged it between his teeth, chewing on the carved end. "Yeah, I reckon that'd be enough."

"We'd be much obliged, Charlie," Ed said.

Tess squeezed her eyes shut. She tried her best to have hope, her very best. But for the first time in her life, her soul felt twisted and empty.

It was all in Jack's hands. He had to admit to *maybe*. And he'd never believed in himself yet.

That night after supper, Tess gathered the girls in a circle on the living room floor. A fire burned low in the fireplace, giving the shadowy room a red-gold glow. The leftover aroma of mutton stew mingled with the sharp tang of woodsmoke and filled the air. Moonlight slanted in a tenuous, broken streak through the small window and puddled in a bluish smear on the couch.

Tess spread a big blanket on the hardwood floor, then dropped slowly to her knees and patted places for the girls.

As Katie and Savannah lowered themselves to the blanket, Tess laid out a precious piece of paper in front of each girl. A pen and inkwell followed.

Savannah looked up. "What do you want us to do with these?"

Tess gazed at her daughter, realizing for the first time how very young twelve could be. Savannah looked impossibly pale and naive in the uncertain light, a girl trying so hard to be a woman.

Tess's gaze moved to Katie. She was sitting Indian-

style, all slumped over, with her little elbows rested on her
bent knees. Her eyes were huge, earnest pools in the
shadow-cloaked pudginess of her face. There was the barest hint of a tremble in her lower lip, the only sign that she
was afraid for her daddy.

Love washed through Tess in a rejuvenating wave.
These children had given her so much—more than she'd
ever dreamed possible. They'd answered a million soundless, aching dreams. Where strangers had once been, there
was now a family.

She didn't have to be strong *for* them; she had to be
strong with them. From now on, they'd be facing a lifetime's worth of good times and bad. Miracles and trage-
dies. And they could battle them one at a time, each of
them stronger for taking hold of the other.

She held her arms out. With a stifled sob, Katie lurched
into Tess's arms and buried her little face against her
mommy's shoulder. Savannah pushed the paper aside and
crawled across the blanket, curling against Tess.

Their love and acceptance gave Tess the strength to take
on the world. She stroked their backs in slow, gentle circles.

"Will he be back?" Savannah asked quietly.

Tess smiled. "That's my girl, Vannah. Always be direct.
Ask what's on your mind."

"Will he?"

The scientist in Tess wanted to equivocate, to elaborate
on the vagaries of the judicial system and the nature of
Jack's fear. But that part of her was small now, and getting
smaller. The mother in her had a simpler answer. "Yes,
honey, he will, but I need your help."

Both girls drew back, studying her. "What can we do?"
Savannah asked.

"See those pieces of paper? I want you each to write
your daddy a letter. I'll take it to him tomorrow."

Katie whimpered. "Oh, no, I—"

Tess touched her cheek. "I'll help you."

Katie let out her breath in a quiet, quavering sigh. "Wuh—will it help?"

"I think it will."

Katie nibbled nervously on her lower lip, then slowly nodded. "Okay."

Tess helped the girls swivel around and stretch out. Savannah lay sprawled, half on and half off the blanket, her legs crossed at the ankles in the air behind her. She chewed on the end of her pen for a long, thoughtful moment, then began to write.

Dear Daddy:

When I was a little girl, you used ta stand by my bed in the middle of the night. You'd stand there, just lookin at me and cryin. I used ta wish so bad you'd pick me up. Every time I saw you in them days, it was through the wooden bars of that bed. It seemed like bein in jail.

Then I grew up, and I learnt that a person don't need bars to be in jail. I always felt locked up and alone and afraid. But then everything changed. Mama started to laugh, and you taught me to dance.

That dancin was something. Sometimes I cry just thinkin about it. That was the night you first told me you loved me. After that, I never once felt like I was in jail.

Daddy I love you. Please come home.

S.

Emotion tightened Tess's throat as she read Savannah's letter. Impulsively she smoothed a stray lock of hair from Savannah's eyes. "That's beautiful, sweetheart."

Katie chewed nervously on her fingernail. "How 'bout if I just sign my name to Vannah's letter?"

Tess hunkered down beside Katie, looping an arm around the child's trembling shoulders. "Come on. Let's give it a try. What would you like to say?"

Katie swallowed hard. "Just . . ." Her voice dropped to a whisper. "Just that I love him."

"Perfect." Tess smiled at her approvingly. "Now, let's get started."

Thirty minutes later, the fire had dwindled to a hazy pile of red and black embers, and Katie's scrawled sentence was finally complete. Her letters were backward and cata-wampus, but the message was crystal-clear. *I love you, Daddy.*

Tess carefully folded the papers into quarters and set them on the wooden mantel, then she brought the girls back into a circle on the blanket. They joined hands and bowed their heads, and together they prayed.

Chapter Twenty-eight

Tess stared at the small brick building. The barred windows glinted in the noontime sun. She suppressed a shiver of horror and tilted her chin upward, plastering a false smile on her face.

Beside her, Charlie and Ed waited patiently.

She cleared her throat. "Let's go." Lifting her skirts, she made her slow, thoughtful way up the jailhouse steps. The men walked a respectful distance behind her. With each step, she felt a desperate tightening in her chest.

Remember the dream. Remember . . .

She took a deep, shaky breath and forced herself to remember what she'd decided. Last night she'd lain awake in her lonely bed, thinking of the good times with Jack, the loving, laughing times. Each memory had driven like a shard of glass through her heart.

She'd closed her eyes, imagining that he was beside her. The warmth of his touch, the sound of his breathing, the scent of his hair, had all been with her, captured in the tiny, reflective place in her mind where cherished memories remained forever.

It was then, in the soft haze of remembrance, that she'd finally slept.

The dream had come with all the color and sounds and sights of reality. She and Jack were sitting in an elegant, wainscoted room. Sunlight streamed through a huge, octagonal window, wreathing a table set with sterling and china and fine crystal. Children were clustered around the table, but they were no longer children. Savannah was a beautiful young lady with a dark-haired man beside her. On her other side was a pink-cheeked baby in a scrolled high chair. Katie, too, was grown-up and smiling, and busy laughing with a heartbreakingly handsome young man who Tess knew instinctively was Caleb. Two younger men sat across from Caleb, their heads bowed together in quiet conversation.

With the dream had come a pervasive sense of peace. Tess didn't believe it was just a figment of her desperate mind; she knew it was a vision. A picture of a future that was destined to be. A future she'd come back one hundred years to find.

And Jack was screwing it up.

She'd be damned if she'd let him.

Tess yanked her skirts up and hurried up the steps. She'd had to die to find love, and now that she'd found it, nothing would take it from her. Nothing.

Not even a stubborn, pigheaded man who didn't know when to say "maybe."

She reached for the doorknob and wrenched the huge oaken door open. It slammed into the brick wall and cracked hard.

A man looked up from his paper-piled desk in the center of a small, shadowy room.

"Hello," Tess said. "I'm Lissa Rafferty, and I'm here to see my husband, Jackson."

The man scrambled to his feet and pulled a clanking set of keys from his pocket. "This way, ma'am." He glanced at Ed and Charlie. "One visitor at a time."

Ed touched Tess's arm. "Good luck, Miz Rafferty."

"Thanks, Ed." Turning away from the men, she followed the jailer down a narrow hallway.

"Rafferty! There's someone here to see you."

Jack scrambled to a sit. He shoved a hand through his disheveled hair and peered through the bars. "Lissa?"

She stepped away from the jailer so he could see her better. "Hi, Jack."

The jailer opened the cell and ushered Tess inside. "Normally I wouldn't let you in, you understand, but Ed Warbass says you can be trusted. No funny business, right?"

Tess nodded and swept into the small, dank cell. The metal bars clanged shut behind her. A key jiggled in the lock, then footsteps echoed down the hall, and they were alone.

She sat beside Jack on the narrow, sagging cot and twisted around to face him. She reached out, took his hands in hers. There were so many things she wanted to say, so many arguments she'd prepared herself to make, but now, sitting here in the filthy darkness with him, all she wanted to do was cry.

"You shouldn't have come," he said quietly.

She snapped her head up to meet his gaze, and the urge to cry disappeared. "I shouldn't have to."

"Lissa—"

"Don't you 'Lissa' me, Jackson Rafferty. I've had enough of your melodramatics, do you understand? No more hiding."

"What do you mean?" He tried to withdraw his hands, but she wouldn't let him. She clung tightly, squeezing hard.

"You know exactly what I mean. I want you to try to remember."

"Don't you think I've tried?"

The agony in his voice tore through Tess's resolve. She had a sudden urge to take him in her arms and stroke his brow, tell him everything would be all right. But she didn't move. Everything wouldn't be okay, goddamn it, if he didn't _try_.

She stared deeply into his eyes, trying to will him to see the goodness in himself. "It's all in there, Jack. In your head. Every memory, every moment, is stored inside. You just have to believe."

"I can't—"

She pressed a finger to his lips. "I'm not asking you to say you didn't kill those people—even though you didn't—I'm just asking you to admit _maybe_ you didn't."

Fear filled his eyes, made his breathing speed up. He shook his head slowly. "What if—"

She let go of his hands and grabbed his shoulders. "What good are your precious 'what if's' to your kids, Jack? Your _kids_, who are sitting at home right now, crying, terrified they'll never see their father again?" She flipped her leather skate bag open and wrenched out the girls' letters, waving them beneath Jack's nose. "Read these, Jack, and tell me they don't matter."

With shaking fingers, Jack opened Savannah's letter. By the time he reached the bottom, his eyes were sheened with tears. He looked up at Tess, his face twisted with pain. "What do you want from me?"

"What if you're not the murderer, Jack? Did you ever think about that? If you're innocent, we're still in danger—the kids and I are alone out at the farm. _Alone._ And I couldn't shoot a barn if I was standing in front of it."

He swiped his eyes and sighed. "Christ, Lissa, who else could it be? I'm the only crazy on the island."

"Joe and Kie Nuanna borrowed a gun from the Hannahs during your blackout. They returned it splattered with blood." She paused to let the facts sink in, then added, "Human blood."

A spark of hope flared in Jack's eyes.

Tess seized on the moment. "Have you ever hurt anyone, Jack? And I don't mean getting to Johnny too late; that was just bad luck, pure and simple. I mean hurting someone yourself. With your own hands."

He frowned. "No. But that doesn't prove—"

"And what about the Dwyers, Jack? You *knew* them, for God's sake. Selina was killed in her own home. She died clutching the baby dress she was knitting. She was soaked in her own blood, and her face was a mass of bruises. Did you do that, Jack? Did you shoot Henry Dwyer in the back of the head, then beat Selina Dwyer senseless and shoot her, too?"

Horror rounded Jack's eyes. The color seeped from his skin. "Christ Almighty . . ."

Tess shook him hard. "Did you do that, Jack? *Could* you do that?"

Jack stared into her pale, determined face and felt the first crumbling sense of doubt. It was nothing really, just a spark, a flicker of hope. "I don't know. . . ."

"You *do* know, Jack."

He squeezed his eyes shut. A memory of last night flashed through his mind. As he'd sat in the middle of this lonely cell, pouring his heart out onto that scrap of paper, he'd felt . . . reborn. And yet here he was now, clinging to the same old fears, reliving the same old horrors.

What if Lissa was right? asked a small voice inside him. If he wasn't the murderer, then someone else was. Someone who wouldn't want Lissa poking her nose into the investigation.

He took a deep breath and released it in a shuddering, frightened sigh. He opened his eyes, and found Lissa still staring at him with absolute trust in her eyes.

His hands started to tremble, slowly at first and then harder. Fear crept through his blood in a chilling, ice-cold wave.

He felt like a man standing on the edge of a black, bottomless pool, poised to dive headfirst into waters that held a thousand deadly terrors.

He looked into his wife's eyes and felt a rush of love so strong, he felt the sting of tears. "You never doubted me, did you?"

Tears glistened in her eyes. "And I never will, Jack."

He swallowed with difficulty. "I'm afraid."

She smiled. It was a slow, bittersweet smile that broke his heart. "So am I."

At her soft words, so filled with love and trust and hope, Jack felt his last vestige of resistance melt away. She was afraid, too, and yet she forged ahead, believing. Always believing.

Christ, how he wanted to be like her, wanted desperately to let himself believe. Not just for her, but for all of them. For himself, for her, for the children they had now and the children they'd have in the future.

He held his breath and dove into the icy waters of that shallow pool—and hoped to hell she was there to catch him.

"Maybe . . ." The word stuck in his throat. He had to force it past his lips. "Maybe I didn't do it."

Lissa threw her arms around him, planting dozens of kisses all over his face. "I knew you could do it!"

He held her tightly, feeling the hot sting of tears in his eyes. Years' worth of fear and self-doubt slid away. Without the familiar armor, he was left feeling frightened and shaky and more than a little lost. "I love you, Lissa," he whispered desperately.

She pulled slowly away and looked up. There was a bright, mischievous smile on her face. "I love you, too, Jack. Now, let's get you the hell out of here."

Three days later, Tess was standing on the windswept hillside above Kanaka Bay, with her arms crossed, staring out across the glasslike water. The shadows of twilight had just begun to fall, casting the world in shades of gray. Ed Warbass stood beside her, and the children were sitting on a huge plaid blanket. Every eye was turned to the Straits.

She chewed nervously on the scraggly nub of her thumbnail. Once again her gaze narrowed, scanned the shadowy water.

"What's taking them so long?" she muttered.

Ed laid a comforting hand on her shoulder. "The telegram said they'd be here tonight. Maybe Jack and Charlie had some paperwork to finish up on the hearing."

She glanced around, noticing for the first time the number of people congregating down along the water. She frowned at Ed. "What are they doing here?"

He shrugged. "Who knows?"

Tess dismissed the question. She had more important things on her mind anyway. Finally her husband was coming home.

She turned her gaze back to the still waters. And waited.

Jack sat in the small canoe, his hat drawn low across his brow, paddling toward Kanaka Bay. A brilliant red-streaked purple twilight sky reflected off the water. In the distance, their destination was a jet black curl of land against charcoal gray sea. He thought about the last few days. He and Charlie had worked side by side, gathering evidence, lining up witnesses, putting together facts, but as it turned out, the authorities didn't need much of it. Joe Nuanna's confession had wrapped the murder up in a nice, neat package.

"Looks like there's a bunch of people waiting," Charlie said quietly.

Jack's rhythm shattered. Awkwardly he rammed his paddle in the water and tried to recapture the even lift-plunge-pull motion. Water slapped against the sides of the canoe.

"Folks make you nervous?" Charlie asked, leaning back in the canoe.

Jack nodded.

Charlie leaned back in the canoe. "Don't be. You're one of us, son. Looks like I'm not the only one your wife convinced of that."

Jack looked up. "Thanks, Charlie. I really mean that. Without you . . ."

He laughed. "Without me, nothing. It was your wife that did all the work, son. You're a lucky man to have a woman who loves you so much."

He smiled, slow and easy, thinking of Lissa. "Yeah, I am."

They lapsed back into silence as Jack expertly maneuvered the canoe into the harbor and up to the sagging wooden dock. The islanders stood back from the dock, their bodies a tangle of shadows that were curiously silent.

Jack and Charlie stepped out of the canoe, their feet splashing in the cold water. Alone, Jack brought the canoe onto the shore and pulled it high on the beach. The wooden hull scraped loudly on the pebbles and sand.

Then, slowly, he turned and faced the silent people.

Charlie was the first to speak. "You all heard about the Nuanna boys, I know. Well, Joe admitted to me that he did the killings. Trial's set for a week from today in Port Townsend."

The crowd rustled around, talked quietly among themselves, then, slowly, Jerry Sikes came forward, his hand outstretched. "Welcome back, Jack."

Jack stood stunned, unable to do anything except stumble forward and take the man's hand. One by one, the other islanders came forward to greet him, welcome him home.

"Good to have you back, Mr. Rafferty."

"Guess it feels good to be home."

"Hope you and Missus Rafferty'll come on over for supper sometime soon."

Jack tried his best to answer all the well-wishers. Finally, overwhelmed, he looked up.

And saw his family standing on the hill. A huge ache spread through him at the sight of them.

"Lissa." Her name came out as a whisper of longing.

"You'd best be runnin' along," a woman said beside him. "She's been waitin' on yah all day."

Jack drew his hand back. The crowd parted as if on cue, giving him room. He ran through the darkened grass and bounded up the shadowy hillside.

"Daddy!" Katie came at him first, braids flapping. She threw herself into his arms. He swept her into a bear hug and twirled her around, reveling in the high, clear sound of her laughter.

When they came to a stop, he kissed her soft forehead and whispered, "I missed you, little Katydid."

He looked up and saw Savannah standing a few feet away. He dropped to one knee and opened his other arm. Grinning, she hurled herself down the hill and slammed into him. The three of them toppled over, rolling breathlessly down the hill.

Laughing, they started to get up. Jack was halfway to a stand when he felt his wife's gaze on him. Crouched in the grass, an arm around each daughter, he looked up. His heart tripped hard, slammed into his throat.

Lissa was close enough that he could see the welcoming softness in the brown eyes, close enough that he could smell the lavender scent of her hair. He swallowed thickly. God, she looked beautiful.

His hands slid down the girls' backs and fell to his sides. Drawn to his feet, he moved toward her. All around them the wind whispered through the grass. Stars poked through the twilight sky and twinkled overhead. A tiny mewling sigh came from the wicker basket at Lissa's feet.

She smiled. "Hi, Jack."

He took her in his arms. She melted against him, her arms circling low and casual around his hips, her face tucked in the crook of his neck. They stood there for a long time, as long as it took the pale orange sun to sink into the horizon. Neither one of them said anything; there was nothing that needed to be said. What they needed now was togetherness, and together, standing in the middle of the shadowy field, with their children gathered around them, they began to heal.

Finally Jack pulled away. Taking her face in his hands, he stared down into her luminous, love-filled brown eyes and felt a surge of emotion so strong, so *big*, he almost buckled at the force of it. "I didn't do it," he whispered quietly. "I . . . remembered."

There was a long, pregnant pause. Tears sparkled in her eyes. "I never thought you did."

"I love you so much." Jack's throat closed up when he said the words.

"I love you, too, Jack."

He leaned down and kissed her. A slow, lingering kiss that held nothing back. Then he pulled away and whispered, "Let's go home."

She looked up at him, her eyes shining with happy, loving tears. "Home."

That's all she said. Just a single, simple word, but Jack had never heard anything as wonderful in his life. The word sank into his soul and caused a glowing warmth. He looped an arm around her shoulder, and together they stared down the shadowy road toward their farm. They couldn't see any buildings, but in their hearts, they saw it all. The picture-memory of it filled their souls, beckoned them to return to the place where it all began.

Home.

Jack bent down and picked up the basket. Caleb blinked up at him and gurgled a welcome.

Jack grinned. "Hey, he smiled at me!"

Lissa slipped her hand in his. "Of course he did." She leaned against his shoulder. "You're his daddy. Now, let's go home."

Epilogue

CHRISTMAS EVE 1873

Tess stood beside Jack, her arm curled around his waist.
Outside, a winter storm raged. Rain burst from the heavens
in a great whooshing sound and hammered the pitched
roof overhead. Running water blurred the small windowpane, turning the glass into a square of undulating silver.

She and Jack stared through the small, waving pane,
their gazes searching the darkness for the small white
cross on the hillside above the barn. The moon slid past a
charcoal gray cloud, sending fingers of blue-white light
across the barren landscape.

Tess felt the tremble in Jack's body, and she knew what
he was thinking. Though the blackouts were no more, a
good hard rain still triggered the painful memories of his
past. She sidled closer, letting her body form to his. Her
cheek rested on the hard ball of his shoulder.

"I still miss him so much," Jack said in a throaty whisper.

Tess kissed his shoulder. "I know."

Together they stood against the storm, staring out the
window. Far in the distance, Tess saw a flash of white in
the moonlight. She smiled softly, remembering the day, not
so long ago, when Jack placed that plain white cross in the

ground. It had been sunny that day, the air tinged with the scent of the sea and a million blooming flowers.

The family sat in a circle around the cross, holding hands. Slowly, through tears and laughter and memories, Jack told his children about the uncle they'd never known.

Such a little thing, she thought, making a grave, and yet it had given Jack a place to go where he felt close to Johnny. A way to say good-bye.

Somewhere a bell tinkled, snapping Tess out of her memories.

"What was that?" Tess asked.

Thunder boomed through the night. Jack shivered and crossed his arms, staring intently at the shimmer of white through the night's darkness. In times like this, when the power of the past was strong, Jack focused on the cross and remembered the good times. "What? Huh?"

Tess eased away from him. "I'll be right back." Reaching for her flannel robe, she kissed him good-bye and left the bedroom.

In the shadowy darkness of the hallway, she paused.

The bell tinkled again. Louder this time.

Frowning, Tess moved toward the living room. The bedroom door slammed shut behind her. She jumped at the unexpected sound. "Hey, what the . . ."

She smelled smoke. And roses. Tess's frown deepened.

From somewhere—she couldn't quite place where— came the rustling sound of fine silk. Suddenly the shadows parted. A pale, rose-hued cloud rolled into the hallway, swirling around Tess's bare feet. The smell of roses intensified, turned sickeningly sweet.

Tess reached blindly for the bedroom door, and found it locked.

"Jack." His name was a whisper from her too dry mouth.

She took a deep breath to calm down. Somehow she'd

accidentally locked the door. Except . . . except the door didn't have a lock.

"Tess," came a hoarse, feminine voice from the living room. "I'm waiting."

She told herself not to move. She didn't want to know what was going on. She just wanted to stand here, waiting for Jack to open the door.

But before she knew it, she was moving through the rose-colored light toward the living room. In the corner of the room, the Christmas tree, surrounded by paper-wrapped packages, seemed to be floating on a layer of stardust and light. The dozens of candles that Tess had blown out an hour ago were burning brightly, sending plumes of smoke into the air.

The holiday scents of brandy and candied orange peels and evergreen were still thick in the house, but now there was another smell as well. Something Tess couldn't identify. A haunting, heady smell like burning roses.

"Is someone here?" she asked quietly.

A breeze caressed her face. On the tree, the homemade paper ornaments rustled softly together. A bell tinkled gaily.

Tess brought a shaking hand to her throat and moved toward the tree. She'd made every ornament for that tree, and there hadn't been a bell.

"Hi, Tess."

Tess gasped and spun around. There was no one in the room. "Wh-Who is it?"

A throaty barroom laugh filled the small room. "Don't tell me you forgot your old friend, Carol."

Relief rushed through Tess. "Carol," she said with a smile. "I should have known it was you."

"Of course you should have. Sex must be corroding your brain."

Tess grinned. "But what a way to go."

"Which brings us to our point. It's time to choose."

"Choose what?"

"Whether you want to stick with this life or move on."

"Are you kidding? I'm staying."

"Your decision is permanent. You won't be Tess anymore. Your soul will remain the same, of course, but your memories of the twentieth century will be gone. Your new memories will start from when you first woke up in this house."

Tess laughed wryly. "Afraid I'll invent tampons and rubber baby pants before their time?"

Carol's throaty chuckle filled the darkness. "Something like that. So, what do you say?"

Tess glanced down the darkened hallway, where her babies slept and her husband waited. At the thought of them, an aching tenderness unfolded in her chest, wrapping tightly around her heart. "All the memories I need are right here, Carol. I'll spend a lifetime making them."

A warm breeze, almost like a breath, touched Tess's cheek. The rosy light faded, became a glowing haze of gold. Then the candles extinguished themselves, leaving behind a heavy scent of smoke. "You've made the right decision," Carol whispered. "Good-bye."

"Merry Christmas, Carol," Tess said softly.

"Who are you talking to?"

Lissa looked up, surprised. Jack was standing at the corner of the room, staring at her. She blinked until he was in focus.

"Was I talking?" she asked distractedly.

"You said something about Christmas carols."

She frowned, wondering why her legs felt numb and her throat was so dry. "That's odd."

He came toward her, moving in that lithe, graceful way that always mesmerized her, and pulled her into a passionate embrace. She curled her arms around him and rested her face in the crook of his neck. The warm, familiar scent of him saturated her senses, reminded her once again how much she loved this man.

"Dance with me," he whispered against her ear.

Lissa smiled up at him. She placed her hand in his and closed her eyes. Outside the storm played on, the wind beating a gentle cadence on the window pane.

Together they began to move, slowly and in perfect time to each other and nature's music. There, in a room that smelled of smoke and Christmas and magic, Jack and Lissa danced.

It was a good day for miracles.

Author's Note

ONCE IN EVERY LIFE is based on an actual series of incidents that took place on San Juan Island in 1873. For the purposes of storytelling, I have changed some of the character names and played slightly with the timing and sequence of events. My account of the events is based in large part on the memoirs of Delilah "Lila" Hannah, my husband's great-aunt.

In the spring of 1873, Henry and Selina Dwyer were murdered in cold blood as they worked their farm. For many weeks, apprehensive settlers reacted nervously to the realization that a killer was among them. They suspected the worst of everyone.

During this time, while the islanders were trying to get a vigilante group together, Minerva Hannah was quietly adding up her suspicions about Joe and Kie Nuanna, who had borrowed a shotgun from the Hannahs only a few days before the murder. Joe and Kie had returned the gun—which did have human blood on the stock—but had not returned the shot pouch. Unbeknownst to Minerva, Justice of the Peace Ed Warbass had found the buckskin pouch in the Dwyers' root cellar.

Ed Warbass telegraphed this information to a special officer in Victoria, and the police arrested Joe and Kie Nuanna and a third young man, called Indian Charlie.

A hearing was promptly held; however, the magistrate

determined that the evidence was not strong enough to convict. The court allowed Special Officer MacMillian to hold Joe for another week only, pending gathering of evidence. It was at this time that Charlie MacKay (or MacCoy) had a fatherly chat with Joe Nuanna.

Joe eagerly pinned the crime on his friend Indian Charlie, who had already been released. He told about the crime in an incriminating level of detail. Later, when Charlie was arrested and could easily account for his whereabouts during the murder, Joe confessed to the heinous crime.

Joe was extradited to the Washington Territory in late October. He was tried for the Dwyers' murder. Most of the citizens of San Juan Island showed up for the trial, and evidence given by Minerva and Lila Hannah was conclusive.

Joe Nuanna was hanged on a cold day the following March. Most of the town turned out for the event, and the young man's last words were reportedly as follows: "People, I am very sorry for what I have done. Now I have to go. All hands—good-bye."

For an exciting preview of
Kristin Hannah's latest novel,
Between Sisters,
please read on.

Available in hardcover in May 2003.
Published by The Random House
Ballantine Publishing Group.

Dr. Bloom waited impatiently for an answer.

Meghann Dontess leaned back in her seat and studied her fingernails. It was time for a manicure. Past
time. "I try not to feel too much, Harriet. You know
that. I find it impedes my enjoyment of life."

"Is that why you've seen me every week for four
years? Because you enjoy your life so much?"

"I wouldn't point that out if I were you. It doesn't say
much for your psychiatric skills. It's entirely possible,
you know, that I was perfectly normal when I met you
and you're *making* me crazy."

"You're using humor as a shield again."

"You're giving me too much credit. That wasn't
funny."

Harriet didn't smile. "I rarely think you're funny."

"There goes my dream of doing stand-up."

"Let's talk about the day you and Claire were
separated."

Meghann shifted uncomfortably in her seat. Just
when she needed a smart-ass response, her mind went
blank. She knew what Harriet was poking around for,

and Harriet knew she knew. If Meghann didn't answer, the question would simply be asked again. "Separated. A nice, clean word. Detached. I like it, but that subject is closed."

"It's interesting that you maintain a relationship with your mother while distancing yourself from your sister."

Meghann shrugged. "Mama's an actress. I'm a lawyer. We're comfortable with make-believe."

"Meaning?"

"Have you ever read one of her interviews?"

"No."

"She tells everyone that we lived this poor, pathetic-but-loving existence. We pretend it's the truth."

"You were living in Bakersfield when the pathetic-but-loving pretense ended, right?"

Meghann remained silent. Harriet had maneuvered her back to the painful subject like a rat through a maze.

Harriet went on, "Claire was nine years old. She was missing several teeth, if I remember correctly, and she was having difficulties with math."

"Don't." Meghann curled her fingers around the chair's sleek wooden arms.

Harriet stared at her. Beneath the unruly black ledge of her eyebrows, her gaze was steady. Small round glasses magnified her eyes. "Don't back away, Meg. We're making progress."

"Any more progress and I'll need an aid car. We should talk about my practice. That's why I come to you, you know. It's a pressure cooker down in Family Court these days. Yesterday, I had a deadbeat dad drive up in a Ferrari and then swear he was flat broke. The shithead. Didn't want to pay for his daughter's tuition. Too bad for him I videotaped his arrival."

"Why do you keep paying me if you don't want to discuss the root of your problems?"

"I have issues, not problems. And there's no point in poking around in the past. I was sixteen when all that happened. Now, I'm a whopping forty-two. It's time to move on. I did the right thing. It doesn't matter anymore."

"Then why do you still have the nightmare?"

She fiddled with the silver David Yurman bracelet on her wrist. "I have nightmares about spiders who wear Oakley sunglasses, too. But you never ask about that. Oh, and last week, I dreamed I was trapped in a glass room that had a floor made of bacon. I could hear people crying, but I couldn't find the key. You want to talk about that one?"

"A feeling of isolation. An awareness that people are upset by your actions, or missing you. Okay, let's talk about that dream. Who was crying?"

"Shit." Meghann should have seen that. After all, she had an undergraduate degree in psychology. Not to mention the fact that she'd once been called a child prodigy.

She glanced down at her platinum and gold watch. "Too bad, Harriet. Time's up. I guess we'll have to solve my pesky neuroses next week." She stood up, smoothed the pant legs of her navy Armani suit. Not that there was a wrinkle to be found.

Harriet slowly removed her glasses.

Meghann crossed her arms in an instinctive gesture of self-protection. "This should be good."

"Do you like your life, Meghann?"

That wasn't what she'd expected. "What's not to like? I'm the best divorce attorney in the state. I live—"

"—alone—"

"—in a kick-ass condo above the Public Market and drive a brand-new Porsche."

"Friends?"

"I talk to Elizabeth every Thursday night."

"Family?"

Maybe it was time to get a new therapist. Harriet had ferreted out all of Meghann's weak points. "My mom stayed with me for a week last year. If I'm lucky, she'll come back for another visit just in time to watch the colonization of Mars on MTV."

"And Claire?"

"My sister and I have problems, I'll admit it. But nothing major. We're just too busy to get together." When Harriet didn't speak, Meghann rushed in to fill the silence. "Okay, she makes me crazy, the way she's throwing her life away. She's smart enough to do anything, but she stays tied to that loser campground they call a resort."

"With her father."

"I don't want to discuss my sister. And I *definitely* don't want to discuss my father."

Harriet tapped her pen on the table. "Okay, how about this: When was the last time you slept with the same man twice?"

"You're the only one who thinks that's a *bad* thing. I like variety."

"The way you like younger men, right? Men who have no desire to settle down. You get rid of them before they can get rid of you."

"Again, sleeping with younger, sexy men who don't

want to settle down is not a bad thing. I don't want a house with a picket fence in suburbia. I'm not interested in family life, but I like sex."

"And the loneliness, do you like that?"

"I'm not lonely," she said stubbornly. "I'm independent. Men don't like a strong woman."

"Strong men do."

"Then I better start hanging out in gyms instead of bars."

"And strong women face their fears. They talk about the painful choices they've made in their lives."

Meghann actually flinched. "Sorry, Harriet, I need to scoot. See you next week."

She left the office.

Outside, it was a gloriously bright June day. Early in the so-called summer. Everywhere else in the country, people were swimming and barbecuing and organizing poolside picnics. Here, in good ole Seattle, people were methodically checking their calendars and muttering that it was *June, damn it.*

Only a few tourists were around this morning; out-of-towners recognizable by the umbrellas tucked under their arms.

Meghann finally released her breath as she crossed the busy street and stepped onto the grassy lawn of the waterfront park. A towering totem pole greeted her. Behind it, a dozen seagulls dived for bits of discarded food.

She walked past a park bench where a man lay huddled beneath a blanket of yellowed newspapers. In front of her, the deep blue Sound stretched along the pale horizon. She wished she could take comfort in that view; often, she could. But today, her mind was caught in the net of another time and place.

If she closed her eyes—which she definitely dared not do—she'd remember it all: the dialing of the telephone number, the stilted, desperate conversation with a man she didn't know, the long, silent drive to that shit-ass little town up north. And worst of all, the tears she'd wiped from her little sister's flushed cheeks when she said, *I'm leaving you, Claire.*

Her fingers tightened around the railing. Dr. Bloom was wrong. Talking about Meghann's painful choice and the lonely years that had followed it wouldn't help.

Her past wasn't a collection of memories to be worked through; it was like an oversize Samsonite with a bum wheel. Meghann had learned that a long time ago. All she could do was drag it along behind her.